THE SPEAR OF ATHENA

GODSWAR
Volume 2

Ryk E. Spoor

THE SPEAR OF ATHENA

Histria SciFi & Fantasy

Las Vegas ◊ London ◊ New York ◊ Palm Beach

Published in the United States of America by
Histria Books
7181 N. Hualapai Way, Ste. 130-86
Las Vegas, NV 89166 USA
HistriaBooks.com

Histria SciFi & Fantasy is an imprint of Histria Books encompassing outstanding, innovative works in the genres of science fiction and fantasy. Titles published under the imprints of Histria Books are distributed in the United States and Canada by Simon & Schuster and worldwide through Unified Book Distribution. We appreciate your support of copyright by purchasing an authorized edition of this book and for respecting intellectual property laws by not reproducing, scanning, or otherwise distributing any part of it by any means without permission. You are supporting authors and enabling Histria Books to continue publishing books for everyone.

All rights reserved. No part of this book may be reprinted or reproduced or utilized in any form or by any electronic, mechanical or other means, now known or hereafter invented, including photocopying and recording, or in any information storage or retrieval system, without the permission in writing from the Publisher. No part of this book may be used or reproduced in any manner for the purpose of training artificial intelligence technologies or systems.

This is a work of fiction. Names, characters, places, and incidents either are the product of the author's imagination or are used fictitiously, and any resemblance to actual persons, living or dead, business establishments, events, or locales is entirely coincidental.

First Edition

Library of Congress Control Number: 2025944904

ISBN 978-1-59211-691-1 (softbound)
ISBN 978-1-59211-713-0 (eBook)

Copyright © 2026 by Ryk E. Spoor

First, to Dean Koontz, whose horror/SF/F novels not only afforded entertainment but inspiration over the years, and who is saluted in a very specific sequence in this novel; anyone who's read the right one of his early novels will surely recognize one of the two major sources for *The Darkness That Devours*.

Second, to my old Pittsburgh gaming group, and in this case specifically Lesley and Chad; the combination of Captain Jeanne Campbell's adventures and the power-armored "Iron Saint" inspired what we see with Clan Camp-Bel today.

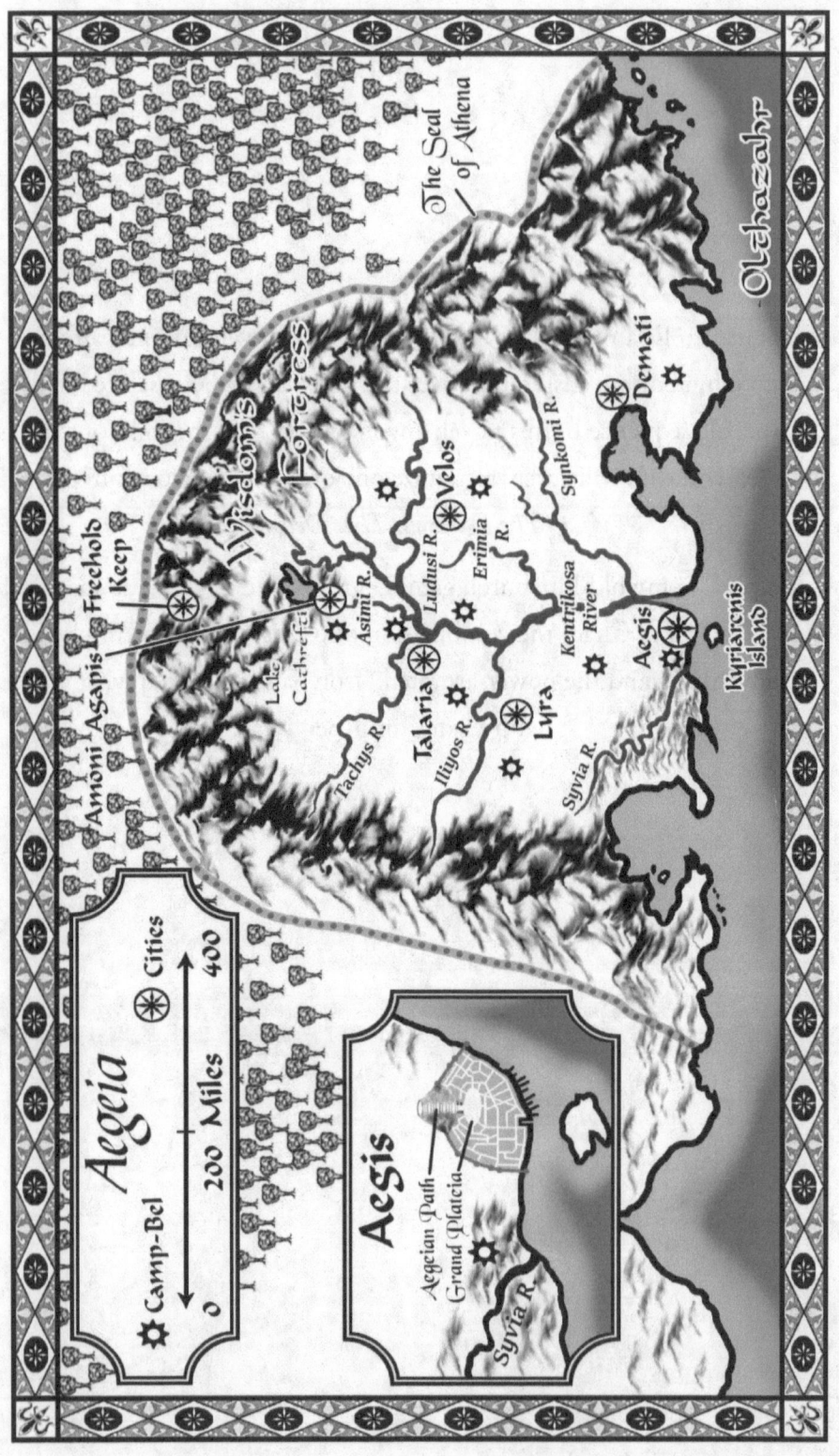

Chapter 1
The City of the Dragon King

"By the Lady's Wisdom..." breathed Captain Pennon.

Ingram chuckled, with a completely silly feeling of pride as he saw the reactions of his fellow Camp-Bels to their first sight of *Fanalam' T' ameris' a' u' Zahr-a-Thana T'ikon*, Zarathanton, the greatest city in the world.

Less than a mile distant, the pearl-grey, shining-polished walls slanted steeply upward, five hundred unbroken feet of invulnerable stone that had stood untouched for half a million years, since before the days of the Fall. They slanted away to both north and south, encompassing a diamond shape more than two miles on a side, with the great Gate visible in the point of the diamond that bestrode the Great Road. Two hundred fifty feet high, glittering with *krellin* and gold and jewels, the gates stood open, the twin gates spanning the entire hundred-yard width of the Road and allowing a steady flow of traffic — on foot, riding on sithigorn or horse or runner-lizard, trundling along on wagons — in and out of those mighty gates.

Despite the immense height of the walls, other great buildings could be seen, the highest of all being the spires of *T'Teranahm Chendoron*, the Dragon's Palace, stretching two thousand feet and more into the sky. Even from this distance they could hear the murmur of two hundred thousand people's voices, motions, actions vibrating the atmosphere.

Both of the main approaches to the city have carefully tended growth and designed curves and ridges along the side of the road that obscure any sight during the approach, Quester's mind-voice noted. *Do you think that is deliberate?*

Ha! I have no doubt it is. The impact of seeing Zarathanton like that? I know if I were the rulers, I'd want to make sure visitors felt it every time.

"By the Lady's Wisdom," Pennon said again. "It seems you might fit all of Aegis itself within a mere corner of it."

"No doubt," Victoria Vantage said with her own smile. "In fairness, that is true of almost any other city I have ever seen. You could fit *all* of the cities and villages of my native Evanwyl in the Southern Quarter and have room to spare."

"Where is your estate, Lady Vantage?" Pennon asked.

"The easiest way to reach it would be for us to pass through the city to the Eastern Gate, then turn north," she answered, gesturing. "It lies a few miles north of the City, at the edge of the Forest Sea. I would welcome all of you there, but as we have been gone quite some months now, it would be unfair to suddenly impose on my staff, who have undoubtedly grown accustomed to merely maintaining the house and grounds."

Ingram found himself nodding. It *had* been a while. Months to make their way south through the Forest Sea, and all the adventures *that* had included, and then, once they'd met up with the survivors of Clan Camp-Bel, turning West and reaching Shipton and hiring onto *Great Turtle*, one of the larger cargo ships, to go as far as the East Twin... months indeed to come full-circle back to Zarathanton.

"Of course," said Pennon. "We will find rooms here in the city easily enough, I should think." She paused, watching the streaming of human, *Artan*, *mazakh*, Children of Odin, and others in and out of the gates. "And here, if anywhere, we will begin to find answers to our questions."

I sure hope so, Urelle's mindvoice said. *Because I have no idea where else we'd go.*

It still gave him a little tingle of a thrill to hear Urelle's voice that way, in his head. Quester had initiated the younger Vantage and her aunt into the mindspeech connection of his Nest on their journey back North. Their sometimes-harrowing southward journey had bound them together, to the point that Quester had come to see them as possible Nestmates as well; the two women, having seen how Ingram and Quester sharing that bond had not harmed but aided them numerous times, had decided to risk it.

It was a unique bond the four of them now shared — and a very, very convenient one. *Well, you still have the Wanderer's Lens.*

I guess. If we really hit a dead-end here, I guess we'll have to risk it. But I truly do not *wish to disappoint him by asking for his help unless there's no other choice.*

Ingram couldn't disagree with that; calling on the assistance of a legend was something to be used with great discretion and reluctance. Although he also remembered the parable of the Always-Worse, in which the boy's wish-ring was never used because things could always be worse; sometimes you had to accept that it would be *time* to use your resources.

But it was definitely not that time *yet*.

As they approached the gates, Ingram saw one clear reminder that things were *not* exactly as they had been before they'd left. Well-armed guards stood by the gates, watching carefully the passage of all, large or small. There were also wagons leaving regularly, heading to the West, emblazoned with the lightning bolt-starburst of Elbon Nomicon and the Sauran Kings.

Victoria went to one of the guardsmen as their party reached the Gate. "Pardon me, sir," she said. "It has been some months since I left the City; what news?"

"Months?" The guard, a slender, long-faced man with skin of deep blue-black and a dour expression, shook his head. "Much news, little of it good. The Black City come to the world? The King of All Hells walking the world? But the beginning."

"Ah, Artaquas, don't paint it *all* with your depressing brush," said another, equally tall and thin but with a bronze-brown complexion and more smiles than frowns written in the grooves of his face. "After the horrors of the start of the war, things are better, at least for now."

"Hmph. Here, maybe, Ichiban. Yes. But with the new King having taken our forces West, to meet those of the Hells? There'll be bad news coming back, I have no doubt."

"New King?" Victoria blinked. "Yes, I suppose there must be."

"*That* many months, eh? Wasn't much of a choice, of course — the Marshal of Hosts being the King's relation and knowing his mind so well."

Victoria giggled, a startling sound for Ingram, who wasn't used to hearing such a... *light* sound from the usually serious old Adventurer. "Oh dear. I'm sorry, but... oh *dear*, poor Toron! He was so often given to remarking how *satisfied* he was not to be the King. And now it's his job." She looked up, gaze sharpening. "So he's taken the war to the gates of the Black City, has he?"

"Such was the plan. Not sure he's *reached* it yet — he was traveling the land route to build his forces, recruit as they went, and give allies, including Idinus himself, a chance to gather. Might be mustering near Hell's Edge by now, though." Artaquas nodded gloomily. "How many of them'll make it through *there* to actually reach the Black City, I don't know."

"Idinus? The *Archmage* is coming to *our* aid?" Ingram realized it was his own incredulous voice speaking.

"So the King told us, and no reason to doubt it," Ichiban said. "Sure, and the State of the Dragon King and the Empire of the Mountain have been at odds before... , but neither of them wants the Black Star here, spreading his power and ruin. I even hear rumor the Archmage may send an avatar directly."

"Wow." In some ways, the idea that Idinus of Scimitar, God-Emperor of the Mountain, had bestirred himself to act in concert with his adversaries chilled Ingram more than any of the other news. There was no greater threat than one that could bring such forces together.

"Well, we thank you for this news. Who is in charge at the Dragon's Palace, then, if the King himself has gone to war?"

"Calladan Mystraios," said Artaquas. "Not a Sauran, but the head of the Academy commands respect enough, at least for now."

"I should think so. An excellent choice," Victoria said, nodding. "I will pay my respects later. Again, our thanks."

"You're welcome. Good day to you. HOY! You! Watch where you're going with that wagon!" Artaquas trotted over towards the offending driver.

"So, where to now, Ingram?" Captain Pennon asked.

"Quester and I will head to the Guild; we've got to get an idea of how to get into Aegeia, and if anyone's going to have ideas, it'll be our fellow Adventurers. You and the rest of the Clan should get yourselves some rooms. I'm guessing Victoria and Urelle will head home?"

"Quite so. Obviously, you will stay with us, and in a few days, we may be able to offer your Clan brethren rooms as well."

"Thank you, Victoria." The kind words did send a twinge through Ingram, because it reminded him of just how very few of Clan Camp-Bel had survived to reach here. Besides himself and the Captain, there were only ten remaining; fifteen had survived the attack that their arrival had interrupted, but four of those had later succumbed to unexpected side effects of the combat — soul-injuries, magically-enhanced infections, and such — and one had been killed on the way to Zarathanton, ambushed by a groundripper.

A lot of the Clan stayed behind, he reminded himself, *including Mother and Father*. Still, there had been a few hundred, close to half the Clan, on the three ships that had fled, and every effort had been made to make it look like it was in fact all of the Clan on board. Never in the Cycles they had served Athena had the Clan lost so many — and these had been lost in what was at least partly a ploy to distract, not an assault force.

And it was all about me. Hiding me. Preventing people from thinking of me as significant. Keeping even me from taking myself seriously, making me believe I wasn't good enough to be a Camp-Bel.

He still couldn't quite grasp that, sometimes. The lengths to which they had gone weren't, in truth, so surprising - Camp-Bel traditions were nothing if not focused on overachieving in every dimension — but the fact that they'd found it *necessary* was. Something about the prophecy they'd been given had managed to get them to swallow their pride and confidence and *not* confront the unknown threat head-on, which was much more the Camp-Bel preference.

What that "something" was, however, none of the Clan survivors here knew.

He was still thinking on all of this when the group separated, the Camp-Bels heading North from the Grand Intersection and the two Vantages hurrying on ahead to the East.

The Adventurer's Guild Hall hadn't visibly changed in the years since they'd first entered, and Ingram felt his spirits lift as they passed the threshold. *We really are Guild Adventurers, and we've got tales to tell, to enter in the annals!*

That we do, Quester agreed. *It is different from the first time we passed these doors, indeed.*

Passing through the front entrance hall and the Hall of Requests, the two of them reached the main Adventurer's Hall, and immediately saw a familiar figure. Nine feet tall with blue-gray skin, bent over a desk with papers scattered about, the Sorter of Querents was clearly the same being they'd met almost three years ago.

He glanced up as they entered, then froze, a letter sliding unnoticed from the huge hand. Disregarding the *Artan* Querent before him, the Sorter shot to his feet and practically ran to them. "Quester! By Chromaias and Kharianda, you're *alive!*"

Chapter 2
History of Horrors

Quester felt his antennae flick involuntarily — the equivalent of an astonished blink. "I am," he agreed, "but from whence this amazement?"

The Sorter was still staring down at him, then glanced back at the *Artan*. "Excuse me a moment; Guild business, you understand."

Without waiting for the Querent to answer, the Sorter grasped both Quester and Ingram gently by the shoulders and guided them through a set of doors and down the hall to one of the private meeting rooms. Only when the door was shut did he turn back to face them.

"Well now," he said. "Well, now. Sorry about that, but… you'll remember back when you applied, we had a talk about your people's Nests getting wiped out?"

"Indeed," Quester said. "You knew of two besides my own."

"Well, then, here's the thing: add three more to that."

"Shargamor's *Water*." Quester whispered the prayer-curse. "And we learned of another on our travels. *Seven*. I… I do not know if there were *more* than seven Nests!"

"No more do I," the Sorter said heavily. "But even that's not the worst. See, there ain't many Iriistiik Adventurers — seeing as how most o' your people are nicely set up in your Nests, you do business outside but ain't got so much reason to go runnin' around gettin' in trouble. Still, there's always a few, just like there's always a few Toads willing to get out of the mud and hop to it. We've had ten on the rolls here, countin' you, that were active." Quester felt his spiracles tightening with dread even before the Sorter finished, "Now? Don't think there's four of 'em left."

Ingram muttered his own curse. "Something's even hunting down the *Adventurers*? The singletons, the ones without a Nest or on long missions away?"

"Seems like it must be, don't it?" The Sorter shook his head dolefully. "Once I noticed the pattern — got a report of a murdered Nest, then two of our Iriistiik members killed — I sent out alerts, but it's always guesses and grabs as to whether they'll get through to everyone. Way you reacted tells me it sure didn't get to *you*."

Quester had been thinking. "We must assume this is a coordinated effort. Yes?"

Ingram's brow furrowed. "Well... I guess, yeah. I mean, maybe one or two could be accidents or coincidence, but it wouldn't make sense that there were two or more groups that just suddenly decided to hunt down your people." His head snapped up. "By *Athena*... The Xiilistiin."

"*What?*" the Sorter snapped. "Xiilistiin? I haven't heard of any of *those* monsters active in decades!"

"I wish *we* hadn't," Ingram said. "They're active and working with someone — we think Ares — inside Aegeia."

"Kharianda protect us." The Sorter seated himself with a sigh. "I'll have to put out another alert to all the Guild Houses. Xiilistiin! Xiilis are bad enough, and gods know we've tried to wipe *them* out, but Xiilistiin..." he shook his head. "Iff'n we weren't already in all-out war, this'd be a top-alert emergency."

Ingram frowned, and Quester could smell his friend's puzzlement. "I'm not arguing — especially after what I've seen — but I didn't realize they were considered *that* bad."

"Prob'ly because after they showed up, weren't a single country or Guild House that wasn't happy to hunt 'em down. Parasite soul-stealers? Ain't much worse'n that, believe you me." The Sorter pursed his lips. "See, stronger their Swarms get, the better they get at their imitations, more they can steal from the people they catch. It's like an avalanche — starts small, but every little bit speeds the thing up, until next thing you know you've buried a whole Chromaias-damned *valley* under it. An' if they get a Patron — god or demon, and they really like to cozy up to some of the *Mazolishta*, Erherveria, and some of the others — they just get worse."

Ingram bit his lip. "Ugh. Okay, I can definitely see that. But what's the Xiilis?"

"They're... well, I guess you'd say the ancestors of the Xiilistiin. Look kinda similar, but not as bright, and they're not nearly as dangerous. Work in broods from one hatching, and their imitation of their prey is a lot less impressive. Don't know how they changed to the Xiilistiin, but —"

Quester clicked his mandibles together as an exceedingly unwelcome Mother-memory surfaced. "I do."

"Beg pardon?"

"It was... our fault, in a way," he said slowly.

"*Your* fault?" Ingram stared, then, "Oh. You mean the Iriistiik?"

"Yes." He slowly lowered himself to a sitting position, his abdomen forming the third leg of a stool with his legs locked. "The Xiilis have always been predators of the Iriistiik, one should understand. Their ability to mimic scent and pose and such exploits some of our species' particular weaknesses, so a Xiili brood could infiltrate a Nest and parasitize and kill us fairly easily.

"Their broods are small, however — eight to fifteen individuals, in general — so they were a frightening but self-contained problem for the most part, and when discovered they could be driven out or killed. Xiilis are not terribly bright, and the powers and abilities they can mimic are limited and almost never as strong as the original. Thus they nearly always preyed exclusively on workers, rarely on warriors.

"But..." He paused. "Understand, there are many things the Iriistiik do not discuss commonly with those not of the Nests. Some of these things may nonetheless be known; do you know how the Mother of a Nest becomes who she is?"

"Not exactly," the Sorter said after a pause. "Seems to me I've heard it's somethin' like bees, right?"

"Very much so, yes. A particular larva is chosen, and raised with a very special... food, you might say, manufactured by the Nest. This Mother's Meal transforms the eater into a Mother; in an emergency — for example, if the Mother is somehow killed — one of the Thinkers may partake of the Meal and transform, though this is much more stressful and possibly deadly."

After a moment to gather his thoughts, Quester bobbed his antennae, inhaled, then went on. "One unfortunate Nest was raided by a strong brood of Xiilis, one that had already taken a small pack of cloakwolves." He saw Ingram wince, sensed his friend's understanding. "Yes. So they were even more adept at hiding themselves from us than normal. The leader of the brood made it to the central breeding chamber and substituted itself for one of the larvae."

"Oh, I'm not likin' what I'm thinkin' here."

"Yes. The Nest was preparing to begin a new Nest, and of course the first step was to make a new Mother. And so the brood-mother of the Xiilis was fed Mother's Meal."

"Athena's Mercy. And so was born the first Xiilistiin."

"Yes. So well-placed was she that she was able to maintain her deception and get four more of her brood changed before the Nest's Mother sensed something wrong." He felt his wingcases tighten and buzz in distress. "Too late."

"They wiped out that Nest."

Quester nodded. "And there made the first Swarm-Heart."

Ingram frowned. "And *all* Xiilistiin are decended from that *one* brood?"

"In a manner of speaking, but not all directly. You see, with the transformation they became, in some ways, related to us, or at least powerful mockeries of us. Their Brood-Queens and attendants make something very similar to Mother's Meal, and they can use it to bring in Xiilis and transform selected members. So they are not inbred nor easily vulnerable."

"Well, the Guild thanks ya for the information," the Sorter said after a moment. "More we know about 'em, the better we can deal with 'em." He gave a wry smile. "But ya didn't come here ta just give me a history lesson. What brings ya back to the Guild? Need a place to stay? Lookin' to buy hard-to-get merchandise? Or maybe just gonna pay yer dues?"

Ingram laughed. "Yeah, they *are* about due, right?" He reached into his pouch, rooted about, and then pulled out the crystal sword they'd taken off one of Ares' servants a few months ago. "Here, that ought to cover us for a while."

The Sorter raised his brows. "An' of course you haveta make it the harder way. You know there's a ten percent assessment and conversion fee this way."

Quester dipped his antennae. "We are aware. But I believe you will find it is more than sufficient. According to our own wizard, it is a quite powerful weapon, fourth-circle with additional enhancements."

"Fourth, eh? I'll have our people check it out, but I'm sure you're right. Sure, that'll keep you paid-up for a while. So what d'you need?"

"Research and advice," Ingram said, "on how to do the impossible."

A booming laugh came from the *bilarel*. "Well, then you've *definitely* come to the right place, Adventurers!"

Chapter 3
An Instructive Visit

"I can only afford you a few moments," said Calladan Mystraios. "Even for you, Victoria."

"I quite understand," she said. "But I believe my friends' questions should be brief. But first, how have you been doing?"

"Well enough until I found myself drafted into being King-in-Proxy," he said with a half-chuckle, half-sigh. "The Academy's been doing quite well, or was when I left. A nice new crop of students, about half sponsored in." His sharp black eyes looked distant for a moment, obviously thinking about the Academy, where his true heart lay.

He hasn't aged, a part of her noted. Calladan still looked every inch the wise wizard — well over six feet tall, trim, sleek black hair with a sprinkling of gray, white at the temples, penetrating gaze, a pointed black beard with a streak of white through the center, elaborate black robes covered with mystical symbols, and the intricately carved ebonwood staff that glinted with both gold decoration and steel reinforcement. He'd looked exactly the same... *was it forty-five years ago? How time does pass...* as he had when she'd first seen him during her brief time at the Academy.

At the same time, he looked... smaller, perhaps a hair less certain, as he sat in the Dragon King's Throne, made for beings far larger and grander than mere humans. The dramatic series of crystal platforms that culminated in the dais that supported the throne made the throne room feel cavernously hollow without the size and aura of power of an Ancient Sauran seated upon that throne.

"And you?" he went on. "I'd heard the Vantage V—" he cut off at her glance. "Er, I'd heard you retired to be one of the Eyes back at Evanwyl."

"If only it had stayed that way. You and I know what is happening to the world. It did not leave Evanwyl untouched. But it would take a long time to go into all that."

"Yes, I suppose it would. Perhaps I will have time later; I would very much like to hear it." He turned to look at the other three. "Now, I cannot *possibly* be wrong in that this young lady is a Vantage, no?"

"My niece and a most accomplished young mage, Urelle," Victoria said proudly. "Had things gone a bit differently, she might have been in your Academy this year or the next."

"And proud to have her, I am sure. An honor to meet you, young Urelle."

Urelle took his extended hand and shook it, looking not a little overawed at meeting the Director of the Adventurer's Academy. "I'm very honored, sir."

He studied her other two companions. "Hmmm. A unique pair you are — for just by the way you stand I see you are partners. Adventurers as well — Guilded here in the city." His eyes narrowed. "That weapon... I have seen its like only once before, a long time ago. Aegeian?"

Ingram grinned. "Well done, sir! Ingram Camp-Bel of Aegeia, at your service!"

"*And* a Camp-Bel! This becomes a most interesting visit." He looked to Quester. "And a Gray Warrior. My condolences for your losses, *Iriistiik*." He pronounced the name with the buzzing trill that few humans could manage.

"How did you know, sir?"

"Put in the position of ruler, I've made it my business to know what is happening in the world, insofar as one man can. The deliberate extermination of species is a clear signature of the powers behind this. The *Artan* are the most obvious, but the losses over the last few years by the Iriistiik make it near-certain that this, too, is part of their work."

"Then... thank you for your sympathy, sir. I am called Quester."

"An honor to meet you, Quester." He bowed to allow his forehead to be touched by Quester's antennae.

Quester straightened. "As we are on the subject... one of our questions was whether you know of any *surviving* Nests?"

Calladan's lips tightened, and Victoria could see the leashed anger — not towards those present — in the tension of his stance. "I wish I did, Quester. I have not had a *thorough* search of the records done, of course, but the overview I have had mentions no other Nests than those we know have been destroyed."

Oh, Quester. She saw the antennae drop, the angular body sway a moment, and felt him cut them all off, for the moment, from his mind and thoughts, privacy in his grief. *No Nests mean no Mothers. If we cannot find another Nest... then the few surviving wanderers like Quester will be the last of their kind.*

After a moment, Ingram cleared his throat. "Um. Well, we have another question. Are you aware of the, well, Seal that Athena often puts around Aegeia at points in the Cycle?"

"I am. And I have heard that it has been done for this Cycle, just recently."

"Okay, that makes it easier. We think that this time it wasn't Athena, but *Ares*. And somehow not right for the Cycle."

Calladan's entire attention was suddenly focused on Ingram. "You mean that Ares is not, for lack of a better term, sticking properly to the script?"

"I... yes, I guess that would be a good way to put it."

Victoria remembered something said by the dying Xiilistiin at the battle where they had rescued the Camp-Bels from being wiped out. "There are even a few implications that Ares may not actually *be* Ares, at least not as the Aegeians have known him."

Calladan closed his eyes. "That would be... extraordinarily bad. But go on. That was not your question."

"We need to know — I mean, we need to find a way to get *through* the Seal and into Aegeia. The Guild said you were the best person to ask, at least anywhere near here."

"I am touched by the Guild's faith in me. Insofar as I know, *no one* has ever breached the Seal. The Aegei may work *within* it, and may be able to speak outside of it, but even they cannot bring anything through the Seal."

He frowned. "A pretty problem indeed, and unfortunately, I don't have much time to devote to it. Yet the Guild must know that."

Urelle's brow had been furrowed in thought. Now it suddenly cleared. "Sir? It might be silly or obvious but..."

"Go on, Urelle. Sometimes silly and obvious is still very relevant, and I have found that often what seems silly or obvious to one is quite opaque to another."

"Well," Urelle said, "I was working with... another really powerful wizard, and he helped me figure out how to break a powerful tracking charm on us. The trick was that even the best spell has... well, a tiny flaw, like a stitch that completes a piece of cloth and could be used to unravel it."

Calladan raised both eyebrows. "Neither silly nor always obvious. This is a truth that is often forgotten, because most spells do not *require* that level of analysis. They can be broken by superior force, or cleverly negating a part of their matrix directly rather than using the extremely complex and time-consuming process of analyzing the spell to find its... keystone, so to speak."

"So would it apply to the Seal?"

Calladan stroked his beard in contemplation. "I do not see why it would not. It is true that the Seal *could* be put in place by pure, unadulterated godspower, which can follow quite different rules... but that would be an incredibly inefficient and power-hungry method. Quick, dirty, and wasteful. Athena does not work that way, and I do not expect Ares would if he could avoid it. So much easier to build a matrix, a structure for the godspower to reinforce — a spell cast and strengthened by the power of the gods, rather than a pure shield of that energy and will. And in *that* case... yes, there would, and must, be such a keystone."

Urelle's face lit up... and then immediately fell.

"What's wrong, Urelle?" Victoria asked, puzzled.

"Auntie, knowing that was really helpful working on the Coins, because I could *see* the whole spell. I could *look* for the - well, I thought of it as a flaw, but keystone works just as well, maybe better - the keystone in context of the entire work."

"Ah." One didn't have to be a wizard to understand the problem. "But you cannot see the entirety of a spell that covers a perimeter of perhaps over two thousand miles. Yes."

"Very true," Calladan said. "If one were possessed of the eyes of the gods, one might do so, but we are far more limited. Still... we may be able to narrow the likely locations down."

"You mean," Ingram said, perking up slightly, "there are limits on where it could be placed?"

"There are *always* limits, young Ingram," Calladan said, and Victoria smiled just a touch as she heard the professorial tone entering the deep voice. "A spell is designed to perform a particular function, and its design is *predicated* on that function, and on external constraints that must be adhered to in making the spell able to perform the desired function in the real world.

"For example, in the ideal case, if one considers a spherical perimeter to be secured, the keystone may be placed at any point upon the sphere, as no point on a sphere is in any way more or less significant than any other."

"But that's not true in the real world," Urelle said, also starting to sound more animated, and Victoria saw even Quester's antennae rising up again. "Right? For example, the Seal is not a sphere."

"Right you are, Urelle. It is not a sphere, but a somewhat irregular quadrangle in general outline, with extensions both above and below ground to prevent intrusion from the obvious third dimension." Calladan was up out of the throne now, sketching an outline of Aegiea in the air and causing a faint, glowing aura to extend up and down from the shimmering perimeter. "Naturally there are also elements to prevent intrusion by dimensional shift, teleportation, shadestriding, and so on, but these aren't relevant to our particular question.

"In addition, this god-spell has been cast many times over the ages; it has a *fixed matrix*, determined dozens of Cycles and two or more Chaoswars ago. That means that its keystone *today* will be — will *have* to be — in the same place it has been in every prior cycle. Now, Ingram, tell me one place where our hypothetical keystone *won't* be."

Ingram jumped at being addressed and looked momentarily panicked, a student being called upon who has no idea what to say. "Um, er... well, not here, along the coastline. That's where almost *everyone* trying to get into the country is going to be, it'd be stupid to put the potential vulnerability there."

"Very good, and correct. We can dismiss this entire area of the perimeter." That section of the perimeter went red.

"Could it not be in the sky, or even better, below the ground?" Quester asked. "Those would be by far the least accessible areas and thus would seem to be the obvious places to put the keystone."

Urelle opened her mouth, then closed it, frowning.

"The answer is no, it could not be in either of these places, sensible though it would be to put it there. Urelle, you had a thought. Can you tell us why the keystone cannot be in either location?"

Victoria smothered a giggle. Calladan was now fully in his teaching mode, down to asking the pupil to explain rather than doing it himself. *He really does belong in the Academy. Gods grant this war is short.*

"I don't..." Urelle stopped herself, then traced the outline. "It's irregular, not a sphere or something. That means the perimeter is the anchor for the above and below ground extensions. They *can't* be keystone areas because all the, oh... stitching, supports, anchors, whatever, have to be along the perimeter. All the *structure* comes together there. The keystone *has* to be somewhere along the perimeter!"

Calladan smiled and nodded. "Excellent!" The transparent above and below-ground extensions shaded to red as well. "Already we have eliminated well over ninety percent of the possible locations. That does still leave us with three-quarters of the perimeter as candidates, however."

"Ingram," buzzed Quester, "did you not tell me that the *Rohila* have strongholds all along this part of Wisdom's Fortress?" His claw traced the western side of the mountain range.

"Yes. And I think on the other side, too. They live all through the mountain range." Ingram shook his head. "They're... not comfortable neighbors, but there's a basic agreement that as long as *we* don't intrude on their space, they will keep their activities within the mountains or outside Aegeia."

"Then we can exclude most of the mountain range," Calladan said, "which suddenly makes our task far easier. There is no possibility that either Athena or Ares will have placed the singular weakness of their spell directly within or adjacent to the domain of those who are not allies. There will have been no few painful and drawn-out negotiations made, in fact, to address where, exactly, the Seal goes within Wisdom's Fortress, or it could cut *through* Rohila settlements."

"Yes," Victoria said, remembering their own experiences. "It would appear to me that the agreement actually leaves the Rohila *inside* the perimeter — that for the most part, it traces the exterior edge of the mountains. Based on where we encountered the barrier ourselves, anyway."

"Hmmm, a most interesting decision that must have been. But I suppose it is inevitable; the Rohila's warrens extend laterally as well as vertically, so that there might be some significant settlements underneath areas of Aegeia that are within the perimeter of the mountains. The only way to not provoke them and still enclose the entirety of Aegeia would be to enclose the mountains as well."

"But if we eliminate the whole perimeter, there's nothing left!" Urelle said. "We've determined that they can't put it above or below, they certainly wouldn't put it along the open coastline, and now you've eliminated the entire mountain range!"

"Not quite, young Urelle," Calladan said. "Ingram?"

Ingram's mouth had dropped slowly open. "By *Athena*... of course."

"What's 'of course'?"

"As Calladan said, there is no way they would put the weakness near one who isn't an ally, and the Rohila aren't anyone's allies. But we *do* have one ally on that perimeter, one that guards the *only* reasonable pass through Wisdom's Fortress." His finger touched the center of the northern wall of mountains. "Freehold Keep."

Calladan smiled broadly. "And we have reduced your search to a manageable area, I believe."

"Thank you so much, Calladan," Victoria said, and seeing that he was still smiling, embraced him. "I had *hoped* you might have some wisdom to give us, but I admit, this is far better than I'd expected!"

He returned the hug. "Now, now, Victoria, I will hardly accept all the credit. I guided the thoughts, but with but a few clues, you and your friends were able to see your way clear." He glanced over and down. "Something still troubles you, young Camp-Bel?"

"Nothing to do with the location, sir. Just... the practicalities."

"How do you mean?" Quester asked.

Ingram shook his head. "One good reason to believe the keystone is somewhere there, or around there, maybe just behind it, is that The Salandaras — the one who's given responsibility for the Freehold — is sworn to hold the pass against any and all who seek to enter once the Seal has been placed. By the Seal's appearance, it's assumed Athena herself has ordered that none enter or leave, and so the Freehold will become an impassable bastion against it."

Calladan gave a shrug. "That is a challenge, but unfortunately even as King-Regent I have no say over the Salandaras; none truly have, save themselves and their unpredictable god. It would seem to me that you have little choice but to attempt passage. Perhaps the uniqueness of your circumstances will move them to make an exception," he smiled wryly, "if you can truly get them to grasp it."

"Yeah," Ingram said gloomily. "That's going to be hard enough. But even if I do, one thing they do real well is keep their word."

"A usually admirable trait, but one that may be troublesome in this case. Still... I have given you what aid I can, I think, and there are many other people I must see today."

"Yes, of course you do. Thank you very much, sir. At least we have an idea of a destination, which is by *Wisdom* a lot more than we had coming in!"

"Truly," Quester said. "Thank you, Calladan."

"Thank you *very* much, sir," Urelle said. "You gave me more to think about, too."

He grinned broadly. "The finest reward of a teacher — seeing his students *thinking!*"

They laughed, and Victoria even smelled a touch of humor in Quester's scent. *He is strong and will recover.*

But my, my, what a challenge we have before us.

Chapter 4
Parting from the Clan

"Ingram, have you taken leave of your senses?" Captain Pennon snapped. "If you are going back to Aegeia, we go with you!"

"No, you do *not!*" Urelle saw the tension in Ingram's whole body as he kept his gaze locked on Pennon's. *He's confronting the Captain of the Clan; I can't imagine how hard this is for Ingram, so soon after finding out that he* wasn't *the humiliating failure he thought he was.*

But it *was* his place to do this, and Urelle and the others had known it was coming for almost the entire week since they'd arrived.

"In the name of Athena, *why?*" Guardian Paschalia asked. "You are four and would set yourselves against Ares? Surely you could use the aid of the Clan, even though we are few." Paschalia's voice was low and earnest; Urelle thought he was still trying to make up for his having accepted the deceptions surrounding Ingram's competence.

"Three reasons," Ingram said, looking around the Vantage's large sitting room. He raised one finger. "First, what little we know about this prophecy or whatever points to it being *us*, not any of you. Which of us, we're still not clear on, but somehow I am involved, and at least one of the others. *We* are supposed to confront or stop Ares somehow. *You* are not in that category.

"Second," he went on, elevating a second finger and cutting off any protest, "We already *know* there's more of the Clan inside Aegeia — or there should be. If there *isn't*, I *will not risk the whole Clan.* Some of us *must* remain outside to be a last hope and nucleus of a liberation force, if the worst happens. And since *I* can't stay, you, Captain, and all your forces, are the obvious choice."

Pennon's normally cheerful face looked like she'd bitten into a puckerfruit, but she finally nodded. "That... makes sense. I hate to admit it, but it makes sense. So, what's your third reason?"

Ingram hesitated, and she sensed a trepidation, as of someone about to do something they had never dared do before. "The third..." He swallowed audibly, then took a breath and straightened up — though his diminutive size made that an unimpressive gesture. Still, he met Pennon's gaze once more. "The third reason is that you'll slow us down, Captain."

Pennon opened her mouth, closed it, opened it again, then just stared incredulously at Ingram. "Slow... you... *down?*"

"Slow us down," Ingram repeated, though there was still a tremor in his voice. "We have to face the truth. The Clan was close to being wiped out when the *four* of us came in and proceeded to wipe out your enemies in a few moments — enemies that had been chasing you a long ways." He looked around the small circle of Camp-Bels. "There is not one of you, even the Captain, who could take on Lady Victoria or Quester, and I don't think you could take me or Urelle, either. I hate to say it so bluntly, Captain, but we would be spending time worrying about *you*, time and effort we can't afford."

Pennon stared at him for long moments. Then she chuckled. The chuckle turned to a laugh, and the laugh to a roar that doubled her over with mirth, left her gasping for breath before she could finally recover, leaning against the paneled wall for support. "Ohhh... Ahh, Ingram, forgive me, I do not laugh at you, but at *myself*. At *us*. The Camp-Bels, the proud defenders... who needed rescue at the hands of the one we had deceived. Who truly — as you say — has no need of *us* to defend him, or his friends."

Paschalia, too, had laughed, with a twist of sadness in his smile. "It's a hard truth to swallow for those of us who were as deceived as you were, Ingram. But... aye, I saw those you felled, and read clearly the *way* in which you slew them. It was something I could not have done, nor, I think, even the old Captain, let alone — no offense! — our new Captain Pennon."

A snort. "No offense taken, Pas. He was the best of us, by far. But you are likely right. You have grown even past where you were when you left, Ingram, and taken yourself beyond our ability to protect." She grew more serious and looked to Paschalia. "And he made an excellent point. We are very few. We do not know if the rest of the Clan in Aegeia will survive. It is our duty to remain here and build our strength; there are those we can protect and assist in the greatest of cities, indeed, and from those we will find others to test, to train, to become part of the Clan."

She gave the same two-stage salute with her arms that Berenike used, first crossing her arms in an X on her chest, then rotating them to stand upward on either side. "Travel swiftly and well, Ingram Camp-Bel, and may the Lady's Wisdom guide you, the Lady's Shield protect you, and the Lady Herself be beside you in battle."

Ingram returned the salute, and bowed as well. "Captain, I thank you for understanding," he said, and Urelle could see that behind his formal words his eyes were bright with tears, for this which was not just *acceptance*, but true and unquestionable *respect* from the Clan he had loved and felt outcast from for so long. "The Lady's Wisdom guide you all, and her Spear go before you in battle, as her Shield wards you from all harm."

Then he flung his arms around Pennon, whose eyes went wide and then misty, as she returned his embrace. "Well spoken, Ingram," she said quietly. "And once more, the apologies and the love of the Clan are yours. You are not Captain... but in this you have the right, and the duty, to command us. Go, then, all four of you, and may the Father of the Gods himself walk with you on this mission."

***

"Okay, Urelle, *that's* just showing off."

She looked over and grinned at Ingram. "What?" she asked, in an overly-innocent tone.

He pointed down. "You're flying *one inch* above the road?"

"I think it looks really mysterious and... what was it the Wanderer said... *cool*, that was his word."

"Okay, it looks... interesting, maybe." Ingram's tone was snippy. "But isn't that a *huge* waste of effort?"

Well, Balance, I do something I think is fun and this *is the way he reacts?* She opened her mouth to snap back, then suddenly realized what was bothering him. "I know it was hard to just leave them behind, Ingram. But please don't snap at me for it."

He blinked, looked angry for an instant, then visibly choked back a response. After a moment, he closed his eyes and breathed slowly out.

Good, Nest-brother, she heard. *I am glad neither I nor Victoria had to intervene and put some sense into your head.*

"Sorry." Ingram bowed to her as they walked. "I still wish they could have come with us."

Aunt Victoria raised her eyebrow. "They would have if you had given them the slightest opening, young man."

"I know, I know! I was the one who told them they had to stay behind and *made* them accept it."

And that, Urelle thought to herself, *was one of the hardest things I think he's ever done. I know he wanted the Camp-Bels with him. But he was right.* "You were *right*, Ingram. You really were. If any of us thought otherwise, you know we'd have said something, right?"

He smiled, then reached out and gave her hand a quick squeeze that sent a tingle through her. "Yes. Yes, of course, you all would have."

A gentle rain was falling as they walked along the Great Road, keeping towards the southern side to allow larger traffic — like the big trade wagon pulled by eight riding lizards — to pass unimpeded. From beneath her travel hood, Urelle looked back to the West, seeing somewhat lighter clouds that hinted at better weather in an hour or so.

"How far is it to Salandar?" she asked.

"About six hundred miles, more or less," Victoria answered. "The average person, in decent health, would do that in about thirty days. With our particular advantages, I would expect to cut that to twenty days."

"A shame we could not all fly there," Quester said. "But all the existing air-cruisers went with the army."

"Yes," Urelle said. "And there's no way I could keep us all flying for any great length of time. It's pretty easy to do for myself, but not for anyone who's not a strong mage." *Which might include Ingram, based on what I sense from him, but not Auntie or Quester*, she thought. It was *odd* that Ingram seemed to have such strong magic about him, but wasn't, by his own account, trained much at all in magic himself. She really needed to sit down with him and discuss it; giving him even a basic grounding in magic could be a big plus under the right circumstances.

"So," she went on, "does anyone here *know* any of the Salandaras?"

"I can't say I *know* any of them," Victoria admitted. "I have, of course, spoken with a few when my friends and I passed through, and roomed there a few times, but none that I would say I know well enough to speak to on such a matter."

"I don't... no, wait, we *do*, I think," Ingram said, his head coming up suddenly. "Quester?"

"Indeed. Indeed. You know the requirements of the Guild membership, of course, Lady Victoria."

"Indeed."

"Then you recall the final test, which seems so simple, yet I suspect eliminates more than other testings might."

"Oh, indeed, the Examination." Urelle could somehow *hear* the capitalization, as Victoria looked to her. "At the conclusion of all other testing, the candidate submits to a direct... survey, one might say, of their soul, to verify that they are who they claim to be, that they are uncoerced in any way, that they have sought to be Adventurers of their own free will, and that they have not merely the will but the *moral and ethical* qualifications to be given the Guild Patch."

"So, every Adventurer has their minds read?" That seemed awfully... intrusive to Urelle, though it obviously made sense to check anyone trying to be an Adventurer awfully carefully.

"Not exactly *read*," Ingram said. "And *soul*, not *mind*. They're not trying to find out your secrets; they're making sure that you won't refuse someone in need, that you aren't carrying an agenda inside you that conflicts with the basic function of Adventuring, I guess is the best way to put it."

"Quite," Victoria agreed, and Quester nodded. "Now, why do you ask, Ingram?"

"Well, we were, um, awfully lucky in our testing. Not only was Toron there to direct the testing, the one who did the Examination was Frederic of the White Robe."

"Oh, my."

Urelle felt her eyes widen. That name wasn't quite on a par with the Wanderer's, but it was very much a name to be repeated with respect. "And so Druyar Salandaras...?"

"Was with him, as you would expect," Quester said, a hint of pride in his buzzing voice — and in his warm-spice scent. "In fact, he was the one who presented us with our Guild Patches."

"Not something even a Salandaras is likely to forget, indeed," Victoria said. "That is a stroke of luck. More than you know."

"What do you mean?" Ingram asked, straightening with hope.

"I mean that he is currently *The* Salandaras, which means that the Freehold is his to ward and watch. If he is present, of course," she went on, her voice cautioning Ingram against too much hope. "He and Frederic are far more Adventurer than they are the sort to stay at home. With the War... they may either have joined the Army of the Dragon, or, just possibly, have returned home to protect their own people. *If* the latter is the case, we may be fortunate."

Ingram nodded. "Let's hope and pray that is the case. Otherwise," he looked grim, "we'll have to convince people we've never met to break the word they've never broken."

Chapter 5
Unwelcome News

Raiagamor smiled in quiet amusement, watching Kerlamion, the so-called King of All Hells, directing the actions of his wide-flung plan. Kerlamion did not realize that the entirety of his actions, of the *plan itself*, were mere distractions, parts of a shadow-play by the true King, *Raiagamor's* King, to allow him to reach a goal that even Raiagamor could only guess.

No comments, my little tenant? he mused. *No thoughts on seeing the world being directed to chaos, from your little country to the very farthest reaches of the world?*

There was no answer. While he could still sense that "tenant" — the final remnant of the true Ares — where he had left it, sealed away within the vastness of his hungry soul — Ares had not spoken to him for a long time indeed. He had railed and pleaded and cursed for the first few months, and then, as he came to grasp his helplessness, spoken less and less. The last time had been... fourteen, fifteen years ago, a feeble protest at the planned murder of a generation of children.

It did not, of course, matter. The tiny core of Ares' essence existed as a salute and a demonstration to the King; what Raiagamor had done, in consuming Ares' power and yet, ultimately, leaving his essential *self* still alive and aware within Raiaga, was something only the King and the Elders could do. By succeeding in this, he had proven himself the equal of those uncountable years older than he — something that had pleased the King.

At this point, it was also something like saving a fine bottle of spirits for a special event; Ares was aging in helplessness, fury, and despair with every passing year, and would be a *fine* celebratory treat at the end. When the time came for even the symbols of the gods to be destroyed, Raiagamor would force Ares to watch... and then, as the remnant god fully understood the totality of Raiaga's victory, he would be consumed.

But Raiagamor needed no commentary from the defeated god to appreciate his unique vantage point on this conversation. Unlike the others participating in this conference — two of the *Mazolishta*, Erherveria, Balgoltha, and more — Raiagamor understood how to use the Scroll given him by his King to *listen*, to *observe*. That knowledge was a little gift given him by the King, a small thanks for the inspiration Raiagamor's own design had given the King in his current project... and one of inestimable value.

It allowed him to watch the unfolding of the scheme of a being who, Raiagamor admitted, was vastly superior to him in every way, and none more so than the ability to manipulate others, to direct their actions down the distance of centuries to culminate in precisely the conditions the King required. It was a breathtaking and, Raiagamor had to admit, an intimidating, perhaps even frightening, thing to watch from the outside, especially since Raiagamor had unwillingly come to the conclusion that it implied that *his own actions* might well be serving the King in ways he did not even guess.

It was not comfortable to realize that your grandest strategy might be only a single move in someone else's great game.

But it *was* entertaining. Especially since, for one outside the circle of plotters and manipulators, it was much easier to *listen*, to hear the hints of quiet deception, to sense that already, perhaps, the Grand Design of Kerlamion had begun to go ever-so-slightly awry. And with the Army of the Dragon now closing in, Kerlamion would have more immediate concerns demanding his attention, distracting him from the more distant problems.

Yes, the King's true plan must be already active, perhaps had been for centuries, but now was guiding the events in ways even the greatest of the Demons had not grasped. *How long, I wonder, until the King no longer needs Kerlamion?* He admitted he would give a great deal to see that conversation... and who knew? Perhaps he would.

At last, the conference was over, and one by one, the others faded from the view of the Scroll. As he reached out to clear his own, the King's eyes turned towards him. "Raiagamor," the calm, pleasant voice said, "bide a moment."

He immediately touched the Scroll in the manner that made it two-way. "Yes, my King?"

"I sensed your observation. Have you any thoughts?"

Raiagamor allowed himself a smile. "It is my thought that it will not be very long before you may have words with the King of All Hells that he will not wish to hear."

"Ha! Indeed, if all proceeds as planned, yes, that shall come to pass in not all that many months." A cheerful smile, so human, yet not. "And have you deduced my own goal?"

"The entirety of it? No, Majesty." Honesty was by far the best policy here. There was no telling exactly what the King wanted, why he had initiated this conversation, and the last thing Raiagamor could afford was to be trapped by his own desire to impress his perhaps-one-day Father. "It is evident to me now, from some of the other conversations I have heard, that the last Justiciar of Myrionar is the focus of your work, and that you have eliminated most of the other followers. You concentrate the power of her god, and weaken it at the same time. But the exact end... No."

"Excellent. If you have not yet seen it, I remain confident that no other shall before it is far too late to stop."

"Was that all, Majesty?" He did not think it had been nearly long enough for the King to need or want a further update, and little had changed; his plans progressed, but nothing remarkable had happened worthy of reporting.

"Yes. Thank you for your..." The King paused, as though a thought had struck him. It was *just* theatrical enough that Raiagamor knew it was purely an act — and that the King wanted him to know it.

This is going to be bad.

"Now that I think of it, there *is* one more thing, Raiaga," he said, in that smooth, deceptively comforting voice.

"How may I serve you, Majesty?" *Best to be as careful as possible.*

"Oh, no, it is not how you may serve *me*. It is that I have some news you may find useful."

It was *here* that the King's essential nature showed itself, even in pleasant-seeming conversation; he paused, the veriest hint of a smile on the human face, eyes glinting with amusement at the tension he was eliciting, and anticipation in whatever unpleasant news he planned to deliver.

But there is nothing for it but that I play along. "Yes, Majesty?"

"Well, you are of course aware that my agent in Zarathanton successfully escaped detection — quite impressive, really, given that he had assassinated the Sauran King in his own palace."

"Indeed, impressive. One of the Elders?"

"Oh, no, no. Not a child, certainly — a descendant of Virigan, in fact, named Alekivir, a mere twenty thousand years old or so." The last part was said without irony; even Raiagamor was more than twenty times older than Alekivir, and he was scarcely newborn compared to the incalculable age of the King and Queen, or even the Elders who had been born of the early days of their reign — and survived the first Great Battle. "Promising, though, with this success."

Another theatrical pause, which Raiagamor had expected; despite this, he found himself restraining his rising temper. "Where was I? Ah. Now, Alekivir has remained in the capital to keep an eye on things, so to speak. I have other spies in the Army of the Dragon King. In any event, one thing he *does* do is watch for interesting arrivals, especially those who seek the counsel of the King."

"But the Sauran King is not there," Raiaga said slowly. "Who is Regent?"

"Calladan, the head of the Academy," the King answered with a smile.

"Hm. A good choice on their part. Not a Sauran, but a well-known name, highly respected, capable." In a way, that was also good for the King's plans. He clearly had no intention of being bothered by *unscheduled* disruptions, and having a strong and intelligent substitute for the Sauran King would minimize the chance of someone using the current chaos to strike against the great City.

And, Raiagamor thought, *it means the most powerful and experienced defender of the Academy... is not there. Useful for anyone seeking to fell* that *institution as well.*

"Yes, quite. But that is of course only a side issue. The *important* thing is that a set of new petitioners appeared a short time ago — one that I think you would have found most intriguing."

Raiagamor raised his eyebrow. "Please, go on, Majesty."

"The most *obvious* point is that several of them were Camp-Bels."

So Deimos' attempt failed, at least in part. "Unsurprising, though somewhat disappointing. Still, they are outside the Shield, and no longer of much concern."

"Indeed, I did not expect that to be of overmuch interest to you. However, there were four in particular of these newcomers that might be of *far* more interest. Two of them were women... and *not* Camp-Bel."

"*Not* Camp-Bel?" That was odd. There had been, as far as he, Deimos, and Phobos had been able to ascertain, no *other* disappearances at the time of the Camp-Bels' departure. "Outsiders, then?"

"Outsiders indeed, but a most intriguing pair of outsiders. You see, their names are Victoria and Urelle *Vantage*."

That caused him to freeze. *This cannot be coincidence.* "Vantage. Related to...?"

"Victoria is her aunt. Urelle, her younger sister." The King's smile had a glint of deadly crystal in it.

"Interesting." More than interesting; anything connected to that family would have some tie to the King's own plans... which made it much more dangerous for anyone, even Raiagamor, to involve themselves. "But how would they have *met* the Camp-Bels? You phrase it as though they were traveling together, yet the Camp-Bels would have traveled from the southern shore to the north, while we know the Vantages had taken up residence near Zarathanton itself."

"Well, yes, they *had*," agreed the King. "But it was only a work of a few hours to ascertain that they had departed that residence, perhaps within *days* of Kyri Vantage's own departure — and headed south." He smiled again. "But not alone. Two others travelled, and still travel, with them. The first is a diminutive youth indeed, with lavender hair, wielding a *most* distinctive weapon that rendered his identification easy: Ingram Camp-Bel."

There was a connection, and a peculiar one. He remembered Ingram vaguely, as the adopted child of the Clan who could never quite keep up with his adoptive family. A pathetic story.

But not so pathetic, not if he was now a companion of the Vantage women. "You said *four*."

"So I did." *Now* the smile was crystal-bladed within the human mouth. "The fourth is *very* interesting. An Iriistiik."

The pattern struck him like a blow, and he froze in order to prevent an all-too-revealing explosion. Only when he was certain that he was under control did he speak. "This is the group that was being tracked. The one Deimos encountered, that was protected by Berenike."

"It would certainly seem likely, yes."

"Then the woman of the prophecy may not be Berenike at all," he murmured, the connections becoming grimly clear. "Or... no, wait."

And then he could not restrain a snarl. "Those *light-damned* cards! It described a person... but did not ever say the description applied to *only* one person! Berenike *is* one threat — and the other *is a Vantage*."

The King grinned savagely. "A *most* interesting development, if so. And I would agree that it is the most direct and obvious conclusion, fitting all of the data we have to perfection... and, as you note, the bent of the Cards to tell the truth while misleading."

"Does this mean that their actions connect to *yours*, Majesty?" The very last thing he wanted was to be directly involved in the King's master-plan; in such a case, anyone — anyone at all — might be a disposable pawn. Perhaps — *perhaps* — the Queen his Mother might not be, but the King would hardly spare a thought before sacrificing Raiagamor under those conditions.

"*Connect*... perhaps. Everything connects in the end, Raiaga. Everything. That is the truth behind all Creation, really. But in the way you mean?"

The King paused then, and for a long moment Raiagamor saw the King truly *thinking*. His eyes flared a blank green, and he sat, unmoving, for many seconds before the alien color faded, and he looked, once more, human.

The human smile, too, returned. "No. Not in the way you feared, Raiaga. The connection is perhaps not *coincidence*, but it is not of my design, nor in any way likely to impact it, so long as neither you nor they approach Evanwyl or the hidden land Kaizatenzei — something I think is most unlikely indeed, given that your interests are already fixed *most* firmly in Aegeia."

"Have you any other intelligence regarding those four?"

"There *was* one more little tidbit of interest, yes," the King said, raising his hand in preparation for ending the communication. "Their current destination is Salandar."

The scroll returned to silvery blankness before Raiagamor had quite absorbed the meaning of those words.

When the meaning did penetrate, he was caught between a gasp of disbelief and a roar of inarticulate fury. Which was fortunate, because the balance between the two gave him a brief moment to regain control of his emotions, clamping down the steely bands of his will upon the raging fire that always burned within his heart.

His eyes went, unwillingly, to the map he had left floating in air a short distance away. Salandar winked from near its center, and just to the south...

The Freehold.

Chapter 6
The Lucky Accursed

Quester smelled Salandar before he could see it. There was a tang of fire and metal, the smell of forges at work; there was the faint understench of garbage and rot from the waste of many people living nearby, but no stronger than that of most places; Salandar must be reasonably clean. The scent of flowers, fields of gravelseed almost ready to be harvested, fresh water flowing; and the many different-yet-similar odors of humans *en masse*.

Sure enough, as they rounded yet another gentle curve in the Great Road, the clear area ahead was populated increasingly by buildings, concentrating to a dense clump a few miles in the distance. There seemed, however, to be something... not quite right about it, and he puzzled over that impression for several minutes before Urelle spoke.

"Why... I don't think they have a *wall* around the town!" she said, disbelief clear in her tone.

"*That* was what was bothering me," Quester agreed instantly, chagrined by the fact the least-experienced of them had seen something so obvious before him. "I see no indication of such a defense." He focused attention narrowly, directing light to be concentrated in a somewhat different way, magnifying the road ahead at the cost of drastically narrowing the width of his field of view. "Hm. There *is* some sort of barrier or impediment, perhaps, but it is not terribly high. Certainly not what we are accustomed to seeing elsewhere."

"Indeed," Victoria said. "You will likely not see anything quite like Salandar anywhere else, either. They have chosen a unique approach to their city, rooted in their individualistic spirits. Every home is a fortress unto itself, and they are connected in time of trouble not by roads, but by tunnels — tunnels patrolled constantly, and enchanted by the allies of the Salandaras to prevent any easy access from below."

Ingram squinted. "So there wouldn't *be* anyone outside if they were under attack?"

"Only those involved in any battle," Victoria said. "All the people you can just make out, now, would be inside."

"What is *that*, Auntie?" Urelle asked, pointing to a peculiar structure located to the south and east. It reminded Quester vaguely of a nested set of pipes that had been cut diagonally, leaving an opening into a central area surrounded by concentric semicircular walls that rose up to the south.

Victoria's mouth tightened as she looked. "The Crucible of Children," she said quietly.

To Quester the phrase meant little, save a hint of something tragic yet proud from the clouded memories within him; Ingram's blink and raised eyebrow showed he, too, did not understand.

Urelle, however, went visibly pale. "The *Crucible*... I thought that was a *story*. A horrid story!"

"No. It's very much real."

"What *is* the 'Crucible of Children', Victoria?" Ingram asked. "I've never heard of it, and I don't think Quester has, either."

"It is a... testing area, one through which all able-bodied children of the Salandaras are sent once they reach no more than ten to eleven years of age," Victoria said after a pause. "The details of that, and the other testing and training the Salandaras put their children through, are not otherwise known."

"It *is* known," she went on, after another pause, "that many of the children do not survive. That area around the Crucible, the one that seems grayish from here, is the Memorial Garden, with a memorial for every child lost."

With a shuddering feeling within his very shell, Quester focused his gaze. Just in his range of vision, the gray abruptly turned to a multitude of distant carven gray stones, interspersed with walkways and dotted with color here and there of gems or flowers or other things in front of the monuments. "Mother's *Mercy*," he buzzed, aware vaguely that his voice must be almost incomprehensible to the others. "There are *thousands* of them."

It would be far less stunning in his own species, of course; larvae were not developed *people* yet, and were often disposed of for various reasons; the Queen could lay far more eggs than any Nest could support as adults. But for *human* children...

"Salandar has stood there a long, long time," Victoria said.

"What kind of monsters *are* they?" Urelle whispered. "Sending children that young to die...?"

Quester directed a spellstunned glance with Ingram. *This certainly does not fit with my impression of Druyar,* he thought to Ingram.

No. But if I've learned anything, it's that surface impressions are often really, really wrong.

"Not monsters," Victoria said. "A people under a most peculiar blessing... and curse. To meet its requirements, they maintain themselves as they are known — which means that even the children will be tested to near-destruction. The curse deprived them of the genius that could have been theirs; the blessing compensates for it, if they maintain the strength of their line."

Ingram seemed far less shocked, and memory told Quester why; the Camp-Bel traditions. Perhaps not so *many* died, but the deaths of both Camp-Bels, and of candidates for God-Warrior, were not few, and also involved those Victoria, certainly, would call children.

"What sort of... curse is this?"

She gazed out at the nearing city. "The Salandaras themselves speak little of it. It may be they know the details but consider them sacred secrets, or that they have forgotten the truth. What I have heard over the years, from sources that might know, is that many thousands of years ago the first Salandar (not their name *then*, of course) and, perhaps, his family, were involved in a great contest of gods; *which* of the darker gods is not clear; some say it was Kerlamion, others one of the Elderwyrm, others still that it was the Lightslayer itself. Their opponent is equally disputed — Terian, Chromaias, Odin, the Triad even. In any event, at the last the Salandar managed to win this contest, but by an act of what the enemy considered sheer, ridiculous luck, aided and abetted perhaps by brilliance, but still offensively improbable. Infuriated by what it considered defeat from a fluke of luck, unable by the letter of the agreement to *kill* the Salandar, it unleashed a tremendous curse upon the helpless human.

"But — again, according to the stories — at the *precise same moment,* the dark god's opponent sent down an equally powerful *blessing*. The two powers contested unexpectedly and dangerously, focused into a single mortal soul... and the result was not what either desired."

A faint smile moved a corner of Victoria Vantage's mouth. "The evil one had intended to reduce his victim to an imbecile and a cripple, one with barely the wit to understand what he had lost and unable to even clean or feed himself, yet long-lived enough to suffer for decades, with none able to undo what had been done. The being of light had wished to reward his successful agent, giving him the best of fortune and ability for so long as his line remained faithful.

"What they *got*..." she chuckled, a laugh that somehow still carried a note of sadness. "What they got was an entire *clan*, a line of descent and of association, whose mental capacities *were* drastically reduced from what they might have been... but not *nearly* so much as the enemy would have hoped."

Understanding brightened within Quester. "Ahh. Thus Salandar, from the Ancient Sauran S'Alandar — without knowledge." Depending on context, he knew, that word in Sauran could easily mean *idiot*.

"Yes; an insult that they embraced and made their own. They were, from the blessing, strong and courageous... and *fortunate*. But they were also bound to *challenge* themselves against the forces of the world, from the youngest to the oldest, and if they failed to do so, the original curse might win out, and this time affecting not just one man, but all those descended from him and bound to his destiny."

"So they're stupid and strong?" Urelle said after a moment.

Another snort of sad laughter. "Less intelligent than they might have been, though not all of them would be called *stupid*. And not, at that, forbidden a certain share of common sense and wisdom. But their *fortune* is the key, and many, even most, believe that what truly happened is that a god of fortune — perhaps the very *essence* of luck — intervened in that clash and took the Salandaras for its own. Those who survive the Crucible, thus, are seen as those *chosen* by Fortune. The others, I assure you, were no less loved, and they do not die unmourned — nor, I think, are their souls left to drift. They are claimed and protected by whoever or whatever their patron is."

She looked forward, to where the buildings were now drawing much closer. "And that is why it is said that any who know a Salandaras well may see their great cheer and great strength and spirit... and sense a sadness beneath, for not one of them who lives does not have a brother, a sister, a friend who went into the Crucible and failed to return."

Quester looked on the strange huddle of buildings and the towering shadow of the Crucible of Children with a new, painful empathy. Cursed to a course they could not escape, they could have broken, died away or become less than they were. Instead, they had embraced the curse and blessing they had been given, and let it become their strength, instead of their weakness. "And thus, they are known to be worthy of trust, for their resolve is shown to be so very strong."

"Certainly my view," Victoria agreed. "I've heard many stories about the Salandaras, but one that I've *never* heard is of one committing treachery. Even the Dragons and the Saurans can't say that about their people."

A tall, broad figure of a woman stood in the road before them. She wore a long coat of mail, emblazoned with a simple device of sword and shield crossed that Quester recognized as the general symbol of the Salandaras. Her hair was dark, fairly straight, and tied back — visible because she wore no helm. She did have a bow and a longsword, with a shield leaning against a low wall nearby. She nodded as they came closer. "Passing through or staying?" she asked after they responded with similar nods.

"We may stay a day or two," Victoria answered, "though we are bound for the Freehold."

"Ah. Many go to Freehold," the woman said after a thoughtful pause. "Not so many here now. War, you know."

Ingram pursed his lips. "So many of those who usually live in town have gone to the Freehold?"

"Right. Safer there. Send workers, farmers if not needed, many warriors. Some stay, keep road safe; Bridgeway, Dragonkill need it."

"What of Artani? Is that road —" Victoria fell silent at the shake of the big woman's head.

"Artani... burned." Her voice was filled with both sadness and anger. "No open road to Empire of Mountain left. Adventurers say Avalanche Gap sealed."

"Great Balance," she murmured. "How, then will the Archmage's forces reach Hell's Edge?"

Quester exchanged quick thoughts with Ingram. "Our guess would be that he will bring them up the Nightsky River as far as Kheldragaard, then march just south of the southern reaches of the Broken Hills to join with the surviving Great Road north of Dalthunia; I doubt that Dalthunia's border guardians will try to oppose such a force as long as it is not trying to invade the country directly."

"I suppose. That will be a much harder journey, though."

"As our enemies doubtless intended." Ingram shrugged. "It isn't our problem, thank the Lady. Guardian... what is your name?"

"Kaydrin," she answered with another small bow.

"An honor to meet you, Guardian Kaydrin."

"Ha! Not true Guardian, just guarding here for moment. But thank you."

"You do the job, you get the title, I think. Is there still an open inn?"

"The Long Bar still open," she said. "Not close *that* unless invaders, and then will fight in bar doorway."

"Excellent!" Victoria brightened. "That's a sight worth seeing. You can *just* make out the start of it ahead."

Kaydrin stepped aside — not that she truly had to, with the hundred-yard width of the Great Road mostly open. "Enjoy. And good fortune."

"Good fortune to you as well," Victoria said, and the others echoed the phrase.

Once they were well past, Ingram glanced back and frowned, puzzlement clear on his face.

What is it, Ingram?

How in the name of the Gods is one Guardian supposed to keep the town safe and the road open?

Quester buzzed in amusement. *I do not know, but I would guess that Guardian Kaydrin is likely not as alone as she appeared, and that she has methods of alerting the town close to hand. They have, as Lady Victoria said, been here for millennia; time for them and their many allies to have placed many subtle and powerful enchantments as well as physical defenses.*

Better believe it, Urelle's mind-voice said. *I did some looking around while you were talking and there's a whole wide band of territory absolutely* saturated *with magic, looks like it surrounds the whole city. I didn't try analyzing it, but I'd bet anything that there's all kinds of alarms and defenses just waiting for someone to be dumb enough to think they could just charge through the guard.* She paused. *Almost as intense as the defenses around Zarathanton, actually, which is* scary. *These people take their protection seriously.*

"As well they should, with their history and interests," Victoria said. "And that means, having been passed inward by their guard and whatever unseen observers and spells there might be, we are much safer now than we have been."

She smiled, her teeth bright in the light of the setting sun. "Now look ahead and see one of the most amusing wonders of the world."

Quester focused his eyes forward again.

"Hello? Quester?"

He became aware that he had stopped dead in the middle of the road, staring in disbelief. "By the *Mother*. That is..."

"The Long Bar," Victoria said, her voice carrying the satisfaction of one who has seen the reaction they had hoped for.

"I'm not clear on what we're *seeing*," Ingram said. He pulled out his far-viewer device. "It looks like something sitting across the... *Athena and Ares!*"

Quester understood his friend's reaction all too well, as he still could not quite believe what he was seeing.

The Long Bar was a gigantic structure that *straddled* the entire Great Road, constructed of blocks of polished stone and massive, ancient beams of wood cut from trees that must have been some of the greatest monarchs of the forest in their day. Twin doors were swung wide — each door fifty yards across and well over thirty high, mounted on immense rollers to swing easily shut, but with signs that they had likely not been shut in years, if not decades. Within the vast tunnel of the interior, Quester could make out counters, storefronts, doors leading to the interior of the building on either side of the road, loading docks...

The gigantic building extended far down the road — at least a thousand feet, perhaps *twice* that, nearly as long as the Dragon's Palace was high.

"Great *Mother*," he buzzed again. "What need for a city have they? *That* is a city unto itself!"

"The Long Bar often *is* a city of its own, when there is no war," Victoria said. "You have seen how busy the Great Road is to the West in time of peace, have you not? This is scarcely less busy, for any traffic bound to or from the Empire, or to and from Dragonkill, must pass through here — and Salandar is the only truly safe location in several hundred miles in either direction."

She smiled again and nodded in the direction of the Bar. "And unlike many establishments *within* cities, the Long Bar is designed with accommodations of all types, including ones to serve beings vastly larger than ordinary humans. Accomodations including markets, private rooms, meeting rooms... and, of course, food and drink!"

She turned back towards the Long Bar, which now showed a faint glow from within as twilight began to fall. "Come, we will discover word of the road to the Freehold, and stay in the most comfortable beds for a hundred miles and more!"

Even though he found himself far more tolerant of variation in bedding than his friends, Quester approved of this course of action.

Chapter 7
The Freehold

"We must be getting close," Urelle said.

Victoria nodded, seeing the same signs as her niece. The path into Wisdom's Fortress was broad, not terribly difficult, but wound somewhat through the foothills. However, the way the slope of the path was changing, and the depth to which they had now penetrated the mountain range, argued that they *must* now be approaching the single pass through the range which was guarded by the Freehold.

"I sure hope so," Ingram said with a grimace, rolling his neck side to side. "Another week on the road after just *one* night in the Long Bar is really getting tedious."

"I, too, appreciate more sheltered resting places," Quester buzzed, "but at least that night was free, thanks to Urelle."

"Well, you all were watching—"

"—but we were not *doing*," Victoria cut off Urelle's attempt to minimize her work. "You found the problem, you undertook to solve it, and you did. The fact that you later discovered we had been observing does not in *any* way detract from the work you did. And Outas Salandar will remember it as well."

"I... I guess."

"By the *Wisdom* he certainly will!" Ingram's voice was affectionate and just a touch exasperated. "Stop minimizing your own work! You're an Adventurer like us, and with the three of us to testify to things you've done, you'll end up Guilded in no time once we can reach a Guildhall again."

Victoria nodded, pleased by the others' vehement insistence that Urelle take credit for her own work. *And it was a good little bit of work; pests damaging the stores which turned out to be a bit more than ordinary pest control might handle, but a wizard with field experience? Not so much a problem.*

They rounded a curve and could see before them... and all four of them stopped dead in the middle of the road, gazing incredulously at the sight before them.

After a few frozen moments, Victoria shook her head, leaning on Twin-Edged Fate as she gave vent to a soft laugh. "The world does not cease to amaze, does it?"

"*How?*" was Ingram's only word, staring forward and up.

She was asking herself the same question.

Twin mountains — the Guardian Twins, she thought they were called — reared before them, fifteen thousand feet high — and they were *smaller* than the ones flanking them. Between the Twins was — *had been* — a pass, a gap that had been narrow on the scale of such things.

But instead of the slopes of the mountains coming smoothly down to a pass, perhaps guarded by an ordinary fortress...

It was a *wall*, but a wall such as she had never seen, a wall beside which the barrier surrounding Zarathanton itself was but a temporary barricade. A towering, squared-off barrier looming fifteen hundred feet into the air, level for its entire mile and a half of breadth, lay before them, composed of the granite and basalt of the mountains, jumbled together as though they were a cross-section of an avalanche.

Glancing upward, she saw sharp divots in the shoulders of the Twins, and thought that — perhaps — that was precisely what the great wall *was*. *Though how in the name of the Balance it became so straight and smooth and solid, I cannot imagine. Only the descriptions I have heard of the walls of Hell's Edge might compare with this.*

In the air above the great wall... was tumult. The air itself flickered like heatwaves, clouds skirled and spun along the length of the stone bulwark, and other shapes danced and dove, in motions that might have seemed random but that Victoria could tell were nothing of the sort. *Even were we to assay to fly over that wall, we would not find the passage easy; the air between the Twins is, itself, a wall, less substantial but I think no less effective than the stone beneath it.*

Exactly in the center of that mighty barrier was a castle — a fortress that in any other setting might have been imposing indeed, but was here, before and against the titanic grey backdrop of that wall, somehow diminished. There was a tower on either side of the path they were following, flanking walls of the castle's own that rose over a hundred feet, with a broad set of double doors in the exact center.

Bright lights glittered along that wall, and flickers of firelight and light globes sparkled from the windows that showed the multiple floors within the fortress. The area before the gates was brightly lit, and as they approached Victoria could see that there were numerous soldiers watching, both from atop the castle walls and before the gates.

"Stop there!" called a guard wearing gold-striped mail. "Who are you? What brings you to the Freehold?"

"I am Victoria Vantage, Adventurer, Zarathanton Guilded," she answered. "With me are two other Guilded, Ingram Camp-Bel and Quester, and my niece Urelle Vantage, a wizard of some skill."

"You advance alone," the gold-striped one said. "We see your patch, check it."

"Of course."

Up close, the guard had black hair and darker skin than the other Salandaras she had seen thus far, but there was still something in his face and bearing that marked him as one of that clan. A scar ran across his face, and one eye was covered with a patch. "I am Nogra Salandar, First Guardian of Freehold Gate."

He tapped her patch, nodded at the response. "Good. You two, we check also," Nogra said, and in a moment Ingram and Quester had passed. He nodded at Urelle and gave a brief smile. "You come long way here. What reason? Freehold is closed — Aegeia has declared Seal of the Cycle. No passing here."

"Surely you would not deny travelers shelter, though?"

A rumble of laughter. "No, we have beds — not many, but we can find four more. War has crowded us; we prepare, in case war go badly."

"Have many Salandaras gone with the army?" Ingram asked.

Nogra nodded. "Many. Half our warriors go with Sauran King's army. Maybe enough. Most of others here... in case Black City does not fall." He glanced at them with a shrewd glint in his eye. "But you ask questions, not answer mine. What reason you come to Freehold? No one take *this* road by accident!"

She heard Ingram exchange thoughts with Quester, so swiftly that she could barely get a sense of it. *They have been linked much longer than either Urelle or myself.* Quester bowed to Nogra. "You are correct. We seek Druyar Salandaras, if he is indeed *The* Salandaras, as we have heard."

The thick black brows came together, then rose. "Yes, Druyar is Freehold Lord, the Salandaras, and he is here. You know him?"

Ingram tapped his shoulder. "It was he who awarded us our Guild Patches, and his companion of the White Robe who administered our final test."

"Hm! Sounds like something he might remember. Good, then. Come in."

The interior of the Freehold was only less impressive than its exterior by the fact that even the Dragon's Palace would have been small compared to the impassable bulwark surrounding and above the Freehold. The entryway was more than sufficiently grand, ornamented in statuary of bright colors that included many figures of warriors, women and men both, and a wide variety of monsters, strange mechanical beasts, and individuals of every species Victoria had heard of, and a few she hadn't.

They didn't have much time to study the scenery, though, because Nogra led them straight through another set of doors, past a vacant throne, and behind it to a smaller set of rooms.

A huge man wearing silvery-polished armor was studying a map with the air of someone trying to focus on a lesson several steps beyond them; next to him, a brown-haired man of average build in white-and-gold robes was speaking quietly.

The big man turned quickly, a student rescued from lecture by an unexpected but welcome interruption. "Nogra! What you bring..." He paused, and abruptly the square, stolid face lit up with pleasure. "Young adventurers! Have not seen you for long! Come, sit, talk!"

Ingram's face had also lightened. "You *do* remember us!"

"HA!" The laugh was quick and cheerful. "Druyar forget many things, yes, but not swear in many adventurers. And never one boy and one bug, no! You are... Ingram, yes, and this is Quester. Remember that. Quest mean adventure!"

"You appear to have made quite the impression," the other man said with a gentle smile. "Of course, I remember you both very well. Thank you, Nogra — you may return to your post." As the guard left, the smaller man went on, "now, Adventurer Ingram, if you would be so kind as to introduce your companions...?"

"Of course, sir! This is Victoria Vantage, also Zarathanton Guilded, and her niece Urelle, who is quite a wizard and should really be Guilded already, herself." He turned to Victoria and Urelle. "This is Frederic of the White Robe, and Druyar Salandaras, Guilded Adventurers—"

"—and Adjudicators of the Dragon Throne, yes," Victoria completed, and bowed low; she saw Urelle copy her motion. "It is an honor to meet you both. Your reputations most certainly precede you."

"As does yours, Lady Victoria, if you are indeed the same who once traveled with our newly-crowned King."

Druyar's brilliantly green eyes brightened further. "Oh! *That* Victoria! Yes, we hear many stories!"

Victoria saw a glint in that gaze that confirmed her suspicions. *He may be far from the brightest man I have met, but he is certainly not as dull as he pretends. As befits a man of his reputation.*

Druyar insisted they all sit, and then bellowed cheerfully for refreshments to be brought. Victoria did not argue; after all the time on the road, a chance to rest and eat would never go amiss. And here, at least, she felt safe, indeed.

Only after they had all eaten something did Druyar lean forward in his chair and speak. "Come long way to see me. Why?"

The others glanced at her. *You want to tell him?* Ingram's mindvoice asked.

I suppose I might as well. It is your mission... but it is ours now. "Because we have a mission which cannot succeed unless we can find a way to enter Aegeia."

Druyar frowned. "Can't just let —"

"Druyar, let the Lady finish," Frederic said quietly.

"Sorry. Go on, then."

"Ingram here," she gestured, and Ingram nodded, "is a native of Aegeia, a Camp-Bel, as I believe you knew. We have found of late that he has been hunted by others representing the god Ares, and have other reason to believe that he, and possibly the rest of us, are specific targets of theirs."

Frederic pursed his lips, but said nothing.

"Moreover, we have learned that Ares' actions are *not* normal for the Cycle. We suspect something far worse is happening, and that it may be a matter of prophecy that we, or at least one or two of us, will be vital to the opposition of Ares and the victory of Athena.

"Of course, we also know that Aegeia has been Sealed. But it is also certain that there is a point at which the Seal is weaker, perhaps able to be passed through by those with the skill to find that weakness and exploit it. Calladan Mystraios, the current Regent, worked with us to determine that the only likely location for that weakness is here, likely in the depths to the rear of the Freehold."

Druyar was silent for several long moments, his deeply-tanned brow furrowed under his peculiarly golden hair. Finally, he sat back with a deep sigh. "How you sure this Cycle bad? Not same as others?"

"Ares hunted down the Camp-Bels," Ingram said. "Half of them fled Aegeia entirely but he sent ships after them, and if we hadn't caught up with them at the right time all my Clan-brethren would have been killed. Assassins were sent out after us, tracking us with magical coins that showed our enemies the direction to find us. And the survivors of my Clan told me that there was some kind of prophecy associated with me, and maybe my friends, too."

"Huh." He paused again, then looked to his companion. "Guardian?"

Frederic — who Victoria now remembered was one of the Guardians of the Wild, serving under Willowwind Forestfist, the Warden of Nature and Chosen of Eonae — frowned and was also quiet for a moment. "Taking your words at face value — and I believe you, for as well as knowing you are Guilded I was the one who administered your final examination — you have, indeed, a powerful reason to find a way to enter Aegeia. And with the importance of Aegeia and Athena to the State of the Dragon King, there is also strong reason for us to support you in this quest."

"But..." Ingram said, speaking the implied word.

"But cannot let through." Druyar's tone was both regretful and final. "Oath clear. The Salandaras hold the Freehold. When the Seal made, we are part of Seal."

Which implies that Athena was very much aware of the one possible vulnerability when first she Sealed Aegeia. And the fact that no one has ever exploited it says that either no others have ever sought to enter that way...

... or that the Salandaras have done very well in their task, Ingram finished bleakly.

Urelle looked up. "The Salandaras are *part* of the Seal?"

"Is way oath worded, yes?" Druyar looked to Frederic again.

"Well... yes, I suppose. The Salandaras and the Freehold 'become the completion' of the Seal, if the ancient records are correct, and 'their wills support and uphold the Seal as one with their oath'."

"Then a *Salandaras* could pass through the Seal without breaking their oath, right?"

Druyar stared blankly at her, but his expression was matched by that of his companion. It was another minute before a smile spread like slow dawn across Frederic's face, transforming his ordinary visage to one of startled amusement. "I... cannot fault your logic, Urelle."

"Then if *you* come with us —"

Druyar cut his hand through the air, chopping the words off. "Defender of Freehold. Need to be here to protect people. If leave, will be to join army against Black City, or protect Salandar. Like to Adventure, but not this way."

"Druyar is correct." Frederic's expression held nothing but regret. "We have too many responsibilities, and there is no telling, first, if we even *can* find a way through the Seal, and second, if we could *return*, having done so. And," he held up his own hand, forestalling the next question, "our other, more formidable, Adventurers have nearly all answered the call of the Sauran King. There are no others here who could be both formidable enough to accompany you, and could be spared from the potential defense of the Freehold."

"But sir..." Victoria could hear the strain in Ingram's voice, trying to stay controlled and reasonable when part of him was so desperate to *move*, to go *forward*, "isn't there *something* you could do? This *is* part of your job too, right? To protect the State of the Dragon King? You are Adjudicators! There must be *some* way!"

"Can't see way. Not many Salandaras, really. Most good ones at battle."

Victoria sighed. *He is right. In a way, it is like Ingram; the Camp-Bels have only so many people, and it will take them many years to recruit...*

She felt a flash of light from Quester. *Recruit?*

"What is it, Quester?" Ingram asked, obviously having felt his friend's moment of enlightenment.

"What if," Quester said, with the deliberation of one just understanding their own idea, "What if... one of us were to *become* a Salandaras?"

Chapter 8
Becoming a Salandaras

Ingram had to laugh. It was typical of Quester to find the straightforward path that no one else saw.

Druyar began to chuckle, too, and soon he and Frederic were laughing together. "That... that funny! Not stupid, maybe good idea. But funny."

"That it was. Quite clever, Quester," Frederic said, a smile still evident. "A most *interesting* idea, in fact. Let us consider it."

"Not much consider," Druyar said. "Salandaras if born, or if married to Salandaras. Yes?"

"Well, that is of course one obvious path, yes. If one of you were to marry into the family, you would be one of them."

That wiped the smile off everyone else's faces, including Ingram's. *Marry?* That was a tremendous thing to ask. *But,* he thought, a trickle of hope beginning to flow, *it's not impossible, and maybe...*

Victoria was the first to speak. "Not... entirely impossible. Marriages of convenience are not unheard of, and while I cannot see this as an option for Urelle or Ingram, let alone Quester, it so happens that *I* am currently unwed."

Druyar sighed and shook his head. "Can't just say words. Have to *mean* words."

"What Druyar means is that you cannot have a pure marriage of convenience — not and be counted a member of the Salandaras," Frederic amplified. "I do not think that it is required that you be in love with your partner, or that there have been any specific period of development for the relationship, but the oaths of marriage for the Salandaras are binding and specific, and you *must* mean them when you swear the oath."

Victoria nodded. "I suppose I should have expected something of the sort. To what would I be committing myself?"

Frederic reached into the small pack leaning on the table leg near him, dug around, and pulled out a small book, which he flipped through. "Ah. Here." He read for a moment in silence, his brow becoming furrowed as he did so. "Most of the conditions seem... not unreasonable, and deal with your proper relationship with your pledged partner — defending them, supporting them, listening to their concerns, and some parts of the oaths deal with the level and extent of exclusivity in the relationship, possessions, other responsibilities... but I am afraid that two of the most important conditions would pose an issue.

"First, you would have to renounce all loyalty to any and all other countries, becoming a citizen of Salandar first and of the State of the Dragon King second, with no others holding your loyalty."

Victoria drew in a breath. "That... *is* something to give me pause. I am a loyal citizen of Evanwyl, and as a Vantage I am technically one of the Eyes themselves, although at rather a far remove at the moment. But go on."

"The second is that you renounce your prior name and family, becoming a Salandaras in all ways."

Ingram felt the spark of absolute refusal from both Victoria and Urelle before the older woman spoke. "*That* is, I am afraid, a dealbreaker indeed. I am a *Vantage*, and I cannot renounce that."

"Neither can I," Urelle said.

"In honesty, I cannot blame you," Frederic said with a sad smile. "But if you cannot pledge those two oaths, then marriage is not an option."

Ingram felt as though a vise was slowly closing on him. *There's no other way into Aegeia! We have to get through here!*

For a moment he considered just charging through, into the rear of the castle, seeking a hint or sign of the weakness of the Seal... but his training simply sat up and smacked him for the thought. *This is a rightful and just ruler, one of those I am to protect, not betray. And even if I would... it's ridiculous. I know the stories of the Salandaras; Druyar would probably beat all four of us by himself.*

"There has to be *some* way, sir!" he said, hating the way his voice wavered, showing his own desperation in his tone.

The two were quiet for a few minutes, then Frederic looked up. "What about that woman, Serena? Isn't she technically a Salandaras?"

"Yah, yah, she is," Druyar said, perking up. But then his brows came down. "But... granted that for *help*. Saved many of us. Fought shoulder-to-shoulder, too, after saving town."

"Yes, I remember now," Frederic said. "It's a perfectly viable route, but you would have to perform some great service to the Salandaras before you could be given honorary acceptance into the clan."

"And unless something uniquely suited to us just happens to turn up in the next few minutes, it would seem unlikely that this could be done in the next few days, or even weeks," Victoria said reluctantly.

"Yes." Frederic's mouth firmed with resolve. "Still, the Salandaras Clan has existed for thousands of years. I have to believe that similar situations have happened before. Let us see if the records have anything to tell us."

"Druyar not sneaky one," the Salandaras said with a grin. "Think straight forward, like sword blade. Let Guardian do twisty thinking."

Frederic smiled fondly at Druyar. "We each do what the other cannot. We both want a resolution to Ingram's problem without compromising our honor."

"Yes. Go look in records. I think here. Maybe slow, but sometimes think of things anyway."

The brown-haired Guardian led the way through a side corridor. "Druyar is not *quite* as slow as he makes himself out to be," he said.

"We had guessed as much," Ingram said. "Even with someone to help you, you don't survive Adventuring for that many years if you're truly an idiot."

"Truly. And he has occasionally surprised me and others by having a moment of brilliant insight. Still, he is right that complex thinking is my major part of our partnership — that and my mastery of natural forces, of course," Frederic said as they made their way down a long set of stairs, and then along another hallway. "The latter will likely not matter in our current problem, though."

"One possible problem," Quester said. "Do these other routes, such as being awarded membership, also come with the same strictures?"

"No," Frederic answered. "Marriage is a choice by the newcomer to become one of us; Clan-Through-Honor, or adoption, is a choice by the Salandaras, and this forces no other choices on the chosen."

They turned right and passed through an open set of double doors, of gray shardwood and bound with polished bronze. *Enchanted,* Urelle's mindvoice informed them. *This whole room is well warded.*

I am unsurprised, Quester said.

The room was over a hundred feet long, fifty wide, and twelve high, and the walls were covered with bookshelves, pigeonhole racks for scrolls, and a collection of other objects of various types ranging from a scattering of green crystals to a white-gleaming skull sitting in the center of one of the tables that ran up the center of the room.

"The Vault of Memories," Frederic said, gesturing around. "Every event of significance, and many of insignificance, throughout the clan's history is supposedly gathered here."

"I hope you have a guess as to where we should look," Urelle said, staring around with no little awe, "because there's no way we have a *tenth* of the time we'd need if we have to search *everything*."

"I do," Frederic said. "But I am afraid it will be the most mind-numbingly boring portion of the records. Over here," he led them to a series of shelves on the far side of the room, filled with rank upon rank of identical books, "are the membership records of the clan — simple notations of births, deaths, and marriages, as well as passage through the Crucible. If there is any other way to become a Salandaras, it will be hidden in these books."

"That makes unfortunate sense," Victoria said. "If we do not become so mind-fatigued that it all blurs out, the entry of a Salandaras who is *not* married or wed to the clan should stand out."

The little group divided up the six shelves of books between them, and began working their way through them. *Six hundred books or I am still an egg*, Quester said grimly. *This will not be entertaining.*

After getting the symbols used by the Salandaras to represent births, deaths, Crucible passage, and marriages firmly fixed in his head, Ingram found the records exactly as mind-numbingly dry as Quester had predicted. Page after page of names did, in fact, blur into each other, as he simply grew used to scanning for the symbols.

"Oh! What's this one?" Urelle asked, her voice shockingly loud after nearly an hour of silence broken only by the turning of pages. "Let me see." Frederic scrutinized the page, then shook his head. "*That* is someone being sloppy. They started to mark *marriage* and then corrected themselves to *birth* — probably they were transcribing a number of events at once, catching up. But they weren't too careful about the correction."

"*Balance*," Urelle cursed. "I had hoped I had *found* something."

Another half-hour passed. "Frederic, I am quite sure that *this* is a new symbol," said Victoria.

"Hmm... My, yes, I have not seen that one before. Let me see..." Frederic muttered something and light danced on the page, was echoed from several of the other books. "Well, that isn't very helpful. Those other volumes will have entries with that symbol, but that doesn't tell us *what* it—"

"Pardon me," Quester said, "but there was also a glimmer from that shelf over there." He pointed to a shelf across the room and about eight feet from the floor.

"Over *there*?" Frederic's puzzlement was obvious. "Let's try again."

Sure enough, a green glint flickered on that shelf for a moment when Frederic repeated his spell. "Well, may Wind and Tree ward us. That's unexpected."

Urelle gestured and all the books near the glint — four or five of them — floated off the shelves and down to them.

"Yes, yes... now what's *this?*" Frederic had found an exquisitely thin book, more like a pamphlet, that had been stuck between two others. He opened it up, and then began laughing.

"What is it?" Victoria inquired.

"Something that would have made both your work and mine much easier had I known it existed. This is an actual *key* to the records — a summary of all the known and allowable markings to be used in the records. Someone — probably decades, perhaps *centuries* ago — put it up on that shelf for some reason, and it's never been put back where it belongs."

"So what *is* the symbol here, then?"

"Let's see... ah. Rather the *opposite* of what we were looking for. This means *exiled from the Clan.*"

"Ouch. I guess *that* doesn't happen very often."

"This is the first I've heard of it," Frederic said, eyebrows both arched high. "But then, I doubt the Salandaras would want to call attention to such things, either."

"More importantly, are there symbols we *should* be looking for?" Ingram said, trying not to let too much of his impatience and worry show in his voice. "If we could find some such, that same spell of yours would really cut down our search time."

"That it would. My apologies, but understand, I spend half my life researching things; discovering a key glossary you never knew existed?" Frederic's brown eyes were practically *sparkling* with excitement. "That's like digging in a farmer's field and striking a vein of *krellin*." He bent over the little booklet again. "Hmm... yes. Here we go. This symbol means *adoption into Clan*. And this one... yes, I remember this in front of Serena's entry, it means *Clan Through Honor*."

"Adoption. Can you find that symbol?"

"Easily done. Everyone, go to the books we have out and sort out the ones that glow."

For a moment, Ingram was worried that most of the books would glow, but then he realized how unlikely that was; they hadn't *seen* that symbol in an hour and a half of searching.

Less than one out of ten of the books glowed this time, and they soon had all of them stacked on one table. They began leafing quickly through each, looking for that symbol.

"Looks like all of the kids so far were adopted very young — I'm not seeing any of them older than about three years old," Ingram said after a while.

"That makes sense, I am afraid. The Salandaras' way is hard, and children must generally be brought up in it to survive. They do not adopt often at all — most candidates for adoption would be brought to other families or cities. And as you see... many adoptees do not survive to be adults."

"The Crucible?"

Frederic bowed his head.

Ingram felt himself smiling. "Then that's the solution, isn't it? If Druyar will adopt me, then I have to pass the Crucible, and then I'm truly one of you."

"What if you get *killed* in the Crucible?" Urelle demanded.

"Look, not to minimize in any way what the Salandaras are like, they're still mostly kids who are what, eight, nine, ten? I'm sixteen years old and a Guilded Adventurer! Besides, if I can't get through this Crucible, how can I expect to survive whatever Ares has waiting for us?"

"The idea has some merit, young Ingram," Frederic said. "But unfortunately, your age argues against it. As you have noted, the Crucible is intended for those significantly younger."

"They can't *all* have been the same ages. I mean, over *thousands* of years haven't there ever been exceptions?"

"It is, I think, simple to check." Once more Frederic muttered words that Ingram could not quite check, and the green foxfire light burned on most of the volumes; a second time, and perhaps half of them glowed. A third incantation, with a bit of strain showing on the Guardian's face, and only a few scattered volumes glowed; another, and only one glimmer was seen, on the table nearest Quester; two more repetitions of the spell, and this time there were no glows at all.

Frederic of the White Robe shook his head. "By combining the simple search of age with the Crucible symbol, I have surveyed the ages of those who passed the Crucible after their tenth year; as you could see, the oldest ever to pass was fourteen." He picked up the last volume to glow, leafed through it, found the entry. He then cast a similar spell again, looking weary, and several volumes on other shelves glowed. He chose one and paged through that one as well.

"The oldest to pass the Crucible was Jorna Salandaras, who had unique circumstances. She was adopted late — at about six years of age — and she was an *Odinsyrnen*, and so matured more slowly. Now while you could indeed argue that you have unique circumstances, I can't see them extending the age limit so far beyond precedent that —"

"I'm fourteen."

Ingram felt a spurt of both hope and fear go through him at Urelle's statement. "What?"

She looked at Frederic. "For another couple of months, I'm fourteen. And I know I'm human, but I haven't had any time at all to be raised in Salandaras society. I'm pretty well trained and I've been on Adventure with my aunt and friends, but I've still *got* to be less prepared than your normal Crucible entry. Couldn't that balance out my age?"

Victoria looked unutterably proud.

She's got to be terrified of the idea, Ingram thought, *but she's not going to let Urelle see that. So Urelle shouldn't see* me *having that problem, either.*

Frederic smiled, though a crease of worry was on his brow. "You realize that the Crucible is meant for Salandaras — warriors, almost to the last person. While this may make some of its challenges easier for a mage, others may be almost impossible. One of the blessings of the Salandaras is their strength, and you are…"

Urelle — only a couple inches over Ingram's height, and slender — stepped over to one of the long tables, gripped it, and with careful, slow deliberation, lifted the massive solid-wood table over her head, then brought it back down again, letting it come to rest without so much as a jar.

"... you are obviously not deficient in that category," Frederic finished his statement. He gave a half-disbelieving laugh. "It is in Druyar's hands, then. But perhaps. We have, at least, precedent, and the fact that we know and understand your urgency. It is, after all, not in the interest of the Salandaras to be *manipulated* by others, and if this is truly a false Ares, we should not be guarding his back door at all."

"Then let us put everything — including your newly-found key — back where it belongs," Quester said. "And then we can see what the Salandaras decides!"

Chapter 9
A Final Consultation

He stood atop Mistveil Peak, looking out from Aegeia to the north and west. Somewhere out there, he knew, the armies of the Sauran King and the Archmage were confronting those of Kerlamion. *That would be a battle to see.* And one that would likely allow him to steal countless souls for power. *Unfortunately, I don't have time for such amusements.*

Raiagamor had come here for a far different and much more urgent purpose. He extended claws rarely seen by any, assumed his true shape for a moment, for what he was about to do was delicate and perilous — if not to him personally, most certainly to his plan.

The Seal of Athena is not quite *unbreachable. Beings such as the King and myself have a unique power to do so. But I must do it extremely carefully, for what I do* not *wish to do is leave a weakened area — or, worse, damage the enchantment so that it unravels.*

What he did then would perhaps have made sense to the young mage Urelle — though she would never have been able to duplicate it. He touched the strands of enchantment, the stupendously complex and immense structure, and found the parts of the enchantment that barred creatures and beings of intellect or power... and slowly, carefully shifted *himself* until he could tell that those forces no longer responded to him, no longer recognized him as anything other than the least of animals.

With that, Raiagamor passed easily through a seal that could have stopped a god, and stood on the other side of the barrier. He walked down the slope, searching, until he found a flat area of stone, perhaps fifty feet long and twenty wide.

Now he could accomplish his goal. Resuming his human form, he produced from his neverfull pack a small table, a chair, and a metal-and-bone tube inscribed with many runes. When opened, the tube released the polished-metal scroll he had used several times before.

Setting the scroll in the holders designed for it, he sat down and touched the smooth surface, willing it to activate. "Majesty?"

There was no response at first, but Raiagamor had not really expected one. The King had his own plans and responsibilities, and would be unlikely to interrupt them for his still-unacknowledged offspring.

That he *would* answer eventually — of that, Raiagamor was certain. The King had given his word, and for all the terrible and true things one could say about him, one absolute was that he kept his word scrupulously.

So Raiagamor waited patiently. His rage was well under control; in this quiet, clean, cold space he felt as nearly peaceful as he ever could. For the moment there were no demands, no conflicts, no decisions, not even hunger. Just the wind and the mist, the faint hissing clatter as small stones shifted, the pure scent of the thin, crisp air. He took this in; let it fill him. Calmness, peace, these were things he knew so rarely, and both things that would serve him well in any contact with the King.

With scarcely a shimmer, the blank gold changed to a dark room and the familiar blond man with his even more familiar half-smile. "Raiagamor, what an unexpected pleasure. What occasions this call?"

And once more to the unspoken contest. "A pleasure to speak with you as well, Majesty. As you know, I had thought that, perhaps, I could and should complete my plan without availing myself of my third opportunity for your assistance."

"And yet you have called. Has something gone wrong?" The smile was a study in twin edges, false sympathy and mockery in one.

"Not at all, Majesty." A tiny but unmistakable uptick of the eyebrow. "At the moment, things appear well in hand. Yet I thought much on this, and it came to me that one who waits *until* something has gone wrong makes the righting of their plan much more difficult; and that one who foregoes a powerful resource out of pride is twice a fool. So I would consult you for a third and final time, now."

A true smile spread across the King's face. "Now that is both well-spoken *and* well thought, Raiagamor. And you are correct; even had your plan succeeded, I would have had doubts still had you not taken advantage of this resource. Pride is our strength... and our great weakness. So come, he who would be my child; what would you have of me? The Cards, once more?"

"No." He smiled with a sour edge to it. "Truthful or not, I have seen how well they seek to mislead; I begin only now to suspect the fullness of their deceptive truths. No, my King, I would have advice. *Your* advice. I will lay before you all I plan, all I know, all I guess, and then ask you to tell me one action that I have not taken that I *should* take to make my victory most certain."

The King pursed his lips, then stood and bowed. "Your thinking is clear and shows you *have* learned somewhat, Raiagamor. Very well." He extended his hand, and it emerged from the surface of the scroll. "Bring me through, for this is best done face-to-face."

Raiagamor grasped the King's hand and pulled; in an instant, the human form of the King stood before him. Raiagamor knelt and bowed his head.

"Oh, no, no need for that now," the King said, and pulled him to his feet. "I am here as a mere consultant, not one to take your oath or pass judgment... yet. Another chair would not go amiss, however."

"Of course, Majesty."

With both now seated, the King studied him from deceptively innocent blue eyes. "And will you trust me enough to take all you know directly? Or must we talk it through?"

Raiagamor considered. "If you give your word that you will take nothing I would not willingly give you, and pass no judgments unasked based on anything you see... then directly would be acceptable, and I think wisest."

The King bowed. "You have my word. I will take only that which you offer, that I must learn in order to properly advise you, and if I see aught else — say, your plans for my overthrow later — I shall dismiss it from my mind and judge you not." He laughed at the faint twitch that Raiagamor was not — quite — able to restrain. "Child, it is of no moment to me. Fully half of my children have entertained such thoughts at one time or another, and no few have gone beyond idle speculation. It is a perfectly reasonable ambition, even admirable if the plotter lays his plans well."

For an instant, the face shifted and the smile was immense, crystal blades beneath blank, yellow-glowing orbs, hungry and perilous. "The only punishment comes if the plotter sets their plans in motion... and *fails*."

In other words, I will be safe as long as I leave such things in the realm of thought and not of action. Good to know. "Then shall we begin, Majesty?"

The King took his outstretched hand.

Raiagamor found himself stumbling back, shaking, horrified and awed and fearful. The King simply laced his fingers together and leaned back, regarding Raiagamor with dark amusement.

It had truly been nothing but a single touch. Yet in that instant, the King's mind and soul had touched Raiagamor's. In that single instant he had *felt* the King locate and gather every element and aspect of his grand plan, every single fact or deduction or event, howsoever small, that might have relevance to the success or failure of the mission, and absorb it, a single drop of water added to the immensity of an ocean. But more, Raiagamor had *seen* the Soul of the King, and it was infinitely grander and more awesome and terrifying than Raiaga had even begun to imagine. It seemed to him that a monstrous shadow loomed up, encompassing not merely the world but the universe, stars and galaxies themselves as motes of dust before infinite hunger, ultimate malice, immeasurable and pitiless amusement at the devices and schemes of beings scarcely able to comprehend the adversary they would face.

"Yes," the King said softly. "Perhaps you *are* of my children, for few others indeed could have seen and understood so much, Raiagamor."

Raiaga was immensely grateful, all of a sudden, for the brief but intense peace he had felt before. That peace gave him a buffer, a cushion that allowed him to fight back against the feeling of insignificance and horrid, hungry menace without letting the rage envelop him — something that would have undoubtedly been fatal. *He expected that reaction; now I must recover, must accept and act as though I have seen nothing!*

He rose and seated himself across from the King. "So you have seen the plan and all things I believe impinge upon it."

"I have. And an excellent structure of intent you have built. It is... worthy of having inspired me. Have you any specific question you wish to ask, or any additional thoughts?"

He took a breath — not, strictly speaking, necessary, but the human body responded to such things, and it was well to pay attention to all aspects of one's masquerade. "I have thought long and hard on these things, Majesty, and one thing that I have, reluctantly, come to conclude from study of history is that would-be heroes, and especially Adventurers, overcome obstacles, even — or perhaps *especially* — when this appears impossible."

"And...?"

"And that means that, improbable though it would seem, I must assume that Ingram Camp-Bel and his companions will somehow find a way through the Seal and all the obstacles I have raised — even though some of those exist on levels he cannot possibly imagine now. I believe it would be best if your advice touched upon them in some way."

"Oh, excellent. Yes, that is one of the most important lessons to learn. Heroes *find a way*. This is not merely a truism, it is, in some very real sense, the way the world works. The Creation prefers creation; we are agents of destruction."

Raiagamor stared at his unacknowledged grandfather. "You mean the *universe itself* assists heroes to their goals?"

"Ha! Not in so crude and direct way as you mean, yet... yes, indeed. It makes our challenges all the more amusing. So! Let me consider your problem."

For long moments, the King sat immobile in his chair, eyes glowing with that unreadable, blankly yellow flicker. The mist surrounding them faded away slowly, yielding to bright sunshine that warmed the stone about them. Raiagamor waited, watching the sun's slow movement, occasionally consuming a minor mote of power from insects that passed too close.

At last, the King stirred. "An intriguing problem to contemplate, Raiaga. I thank you. So rarely am I presented with something so worthy of thought, or — in truth — a plan so well-wrought, overall, in both its functionality and its ability to eventually bring about confusion, pain, and suffering." He nodded. "And you have chosen *excellent* allies. Powerful, flexible, deadly to almost any... but no threat to you if you remain aware of them. Yes, these will serve you well."

"Thank you, Majesty."

"It is a pleasure to see, so thanks to *you*, Raiaga. Now, to the matter at hand. You were wise to speak the Camp-Bel's name first. This is not to diminish the significance of his companions; two Vantages in a party are, I am afraid, two too many, and that Iriistiik warrior is an unusual creature.

"But the Camp-Bel is the center of this. Oh, he may not be the one to directly endanger your plan — aspects of the Cards' prophecy argue against it — but I believe he is the crux, the one who will trigger, or possibly plan, the events that could threaten your grand design."

Raiagamor nodded. "And your advice, then?"

"Hmm. Well, as you have done everything reasonable to prevent his entry, I will focus on the likelihood that he and his friends pass all your barriers." The King frowned in thought. "Given his demonstrated prowess, we can both agree that Ingram Camp-Bel's purported incapacities were a blind, a ruse — and a cleverly enacted one. Yes?"

"Yes. Extraordinarily well enacted. I had not the slightest suspicion that this boy was anything other than a disappointment, and I would swear that no others did, either."

"Quite so. Thus, there must have been an equally extraordinary reason, and given other aspects... the Camp-Bels were in possession of knowledge of his future importance. A prophecy, the direct word of a god, even perhaps a forecast from some combination of their advanced technology and their peculiar connection to other forces."

The King glanced at Raiagamor, saw his nod, and went on. "It is my belief — one based on some knowledge I have that you do not, as well as on your own — that as of this moment Ingram Camp-Bel still does not know the details. He obviously knows, by now, that the Camp-Bels deceived him, and presumably since he still associates with them that he has accepted the benevolent, or at least neutral, nature of their motives in this."

While he didn't have whatever other information the King had, he felt the statement was reasonable. "Go on."

"This means, of course, that the other Camp-Bels have not told him, and I incline to the theory that none of the survivors *know* the details. The Camp-Bels are very much aware of one of the most ancient facts about such covert operations — as phrased by a human some years back, 'three can keep a secret... if two of them are dead.' They would not *dare* spread the true knowledge around very far. It would inevitably leak out. Since the highest ranked survivor of the Camp-Bels with Ingram was Pennon — formerly third in command — it stands to reason that of that group, only the original Captain and possibly his second in command would have known the secret."

"So... Ingram Camp-Bel no longer has a way of *discovering* his purpose?"

"Tsk, tsk, Raiaga. You have made a cardinal error — a small one amidst all the other work you have had to do, but still a potentially fatal one. You have accepted that the fact that your searches for remaining Camp-Bels have turned up nothing means that there *are* no remaining Camp-Bels. I believe that not only are there remaining Camp-Bels, but that it is likely close to half of their original clan."

Now a spark of rage ignited, and he clamped down on it ruthlessly. The King was in a fine mood, barely trying to tweak him today, and offering valuable insight. "I... see. You believe they were capable of hiding even from my best agents?"

"Say rather that they were capable of devising a way to disappear that would deceive such agents, with the distraction of the other part of the clan, especially if such agents had other interests and responsibilities. I do not believe — especially with some of the most capable allies you have — that they can remain hidden overlong against a search directed with the knowledge that there is something to find. But it will require some little resource and time to find them."

Riagamor considered this. "Yet how does it matter to this specific problem? Yes, they would undoubtedly be useful allies to Ingram and his friends, and for that reason must be destroyed, but, by your own words, the two who knew the truth are dead."

"Ahh, but think! There are — must be — two others who know the truth, *had* to know the truth."

Rarely did Raiaga think himself *stupid*, but this was one; even as the King spoke he saw his error. "My apologies for my blindness. His parents, of course."

"It would seem likely, would it not? The two closest to him must understand what he is to face, what he must do, and must make sure that — even as he is convinced he is the least of the Clan — he is trained to be equal of any task. This could never be accomplished unless those directly and intimately associated with him knew full well what they sought to do."

"And so, your advice..."

The King smiled, and this was the smile of his true form. "... is that the Camp-Bels be found. As a group, naturally, they will be fine bait, drawing your nemeses into a trap. They must suspect nothing.

"But you — and your agents — must ensure that Ingram Camp-Bel never speaks to his parents again."

Chapter 10
The Crucible of Children

Urelle stared at the crescent of carven cylindrical columns before her, columns cut off in a manner that made them look like stalks of grass sheared off by an errant sword-stroke, and shivered. At the center of that crescent was a single dark, unadorned archway, ten feet high and wide.

The entrance to the Crucible of Children.

She glanced backward, saw the figures outlined against the dawn: the tall, angular shape of Quester, the broad crescents of Twin-Edged Fate over her aunt's shoulder, the tiny figure of Ingram watching tensely, and to the side, the simply robed form of Frederic next to the massive height and breadth of Druyar Salandaras. All of them watching.

And if I fail, Ingram's hope is gone.

No! His mindvoice showed he had heard her thought. *Don't carry that around with you into the Crucible, Urelle! I... I'm more worried about you than my mission, okay?*

Really?

Really. I mean... I'm terrified about what might be happening to Aegeia. My parents, my Clan, our countries. But I didn't travel with them through the Forest Sea, all the way to the Wanderer's Stronghold and the shore and back. You don't worry about me, or anyone but yourself. Understand?

She could feel a strange emphasis beneath his words, a current of thought that lent even greater weight to what he said. *I understand,* she answered, even though she didn't, not exactly.

"Hey," Druyar rumbled. "You doing that think-talk thing, yes? Remember, no doing that in Crucible. Just you, no one else, nothing else. Can't pass unless is all you. Right?"

"Yes, sir," she said. "Quester, can I... turn this off?"

"I can do so for you," Quester said. He advanced to her side. "Stand still for a moment."

The touch of his mind was not nearly so disquieting as it had been the first time, months ago, when the Iriistiik had first bonded them. There was a tingle, a chill — and suddenly the *sense* of the others near her was gone. She felt momentarily desolate, her heart itself gone cold. *It's only been a few months... but I've already grown so accustomed to that connection.*

She glanced at Quester as he moved off, and was abruptly seized with a powerful understanding, an aching empathic grasp of the depth of suffering Quester must have endured upon the loss of his Nest. *I miss it terribly, after only a few months. He was born to such connections. Yet he has shown so little of the emptiness it must have visited upon him.*

Urelle straightened and gave them all a smile. "See you in a while!"

She made herself walk steadily and calmly towards the entrance to the Crucible, gesturing with casual grace as she approached the dark doorway, summoning a gleaming orb of light to hover near her as she passed into the Crucible.

Immediately she slowed her pace. The Crucible was never *identical* from test to test, but there were many constants about it — one of them being that even the footing could be treacherous, or worse.

"Interesting."

Urelle whirled, looking everywhere, but the quiet voice had no visible source. At the same time, it *was* a voice, not something in her head. "What's 'interesting'?" she asked, managing to keep her voice nearly steady.

"You, child." It sounded like a woman's voice, someone about as old as her mother would have been. This time it spoke from above her right shoulder, and she restrained the impulse to glance that way. "It is long and long since one such as *you* entered the Crucible." The tone shivered along Urelle's spine; it was amused, cold, analytical. This was not a voice to comfort.

"You mean someone who wasn't a born Salandaras," she said, returning her attention to moving cautiously along. She muttered another set of arcane words, focused her will, and now she could see in the other forms of light; cracks around openings, she knew, would often become obvious in the vision of heat when they might be nigh-invisible in ordinary light.

"That, of course," the voice agreed, so clearly in front of her that her eyes tried once again to focus on something nonexistent. "But more, a *magician*. Rare they are in any of the Salandaras, and those adopted are usually of martial bent, as well."

Urelle sensed a sudden flare of power — not magic, but perhaps *beyond* that — and dove forward instinctively.

One of the great stone blocks of the ceiling dropped, a fifty-ton hammer sending a shock through the floor and pulverizing the rock below, a spray of grit and powder carrying the scent of heat and brimstone.

As she was completing her roll, Urelle saw a darker line on the ceiling, not two feet ahead, and checked herself with a spurt of fear. A metal grate slammed down not one inch from her left boot.

"Good reactions," the voice said calmly. "Perception and reaction, in efficient unity."

Urelle lay there, letting her frantic heart slow and her breathing steady. *Balance, that was close! On both sides!*

There was no moving the immense block behind her. Oh, if she took enough time she could find a way around it, through it, under it — magic *did* have its advantages, especially for a Shaper — but the *point* of this little trap had been clear: "you can only move forward, not back".

Of course, now a strong iron grate was telling her that she couldn't move forward, either.

"Who are you?" she asked finally, rising to her feet to examine the grate.

There was a pause, long enough that Urelle began to wonder if her unknown observer had departed. But then, "An interesting question. I am not sure I know the answer."

That was an unexpected response. "You don't know who you are?"

The grate was of a fairly standard design — a set of bars spaced six inches apart, inch-thick rods of blackened steel, set in a framework three or four inches wide, also of blackened steel. She'd caught a glimpse of wickedly sharp points as the grate came down, so from that momentary impression she deduced that the rods ended in about one and a half to two feet of steel below the framework now resting on the ground, pointed to impale anything below. The whole thing would weigh many hundreds of pounds, maybe more than a thousand.

"Child, I know who I am. But I am not sure of the answer that would tell *you* who I am."

"Are you the Salandaras' patron? Their god or whatever power they rely on and are bound to?"

"They have many patrons, the Blessed and the Cursed. Their fortune and misfortune have made them many friends indeed. But in the way you mean... yes, I am."

Urelle studied the perimeter of the gateway closely; squinting ahead, she could see a windlass or similar structure that could be used to raise it. There didn't seem to be any latching mechanism, although it was possible there was one hidden below the ground, where the ends of the bars were.

But if there wasn't, there might be a fairly easy way around this. "Do you speak to all of the children?"

"Not to all. To some. Those who need it, those who pique my interest. But it is not uncommon; even those raised in the Salandaras may find that they need someone to reassure them, in the darkness of the Crucible." The same chill amusement clung to every word.

"Begging your pardon," Urelle said, "but you don't sound comforting at *all*."

She focused on the grate. *Just like the airwing spell.* Airwing let her fly — not terribly fast — and part of that was negating her own weight. She had also done a number of spells involving moving objects around with magic.

Admittedly, those were generally *small* objects, and even with all her equipment Urelle wasn't sure she weighed a tenth of the mass of that grate. But on the other hand, she didn't really need to *move* it — just make it, for a few seconds, lighter than air, so it would float up of its own accord and let her pass.

"I did not say *you* were in need of reassurance," the voice answered. "You present a *problem*, Urelle Vantage. An interesting problem, even a worthy problem and candidate, but nonetheless a problem, a riddle to be properly asked and answered."

She brought up the magic, and began what was one of the most straightforward, yet difficult, Shapings: changing how the very shape of space saw something. She saw the grate surrounded by what seemed a whirling funnel that plunged sharply down below, the pull of the world upon the grate. She reached out and concentrated, feeling the weight not with her body but her *mind*, bearing down upon her like a blanket of lead and gold, a blanket that could not be grasped yet was more absolutely real than the actual metal.

Slowly she raised her hands, willing the whirling, immobile vortex of mass to quiet, to shrink, to rise.

"And I think part of the riddle must be asked *now*."

A door slammed shut on her mind, a door of *krellin* and ironwood a dozen feet high and three thick, and she screamed, a short, incredulous grunt of pain and shock. In the same instant, her mystic vision vanished, and the glow-orb was extinguished; darkness absolute as the grave rushed in to fill the void.

Minutes passed before she could recover from the impact of something she had half-expected, yet had never really imagined, had heard of only in ancient Adventurer's tales. "You... you *shut away my magic!*"

There was no reply, but somehow, she had a sense of distant laughter... and keen, icy interest.

Urelle touched her neverfull pack, found it sealed; the space between space that held her equipment could no longer be reached. *Myrionar's Sword, that's going to be... what if the connection was severed?*

She knew the answer, of course. If the enchantment that made the neverfull pack work hadn't just been temporarily inactivated but was destroyed, then she would likely never find anything that had been in there again; it would be lost between, found only by sheer luck or by the strange and sometimes lethal beings that prowled the shadows between the layers of reality.

On the other hand, if she didn't get out of here, it wouldn't matter if *anyone* found her stuff.

"All right. Forward," she said.

She wasn't at all sure where *forward* was at the moment; there was not the faintest trace of light in any direction. She thought she remembered seeing, just beyond the windlass, a shadow that might be a torch or light-orb holder, but that did her no good here.

Worse than the lack of light, though, was the lack of *sense of the world*. She had been aware of the magic since she could remember, and though it could not, usually, substitute for sight, it had always been there, giving her a clear awareness of existence, of there being walls and wind and iron, fire and light and dark, power and promise rippling in bright mists throughout the entirety of creation.

Now she was trebly-blinded within an hour — first losing her newest perception, the connection with her friends, and now bereft of sight and mystic senses.

All she *needed*, though, was light. The Crucible did not want to encourage her to magic her way through all obstacles. But she was still living; the stones were still solid and cool, the metal, when her hand found the grate, as smooth and immobile. Matter was still itself.

She backed slightly away from the grate, felt in front of her and brushed at the stone, carefully cleaning away every trace of dust or stone chips she could find. Then she reached into one of the pouches at her side, glad that she didn't carry everything in the neverfull pack... and that she always, always arranged her materials in exactly the same way.

Sure enough, the small vial she remembered was there and — she shook it — still filled with the essence of water. With infinite care she set the vial on the floor before her, and practiced reaching out to touch it several times, to make sure she knew *exactly* where the vial was. *I have only one; I can't make a mistake here.*

Alchemy *should* still work. Alchemy was bringing out the essences of physical materials, with some symbolism to focus the *manner of expression* of the essences. The field of enchantment, or whatever, that the Crucible's resident or overseer had put into place still left Urelle's spirit and thoughts untouched, left all the materials unchanged; Urelle was pretty certain that it couldn't inhibit alchemy to anything like the extent it shut down more separate and independent magical forces.

And, fortunately, this wasn't a difficult alchemical challenge. She needed a Vial of Light, and while there were many ways to make one, the easiest and most straightforward (if rather wasteful in terms of materials) was the Endless Burning Water, made from the essences of four of the five key elements — earth, air, fire, and water. The vial was already infused with the essence of earth, and it held the essence of water. That provided an anchor for fire, which could not burn alone, and water to shield and moderate the power of flame. However, water and flame together would result in flame being swiftly extinguished, so one had to introduce air, to support the flame, at the same time and in the same amount as fire.

Fire essence capsules — tiny spheres of glass filled with the essence — were very useful tools in any alchemist's kit, and Urelle had a tube packed with pearlseed fluff that cushioned six such tiny spheres. Larger spheres of fire essence, of course, were used as weapons; the False Justiciars had used them in the attack that had killed her parents. Her little fire essence spheres came from the far-right pouch.

On the far-left pouch — as far away as could be from the fire-essence capsules — were the air-essence capsules — similar in appearance, though fire-essence glowed a brilliant red and air a barely-visible blue-purple. *Neither of them bright enough to be a light by themselves, unfortunately.* One did not combine the two casually, since that could create an explosion as the air fed the fire in the most perfect conceivable fashion.

The real problem's going to be actually adding *these.* The thin glass capsules had to be broken *inside* the vial, after the top was sealed; you couldn't pour fire essence and air essence into a bottle like water or ground earth, at least not without a good lab and magical assistance she couldn't use here.

With extreme caution, she removed one fire essence capsule from its tube, sealed and replaced the tube, and then felt gingerly about until she found the little glass vial. She inserted the capsule into the neck of the vial by feel, and then let go; the lack of reaction, and the shimmering of the red-gold dot, told her the delicate capsule was still intact in the water essence. She repeated the operation with the air essence; now the two capsules were where they had to be. But how would she *break* them, after she sealed the top? Not only that, but she'd have to break them both *quickly*. Oh, if the air capsule broke first, it wouldn't be a problem, but if the *fire* capsule broke first, there would only be a few seconds before the water essence extinguished it.

Holding the stopper in her teeth and the vial in her left hand, she moved carefully away from the grate and nearer to the fallen block. Her right hand touched the ground, felt around, locating several chips of dense rock. The first few were too large, but finally she found one that *just* fit through the neck of the vial.

She placed it in the neck, barely holding it up, and prepared herself. Then she let it go and whipped her hand up, grasped the stopper, and began screwing it into the top of the vial as fast as she could.

Nothing happened, which was a relief. She'd had to act as though the pebble would drop on one and break it, which probably would've been a disaster — she doubted that, fast though she was, she'd actually have even gotten the stopper *positioned* before the break happened. But now, with the stopper in place...

She bit her lip, took a deep breath, and then began shaking the vial as hard as she could. A few seconds passed, and then there was a red-orange flash. *Balance! That's the fire capsule!*

The momentary flash of light was already dimming, and Urelle redoubled her efforts, praying while the light guttered, faded...

And then flared out brilliantly as the air essence burst free from its capsule and filled the water-essence with its own flame-nourishing matter. The Endless Burning Water illumined the area almost as brilliantly as her magical globe, with a cheerful warm yellow flame-light, burning within the liquid in skeins of rippling fire that danced, miniature dust-devils of flame, from the bottom of the vial.

The "Endless" was an exaggeration, of course; the Vial would eventually shatter, once the fire had consumed enough of the crystal to weaken it, but that would take days, weeks, perhaps months. She breathed a sigh of relief; she had been right about alchemy. That might give her a few more resources to work with — though precious few. She relied on the neverfull pack to hold almost everything. She then tucked the Vial into a loop on her belt and turned back to the grate.

It hadn't changed since she last looked, and she saw no way around it but that she would have to try to lift it by main force — and somehow get it high enough that she could duck under it before it fell. There wasn't anything big and strong enough to support it — the largest pieces of rock the fallen block had made were barely the size of her fist.

The silence in the Crucible felt deafening; she had never realized how used she was to *some* kind of sound, even merely leaves or grass rustling in a breeze, or how ominous their absence would be. She ignored the foreboding sensation and first removed her pack; without anything actually inside the main compartment, at least for the moment, it was easy to squeeze it through to the other side of the bars. She didn't want anything on her that might make her a larger target, or possibly snag on pointed steel bars as she was making her way through.

Then she put on the thin leather gloves that she had tucked in her belt, to protect her hands and give her a better grip, and started stretching, giving every muscle a little workout to wake it up, prepare it for the next few minutes. Finally, she stepped up, grasped the crossbar that was about a foot or so from the ground, and lifted.

She did not, of course, put her full effort into it yet. She wanted to make sure she had grasped it properly, that her feet were positioned *just* right to take the pressure, and so on. She'd done more than a few heavy lift practices with Lythos, and though both her brother and Kyri had done a lot more, she knew very well the risks and techniques.

And there was, at least, *one* advantage with the grate: it was set in guide channels. There was no chance of it unbalancing and tipping her forward or backward, or falling sideways on her. If she could lift *strong* and lift *straight*, it should come up.

If it wasn't too heavy for even a Vantage to lift.

She set her feet, gripped the bar again, and heaved.

For an instant, she thought it *was* too much, that it was not going to move. But then there was a quiver, and the gate grated upward an inch, two inches, and it was a hair easier now that it was moving, but *by Myrionar* it was heavy, feeling like she was lifting her brother *and* sister, one on each end of the crossbar, both in full armor, to boot. She heard her voice echo around the Crucible, a strained, gutteral groan as she threw more effort into the lift, felt the bar still rising, and *there!*

It was up, resting with grinding force on her palms that had now shifted under the crossbar. But below her was the base crossbar of the gate, and below *those*, still only a few inches from their sockets, were the spearlike points of the bars. She had to get it much higher. And that meant she was going to have to somehow lift it high enough, and then move *fast* enough, that she could get the bottom bar to her chest area — and then swap grip from the higher to the lower crossbar.

No time to waste. She already knew that she might never get it this high again if she dropped the gate now. She threw her full effort against the bar, and after another infinitesimal, terrifying hesitation, it ground upwards again. Urelle forced it up, past her face, past her head, and for an instant stood, arms above her head, the edge of the crossbar digging into her upper arms.

With a grunt she *shoved* upward on the bar, then dropped both hands down — ripping her left arm open on the steel as she did — and caught the bottom bar just as it began to descend.

That very nearly ended her; she felt something starting to tear in her arm as she halted the downward motion, forced the grate to stop, then climb higher, higher. She gave another harsh groan, pushing with everything she had left, right bicep filled with a bright-flaming pain, and then fell forward, rolling. The gate rammed down behind her, nicking the heel of one boot.

She lay there, panting, her muscles twitching, feeling the hard, dusty stone under her cheek, the light of the Vial emanating streakily from underneath her. Urelle rolled over onto her back, rested a few more moments before climbing to her feet.

"Strength and control of mind and body. Good." The voice was a deep bass, accented with a hint of the far North, possibly Skysand.

Yet somehow Urelle *knew* this was the exact same speaker. "You knew I was strong before, I'm sure."

A laugh floated from above. "But I did not know how much was *magic*. Oh, there is strength beyond the mere muscle within you, but it is a part of you, one that simple magic repression can never touch; that, I see now, I could remove from you only if I were to unmake you."

These were interesting comments, but she had to concentrate on why she was here. *Without magic, I'm at a real disadvantage if I have to fight*, she thought. The records of the Crucible often mentioned various deadly creatures within the shifting maze.

She moved forward with care, looking around. There was the windlass, and in a niche to the side, a long lever that probably was used to trigger the descent of the grating if it had to be done by hand.

The lever interested her. It was long — four feet or so — and fairly slender. It was also held on only by a large setscrew, which Urelle rapidly removed with some of the tools she could still access.

The lever was somewhat heavy, but still acceptable for a staff or an oddly narrow two-handed mace. It was of thick rolled steel and could probably take a lot of punishment. *All right, I'm at least somewhat armed.* The air and fire capsules and a few similarly touchy materials would give her a few other options, though she hated to use them up.

"So you test people for... what? Strength, I guess. Resilience. What else?"

"Do you believe it is always for the same things?"

She paused, moving forward, seeing the corridor finally widening out ahead. *That could be good or bad.* "I'd guess that there are *some* things you're always interested in. The others... probably depends on the kind of person."

"Indeed. For those *born* Salandaras, I already know much of them — of their minds, of their bodies, of their ancestry, for all of them have passed through here; their mothers and fathers, the parents of their parents, and so, until the beginning.

"But *you*... you are a child of distant lands indeed, one with her own secrets — some she herself does not know, does not understand how to know." Another chuckle. "For you, the questions are many, if you would also leave here alive and take the name *Salandaras* as well as *Vantage*."

In the light of the Eternal Burning Water, she could now see that there was a chamber before her, one with three exits on the far side... and something else, a dark, sinuous form that shifted as she entered.

She gripped her improvised mace-staff tighter as the thing finished rising and turning. *A valakass; a* wild *valakass, and a* big *one!*

Tame valakass were riding lizards, low-slung but powerful mounts or harness beasts. They could be quite large — some up to five hundred pounds — and if angered were dangerous, but the domesticated ones really took effort to make angry unless they were starving.

Wild valakass were something very different — and could be much larger. As this one stalked closer, with the deceptively slow, smoothly-oscillating side-to-side gait of such large reptiles, Urelle swallowed hard, her throat suddenly tight, her mouth unexpectedly dry; this one was a *monster*, probably over a thousand pounds and fifteen feet long, maybe more. Its head came up nearly to Urelle's chest; dark, beadlike eyes glinted hungrily, and she could see the gray-green beaded skin shifting with the working of the muscles — skin that, she knew, was filled with embedded bone, armoring the creature against any ordinary blows. The wedge-shaped head tracked her movements, and the jaws parted for a moment, showing wickedly sharp, backwards-pointing teeth and ropy strands of venomous saliva.

She brought up her weapon and shouted as loudly as she could. *I don't want to fight this thing — I've got to convince it that* it *doesn't want to fight* me!

The hostile motion and noise did cause the valakass to slow, shift its pace slightly. It was still approaching, but on a curved path, circling her — maybe looking to see if she was vulnerable from some particular direction.

She turned to face it, judging angles and distances. She thought about trying to just run, but she instantly discarded that thought; that would mark her as prey, and she'd seen how fast even domestic valakass were. The thing would be on her before she'd crossed the room.

No. The only way out was to either convince it she wasn't prey... or beat it in a fight.

A smooth, forked pink tongue flicked out, pulled back, flicked out again, tasting the air, judging her scent. *If it can smell my fear, it's going to* really *start thinking of me as prey*. She remembered Lythos, his constant instruction on control, on perception, on action:

"Urelle, I know you do not intend to be a warrior; yet even those who are not warriors may find that they must fight. If you fight through fear, if you fight through anger, you will nearly always lose. You may *feel* fear; you may *feel* anger; but you must always discipline your feelings when it comes to battle. Draw *from* those feelings for strength, for swiftness, for determination and purpose; but never, ever allow them to dominate, to draw from you."

As the thing circled, she drew in a breath, let it out, imagining fear leaving her body in a yellow-green cloud, breathing calm blue in, exhaling bilious yellow fright. Her hands steadied just a touch, and she turned to watch the creature more carefully. It *was* huge, no doubt about it, although maybe she had slightly overestimated it on first sight. Still, from the point of view of fighting it, there was little difference between an eight-hundred-pound lizard and one three hundred pounds heavier.

She saw something — a tighter ripple in the muscles, a shift in the rhythm, a raising of the body for an instant — and lunged aside, as the valakass *charged* towards her. Even as she dodged, she swung the windlass lever as hard as she could.

The impact buzzed in her hands, almost made her drop the metal shaft, but there was a sharp *thud!* and the huge lizard hissed and shied away, scuttling back to its former distance.

"Come on! Go! Get out of here! Or just leave me alone!" she shouted. "I'm not prey!"

It hissed at her but continued circling. At the same time, though, she noticed it was favoring one front leg; she had struck it hard in the shoulder, and the blow had at least done some damage even through the natural armor.

I have to try to make some progress, maybe force the thing to change its approach or give up. As it circled, she tried to take steps to move her slowly towards the exits on the far wall.

It lunged at her again, but she had already thought through her response; she dodged in the *other* direction and this time brought the mace-staff down *hard* on its head.

It had shied away just as she struck, but this turned out to be a terrible mistake; instead of crashing down on the broad skull, the point of the long mace hammered with crushing force onto and into the right eye socket.

The creature gave a metal-tearing shriek and scuttled away, putting distance between itself and the little but powerful human. *Okay! I've scared it now!*

Still keeping an eye on the creature, which was both limping and moving more tentatively with only one good eye, Urelle began moving briskly towards the far exits.

But then the thing gave a louder hiss and whipped around, scuttling towards her with a confused but still powerful limping gait, fury deadly clear in its remaining onyx eye.

It's limping, was the partially-formed thought, but she didn't wait for the whole thought; without a moment's hesitation, she turned and ran, sprinting all-out towards the central corridor.

The thing's claws made a scraping, stacatto rattle behind her — but not, at least yet, one getting closer. *If I can just keep up this pace, it might run out of breath first!*

But then, as the light from the Eternal Burning Water ran over the ground before her, she saw a line, a suspiciously *straight* line, crossing the path from one side to the other.

There was no time to stop; even if she could have seen it in time, there was a monster right behind her. So she did the only thing she could: gathered herself just as she reached the mysterious line in the rock and *leapt* up and forward.

She saw the ground pass below her, and *another* line across the hall — and yet another, ahead, getting closer...

She did not — quite — make it.

But it was the valakass that ran straight onto the trapdoor first.

A section of the corridor twenty-five feet across abruptly dropped away, and both giant lizard and little Adventurer plummeted downward.

In the light of the vial, Urelle suddenly saw the bottom of the pit was covered with ranks of sharp stakes, the points unnaturally dark, and twisted herself desperately in midair to try, somehow, to evade the spikes as they rushed up to meet her.

The valakass, unfortunately, had no possibility of doing so; in every dimension its body was wider than the maximum separation of the spikes, and its mass and the fifteen-to-twenty-foot fall drove it onto the sharp points with irresistible force; it struck with a crunching, squelching noise and a suddenly cut-off shriek.

Urelle struck hard, feeling a twisting agony in her shoulder as she hit, and at the same time a tremendous burning, acidic pain ripped through her right leg.

She gasped, the red-bright pain blotting out her vision, almost taking her consciousness; several moments passed before she could even breathe enough to drive the shadows back from her vision. Hardly daring to look, she forced herself to look down the length of her body.

She had fallen almost entirely *between* the lethal spikes; only one had struck her, and that one through her right calf.

She recognized the pain and sense of *wrongness* in her shoulder. It was dislocated, not broken. She *might* be able to pop it back in place, somehow. But her leg...

"You sought fortune when needed, and fortune found you," said a rough, gravelly voice — a voice that was, nonetheless, the same as before. "A good indication."

"*Fortune?* I'm at the bottom of this pit with a poisoned spike through my leg!"

Another laugh, this one sounding the same as the others even though it also sounded like rocks grinding and splintering against each other. "That is still great fortune indeed, little Adventurer. To fall so that only a single spear touched you, and that one in but a single extremity? To have broken not a single bone in your fall? You might practice that for a year and never duplicate the feat. No, fortune smiled upon you in that moment." Somehow, a sense of a grim smile. "But still, it gives you a new challenge to face..."

Feeling the burning, acid sensation increasing, Urelle focused, lifting her leg. She could feel the spike *dragging* on her leg, and nausea rolled in waves through her. *Can't stop now. Myrionar, help me! I don't think I can do this...*

For just an instant, she suddenly felt... a *presence*. Not the ironic, cold one behind the voice, but someone... someone *warmer*, tall, strong, just behind her, almost holding her. *You can do this*, it seemed to say to her... and she had a phantom sense that the arms that encircled her were ones she knew well.

With a stomach-wrenching effort she pulled her leg free, fighting off unconsciousness and nausea with the memory of that moment, the echo of the hands gripping her shoulders. For a few moments she lay there, gasping, letting it bleed. *It'll cleanse the wound some.*

But she couldn't afford to lose too much blood. She gritted her teeth and sat up, feeling with her good hand for anything she could use to bandage the wound.

Bandage? I'll need two hands for that. I'll need two hands for just about everything.

Urelle felt her body shaking with shock, cold sweat trickling down her face, and for a few instants she just could not move.

But I am a Vantage. She knew what her brother would have done. She knew what her sister, her mother and father, and especially her aunt, would do.

Relax. She remembered Lythos talking Rion through reducing his shoulder, which had been dislocated in combat practice. "You can do this yourself — and should try to, now, for you cannot be certain of having any help elsewhere."

Relax the muscles. The pain tried to make her tense everything, fight the pain — but that would just make it worse, far worse. The entire trick to reducing, or re-setting, the shoulder wasn't a violent motion, or tense muscles, but the opposite: a slow, careful motion that began with the extension of the arm, and a gradual reaching around and behind the head, eventually to attempt to grasp the opposite shoulder.

Relax. She breathed slowly and evenly, despite her body's shock and pain and the blood flowing freely from her wound. She had her arm extended now, and it didn't hurt as much as she had feared. This helped her to keep the shoulder and neck muscles relaxed. *Up now, slowly...* A spark of pain, and she paused, breathing, concentrating. The pain faded, and she reached up, up, over... now her hand was down, rotated, as though she needed to scratch her own neck. Another breath, and now the final reach, towards her other shoulder —

Pop!

There was a spark of new pain, but instantly a far greater feeling of relief, of something wrong suddenly become *right* again.

She sat up and immediately looked at her leg.

There was a bloody hole an inch in diameter through the leg — or it *would* be an inch in diameter if the muscle held the shape. Bleeding badly. *Healing draughts all in the unreachable pack. Don't have any actual bandages. Could improvise a tourniquet, maybe?*

That seemed the best route. She *could* try to cauterize it with one of the fire-essence spheres as a last resort, but there were all sorts of ways that could go wrong. But she had a knife, strong cloth she could cut to a wide strip...

In a few minutes, she had cut a strip from her undershirt and wrapped it tightly around her leg above the wound. In one pouch she found a straight, strong stick she'd been thinking of enchanting into a luminance wand; that made a good windlass; she turned the stick multiple times until she was pretty sure the bleeding had stopped or at least really, really slowed down, maybe enough to clot. Another strip of cloth and another knot and the stick was anchored so it wouldn't just unwind.

At last, she let herself rest a few minutes — dug out a strip of dried fruit and drank water from her meager supplies. The burning from the wound had not stopped, and she could feel something *wrong* inside her. *Poison... or maybe a really fast-acting infection.*

I have to get out of here.

The pit's walls were sheer and while not polished, the rough stone offered little hope of purchase; there were no handholds she could see. The one-eyed corpse of the valakass offered no useful suggestions, and while big, it wasn't nearly large enough to give her any method to climb out.

A rope with a grappling hook, or something like it, would have worked... but all her rope and most other equipment was inaccessible now. Her alchemical materials might be useful for other things, but she didn't see any way they could provide her with a way to fly or climb out of a pit. Some of the ones she couldn't access might, but that was useless thinking.

Her hand strayed to another pouch — a small one, hidden behind her belt — which held just a single, precious object: the tiny Lens, the token the Wanderer had left her. *Do I use this now?* she asked herself. She was certain it would work, even here in a magically-suppressed area; the Wanderer would have made his token as best he could. *And I don't want to follow what Ingram called the Parable of the Always-Worse. Things* could *get worse... but if I don't get out of here...*

Finally, she shook her head. *Maybe. But try again. The Salandaras and their patron don't want to simply kill the candidates. I have to believe that there is some way out of here if you survived the threat. For every threat evaded, there* must *be a way to move forward... involving solving another riddle, or facing another threat.*

Urelle looked around, surveying the area more carefully. Aside from her and the dead valakass, there was nothing else in the pit except the carefully arranged array of spikes, separated by just barely enough space to walk between, arranged in a perfect, ordered array except where a few had been broken by the valakass' tail in its final convulsive thrashing.

Something about that nagged at her, but it was hard to focus with her leg throbbing and the uncomfortable hint of burning within the rest of her body. *Think. Why is it significant that some of the spikes were broken?*

No. It wasn't *just* that they were broken. It was something else... associated with her other thought.

Nothing else in the pit with us.

Now, it might be that the Crucible was an entirely magical place, literally shifting and rebuilding itself for every candidate. But she'd *felt* the effort of her unknown watcher to bring down the stone. That was a directed choice. It wasn't the feel of simply activating a known change, any more than the sudden suppression of her magic. Yes, that *challenged* her, but if the Crucible of Children were infinitely mutable for every entrant, it could simply have shifted to present her with appropriate magical challenges.

"That's why I presented a 'problem'," she said to herself. "Most of the Crucible is fixed. Maybe there's a lot of different paths through it, and each candidate gets a different combination of those paths, so no one candidate's likely to see the same things, but each path is *real*... and most of the challenges in the Crucible are made for strong fighting types. That's why my magic had to be shut down. And since they're children, they won't have much equipment on them, so my neverfull pack had to be negated too."

The unseen voice did not answer, but she pursued the thought, a cool excitement now balancing the heat of the poison or infection working its way through her. *Nothing else here? Perfect except for where the valakass fell?*

Someone had to *maintain* this pit. Almost certainly it would be Salandaras, or someone close to them, who did it. They could just climb down into the pit, but no matter how careful you were, that could be risky; you didn't want your maintenance people falling onto poisoned spikes.

So much easier if you could just walk in...

As soon as the thought was clear, she could *see* where the entrance had to be: under one of the two doors. There were no spikes directly under the open doors, leaving about three feet of clear space on each side — not useful for people falling, but for someone entering or leaving, it would be perfect. The pit was twenty feet deep, and with a twenty-five-foot span that meant each door was only twelve and a half feet long; that left a space beneath each door that was seven and a half feet high — comfortably high for an exit or entrance door.

Knowing what she was looking for, it did not take long to find it: a narrow, perfectly rectangular crack on one wall, outlining a door. The question was, could it be opened from inside the pit?

Urelle thought it could. There were no marks anywhere on the walls, but there had been no list of allowed equipment, no discussion of what she was to carry; the children were evidently free to bring what they wanted. The magic-negating field on her had been a *special* action, not an ordinary one, so it might be that even neverfull packs were normally fair play. Some of the candidates *must* have carried rock-climbing gear, and those would leave marks.

So the maintenance people carried something, probably a minor stoneworking charm, that let them erase small piton holes or such. But that would *also* let them seal the door when they left, eliminating the cracks entirely.

The fact that they hadn't argued that they intended a candidate who survived the fall to have a way out, even if they hadn't brought climbing gear, as long as they were smart enough — or, more likely, methodical and determined enough — to search the walls.

With that deduction, it took only a few minutes to prove she was right by testing the nearby spikes and finding that one could be pulled up just a short distance and then turned. The door swung open with barely a whisper of sound.

Elation was also met by a wave of nausea; she did not — quite — lose her lunch, but it was a near thing. *I've got to get out of here. My leg's hurting worse, and I don't have an antidote or healing draught for the whatever-it-is that the spike put in.*

And I have to get out of here because unless I do, we can't go on.

Her will alone focused against her pain, Urelle Vantage gripped her weapon and moved forward into darkness.

Chapter 11
The Agony of Victory

"How long do we *wait?*" Ingram heard himself demanding again.

"As long as we must," Victoria responded from the dimness of the pre-dawn.

Even without more light, Ingram could see how exhausted Victoria was, dark circles beneath her eyes, the eyelids heavy, the mouth bracketed with lines of worry and weariness. *I look no better, probably. It's been more than two* days.

Quester was sleeping, at least; he could feel the vagueness of presence that told him his friend was not awake and alert. But neither Ingram nor Victoria had been able to rest much. "But shouldn't she have come out by now?"

"It is somewhat worrisome," Frederic's voice answered from behind them. "But many have taken days to pass the Crucible."

"How do you know when to stop watching?" Victoria asked quietly, gazing at the door to the Crucible of Children, gray and closed as it had been since Urelle had entered.

"When the door opens," Frederic said after a pause. "Either the candidate is there, and in passing through that doorway becomes a Salandaras in truth, or no one waits behind the door... and someone must go inside to retrieve the one who failed." His voice was soft, but Ingram could hear the sadness within, and the anger.

"Is there no way to change this?" Victoria asked. "No way for the Salandaras to stop sending their children into a deadly gantlet?"

"None that has been revealed to them, to their allies, or to me, Lady Victoria," Frederic answered. "Not without destroying that which they are, and perhaps destroying all they have built upon being who they are. We do not even know, as we said, the identities of the two beings who clashed over the destiny of their ancestor, nor whatever power it is who is their patron now. Those three, together, might do so, but without knowing who and what they are, it seems impossible to me that an acceptable ending might be made of this."

He shook his head. "And so, the children must go, beloved and feared for... sometimes never to return."

Ingram shuddered. *I wish I could have done this. It's my job as a Camp-Bel, to take these burdens and risks upon myself, not put them onto others.* But that had not been an option.

So now he sat, and watched an unmoving gray door, and felt acid and tension within his gut.

The light brightened, and suddenly a brilliant ray of sun washed across the scene, touching everything with ruddy gold light. Ingram blinked.

Then he realized that the gray doorway had gone black. It was no longer closed, but open.

And there was no figure visible in the doorway.

"Athena, *no...*" he whispered, horror spreading in an icy constricting wave from his heart throughout his body. "No."

Victoria gasped and sagged to the ground, gaze fixed on the dark, empty archway, hands covering her mouth to hold in a mother's screams. Quester's mind was shadowed and the Iriistiik's head sank, both his sets of arms sagging.

Ingram forced himself to stand. *She died for me. For everything that no longer matters, because I don't think I care for the mission one* bit *now. But I will find her and bring her out into the mocking sunlight.*

I won't let anyone else be the one to find her inside this death trap.

As he started for the doorway, Druyar Salandaras bellowed, *"STOP!"*

He paused, glaring back at the huge warrior, who was also staring intensely at the entrance to the Crucible. "Why?"

"Is not yet over."

He whirled back, seeing Victoria rising to her feet, and only then did he see it. A slight movement, from a tiny shape in dark clothes, collapsed at the very threshold of the door. *"URELLE!"*

Frederic caught him as he sprinted forward, Druyar doing the same to Victoria. Quester was there now, great faceted eyes taking in the scene, only hesitating when he saw the desperation with which his two friends were being restrained.

"No!" Druyar said, and his voice was hammered iron. "Not over! No help! She must cross threshold herself! Do not undo all she has done!"

That last was the only thing anyone could have said to have stopped him — or, he was certain, Victoria and Quester. For Urelle moved with the slowness of one not merely exhausted, but wounded, dying, with perhaps minutes remaining and only their iron will driving them forward. Neither he nor her aunt could have failed to go to her... if it were not for the fact that they would then make all that Urelle had done pointless.

"Okay. Okay. We'll stay out of it until she crosses the threshold," Ingram managed to grind out. He saw Victoria nod, Quester's head dip. "We promise. But let us go closer. Be as close as we can."

Frederic's grip on his arms eased, and Ingram hurried forward, Victoria at his side.

Had they not promised, Ingram wasn't sure he could have stopped himself. For he had never *seen* Urelle so badly injured.

A makeshift tourniquet gripped her swollen left leg above a vicious wound in her calf. Blood caked the leg, which was also leaking pus. Urelle's face was smeared with blood and other things in a streaked red-black-yellow pattern of filth, and even her dark skin seemed both paler and darker, with hints of hectic red on her cheeks. One hand gripped a battered length of metal, jamming one end into the stone to help drag herself forward. There were burns on her clothing and her hands, and scorch marks on her face. Her eyes stared intensely, looking only in front of her, a few feet before her, and Ingram knew she was utterly unaware of anything except the goal that lay before her, such a short distance away.

A gasping grunt, and she dragged herself another six inches forward; her other leg pushed, but it, too, was not uninjured; the ankle was puffed to nearly twice its normal size. The one with the tourniquet did not move at all, dead weight that was simply impeding her progress. Her lips bled, as though she'd bitten them in her pain.

But she extended her arms again, anchored herself, dragged forward. Tears trickled from the corners of her eyes, and Ingram felt his own splashing onto his clenched fists, hearing her agonized gasps and knowing he could do nothing to help her... or all this pain would be for naught.

Another six inches. Another, and her feet were near the threshold. She gave a whine and a growl, inhuman in their intensity, and pulled herself forward once more... and her feet slid past the border of the entranceway. "It is done." Druyar said, sadness mingling with satisfaction in his voice.

And - from where, Ingram could not say — a phantom voice whispered "And will beyond that of iron... well enough, little one."

Ingram and Victoria were instantly near her. "Urelle, Urelle, you did it, you *did* it, understand us? It's okay, we're going to help you now."

Her eyes refocused, slid past Victoria, fixed on his face, looked into his own, and those cracked, bleeding lips curved up. "It's... okay now... Ingram..." she whispered.

Then her head dropped to the pavement and the metal rod, so fiercely held, tumbled from fingers gone limp.

"*NO!*"

"Calm yourself!" Frederic snapped. "She is not dead — not quite — and by Shargamor and the Water of Life, she will not die if I can help it."

The Guardian of Nature laid his hand on Urelle's, and instantly, deep, rippling green light flowed across the girl's form. "Unloose that tourniquet," Frederic said, and Druyar bent and did so with the smoothness of one long accustomed to following this man's directions. "Ah," Frederic said distantly, "both infection *and* poison. A cruel combination. The leg itself may have passed the point of salvage."

No! Ingram breathed the word.

"Can it not be restored, if severed clean?" Victoria asked, her voice unnaturally calm.

"There are those who could do so," Frederic said. "None of them are here, however, and you have no luxury of time to seek one out. But I did say *may*. It is possible that I may still be able to help her body to defeat the forces that seek to destroy it."

"Do you need anything? Ingredients, healing draughts — Athena's *Name*, why didn't she use her own healing?"

"I have all I require for the moment," Frederic said. "As to why... I would have to guess that she *could* not. Her pack may have been sealed. Even her magic, perhaps, was no longer hers to command."

"*Founder...*" Ingram whispered, feeling the horrific weight of helplessness once more. *It's like watching Victoria dying. Once* again, *I can do nothing to help!*

All he could do was pray to Athena and Urelle's own Myrionar to help her.

The lines of concentration on Frederic's face, as he threw his powers and those of Shargamor against the terrible injuries Urelle had sustained, were also hauntingly familiar. The Wanderer's face had looked the same.

Frederic sat there for long minutes, quietly intoning spells or prayers in a strange mixture of languages. Was Urelle's face relaxing, smoothing out? And if it was... was it because she was getting *better*, or because the end was approaching? Ingram swallowed, feeling dust and splinters of fear in his throat.

The rippling, leafy, emerald light danced up and down the girl's form, returning always to focus on the savage wound in her calf, from which blood was trickling, mixed with yellow-green corruption. Frederic was breathing faster now, and Ingram saw sweat standing out on the older man's brow, beginning to soak the neck of his famous White Robe. "Druyar," he said, strain evident despite an artificial lightness of tone, "I must say, your patron has angered me once more. There was no need for *this*."

Druyar bowed his head. "Not think so either, but she not listen to me."

"If Urelle dies," Ingram heard himself snarl from between gritted teeth, "your patron will *by the Founder* hear something from *us!*"

The golden-haired warrior raised his head and looked with stern sympathy into Ingram's eyes. "Was her choice. Was her risk. She want to help you." He sighed. "Know that hurts. But don't blame Her, Mistress of Twilight, Fortune. All Salandaras take risk." An aching sadness passed across the normally-cheerful features. "Me and sister, Daryana, we go in together. Take different paths. I come out. She carried out."

"How can you *stand* it?"

Druyar straightened. "Is part of *who we are*. Hear your story, yes? Why Camp-Bels die in training? Why God-Warrior training kill so many? Because is what must be." He gestured to Urelle. "Not want to see her die. Trust Guardian will heal. But if not? Soul is safe. She go where she belong."

"But she will have died for *nothing*!"

"No," Druyar said firmly. "She made it. She Salandaras now. She still alive. Made promise. If die, is now *our* promise."

It should have been wonderful news: Druyar — who right now was *the* Salandaras, the leader — was saying he took Urelle's oath as his own, that no matter what, one of the Salandaras would guide them to the Seal. But all that promise managed was a miniscule lightening, a feeling that it wouldn't all have been for naught. But, looking at Urelle's too-thin face, he couldn't bring himself to care.

"It is... very bad," Frederic gasped, still pouring the forest-jade power into Urelle's slender form. "There is a touch of something else, not mere magic, something greater, associated with all of this. I need a connection, something of our own, to combat this."

"But," Quester buzzed in puzzlement, "but are you not a holy man yourself? A Guardian is a servant and channel of Shargamor, yes?"

"Yes," he admitted, "but not *directly*. I gain the strength, the energy, from Shargamor's blessing, but it is not the power of the gods. Such is not for ordinary humans to channel. I need a touch of the true power, or something else that lies beyond the realm of the ordinary magic I wield."

Ingram's head came up. "Something connected to the gods?"

But before he could concentrate, could focus his desperation into the cry to call forth his oldest friend, he saw Victoria Vantage, with a peculiar expression, extend her hand. "Would this suffice?" she asked.

Frederic, confusion obvious, took her hand.

A faint shimmer showed about their hands, and to his surprise Ingram saw faint red-gold sparkles flowing over Urelle along with the leaf-green. Frederic stared, astounded, into Victoria's eyes. "But... I don't understand."

"It isn't necessary to understand — as long as it is enough."

"It... yes. Yes, it is. I feel a resonance between your... power and Urelle's. Perhaps the connection of mother to child, despite your surface relationship... but I feel the infection weakening. The poison begins to disperse, diluting in the flow of power and will. Urelle's spirit... her spirit is with us now, helping." Despite the sweat and strain on his face, Frederic smiled. "She will recover."

"Thank the Lady," Ingram heard himself say, and sank to the ground. The tears still trickled down his cheeks, but at last, for the first time in days, Ingram smiled.

Chapter 12
Godsblooded

"I think," Quester said, trying to balance gentleness and firmness, "it would be good if you could explain what happened yesterday, when you assisted Frederic."

Urelle looked up from her bed, and Ingram, who was sitting in a chair nearby, glanced to Quester and Victoria. "What happened yesterday?" she asked.

Ingram's brows drew down. "Frederic encountered... difficulty in healing you." The subtle tightness in his voice echoed the fears Quester felt in him, the memory of seeing the young Vantage nigh-dead before them. "He said he needed a... connection to something greater than his magics. I thought about calling Berenike, but before I could, Victoria offered her hand... and somehow that was enough." He looked to Victoria. "She's going to be fine, and that's all I need to know. You don't have to explain anything to me."

Victoria looked around the room, then the right side of her mouth turned up in a half-smile. "It is true that I do not *have* to," she said after a moment, "but Quester is, I think, right. It would be good for us to have few secrets of *import* from each other." In the mindspeech, she added, *and after all, how well can we hide secrets if we can speak by thoughts? Eventually, I suspect, anything you dwell upon will come out, or at least hint at its nature.*

"That is perhaps true," Quester admitted. "But as you are not of the Iriistiik, and accustomed to being alone in your thoughts, perhaps not quite so much as you might think."

"Still... yes, I think you are correct, Quester." A swift procession of emotions flickered like shadows across her face; worry, pride, disbelief, awe, tenderness. "In all honesty, though I knew this secret before, it was something in the manner of a test that I offered my aid to Frederic. I do not think I entirely *believed* it before then."

"Well, what *is* it, Auntie?" Urelle said, after a moment's silence.

Victoria shook her head, smiling with that same subtle incredulity; a strand of her black-and-white hair waved, accentuating the motion. "Well... I suppose there's no point in trying to lead up to it. Kyri — your sister Kyri — is Myrionar."

Quester tried to make sense of this fantastic statement, and couldn't. But his, and Ingram's, confusion was nothing compared to Urelle's.

"Wha... Auntie, *what*?"

"I know precisely what you are feeling, Urelle. But I also know precisely what I am saying. You all recall when we first encountered the Wanderer? How I pointed out that anyone could claim to be a legend, but that I required proof?"

Urelle nodded. "Yes. He said you should pray to Myrionar, and that Myrionar would answer. And when you came back, you said you had been answered, and that this was indeed the Wanderer."

"Yes," Ingram said, brow furrowing again. "And I remember both Quester and I thought you looked... *stunned*, behind your usual veteran Adventurer face."

"Urelle undoubtedly would have seen the same thing, if the idea of studying with the Wanderer hadn't rather distracted her," Victoria agreed. "Then here is what happened: Myrionar did answer my prayers. Myrionar spoke to me. And it spoke *in Kyri's voice*."

They stared incredulously at her. Then Quester said, "But — Lady Vantage — this is, after all, a god. I do not doubt that Shargamor or Athena or Terian, or any of them, could speak in the voice of anyone they chose."

"Undoubtedly, Quester," she said, the half-smile still on her face. "But the voice came with the absolute conviction that this was the true voice of Myrionar. And my subsequent conversation with the Wanderer verified it. Kyri is — will become... *did* become Myrionar. All at once, so to speak."

Quester tried to make sense of this. The god Myrionar had existed for a very long time; after he and Ingram had become employees and, later, friends of the Vantages, Quester had done some studying of their faith, assuming that it would help him understand these friends just as understanding Ingram's faith had aided in understanding the young Camp-Bel. There were some traces indicating that Myrionar had existed many Chaoswars back. Yet Kyri Vantage was young, only a few years older than Urelle; how could she be Myrionar?

Abruptly, Ingram began laughing. "Oh, now it makes *sense!*"

All three of them stared at Ingram. "I must say that I cannot see how this... unique situation can make sense of *anything*," Quester said finally.

"Oh, it's all simple, it's a closed time-loop. Some of the Founder's writings talked about this, although it was usually in the context of ancient stories. No, what makes sense now is the 'Vantage Strength'. Kyri becomes Myrionar, and somehow has to go back in history to whenever Myrionar first shows up. But she has to make sure that cycle keeps happening, right? So she has to make sure that the Vantage line shows up..."

"... and since they're *her* family, they need that touch of godspower that gives them the strength," Victoria finished. "Yes. Yes, that is obvious now." She shook her head again, smiling. "So we've been worshipping our own family. Perhaps we are descended of Kyri, somehow."

"But becoming a god... that's got to be something really difficult," Urelle put in after a moment. "So, that means she has to let all the bad things happen."

Victoria closed her eyes. "Oh, *Balance*, of course. By all that is, Kyri, how it must hurt, even as a god. The very course of events that made you... you cannot change. Or Myrionar will never exist, and all the good you have do will never come to pass."

Thinking about that terrible concept, and then about their journey, triggered another thought. "I think I understand something else, too."

"What, Quester?" asked Ingram.

"Well... perhaps. We have wondered why our opponents at times seemed confused as to the nature of their target, and especially as to why, instead of you, they appear to be focused on Urelle — or, perhaps, Victoria."

Ingram's eyes widened. "No. Yes. By *Athena*, yes. It's Urelle. But Victoria's connected to her by the same power. That's why it's confused."

"Would you explain, Ingram?" Victoria asked, polite steel in the words.

"Oh! Sorry. Look, if we're dealing with either a crazy or a fake Ares, either way they've probably done their best to wipe out all of the possible candidates for Athena, or any of the other gods, to incarnate. We've never known what's involved in the selection; but now it seems awfully likely that it's bloodline — incarnate gods *have* to come from someone who's either been prepared to survive the godspower, or," he looked at Urelle and Victoria, "are *born* with a connection to it."

"I am not becoming any kind of god!" Urelle said, as firmly as her still-recovering body would let her.

Ingram sighed and looked down. "You already risked everything, I'm not asking you to risk anymore."

Quester studied his friends and sensed, delicately, the thoughts and feelings radiating from them. "Urelle, I do not believe your sister planned to become one, either."

"Not the same thing," Victoria said sharply. "If we understand this at all... Kyri *has always been* Myrionar, in a sense. Myrionar was never anyone else, although It took on the guise It wears for the sake of the justice Kyri fought for. This Athena is her own god, not any of her worshippers."

Quester turned his head towards his friend. "Ingram?"

Ingram shrugged. "I can't argue it directly, Victoria. There *was* no incarnate Athena in my lifetime. But I have read the histories, pretty carefully. I think... and I admit, it's just my own impression, but I *think* that the gods don't wipe out the person they incarnate to. She sort of chooses someone who fits with being Athena, and makes them... more of who they are. Yeah, they'll get Athena's knowledge and power, but they're not erased."

"Ingram, the 'knowledge and power' of something that's lived through dozens of Cycles... I couldn't *possibly* be the same person after I got that!"

"No." Ingram bit his lip. "And I wouldn't ask you to do that."

Urelle stared at him, then smiled. "I know you wouldn't. But now I'm worried about going to Aegeia. Am I going to suddenly just turn into this incarnate goddess as soon as I enter?"

Ingram stared at her, and Quester could feel the conflicting worries churning within his friend. Ingram's oath made it imperative that he return, help his Clan, stop Ares. Yet Ingram's personal attachment — an intense affection, perhaps more that Quester could not precisely sort out — to Urelle was equally powerful. He could not risk his mission, yet nor could he risk Urelle.

And Ingram could not move forward on his mission without Urelle. Even if another Salandaras were willing to lead them, Quester could not imagine that they could simply walk through the Seal. It would take a skilled master of magic to take advantage of the single and singular flaw in the otherwise perfect barrier.

There was silence in the room for several moments.

Victoria shifted, and then looked sharply towards Urelle. "We need answers, it would seem, and the answers lie beyond us."

Urelle looked up; for a moment, Quester saw only puzzlement on her face, but then her eyes widened. "But... I thought that should be saved for desperate moments."

Ingram caught on at the same moment Quester realized what they were talking about. "Wait, no, we shouldn't call him over such a..." he trailed off.

Victoria's eyebrow had lifted, and a small, cutting smile appeared as Ingram stopped. "You were going to say 'trivial matter' or something of the sort, I suppose?"

Ingram nodded, face clearly reddened.

"Well, at least you had the sense to realize your mistake. This is *vital*. We have questions that *must* be answered, or we cannot move forward. Yes?"

Ingram exchanged glances with Urelle, and both nodded. "Yes."

"And none of us believe those answers can be found here, yes?"

Quester thought on it, but he agreed with that conclusion. If Ingram didn't know how the incarnations worked, it was highly doubtful the Salandaras would... and these were not ordinary times, in any case. The rules might have changed. "Yes. I do not believe those answers are here," he said, and saw the younger two nod.

"Then we are in need of some means of resolving our questions, or our mission — *your* mission, Ingram, which has become ours — fails here, and Urelle's efforts truly *were* for nothing."

Ingram muttered a curse under his breath.

Quester sketched a bow towards the girl in her bed. "Urelle? Would you be willing to try?"

Urelle hesitated, her storm-gray eyes distant. But after a few moments, she nodded. "I think Auntie's right. We don't have any way to answer these questions, but if anyone can, it's him."

She gestured towards the closet where her clothing hung, and a tiny glittering object flew to her hand. She stared down at it, and Quester could feel her tension rising, a tension not unmixed with excitement and anticipation. "I will try to call the Wanderer."

Chapter 13
Outside Assistance

It was not, Victoria admitted to herself, a sufficiently dramatic method of invoking a legend. Urelle simply gazed with full concentration into the Lens, a small girl with her black hair hanging in her face, staring intently at a little crystal object barely larger than her pinky nail. Faint glimmers came from it, so faint that she could not be sure it wasn't merely reflection from the light-orbs in the room. Then she spoke the single word: "*Arisia*."

The Lens flared up with a brilliant polychromatic refulgence that was nearly a solid thing, a shining, shifting rainbow of nigh-living light that enveloped the entire bed on which Urelle sat, then filled the world with spectral luminance.

When the light faded, the Wanderer was there.

He is... different, Victoria thought.

In appearance he was little changed; the light blond hair, the extremely fair skin, the piercingly blue eyes, the black cloak clasped with silver at the throat, the dark clothing with hints of strange, squarish armor similar to Ingram's beneath, and the tall, elaborately enruned Staff of Stars crowned with its blue-white glowing crystal within the twined cage of metal.

But his pose and expression were different; he stood as one ready for combat, Staff raised, the other hand poised. A long sword of unknown design was sheathed at his side, and about his body flickered the light of mystic defenses. Though he still looked as human as ever, there was about him a sense of power and peril greater than anything Victoria had yet encountered, save perhaps her momentary contact with Myrionar itself.

That gaze flashed about the room, taking in the entire situation — and abruptly the man in front of them was the same relaxed, faintly smiling Wanderer they had met in his fortress, months before. "Well, that's a surprise," he said. "A pleasant one, but still a surprise. I'd expected to be called when you were in some terrible danger."

"Not a danger, exactly," Urelle said, apology strong in her voice, "and I hope you won't think it's wasted the Lens' power, but... we have a problem we can't solve."

"Well, whether it's a waste... we'll see, after I hear about your problem." He glanced around, his fingers moving casually through arcane symbology. "Well, the *Freehold*. Okay, then your problem's something that can't be solved by hitting it harder, anyway. So tell me."

Quickly — with some interjections by Victoria herself, Ingram, and Quester — they summarized their journey here, Urelle's testing, and their sudden realization of Urelle and Victoria's nature, and what it seemed to imply about their entire quest. "So... I guess you understand now, right?" Urelle finished.

The Wanderer sat down slowly on one of the chairs, the Staff of Stars floating away to lean in a corner. The young-looking face suddenly flashed out a grin that grew wider, then became a chuckle, and finally a full-fledged laugh.

"It's not *that* funny!"

"Oh, it's *easily* that funny if you've got my perspective, Urelle," he said. "Being funny doesn't mean it's not also serious, and believe me, I'm taking this *very* seriously."

He bowed deeply to her. "And a *Salandaras*, now, there's a name I've never imagined as one that would be attached to an apprentice of mine. I respect them immensely — considering their average size, it's kind of hard to respect them any other way — but mages, they generally ain't. I hope you realize the honor you've earned."

"I think so," Urelle said after a moment, looking to Victoria.

"We *all* appreciate it, perhaps more seeing what a terrible price she had to pay to attain that honor," Victoria said. "But if we are stopped here, it becomes little more than an honor."

"Do not underestimate that honor, any of you. The Salandaras are a power unto themselves, and to be accepted as one of them is to have that power as your own." The lopsided smile flashed out again. "But still, I know, all the power and honor doesn't matter much if you can't get where you all have to go."

"So?" From her interactions with the Wanderer, she had come to grasp that he was a man of paradoxes — immensely ancient, possessed of fantastic breadth and depth of knowledge that only someone literal ages old could have... and sometimes with the maturity and sense of melodrama of a boy scarce older than Ingram.

"Have you any answers to our questions? Will Urelle suddenly become Athena if she enters Aegeia? Is Ingram's guess about the entire situation, correct? If Urelle *is* chosen by Athena, does it mean my... does it mean Urelle is suddenly no longer... herself?"

She realized her phrasing had become more... personal than she intended, but despite a brief twinkle in his eyes, the Wanderer showed no notice. *And really... why should I pretend?* "Because that is something I will not countenance, Wanderer. I bore no children of my own, but Urelle is nevertheless my daughter, as surely as I live."

Urelle's eyes filled with tears and she reached out and gripped Victoria's hand tightly; she felt Quester's pleased reaction, and saw Ingram smile.

"No one who had seen you together for even a few minutes would think anything else," the Wanderer said. "And I can't blame you. No matter how really great it would be to have an incarnate goddess on your side, it'd still suck for that to cost you a friend. Read a book that had an ending like that, it was a really unpleasant jolt. Lot worse to have happen in real life.

"So, to address your questions... let me think. And do a little research."

So saying, the Wanderer reached into his pack and pulled out several books — blowing the dust off of one. "Man, *that* one has been in there a while."

Ingram leaned forward. "Wait... that's the *Camp-Bel* sigil on that one! And that other one... that's *Athena!* Those are sacred!"

"Whoa! Whoa!" the Wanderer tumbled back as Ingram tried to snatch the books out of his hand.

"Ingram! Control yourself!" Victoria snapped, though she could sense, through the link, the emotions driving the boy.

Ingram hesitated for an instant, giving Quester a chance to drag him back.

"Holy Jebus, give a guy a chance to explain before you try to grab his books!" the Wanderer said. "I was *given* these, one by the then-Captain, the other by one of the God-Warriors some Cycles ago — the Lady knew I collect useful info and this was my reward for helping the right side out a bit. Yes, they're probably sacred books for your people, but they're *my* sacred books, given me by the people they're sacred to, so sorry, I'm keeping them."

Ingram flushed visibly, then bowed. "My apologies, sir. That was... rude, uncalled for, and stupid."

"No one's hurt, it's fine. Just let me work now."

For a while they all waited, silence broken only by the turning of pages and the occasional murmur of some kind of spell.

I'm feeling... kind of disappointed, Ingram thought to them.

In what way? Quester's thoughts were genuinely curious.

Oh, I know what Ingram means. It's kinda... well, no, really silly, but I think both of us expected the Wanderer to just, you know, answer everything.

He is, after all, still a human being, Victoria reminded them. *Ancient, and peculiar, I will grant you. But he himself emphasized that while he could sometimes play in the 'Great Game,' he was still more one of us than a cosmic power. I am afraid he has the same limits as most of us, just much more experience.*

I know that, Auntie. I just... expected more.

"No help for it," the Wanderer said, his voice startling in the former silence. "I've got part of your answer, but I've got to get a consultant for the rest."

"A... consultant?"

"Yeah, one of my colleagues who knows a lot more about specifics of how the gods and such work. Everyone stand clear."

Assured they were well away, the Wanderer waved the Staff and a complex magical circle appeared in shimmering light on the polished floorboards of the room. Victoria could only read small parts of the symbology, but it was clearly one of considerable power.

The words the Wanderer intoned then were of no language Victoria had ever heard; it was rhythmic, musical, with some hints of pronunciation and emphasis that sometimes echoed the sonorous sound of Ancient Sauran, but with the flow that only a truly human language could have for a human speaker. He repeated the same chant three times, four, five...

Upon the seventh repetition, a seven-pointed star flared into existence about the circle, and within the circle a huge shadowy shape appeared, tall and forbidding, vaguely human in outline but so dim and blurred that Victoria could make out little else except that its head seemed broad and flattened, the body nigh-shapeless or perhaps clothed in robes. A deep voice echoed faintly from the wraithlike shape.

The Wanderer replied, still in that unknown language; for a few minutes, the two conversed, the Wanderer's tone becoming more insistent. Finally, he broke into common speech. "Okay, you need to actually *come here*!"

There was a shockwave of displaced air and — with not even a moment's transition — the shadowy form solidified into full reality.

It *was* a man, Victoria realized now — an extraordinarily tall man, over seven feet in height, wearing a strange five-sided hat, gripping a staff even more elaborate in design than the Staff of Stars, wearing robes of brown and gray and blue. "Wanderer, I am currently — by Torline's *soul*, how *dare* you?"

"Shut *up*, you meddling old fraud, this is right smack-dab in the middle of your bailiwick, and this will go a *lot* faster if you take a look around in person."

The other's hand — a powerful, huge hand, fully in proportion to the figure's height — gripped his staff so tightly the knuckles went white. "You... *child!* I was on the *front lines of the battle!*"

"They'll just think you teleported to go mess things up somewhere else. And do you want me to remind you of the time that you —"

"Enough! Very well."

The Wanderer, only partially hiding a triumphant grin, turned to the rest of them. "Allow me to introduce the possibly even more legendary than me wizard, Konstantin Khoros."

Victoria felt a chill across her whole body and gripped her hands together, seeking a trivial comfort. The younger members of their group might know only the name, but she had heard tales of the ancient soul-mage from Toron and others during her adventures. On the side of the Light Khoros might be... but he was one of deep maneuverings and hard choices, and whenever he appeared, danger and disaster were never far behind.

The Wanderer continued, either oblivious to her reaction or simply ignoring it. "Khoros, I know you know who everyone is already, but that extremely distinguished woman is Lady Victoria Vantage, the bandaged girl in the bed is Urelle Vantage — my *apprentice*," he added, causing an intake of breath from Khoros, "the lavender-haired boy is Ingram Camp-Bel, and the Iriistiik is called Quester."

Khoros bowed briefly to them, then rose. "An honor to meet you all," he said in that startlingly deep voice. Victoria noted that despite the illumination, Khoros' face remained in shadow at all times; hints of expression were visible, but no detail.

"I apologize for the unseemly conflict. I should have expressed my displeasure later, privately."

"Now," he went on, "I understand what you are asking, Wanderer. I will first verify what I suspect."

The staff in his hand chimed and gold-crystal light pulsed out from it in concentric circles like ripples on a pond.

The light... *tingled*. It was a wave of sparks and snowflakes, kissing the skin with melting chill and sharp warmth all at once, soaking into her with the bite of a high-mountain wind and the comfort of a long-awaited bath; at the same time, she heard whispers of words she could not understand, and a deep song that resonated in her heart and soul.

For an instant she saw, not bodies, but *light*. Khoros was a blinding sun wrapped in dark mist; the Wanderer, a dancing skein of rainbow gems that receded into infinity in all directions.

Where Urelle lay there was a girl of crystal, of limitless complexity, each facet made of innumerable others, every edge limned with violet fire, every plane seething with the colors of eternity. Standing next to her, Ingram Camp-Bel was a blazing statue of gold behind smoked glass, and Quester was a sphere of emerald luminance that touched somehow upon the rest of them while remaining, at the same time, itself; a point of pure white, more intense than a dozen suns, burned at the very core of the emerald globe.

The vision ended before she thought to look at herself.

Khoros' shrouded face surveyed them slowly, then he nodded, the hat with its unknown symbols emphasizing the motion. "Not entirely unexpected, but it is still good to be certain. Now, pardon me for a few moments, as I must also ascertain certain things about the state of Aegeia and the gods."

Ingram narrowed his gaze. "And you can do that from here, through the barrier?"

"*Through* it... not precisely. *Past* it, yes, in something of the manner in which you will have to enter, though — as I need not travel thence physically, and have rather more knowledge and experience, it will be done more quickly and will seem easier. Now please, a moment of peace."

Khoros did not make a circle on the floor; instead, he held his staff vertical before him with his right hand, while the left sketched complex mystical symbols and formulae in the air, in streaks of blue-white fire. Victoria noted Urelle leaning forward, attention utterly focused on following the ancient magician's every move.

An aura of that same blue-white fire enveloped the soul-mage, shimmering and rippling like burning water; again, Victoria had the impression of voices speaking words she could not catch.

Long moments went by before Khoros let his staff sink to rest on the floor and the luminous aura faded. "So. I believe I can answer your questions.

"First and foremost, no, none of you will find yourselves suddenly possessed by the essence of a god — or, I would expect, anything else — upon entering Aegeia. Your enemy — who is surprisingly closed to me; I can distinguish nothing save only to confirm your suspicion that he is not, in fact, Ares — has expended a great deal of effort and subtle craft to ensure that it is virtually impossible for Athena to be reborn."

Ingram went so pale that Victoria was afraid he would faint; he *did* sway unsteadily before Quester caught his arm. "*Impossible?*"

"I said *virtually* impossible, but yes. His intentions are fairly obvious, even though I can, as I said, distinguish little of his true nature or the mechanisms he is employing. He attempts to subvert the Cycle and, by ensuring that Athena cannot appear at the requisite time, break the Cycle."

"*No!* That would be... that would be a complete *disaster!* Athena and the Cycle —"

"I assure you, young Ingram, I am at least as aware as you are of the consequences. It is the importance of these things that justifies the time and energies I am expending in talking with you, here, when a few thousand miles from here the armies of the Sauran King are in pitched battle with the forces of Kerlamion and his accursed City."

"Wait," said Urelle. "Sir, if you could so quickly divine the situation within Aegeia, could you not then at least send us through the barrier yourself?"

"*Could* I? Yes; I expect that you will find a way through on your own, and thus I would be certain that I could do it. However, what is swiftly — though not easily — accomplished with pure magic and divinations is not done nearly that quickly with living persons, physical beings that must be moved through the barrier. As an analogy, you have spells that will easily enhance your sight and hearing; this does not eliminate the difficulty of escaping a locked room, despite being able to hear and see what passes beyond that room."

Victoria caught both Khoros and the Wanderer in her gaze. "What else *can* you do? I admit it is useful to know that we can move forward without risking my... Urelle's self, and possibly to know the general goal of our adversary..."

"Hey, the first bit was the main concern, right?" the Wanderer pointed out.

"Not *now*," Ingram said, shock and horror still evident on his face. "If Athena can't be reborn, then the Cycle is *over*. So what's the *virtually* part of your 'virtually impossible'? We have to know that."

Khoros sighed. "Yes, you do. Yet I cannot give you a detailed answer. All my divinations tell me is that your enemy has, first, prevented the rebirth of Athena in the normal fashion. Second, has produced a very convincing false Athena so that none will suspect the problem even exists."

"By the Mother..." buzzed Quester. "He can not only imitate *one* god successfully, but also make *another* false god?"

"So it would seem. *But*! While your enemy has closed off most routes, there remains one possibility to awaken Athena. I cannot tell the details, but I know that it will require some one of a very few symbols or artifacts of her worship, and it will require some very specific conditions. On the positive side, I know that more than one of you could, under the right circumstances, meet those conditions. It is also possible you will meet someone else who will be an appropriate candidate.

"And," Khoros went on, "your group's existence is not accident or coincidence. If there is indeed 'destiny' at work, it guides you to the confrontation. I must believe that — if you win through — it may also help guide you to the solution to this mystery."

He surveyed the group again. "I will also caution all of you against *assumptions*. The greatest danger is the falsehood that you believe without realizing you believe it. Whatever your enemy may be, he is a master at manipulating *appearances*, at cloaking a vile truth within an obvious lie that no one questions. The fact that he can do this with the gods and not have his lie revealed by the priests? This tells us a great deal — most importantly, that he will prefer to hide even his vulnerabilities with assumptions; in some fashion they will be plain to see, yet passed over."

The Wanderer grinned, a startling flash of optimism. "But you've got one big advantage; you're on the right side."

"Yes," agreed Khoros. "True in more ways than they know. Oh, one other fact that may be of some comfort: Ingram's impression is correct. Those who become the vessels of the gods are not erased, not turned into duplicates of some particular incarnation of the god. They retain their selves, even while also being connected to the essence of Athena or whatever other god they might be.

"On the other hand, it is also true to say they will not remain the 'self' they were before the incarnation. The access to the knowledge and history and spirit of Athena will change any who suddenly acquire them. Yet... we are, none of us, who we were before any particular significant event. *Life* changes us. You know this well, Lady Victoria."

"Yes," she admitted after a moment's hesitation. "But is there no difference?"

"In degree, perhaps. It is each person's decision as to what degree of change is acceptable." Khoros turned and bowed to the Wanderer. "My apologies again. You were correct in choosing to bring me."

"Don't worry about it; I should've been more polite about asking. It's not like another ten seconds would've made any difference today. Want me to send you back?"

"At this point?" Khoros hesitated. "Ahh. Yes, send me back... to a point one hundred fifty yards east and two hundred south of my prior position."

"By your command," the Wanderer said in a peculiarly metallic voice, then grinned. "Good luck, and keep your head *way* down."

The Wanderer brought his staff down three times; upon the third strike, a blaze of gold and blue enveloped Khoros, and the huge mage vanished.

"Well," the Wanderer said, "That at least got us the answers you really need. You can move forward now, yes?"

"Yes," Ingram said, his color having finally returned to normal. "At least we can do that."

The Wanderer put his hand on Ingram's shoulder; Victoria noted how *pale* the Wanderer was, even next to Ingram's skin, which was far lighter than hers or Kyri's. "Look, Ingram, don't worry too much. I know the idea of the Cycle ending is scary, and possibly disastrous, but have some faith. The gods are *all* playing this game, and that means there's plenty in your corner too."

Ingram's gaze searched the Wanderer's crystal-blue eyes for a moment, then the young boy managed a smile. "All right. Thank you, sir."

"You're welcome, Ingram." He spun his staff in a lazy circle. "I've got to get moving myself; I wasn't in a battle at the time you called, but I do have things I have to finish."

"Will you... I mean, is this used up?" Urelle asked, holding up the tiny Lens.

The Wanderer smiled. "Not yet. Good for one, maybe two, more shots. You made a good call using this one; trust yourself to use it when the right time comes."

"Will it work through Athena's Shield?" Quester asked, antennae inclined in a quizzical manner. "Given that it bars the gods...?"

"Ha! First, remember that I'm the guy that gets to do the things no one else can. But more seriously, yes, because you have the Lens with you as you travel *to* Aegeia. Your... location trace, for lack of a better term, tells the Lens and me how to get through the Shield, by following your own path. Not that I'm going to physically follow the path, that is, it's more that I know what the sequence of locations in space-time-dimension is that corresponds to a passage to Aegeia."

Victoria could mostly follow that; she wasn't sure that Ingram did. Urelle probably understood more than Victoria. Quester's face was, of course, hard to read. "But we can only pass through because we have a Salandaras with us, as I understand it."

"Me and the Salandaras go way back. I'll pass, don't worry." He gave a bow, with a flourish of his cape, and vanished in a flash of smoke and flame.

"We need to get ready!" Urelle started to slide out of the bed — then almost fell to the floor as her knees gave out.

"*You* need to stay in bed, young lady!" Victoria snapped, feeling an unreasonably intense worry at the sight. "Until you are recovered from your ordeal, we are not moving *one inch*. And given what you went through, that will be a day or three even now."

"She's right," Ingram said, with an intensity that made Victoria smile inside, and took Urelle's hand. "You stay right there until you're all better."

Urelle's own smile flashed out.

Quester's mindvoice echoed in Victoria's head with gentle humor. *It seems to me that she just* became *all better.*

Chapter 14
Preparing a Welcome

"We have found them."

Raiagamor could not blame Deimos for wearing a self-satisfied expression; it was a great achievement indeed, and especially so given what Deimos had gone through before. "You know where the Camp-Bels went to ground?"

"We do. Even once we realized they had survived, they had left many subtle false trails, but one of our scouts finally located them. They are in a very well-hidden and defended redoubt not far from Amoni Agapis, in the Iron Forest."

"The Iron Forest?" Raiagamor found the name amusing. The true name had meant *Forest of Heroes*, but the language and time had shifted long since. "Coincidence or planning, I wonder?"

Deimos shrugged. "Planning for what? It's true that Amoni's the last holdout at this point, but if you're able to hide as well as the Camp-Bels are, that wouldn't matter; being hidden within our pacified lands would be at least as useful."

"It should be obvious." He paused, and then saw Deimos' face go inhumanly rigid as it sometimes did when the demon-Xiilistiin was chastising himself.

There was no reason to describe your weaknesses to even your allies unless it became necessary, but fortifying the northern pass and planning for the intrusion of Ingram and his friends had made it necessary to explain to Deimos, Phobos, and the false Athena, the Shadow-Queen of the Xiilistiin, the one flaw in the barrier.

If the Camp-Bels *had* planned this, that meant someone within their ranks had deduced the location of that weakness and planned to be nearby when and if help — in the form of Ingram Camp-Bel and his friends — arrived. Overall, Raiagamor doubted it had been planned, but it didn't really matter at this point. "Your scouts have not yet acted?"

"No, sir. Your instructions were precise."

"Show me the layout as best you know it."

Deimos caused an image of the forest to appear, brought the point of view to focus on a particular location about forty miles north-northeast of Amoni Agapis. This was not far from the northern bounds of Wisdom's Fortress, rough, hilly country with many massive outcroppings of stone. The view enlarged a single hill, and finally showed a concealed entrance between two huge boulders. "We suspect there is at least one other entrance or exit; the Camp-Bels would not let themselves be cornered with no way out."

"No, they would not. There are likely at least three or four exits, all of them heavily fortified. Have we seen any activity, movement in or out?"

"They send out small, impressively stealthy patrols periodically."

Raiaga smiled. "And can your people ambush and replace one of these patrols?"

Deimos considered. "I believe so. We can move a sufficient number of our forces there so that such an ambush can be done with such swift finality that they should be unable to send any message out. However..."

"... yes?"

"I, and Shadow-Queen Athena, am not confident that even one of our people could avoid detection upon entry. They may have god-sight or something similar, or even some of the Founder's technology."

Raiagamor chuckled. "Yes, they might. But I have an answer to that. Send those who would be replacements to me, and I will ensure that they can walk unsuspected even by the gods themselves."

That was, of course, something of an exaggeration. He couldn't truly make these creatures into Great Wolves, let alone the unique being that he was, and a being of sufficient power and suspicion might still pierce their disguises. But he *could* improve dramatically on the Xiilistiin's impressive native ability to deceive, and that should be sufficient.

"Very well. Once they have entered, should I presume they should find, eliminate, and replace Ingram Camp-Bel's parents?"

When Raiagamor did not immediately respond, Deimos opened his mouth to repeat the question, but stopped instantly as Raiagamor raised a hand. "Wait."

Should they replace the parents now? At first glance it was the most obvious, simple, and direct way to achieve the goals: it would leave the bait there to draw in Ingram Camp-Bel and his friends, yet the bait would also be poisoned and there would be no way for Ingram to hear what his parents would say.

But.

Yes, *but*. The problem there was that whatever Xiilistiin took the parents would gain something of their knowledge and so on, but — in all likelihood — not all of it, especially as taking someone inside the fortress would almost certainly be a rushed job. The patrols, if successfully ambushed, could be converted slowly, taking as much as the Xiilistiin could drain from them and incorporating it into their knowledge. This was exceedingly unlikely to be the case with the parents.

And *that* meant there were two areas of concern. The first was that the lack of some amount of their knowledge could betray them to the Camp-Bels at any time — and there went the chance to ambush the returning hero and his allies.

Second… Raiagamor *did not know* what it was that Ingram's parents knew. They held a secret, or perhaps many secrets, of great import and these had to be conveyed to Ingram Camp-Bel in order to, somehow, give him a chance to, as they might say, 'put things right'. But of what those secrets were, Raiagamor had not the slightest inkling, and that was dangerous. The Xiilistiin were *currently* his allies. But you kept allies like the Xiilistiin at your peril, and did so best by hiding your weaknesses and emphasizing your strengths.

What if Ingram Camp-Bel's parents knew something about him — about his one true weakness, for example, or the remaining way to revive the true Athena? This would give the Xiilistiin leverage against him that he had no intention of allowing. And the one replacing them would have an excellent chance of learning such secrets.

He did, of course, have his own backup plans, his own leverage, and some very specific controls on Deimos and Phobos, but it was still a terrible risk. And a risk that, ultimately, Raiagamor felt he should never run.

Leave them alive until Ingram arrives? That he had also discussed with his aides, and would certainly eliminate any risk that the other Camp-Bels would notice anything awry about those two vital persons. In addition, it would make them excellent, if unwitting, lures for Ingram. However, that also made it possible, if unlikely, that they could get to speak with Ingram, no matter how quickly the Xiilistiin spies acted. The Camp-Bels had their reputation for a very good reason, and if they anticipated the strike by so much as a second…

"No," he said at last. *Better not to make things overcomplicated.* As he thought that, he felt better, more certain. The love of a complex plan for the plan's sake was a weakness he shared with the King, but he was *not* the King, and it was best to remember that.

"No," he repeated. "Infiltrate until you are in a position to strike, then kill *everyone*."

Deimos raised an eyebrow. "I thought you intended —"

"—a friendly-seeming trap? Yes, but as long as all our infiltrators aren't killed in the slaughter itself, we can likely arrange that ourselves. But if we kill all the actual Camp-Bels, then they'll never be a problem. Leaving any alive, or attempting to be too subtle? Too many ways for that to go wrong. I would rather lose a bit of information and leverage but be certain of their demise."

"And if Ingram Camp-Bel and his friends approach, we are to attempt an ambush."

"Correct. Lure them in if you can — if you can convince them that his Clan awaits within, it should be a simple matter to make their refuge a killing ground. But if they will not be deceived, slay them."

"As you wish." Raiagamor could see Deimos' hidden approval. The demon-Xiilistiin apparently had not liked the more complex plan either, but been hesitant to mention it. *Important to remember; I must ensure that he and Phobos understand that I want them to tell me if I am making a mistake.*

"I also have a specific task for you and Phobos," he went on. "I want you both to go and personally oversee securing the area in the north."

"Again, as you wish, Lord Ares," Deimos said, eyes narrowed, "but why should we not be directly active in the infiltration of the Camp-Bel fortifications? We are superior to those *hiijaa*." The word signified the rank-and-file Xiilistiin, those converted from ordinary human beings and given no special enhancements.

Raiagamor nodded. "Indeed, you are, and if that were my primary means of dealing with the problem, I would place at least one of you there. However, I would prefer that the trap is never sprung at all. Therefore, I want two of my most trustworthy and powerful agents there to intercept and kill the intruders if and when they come through.

"Also," he went on, before Deimos could speak, "I may find I need either or both of you for other services; the God-Warriors of Ares are, after all, supposed to be highly visible in my court. If you are in a hidden redoubt playing the part of some vital Camp-Bel guard or officer, you can hardly just disappear for a day or three."

The false God-Warrior's mouth closed. "Ah. Yes, of course, Lord Ares. That is eminently sensible. Will there be anything else?"

"Yes," he said after a moment. "While our *plan* is to eliminate all resistance long before it could possibly threaten our hold on the main cities, let alone Aegis, I want to take as few risks as possible. You, Phobos, and Athena will work with me to devise the most effective inner Seal, a defensive shield that will prevent any intrusion into the Aegeian Path at all."

"Such a seal, if it is to stop Berenike, as well as her friends, will take time and considerable effort — as well as another tithe of your godspower — to construct," Phobos said after a moment. "Have we sufficient of either to make this effort worthwhile? We do not know how long it will take them to pierce the Seal once they reach the key point."

Raiagamor laughed. "More time than you might think, Phobos. Yes, they have located the one weakness of the Seal... but to call it 'weakness' is to trivialize the process of passing through. If — and I say quite honestly *if* — they manage the passage at all, it will be itself a heroic effort, and one costly in time as well as in peril. At the *least* I give them two months to pass the Seal. At the most, several months before they arrive, perhaps half a year."

"In truth?" Phobos and Deimos both regarded him in surprise.

"Even I, with my own advantages, would require time to pass through the barrier by that method. Mortals, howsoever skilled... I assure you, it will not be easy at all. I studied the structure of Athena's Seal most carefully, and I do not believe any of you quite understand what was wrought there." He waved the issue away. "No, we have time, and I have more than sufficient power to spare as well."

The two saluted him. "Anything else?" Phobos asked.

"No, that will be all. Take whatever you need to secure the calculated area of emergence; you know what forces are already in place. I will speak with the Shadow-Queen myself."

"Whatever we need? Including our particular ally?"

He thought a moment. *Yes, this is the right time. I do not wish that particular being to have any closer access to this stronghold, but deploying it within Aegeia... yes, that is ideal. Even without Deimos and Phobos, it should be more than adequate to deal with our Camp-Bel friend and his party — and possibly even Berenike.* "Yes. In fact, I insist. It is time we took advantage of its particular abilities. In fact, while you await our anticipated guests, it might assist Athena in reducing the last stronghold of our enemies in a particularly unnerving way."

"As you command, sir." The two bowed and departed.

Once sure they were well on their way, Raiagamor leaned back and concentrated. *Athena?*

Here, my love. The words were deliberately ironic. One of the newer scandals promoting unrest within the nearly-unified Aegeia was that the Incarnate Ares and Incarnate Athena had rekindled the relationship their mortal forms had had. While such relations between the gods were not — entirely — unheard of, *Athena's* reputation did not generally admit of such things; if Athena had any romantic relationships at all, they were things of great propriety and deep personal attachment that evolved out of her own journey towards the unification of Aegeia.

This would be a concern if the true goal was to rule over Aegeia as it was, but Raiagamor intended to *break* Aegeia, shatter the Cycle, and take advantage of the power of the Chaoswar now beginning to turn Aegeia into something quite antithetical to anything it had ever stood for. This situation served him well. *What is the status of the armies?*

She showed him a vision: her own golden tent in the center of a veritable ocean of other temporary shelters, guarded by the armies of Aegeia and four of the five other great cities, showing the colors and symbols of Apollo, Demeter, Hermes, and Artemis. *We are preparing to move on Amoni Agapis tomorrow. The forces of the Anvil and the Mirror are likely trying to fortify the main pass into the city.*

Raiaga nodded. Amoni Agapis sat within a nearly circular valley ringed by low but steep mountains, with one large pass to the south-southwest through which the Asimi ran, warm and broad and smooth, from Lake Cathrefti, the Mirror of Aphrodite. That pass was the obvious defensive point for the city -- though obviously their forces would try to slow any approach to the city as best they could.

Take your time. The pressures of war allow me to take many measures that, once in place, will help erase everything of human value from this civilization. Though I will require your assistance on another project. He outlined the need for the secondary Seal on the Aegeian Path. *You comprehend?*

Clearly, my Lord. I believe I already see the best way to achieve this, anchoring the enchantment in the solid stone of the Pathway Obelisks. As for the other, I will make the ending of the Anvil of Love as torturous as you desire. But I do have one request.

That was a surprise. *Name it.*

I understand from Deimos and Phobos, as well as from our discussion of this new Seal, that you do expect the four Adventurers to enter, even through the Seal of Athena. Is this true?

I have no doubt they will, now. I was given warning by… someone I have every reason to believe. What of it?

The Iriistiik. Give him to me and the Swarm.

You wish to kill him?

No. An impression of a great alien amusement and dark hunger. *We have a far better use for the last of their kind. Tell them that they must not kill the Iriistiik.*

He shrugged. *I have no objection; without the others, that insect is of no threat to me.* He concentrated. *Deimos, Phobos — your Shadow-Queen wishes the Iriistiik captured, not slain. See to it.*

A sense of slight annoyance. *This complicates the problem, sir. Slaughtering everyone is a simple directive; killing all but one,* much *harder.*

Nonetheless, that is my command. I realize that it may not be possible, but make every effort to keep the Iriistiik alive. She has some use for him. And warn your pet of this requirement, or I have no doubt it will eat him without a second thought.

Deimos and Phobos conferred a moment, something he could sense faintly. Then, *It will be as you wish.*

Excellent. About your business, then. He returned his attention to Athena. *It is arranged.*

Thanks of the Swarm to you. You will be most pleased when you see the result.

I look forward to it.

Breaking the connection, Raiagamor rose, stretching the muscles of the human body. He felt the phantom sensations of hunger, turned to make his way to the dining-hall.

Only his long-honed sense of self-preservation and paranoia saved him. As he opened the door, he saw the faintest difference in the play of light, a darkening that meant that the wall nearest him, out of line of sight, was somehow no longer reflecting like the white marble it was.

He leapt backwards even as an immense figure covered in shaggy brown-black fur lunged, glittering crystal claws cleaving the door into four pieces and gouging cuts into the stone itself. *An assassin? An assassin of my* King's *people?*

The other paused in the doorway, his surprise having been ruined. "Quick you are, abomination."

"I have lived long enough to learn speed," he answered, feeling the hunger and rage rising within him. *Oh, it has been* long *since I killed, and far longer since I killed one of* them. "What fool are you, who tries to murder me within my own stronghold?"

"Stronghold." Contempt dripped from the word. "One disgusting mistake surrounded by prey and servants. But yes, I will give you my name. I am Morinavir, and to me is given the honor of cleansing the universe."

Raiagamor shifted now into his own true form, and could now stare with hungry humor *down* into the eyes of his opponent. "This 'mistake' is favored of the Mother and tolerated, if not loved, by the King."

Morinavir snarled, and there was a brief passage of claw and tooth; furniture shattered, walls were cut, but no blood drawn, no souls ripped — though Raiaga felt the tug on his essence, and drew close to the essence of his foe, before they parted. "We are aware. We are also aware of what you do here."

Raiaga laughed; the amusement blunted his rage for a moment. "Are you? I think you have not the first idea of what I am doing here. But now I know you *fear* what I am doing. You fear the worst of all: that the King may *recognize* me, and set me up above all but the Elders themselves!"

"That will *never* happen!"

The Great Wolf closed on him in earnest, and Raiagamor found he was fighting for his life. Morinavir was no Elder, but he was *old*, old enough to have controlled his spirit to the point that even Raiaga had not sensed his approach, old enough to have steeped himself in the ways of combat for perhaps even longer than Raiagamor.

But he fights me as a Wolf, Raiagamor thought with rising hope, as each of them inflicted cuts on the other, and he began to read the other's patterns. *For all they call me 'abomination' and 'monster' and 'mistake', still in the end they think I am like them. That is why they hate and fear me; because if I am like them, I may be no mistake.*

Yet I am not *one of them.*

I am better *than they are.*

Claws blocked claws, legs slashed out but failed to rip through flesh and soul, mouths snarled but could find no safe place to bite. Raiga was being driven back, having to duck away just a little more often than his opponent, slowly but inexorably finding himself approaching a corner, a part of his apartment built into the living rock of the mountain.

Then he was *in* the corner, and his elbow bumped the stone at just the wrong moment — and a taloned hand flashed past his guard, long glittering diamond claws aimed straight for his heart.

The impact slammed him into the wall, but far worse was the result for his opponent, as Morinavir's claws *shattered*.

The Great Wolf staggered back, agony clear on his savage face. "Wh... what?"

Raiagamor shrugged off his robe, revealing the shining metal covering much of his left breast. "I drew your energy out as your claws neared me, making them naught but tough crystal indeed — but then they struck upon this, of *krellin* mined from the Khalals, and were broken."

Smiling, he lunged forward now and struck off the other's right arm, rending the spirit and swallowing the energies of a Great Wolf. "How ironic that you struck the center of one of my secrets — and yet, even had your strike gone true, it would not have slain me, for what I am is something beyond *you*."

The other managed to drive his claws home in Raiagamor's thigh, but Raiaga merely winced, and caught the clawed hand, *held* it there, watched his opponent as his eyes widened in realization, feeling his life-force being consumed, his own claws serving as conduits.

"Only two ways can I be slain, little assassin," he snarled, smiling and raging at the same time. "Only two, and you have brought neither. The first to be so strong with the Hunger that you can surpass my own; that is given only to the Elders, our Queen, and our King.

Morinavir sagged down, and Raiaga remembered a similar expression of shock and horror on Ares' face, so long ago. "And the second? Too late to learn it."

With a single effort he tore the other's spirit from his body, and consumed it entirely.

The massive, shaggy form fell heavily and did not move.

Energy flowed into him, and he laughed, his rage now completely dissipated in triumph and power. *Send me more assassins, my jealous and fearful lesser siblings! Send them* all! *You will but make me a thousand times stronger!*

His hunger for power almost sated, he put back on his robe and went to satisfy the merely mortal cravings, leaving the assassin's corpse behind.

Chapter 15
The Seal of Athena

Urelle watched as Druyar methodically unlocked the seven different locks sealing shut the immense door that was at the end of the lowest corridor in the Freehold, five levels below the ground, through other locked and guarded doors.

The big man very carefully examined each lock, laboriously comparing the symbols on lock with those on the seven keys he had taken from inside his armor. After selecting a key, he then compared the symbols on the key to those on the lock three times before inserting the key and turning it in the lock. Only once he had heard the loud *click!* from the lock did he attempt to draw back the associated bolts.

Why's he so careful about it? Ingram asked in their silent mental link.

Not sure. Wait a minute. She focused, then *looked* at the door with magical sight. *Balance and Sword, that's why. Those locks are* covered *with powerful defenses. I'm guessing if he put in the wrong key, he'd be in for a* lot *of pain.*

"Of course," Victoria murmured aloud. "One would expect the door itself to be a formidable barrier, and an active one as well as passive, to something so crucial to another's security."

"Yah," agreed Druyar. "Locks very magical. Have traps, too, not just spells. Fire, poison, thunder, light, cold, others. Do wrong, you die, or at least be hurt very bad."

"But as you can see, Druyar is very careful for us all," Frederic said. "Is it open, Druyar?"

"Think so." Just as methodically, the Salandaras surveyed the circular door all the way around its perimeter, then nodded. "Yes. All locks turned, all bolts drawn. Can open now, if want."

The four looked at each other; Urelle finally looked up and nodded. "It's time, sir."

"Yah," he said again, but then he knelt down, so that his head was now level with her eyes. Druyar's bright green eyes studied her, and he gave a broad smile.

"You Salandaras, now. You one of us. Won't say don't be afraid — that *really* stupid. But you remember you Salandaras too, when you afraid. You prove you strong, stronger than fear, stronger than pain, stronger than monster or trap or ghost or god that try to stop you." He tapped his chest, pointed at her. "Heart of Salandaras make you strong. *Luck* of Salandaras keep you strong."

Urelle could feel the absolute faith behind the huge man's words, and more: the absolute *acceptance* of her, that what she had risked meant everything to him and his people. She felt a sting in her eyes and then stepped forward and gave Druyar a hug, wrapping her arms as far as they would go around the massive armored chest. "Thank you so much, Druyar. And... I'm proud to be one of you. And so very humbled and sad for the price you pay to be one."

The green eyes showed that glint of sadness mingled with pride again. "Yes," he said, more clearly, some of his accent momentarily faded. "Is sad. But brings us people like you, too, so maybe not so sad. Now you go, and remember what names are yours."

Frederic nodded, and accepted her embrace as well. "I have married into the Salandaras, of course," he said, glancing at Druyar, "but had it been necessary to take the Crucible, I admit my courage might have failed. Fare thee well, Urelle Vantage Salandaras, and for what it may be worth, take my blessing as well." He sketched a symbol in the air, and she felt the magics of the world concentrated, brought to their essence and then dispersed to each member of her party.

The others said their goodbyes as well, as Urelle gazed upon the door and the circular wheel set in its center, like one she had seen in a picture of an *Odinsyrnen* vault.

Then she reached up and turned the wheel, once, twice, three times, and there was a *CHOK* sound as massive bolts disengaged. The door swung open easily, revealing a dark cavern beyond. "Let's go."

The four of them trooped through the circular doorway; once the last of them, Quester, had passed the threshold, they heard Druyar mutter one more "Good luck," and the massive portal swung shut and the many locks re-engaged in a shock of metallic sounds, the finality echoing through the cave and Urelle's heart. *No turning back. Even if we wanted to, I don't think they could even* hear *us on the other side.*

"So, are we through the Seal?" Ingram asked. "Was that door part of the Seal?"

"I don't think so," Urelle answered. "That doesn't fit with what the Wanderer said, or with how I would've set it up. But it must be very nearby."

She brought up her hands, focused, and looked.

Slowly, she became conscious of someone shaking her. "Urelle! Urelle! Lady of Wisdom, help her!"

"I... I'm okay," she managed after a moment. "No, really, just... just give me a few minutes."

"What happened, Urelle?" Quester asked, as she sat there, eyes closed, trying to recover.

"I did something... really stupid," she admitted. "I just threw up my most sensitive spell and looked through it, forgetting what the Seal barrier looked like even from yards away out there on the beach, months ago. It was like stepping out of a cave and looking straight up into the Sun, only worse, because that kind of spell... well, it hits all your senses at once. So it was like I punched myself in the head really hard."

"That *was* foolish, Urelle," Victoria said, in a half-chiding, half-relieved tone. "I hope you will not make such mistakes again!"

She laughed, getting — a touch unsteadily — to her feet. "Oh, Auntie, I'll probably make dozens of such mistakes again. I just have to hope it's always when I'm not about to get killed."

She took a breath, then focused again. "Let's try this the *right* way this time."

Even with her strongest filter charms active, the Seal was almost blinding in its brilliance, a living latticework of golden power that lay only a few feet in front of them and extended outwards in all directions, into the cavern floor, through the walls, through the ceiling, to eventually encompass the entirety of Aegeia.

But...

But here, here the latticework was not the absolute perfection she had seen months ago on the southern shores of the continent. In front of her the crystalline symmetry bent, puckered in, swirled in a vertiginous complexity that dizzied her, a knot of godsfire and geometry — no, a dozen knots, a hundred, a thousand, each one re-tying itself and then untying into the next in a fountain of sunfire convolutions.

"Balance..." she breathed. "It's... *beautiful.*"

She saw Ingram near her, squinting, face strained. "I... I almost think I see something. Like a glittering heat-shimmer that spans the cavern."

She nodded absently. "You have a *lot* of magical potential, Ingram. We have to look into that sometime soon, but yes, I think you're sensing it, somehow."

"Beautiful is well and good," Victoria said, "but can you *open* it?"

"I... I'll have to. But I don't quite know how. Yet."

She felt Ingram's impatience, instantly squelched; he knew she would be trying her best already. And she was. But... *how*? A simple barrier or the spell she'd been able to see on the Coin, those were something like a matter of cutting a single knot, unraveling a weaving once you found the right thread. This thing... it had *many* "right threads" and she wasn't sure how...

"*... path in space-time-dimension...*"

She felt her breath catch in her throat, even as the true meaning of the Wanderer's deliberately casual description suddenly burst in upon her.

All of the... knots, keystones, threads she was seeing weren't really doing and undoing themselves; that was just the way her sight was trying to *interpret* something beyond normal human perceptions. They were all there, all at once, in one place and yet infinitely far away. The Wanderer, when showing her some transportation magic, had alluded to "crossing dimensional boundaries". And in his Book...

She reached into her pack, pulled out the Wanderer's Book, paged through it, her fingers and the Book's faint magic guiding her to the right section. For long minutes she sat and read.

"Are you... okay, Urelle?" Ingram finally said, hesitation in his voice. "You look... well, a little gray, pale, like something was really wrong."

She stared at him a moment, mouth opening but nothing coming out. After a few seconds, with the others staring at her in increasing concern, she found her voice. "Not... *wrong*, I guess, but... by *Myrionar*." She shook her head. "You know that the Seal keeps out pretty much everything — even including the gods, right?"

"That was our assumption," Vitoria agreed, "and those we have spoken to appear to confirm it. And?"

"And if that's true, then it has to block them... well, from *every* direction. The gods can walk in different worlds than this one; their own realms, those of their compatriots, maybe... maybe even many different worlds like this one." She waved vaguely at the book. "That's what the Wanderer's written here; he says that there is an infinity of worlds, as near each other as one written page is to another, yet as distinct and separable as those pages. Athena's Seal exists through *all* of those pages, or at least all the ones that you could ever expect even the gods to reach and try to enter by."

Surprisingly, Quester nodded. "Yes. The Mother-memories say this is true. Perhaps... perhaps even that we ourselves have been on other worlds than this."

"So what does that mean for us, Urelle?" Ingram asked.

"It means..." She stared at the Seal again, took another deep breath, "it means that getting *through* the Seal isn't just a matter of unraveling it here, or pushing through a hole. The way through is... well, through multiple *worlds*. I will have to find a way to open the Seal in stages, find our way from world to world and work our way through the seal until a way opens back into our world... within Aegeia."

"Founder's *Name*," muttered Ingram. "But you said there's an *infinite* number of worlds! Even if we spent fractions of a second in each one, we'd take the lifetime of the universe getting through!"

"Oh!" She smiled. "It's not *that* bad. The... knots, whatever, all connect back in Aegeia. A lot of those connections won't help us, but there should be a reasonable-length path to the, well, nexus on the other side, where all the other ends of the knots or keystones connect." She waved the Book again. "That's what I get out of this. He says making something like this requires you set up... what does he call it... a *cascade* of seals, that self-replicates throughout the entirety of reality. But the cascade's based on one... set of seals you, the mage, have to design yourself. To do *that* you have to hold the entirety of that set in your mind when you cast the spell, and then the spell goes on from there, I guess... Grouping each new set of worlds in the same way that you grouped the first."

Ingram frowned, then nodded. "I think I get it. So, there's *a* path to the center, to Aegeia, through each of those sets or sheaves of worlds?"

"Sheaf, that's a good word. Yes, that's what I think. You have to work through a given sheaf. The only danger is if you make a transition through to a neighboring sheaf, then you have sort of re-set yourself. But that *should* be fairly easy to notice. I have to assume there would be some form of discontinuity between separate-though-connected sheaves."

"And do we have any idea how *many* worlds are involved in one of your... sheaves?" Victoria asked.

"It has to be something a god — an *incarnate* god — could keep in their mind while setting up the seal design. Gods are, I guess, better at that kind of thing than we are, but... well, I wouldn't expect fewer than ten, and probably no more than a hundred."

Ingram winced. "A hundred worlds?" He shook his head. "Well... at least it's a lot better than infinity. Can we just pop from one to the next to the next?"

"I... maybe? I don't know if there will be a physical offset in the location of the seal. Probably not *much* of one, but when we come through there will likely be some amount of error." She thought. "Have to be, I think. Each world is different; there *can't* be a hundred percent correspondence between them, so the corresponding location of the flaw in the seal will be different too... though it won't prevent passage anywhere in the other worlds, only passage to *this* one, so no one on those worlds should be able to detect it. I think. So, I'll have to locate the Seal each time before we can leave."

Her friends looked at her, then at each other; Quester flapped his wing-cases in a shrug. "Well, the more we wait, the longer this will take, yes?"

"Let's go, then," Ingram said. "Do we hold on to each other?"

"Yes. Physical contact will let me draw you all with me."

Aunt Victoria's hands rested on her shoulders in a reassuring grip; she could sense Quester's second-hands take a firm grasp of Victoria's armored coat, and Ingram hold tight to one of Quester's first-arms.

She closed her eyes, then opened them again, seeing the fountaining, ever-changing yet constant maelstrom of the Flaw in the Seal, the Keystone between worlds. She remembered the Wanderer's descriptions of teleportation and similar motion-magics — ones she had tested with him, but hadn't — yet — used in the field. This would be like, and very *un*like, those.

But the basic principle was the same. She reached out her hand, surrounded it with magic and focus, with symbols that resonated with the *motion* of the Seal, that picked up the patterns of its unmoving motion, and... *grasped* the fabric of reality, *pulled* with first one hand and then the other, opening a loop of that coiling fountain of power and possibility...

... and the fountain erupted around them in golden fire and the impersonal violence of a tornado.

Chapter 16
A Dark Beginning

Victoria rolled from her back to her hands and knees and wavered there, unable to rise, trying to keep her breakfast from ending up on the ground beneath her. From the scrabbling and gagging sounds around her, the rest of the party were doing no better.

It seems intrauniversal travel is... unpleasant.

It took several minutes for her stomach to finally accede to her demands that it behave itself. *I must be getting old. I've been through worse. That time Cillerion decided to* sing *us away, now...*

But at last, she felt steady enough to rise to her feet and check on her companions. Urelle *had* lost her breakfast, alas. Unsurprising, of course; if it was bad on them, it would likely have been worse to the one *doing* the work.

Ingram was already up, but his attention was focused on Quester, who was showing little inclination to rise at all. Even the Iriistiik's thoughts were jumbled and incoherent, though clear enough to show that he was slowly recovering.

"Oh, *Balance*, I'm so sorry," Urelle said, then gagged again and spat out a mouthful of slightly-chunky saliva. "Ugh ugh ugh." She sketched a quick sigil in the air and gestured; light flickered on her hand.

Victoria saw Urelle's forehead wrinkle again and her mouth tighten. The light flickered again, steadied, and then the cleansing spell activated. "What happened, Urelle?"

"With what, our travel or that spell?"

"Both, I suppose."

Urelle sat down on a rock, holding her head in her hands for a few moments; Victoria joined her, putting an arm around the smaller girl. "I've never done anything like *that* before — the, well, cross-universe jump, let alone doing it by trying to squeeze... Myrionar's *Sword*, there aren't even good *words*... past, around, through whatever, a hole-that-really-isn't-there." A corner of her mouth turned up. "But now that I've *done* it, I think I can have a *little* more control the next time."

"And your cleansing spell?"

"Conditions here are... *different*. Magic still works, but the environment, the *way* it works, it's not the same. I can *force* it to work the way I want, the way I know... but it's hard. I'll have to adjust every time we go somewhere else, I guess."

"Will... this have... any effect on the rest of us?" Quester buzzed weakly.

"Lady's *Wisdom*, don't talk!" Ingram said, voice thin and shaken. "You were *unconscious* for a few minutes there."

"I am... recovering. And my question is relevant."

Victoria saw Urelle gesture vaguely. "I... don't know? In an infinity of worlds, I'd guess there must be some that would be *terribly* different from ours. But if they're ones in which magic doesn't work *at all*, or is so restricted that nothing I could think of would work, I'd guess they're ones that the gods and other forces would have a very hard time passing through, so probably didn't have to be shielded against." She shrugged. "We'll have to *hope* so, anyway, because if one of our sheaf of worlds is like that, we'll never get past it."

"I suppose the next order of business is to find the Seal connection in this world to the next in our sheaf, yes?" Victoria said, rising and dusting off her battle-jacket. "So where..."

She trailed off, because for the first time she took a real look at their surroundings.

Great Balance, it's hideous.

Surrounding them was a cracked, seamed plain, black and grey, covered in places with a grey-white powder that looked at first glance like gravelseed flour but smelled of brimstone. *Volcanic ash*, she realized as she raised her head and saw, miles off, the towering cone of a mountain with a pall of black smoke rising from it, one that spread out in all directions and left the world shrouded in a grim twilight — a twilight out of which the sulphurous dust sifted slowly down.

The terrain itself was jagged and broken, a gigantic version of the chaotic, split surface seen on a field of mud that has baked to stone-hardness under the sun. Vague shadows in the distance indicated that this might be a caldera — a huge mountain-ringed valley — of which the great volcano looming above was but a single vent left from a cataclysmic past.

"Athena's *Wisdom*, this looks terrible," Ingram murmured.

"Feels that way as well," Urelle said, and shuddered. "Like we're... I don't know, maybe closer to the Black City."

Victoria could feel it, too. The oppressive, hostile miasma that had covered the world when Kerlamion brought the Black City to Zarathan had become a part of the background of their lives... but here it weighed heavier upon them. *Or, possibly, is added to; there is some additional note, a* personal *malevolence that I do not recall from our first sense of the Black City's arrival.* "This is not a place for people to live long."

And yet not uninhabited, Quester noted.

His thoughts pointed them to the middle distance, down a ragged slope from them, where a clear road led, straight and true, across the wasteland, intersecting with another farther on. Moving dots showed that there were people of some kind traveling on those roads.

Ordered in travel, Victoria noted. The dots were organized in clear groups, not merely random scatterings. Though she could see nothing else, the sharp lines delineating each group said *military* to her. "Troop movements. We had best keep well clear. We are not staying here, and we don't want to be caught."

Ingram had his long-viewer glasses out. "Definitely not. They're not human, whatever they are, so we'd stand out. Urelle?"

"I'll look. It might take a few minutes just to figure out the direction, though."

While Urelle focused her power to try and locate the Seal intersection in this world, Victoria borrowed the long-viewer. The marching dots leapt into clear focus; humanoid, but definitely inhuman, the creatures wore functional but, from Victoria's point of view, very ugly armor, mostly of black iron and hide and chain, with equally ugly but clearly effective weaponry — short bows, chopping/thrusting swords for use in formation, spears. They were broader on average than human beings — somewhat like shrunken-down *bilarel*, but instead of being grayish, these were darker-skinned with a touch of green. There also appeared to be at least two classes, or perhaps subspecies, involved, as some groups were a foot or so smaller than the others, and in at least one group she noted a couple of figures even smaller.

I dislike judging on appearances, but they do not inspire me with any desire to get closer.

I agree, Quester thought, seeing the images in her mind. *Even if they are not inherently bad, armed troops marching to apparent war through this sort of terrain will be short-tempered and suspicious of strangers, regardless.*

"Over this way!" Urelle said. "I can see it... it's like a glow of gold. Over that ridge," she pointed to a jagged stone line fifty yards high and about half a mile away.

The four of them moved in that direction, Urelle leading, Quester and Ingram flanking and slightly behind her, and Victoria watching the rear. It was difficult going, picking their way through cracked blocks of obsidian, razor-sharp shards threatening to penetrate even her enchanted battle-coat and boots, low drifts of ash, tumbled basalt boulders. The only signs of life, other than the distant marching warriors, were occasional low, thorny bushes that clung precariously at the intersections of ridges that must channel the infrequent rains. A distant *boom* reached her ears, and Victoria looked back to see a larger, red-lit plume of smoke and ash rising from the volcano.

This is a terrible place, she thought. *Myrionar grant that not all the worlds we must pass through are like this.*

They rounded the ridge, and saw ahead a steep declivity that led down to a little valley — one with a very small but visible pool of ash-tainted water, surrounded by the thorn-bushes. Urelle quickened her steps, gesturing, and in her mind, Victoria could see the sparkling gold of the Seal just on the other side of the pool.

Ware!

Quester had sensed motion — perhaps with his sensitive antennae — and his warning came just in time. A thing like a monstrous wolf burst from the thornbushes that had camouflaged it, heading straight for Urelle.

Urelle had been fixed upon the vision only she could truly see, so the beast might have taken her unawares; but Ingram and Quester lunged to meet it. Despite the armor it wore — showing the thing was a mount or warbeast of some kind — the creature was no match for the two adventurers. The *anai-k'ota* jerked its forepaws from under it, and it gave a frustrated, whining howl — a howl abruptly cut off as Quester's longmace crushed its skull.

"Thanks," Urelle said. "Now just make sure I get a few minutes to open this."

Gutteral, snarling voices came from beyond another ridge nearby. Victoria unlimbered her bow and set herself between that direction and her niece. "A few minutes may be all we have."

She felt the mystic energies building around Urelle even as scrambling noises approached from the other ridge. "Balance and Blade," she heard Urelle mutter, "harder here, too. Magic's... *off.*"

"Can you do it?" Ingram asked, tension vibrating in his voice as he flanked Victoria and Quester took a position on her other side.

"Yes... just not fast..."

Dark, armored forms — the same, Victoria thought, as were marching far below — appeared on the high ground above. *Scouts, likely. Outriders making sure there were no spies or ambushes. Our bad luck to run into these people.*

I think that wolf-thing was calling. That howl wasn't just anger or pain, it almost sounded like words. And look, there's two more of the things with those armored forms. Ingram took a full combat stance, stepping slightly away and in front so he could use his weapon to full effect; Quester did the same, leaping lightly to a taller boulder from which he had a better range and vantage point.

The unknown adversaries confirmed her negative impression by allowing no time to parley; they drew their short, powerful-looking bows, and arrows stitched the air between them.

One glanced from her battlecoat; the others missed, but that was no surprise. The others were taking their first shots at unfamiliar targets in poor lighting and terrain. The fact they'd struck so close was, in fact, worrisome; these were trained and competent warriors. *Best to take no chances.*

So thinking, she focused her will through the bow, into the arrows as she aimed, loosed, aimed and loosed again, picking one on each side of the detachment of five humanoid and three wolf-like opponents that stood on the ridge.

The arrows blazed with white fire, shockingly clean and bright in the lowering gloom, and struck with devastating flares of brilliance, blowing their two targets backwards off the ridge and knocking the others nearby to the ground, several of them now in flames.

A fine strike, Lady Victoria, Quester said, *but that light could likely be seen for miles.*

"Yes, I should have thought of that. However, with fortune we have enough time that it should not matter."

That certainly seemed to be the case; the survivors of the band of scouts had dropped to the ground, some rolling to extinguish flames, and seemed reluctant to make targets of themselves again.

"Almost... got it," Urelle said. "It's just... very strange. I have to shift the way I, well, grasp the forces, and —"

The harsh, braying call of a horn echoed across the desolate landscape, and somewhere far away, it seemed to be echoed by a cry like a hunting bird — but a bird filled with hatred and an evil intelligence.

Without warning, Victoria staggered under the sensation of something *looking* at her, a vast and malign intellect that had suddenly become aware of their presence. She sensed surprise, consternation, and fury, and that demonic bird-of-prey screamed again — nearer, it seemed.

"Mother of Nests, what *is* it?" buzzed Quester, gripping his weapons tighter. Ingram's eyes were wide and fearful, despite his Camp-Bel control.

"I don't know," Victoria whispered, but took a breath, set herself, and refused to let the unseen yet tangible hatred of that distant regard cow her, raising her will against its force of detestation.

It... *lessened* for an instant, lessened in what she sensed was sheer, unadulterated surprise that she met its malevolence with unabashed courage and a disregard for its power or reach.

But that screaming *thing* was closer, and she could tell now that it was an ally, perhaps a focus, for the being whose attention they had drawn. "Urelle —"

"Grab on! Now!"

She scrambled to Urelle's side, the others sheathing their weapons as more armored figures appeared on the ridge above, and gripped her niece once more, feeling her other companions also getting a firm contact.

In the moment the golden light exploded around them, Victoria thought she saw a monstrous bat-winged form descending from the black clouds... a few scant seconds too late.

But what awaits us in the next world?

Chapter 17
A Private Eye, Chicago Style

"*DUCK!*"

Ingram obeyed Quester instinctively, and the glittering red-razor shards passed through the area his neck had just occupied, severing several strands of his lavender hair. He tumbled forward and dodged sideways, as Quester cast his last javelin.

The adorable blonde girl — seemingly younger than Urelle — with the frightening red eyes and glittering crystal-skeleton wings dodged the hard-thrown spear as though it had been a pillow and laughed delightedly. "You're very good! I'm glad we're getting to play!"

This monster's idea of play is something we're not going to survive. Victoria's thought was matter-of-fact.

Ingram, looking back over the smoking ruin of the formerly beautiful, lush landscape behind them, had no argument. *If she didn't consider it play, we'd be dead already.* Urelle —

Found it, but you have to hold her off! Magic's too powerful here! If I do this wrong, I have no idea where we'll end up — maybe a dozen sheaves in the wrong direction, maybe so far off course that I'll never find the Seal again!

He looked at the others, saw Quester's antennae drooping, Victoria's eyes determined but hopeless. *There's no way.*

The girl — wearing some kind of brief red party-dress which, by all rights, shouldn't have survived a single passage-at-arms, but which instead seemed utterly untouched — was descending towards them, and a thousand balls of glittering energy began to coalesce in front of her.

Lady, aid us! He concentrated then, grasping his desperate *need* and focusing it on the face he remembered better than any other's, calling, calling out *BERENIKE!*

A maelstrom of blood-red sparks streaked towards them, impossible to evade, a hell of sanguinary lightning spheres. Ingram dove for Urelle, trying to defend her, knowing it was already too late —

Auric light streaked from above and a concussion rocked the hills, blowing trees down like blades of grass. "Now *that* I shall never allow!" shouted a clarion voice.

The flying girl's eyes were wide and surprised, and then she smiled, showing tiny, somehow adorable little fangs. "Ooooh, *you* look like you'll be *fun* to play with!"

Berenike shimmered before him through a heatwave, her energies far greater than the last time he had seen her. "If combat is your play, you shall find me a *most* interesting playmate!" she said, with her own smile. "But take a care your toys do not harm my friends!"

Ugh! I mean, I'm glad Berenike saved us, but she's completely disrupted the magical patterns!

"Berenike, you have to keep her away!" Ingram shouted. "Urelle can't do this with magic being thrown around everywhere!"

He could see her take in the situation in a glance — then streak forward, slapping aside another barrage of energy balls and taking the laughing, chandelier-winged girl over the horizon in a literal flying tackle.

With the threat and distraction removed, Urelle began murmuring to herself, preparing the jump once more. Ingram couldn't really make it out — he was too distracted by wondering how long Berenike could hold off the insanely powerful girl-child, and whether it'd be enough.

"We had best gather close," Victoria said, recognizing Urelle's invocations. "But what about Berenike?"

Ingram blinked, feeling stupid, before he realized what she meant. "Oh! Don't worry about her. She'll find her way."

Urelle flicked a quick, concerned glance at him and the distant horizon — where red and gold light momentarily overbore that of the sun. "She'd better. Ready!"

Once more they linked hands, and the light of the world reached out and hurled them across the void between worlds...

... to smack his face *hard* into a wooden door. Then Quester's ridged arm jabbed him in the back as the Iriistiik toppled over, Victoria on top of him, and Urelle dropping to send all four of them crashing in a heap to the floor.

"Oooough!" The impact drove most of the air from his lungs, and he fought to drag in enough air to protest. "Get... off!"

"Sorry!"

"Not your fault, Urelle. Though it is odd we arrived so... clumped," Victoria said as she untangled herself from the others, and extended a hand to help Quester up.

"Not so odd, Auntie," Urelle said. "You *can't* materialize inside a wall or anything, so we all had to come out in the same room, and this is... a really small room."

It was also a very strange room, Ingram thought. It was evidently some kind of washroom, but the particular design of the tub and other fixtures was utterly unfamiliar. "Where are —"

"What in the name of Christ and the Dagda is goin' on in there?!"

The sharp tenor voice *cut* through the air. There was something about it that made all of them freeze in place.

The voice was distinctly annoyed. "I better start hearin' some answers—and the right ones—or we're gonna have ourselves a real ugly disagreement."

All four of them exchanged glances, then Ingram shrugged and turned to face the door. "Sorry, sir. We... um, didn't mean to intrude."

"That so?" The tone was nonplussed, maybe confused by the polite response. "You figure I'm dippy enough to buy that you snuck into my bathroom by *accident*?"

"That's... a long story."

The sigh was audible through the door. "Seems like I don't ever hear any other kind. All right, how many of you are there? Sure as hell more'n one."

"Four, sir."

"In *there*? That's gotta be nice'n cozy. Okay, I'm opening this door. Anyone moves funny ain't gonna be laughing very long, savvy?"

"Understood," Victoria said. "You have nothing to fear from us."

"Swell. I were you, though, wouldn't make any assumptions about the reverse just yet." The door opened.

Framed in the doorway was a tall, slender figure, with sandy hair, blue-green eyes, a narrow face, and, Ingram noted, pointed ears not quite completely concealed by the hair. He wore some kind of long coat, worn and patched, and an odd sort of formal-looking and equally worn suit. Of more immediate interest, though, were the rapier in one hand and the delicately-carved wand in the other.

Magic and martial skill combined? This man is likely quite formidable, Victoria thought.

The ears look Artan, but he looks more human otherwise, Quester observed.

I don't recognize the wand design, and I can't tell what enchantments might be on the blade, Urelle informed them.

Important thing is to not have to find out the hard way, Ingram replied. *We just stay still until he's satisfied we're no threat.*

For his part, the stranger was staring with narrowed eyes at Quester, disregarding the others. "And what exactly are *you*, bo? Never seen your kind before, and your aura don't taste like this world or the Other."

Quester tilted his head. "I am an Iriistiik. We are from... very far out, so to speak. All of us. I assure you we are no danger to you, sir. May we at least exit this very small room?"

The man darted his gaze around, his eyebrow rising as he took in the rest of their party. "Yeah, sure, why not? Office is big enough. Watch out for the typewriter."

The "office" wasn't a very large room, though compared to the washroom area it was quite spacious. A large, battered desk occupied a good portion of the floor space, with one chair behind it and a peculiar black-metal device whose purpose Ingram couldn't imagine.

The man returned his wand to a holster under his coat, and put the sword on the desk, hilt still near enough to grab, before he sat down in the chair and glanced around. "Okay, start singin'. Who, why, whaddaya want, all the usual questions. I'll speak up if I think of new ones."

"First, might we have your name, sir?" Victoria asked.

"Might as well, since you already been in my bathtub. Mick Oberon. Now who're you, sister?"

"Sister"? The vernacular here is strange, Ingram thought.

No doubt ours will sound strange to him as well, Quester said.

"I am Victoria Vantage," she said. "These are my companions: my niece Urelle Vantage, and Guild Adventurers Ingram Camp-Bel and Quester. A pleasure to meet you, Mick Oberon."

"Just 'Mick' is fine, or we'll be here all day. Now I'm gettin' sick of hearing myself ask, so spill."

"As I said, it may be quite a long story. The shortest version is that we are traveling from... well, one world or reality to another, trying to pass a barrier that has been set up in our own world to prevent any from entering a place that we absolutely must reach. Your bathroom was just the location we happened to come through into yours."

His eyebrows had climbed high enough to almost reach his hairline. "*Another* 'other' world? You puttin' me on? No, of course you're not," he answered himself. "Even if I couldn't taste it on you, your bug-man's no Fae *I* ever heard of." He grinned wryly. "You people had some of the damndest luck, though; almost as whacky as mine. I don't figure there's five people in all Chicago that'd buy a yarn like yours, and most of the mugs here woulda filled you full of lead after one slant at Quester, there."

"Chicago is the name of this world?" Urelle asked.

Mick visibly restrained a laugh. "The city. The world's called 'Earth,' because most humans got the imagination of this chair I'm sittin' in. And believe you me, most of 'em would run screaming from your buggy friend there, or else write him a real long letter on a Chicago typewriter."

I'm not sure what those last few words mean, Victoria said through the link, *but at the same time I believe I know* exactly *what he means.*

Yes. This world is, I presume, then, inhabited almost entirely by humans or very human-like people. Quester sounded unsurprised.

"So, you, yourself, aren't human, sir?" Ingram asked.

"You know, that ain't normally a question I'm too honest about answering, but..." He gestured towards Quester again. "Nope, no human here. *Aes sidhe*, if you know what that means. Fae'll do, if you don't."

"'Fae'," Victoria repeated. "I know what that word means in our world, but you would not fit the description. What does that mean here?"

"Huh. That's a little more complicated. It means... Uh, me. Pixies? *Brounie*? *Bean sidhe*? *Dverar*? *Huldra*? No? Crap.

"All right. If it's supernatural and it ain't a human witch or maybe a ghost, it's one of us, see? And we vary. Most of us ain't quite as, uh, *distinct* as your pal here, but there's a few... Anyway, me, I get to walk down the street like any mortal. Lucky me." Mick leaned back in his seat. "So, you're just passing through? How're you gonna get back on your course?"

"That's not too hard," Urelle said. "I've developed a spell to show us the way to the next, well, link in the chain of universes. If you don't mind, I'll try that right now."

"Knock yourself out. Ain't every day I get to witness magic I've never seen before."

Mick did watch intently as Urelle performed her now-familiar spell to detect the next destination. She sat back, startled. "Oh! It's close!"

Through her eyes, Ingram saw a bright glow — just over to one side of the room. But, as he thought about it, there was something *different* about the sensation, compared to the prior uses.

Unsurprisingly, she felt it too. "But... it *isn't*. That's... strange."

"So, it is and it isn't. That's real helpful. Say, the part of the world you come from didn't have a real big sign on it readin' 'lunatic asylum' by chance?"

"Well, I can sort of *see* it, just over to the side there, but at the same time, it feels like it's very far away."

Mick's eyes narrowed. "Show me exactly where 'just over to the side there' is."

She pointed. "In that little empty nook on the side of the room." She pointed to the corner, where Ingram could see there was nothing except maybe a little mold and mildew clinging to the walls. "But then it looks like it's somehow a long, long way *past* that corner, too."

Mick closed his eyes with a wince. "Of *course* that's where it is. This was just feelin' way too easy."

Victoria regarded him with surprise. "So, you understand the answer to this riddle?"

"Your gateway, seal, whatever you wanna call it? It's in Elphame. The Fae realm. Sideways, the Otherworld. You're pointin' right to where I keep my own entryway."

"Wait, there's more than one world *in* this world?" Ingram said, trying to keep his tone from being incredulous and more just curious.

"It's hardly a surprise if you think about it, Ingram," Victoria said. "After all, our own mundane world also shares its existence with dozens, hundreds, of other worlds, such as the various god realms, afterlives, and so on."

Urelle nodded. "Probably most of the worlds we have gone to are multiple worlds within an individual universe. Universe being defined as some... oh, set of overarching metaphysical laws that distinguishes things like how magic and such work in each. That's why I have to adjust my spells each time I come through — although I *think* we're bringing a lot of our rules with us. So we can act, *mostly*, like we do back home, with just a little fiddling."

"A good thing, too," Ingram said, thinking about the implications. "If we *didn't*, you'd have to learn an entirely new tradition and approach to magic every single time we came into a new universe. It'd take us years and *years* to ever get home."

"This is all real interesting," Mick said, and Ingram thought that despite the cynical tone in his voice that the older man did find it interesting, "but you got yourself a problem. Elphame ain't safe even for *me*. You mugs got no idea how dangerous it is, and I don't think you can get there yourselves. Leastwise, not quickly, and you made it clear you're in kinda a hurry."

"But *you* know how to get there, right, Lord Oberon?" Urelle asked.

"What part of 'Just Mick' sounded like 'call me Lord,' doll? I gave up all that hooey before your grandparents were born. Yeah, I know how, but it ain't something I'm real eager to do."

Based on the way he was standing and the tone of voice, Ingram figured that Oberon was understating the case. He *really* didn't want to go. "You... left Elphame for your own reasons, I guess?"

"Real good guess. Not a lot of folks there are too fond of me, and a whole mess of 'em might just tolerate the touch of cold iron long enough to help nail me to a floor."

"This is an office," Quester began. "You said it yourself. What kind of work do you do from this office, Mick?"

"I'm a PI." Then, at the blank expressions, "Private investigator. You got a problem, can't do the legwork yourself, you come to me. Why?"

"Well, we have a problem that we can't do the 'legwork' of ourselves, as you see. Could we not hire you to do it?"

He paused a moment. "In theory, sure. But I don't usually work just for dough—and even if I did, I don't figure you're carrying much of the local currency."

Victoria nodded. "That could be a problem. But we might as well see; would this be of any value to you?" She took one of her smaller pouches and dumped it on the desk — from what Ingram could see it was about ten or so Scales and an assortment of smaller coins, mixed gold and silver.

Mick almost overturned his chair. "Holy hell, don't just go flashin' that around! People get *rubbed out* for that kinda scratch!" He reached out, picked up one of the Scales, bit it. "Well, whaddaya know. That's the real stuff."

"I take it, then, that this is of value here?"

"Uh, yeah. Yeah, Victoria, gold's worth plenty here."

"Then," she reached down and separated out four more Scales, "I offer you the one you have and these four in addition. Will *that* be sufficient to convince you to open the way?"

"You know, normally I ain't sure even this'd be enough to convince me to open that door. But that'll buy a helluva lot of milk. More to the point, last thing I need is you bunnies wanderin' around gumming things up. I got enough trouble comin' from two worlds, last thing I need's a third. So, all right, sister." A slow grin spread across Mick Oberon's face. "You just hired yourself a tour guide."

Chapter 18
Elphame

"All right, listen up," said Mick. He was now dressed in a leather jerkin, his wand in a holster on one side, a basket-hilted rapier on the other. "If we're lucky, your Seal, or whatever, is just a little ways inside Elphame, right near the path, and so you can just be on your merry way. Sometimes my luck's like that. But sometimes it really, really ain't, and you poppin' up in my bathroom makes me figure your luck, at least in this world, runs a lot like mine. So there's no guessing just how far it is or what you might run into. We gotta get some ground rules clear — or none of you mugs is gonna make it home."

"It's *that* dangerous?" Urelle asked. Mick Oberon seemed *really* worried.

"More, really, but we ain't got time for the whole rundown. Biggest point to remember is that it don't always *look* dangerous, but for mortals, it *always* is. And even not bein' locals, that's still you guys, even Quester there. So, first, do *not* eat or drink *anything* you see there, no matter how good it looks, no matter how hungry or thirsty you are. You'll be happier starving to death."

"What happens if we do?"

"Short answer? You ain't ever leaving Elphame. It'll bind you, and doing the *un*-binding? Near impossible when it ain't *completely* impossible."

Urelle shuddered. "Really?"

"You figure I'm pulling your leg to hear myself talk, you go right ahead and try it.

"Meanwhile, second point. You meet anyone, and I mean *anyone*, do *not* make any agreements, bargains, or deals with them, no matter how small. Fae got a way of screwing with any mortal that makes a deal with 'em, and while it ain't something they *gotta* do, most of 'em will just because they can. Trust me, I'm one of 'em, I know what I'm doin', and I've still got a web of debts and favors around me so tangled it'd make a spider vomit. You dig?"

Urelle nodded, seeing the others doing the same.

"Third, watch your feet. Grass and dirt are okay, but *don't* step on little toadstools, holly bushes, whatever. Never know who's got a claim on 'em, and there's not a lot worse than an offended pixie. Trust me, it *is* possible to annoy someone to death."

At their nod, he went on, "Elphame don't make much *sense* from a human— uh, mortal—perspective. Just accept what you sense and move on. I get you there, Urelle here uses her mojo to find your Seal, and you're on your way quicker'n a kelpie with the trots. Everyone clear?"

"Quite clear, Mick," Aunt Victoria said. "We appreciate the assistance."

"I don't need you to appreciate, just to listen." He looked them over with a critical eye. "At least you're dressed for it. More for there'n here, anyway. And I get the impression even the kids know how to handle 'emselves in a scrap."

"Guild Adventurers all can, yes," Ingram said. "And Urelle's a wizard you don't want to fight, too."

"Good. Might even make a difference, if we wind up behind the eight-ball. C'mon, let's get this over with."

Urelle brought up her best magical viewing spells while Mick prepared to bring them through, staring at the very unprepossessing corner of the nook. He'd explained that it formed a link to Elphame simply by being a place where he let nature pretty much take its course — as much as it could in a city like this. *Which implies... what? Mold, fungi as the link? Will we come out in some kind of rotting log?*

Mick began to *waver* under her gaze; he seemed at once much smaller, and vastly greater than he had been, and she got a glimpse through... a shell, a *seeming* that he must have built throughout years, perhaps centuries, of existence, of something so terrible and bright that she gasped in awe.

But now she could see... something else, some*where* else, becoming visible, almost as though two places were becoming one under the power that Mick Oberon was calling to him. *Oh! Oh,* that *I think I understand!* It touched on another part of the Wanderer's teachings, somehow connected both with the various transportation magics and the enchantments that made neverfull packs. *Worlds within worlds, exactly!*

With a single effort, Mick swept one reality aside and another took its place.

Urelle cried out, and heard the others gasp or curse.

They were in some kind of shallow cave, an earthy, loamy tunnel that was... more like itself than anything else they had ever sensed. The smells were the *essence* of being within the earth, a part of soil and the gentle decay of humus. The dimness of the light vied with a paradoxical sense that it was more *light* than any light from the mundane world.

"Follow me," Mick said, breaking her momentary paralysis.

His warning was inadequate, Quester observed. *To be fair, I doubt greatly whether any warning couched in words would have sufficed.*

Understatement remains one of your strong suits, nest-brother, Ingram said with a mental grin. *This is... I don't have words to describe it, and I'm seeing it.*

To Urelle, as they moved farther along, approaching the mouth of the tunnel, everything had the strange luminous aura she associated with a fever dream she had had as a child. Mushrooms and toadstools of every size, from tiny buttons to ones taller than Quester lined the pathway, and she saw some simply *pop* from the ground, rising to full height in a smooth, graceful motion. One of them tilted its cap... and *nodded* to her with a faint, sourceless giggle.

"What - did that mushroom *laugh*?" Ingram demanded.

Mick chuckled — and it was then that she really noticed that he had indeed shrunk, by about six inches, and his features were both sharper and more distinct. "Certainly could have, though mushrooms ain't real known for their sense of humor. Most of what lives here is conscious, more or less—a lot less, if we're talkin' about the fungi. Try not to pay anything much mind, though. We don't want attention, and they'll forget us fast enough if we don't give 'em reason not to. And remember — watch where you put your feet."

They emerged into a lightly wooded area, into light that seemed like sunshine... except that when she looked up into a sky that was so blue that she realized she'd never seen *blue* before, there was no trace of a sun, or source for the light. It was just... *there*. Tiny, humanoid winged figures darted here and there, and the closest were calling things — that sounded like taunts — in high, sweet-yet-sharp voices.

"The... *colors*," murmured Victoria.

After a moment, Urelle was able to understand the *difference*. It wasn't just that the colors were tremendously purer and more intense; it was that they were *absolutely* demarcated. There was no blending between one color and another; a brilliant red flower with a yellow center had not the slightest transition between *red* and *yellow,* or the *green* that made up the stem and leaves; the colors actively maintained a total separation, refusing to blend or even dim their shades.

This is the most magical place I have ever visited, Quester thought quietly.

It is. A different magic, but tremendously intense. Urelle decided she would need to be *very* cautious with her spells here.

As though he'd heard the thought, Mick turned to her. "Okay, we're through," he said, and she noticed at that moment that the tunnel they had walked through was gone. "Crank up your spell, doll, so we can suss out what kind of trouble we're gonna have getting to your Seal."

Urelle paused and focused herself for a few moments, and then tried a few very simple preliminary spells — a minor light spell, summoning a small gust of wind, things of that nature. It took several tries before she could determine exactly *how* to limit their effects, during which she temporarily blinded everyone with a flare of sun-bright light, annoyed a number of the little flying taunters with a momentary gale, and soaked herself from head to toe with what *should* have been a tiny stream of water suitable for filling a small cup.

But after a few more tries she understood what was happening. "Yes, magic *is* stronger here, and I had to figure out how it responds to control as well," she said finally. "I think I've got it now, though."

Mick smiled wryly. "Hope so. I like my peepers usable. But I haveta say, the way you're goin' about it, that's *way* different from how magic works here."

"One more piece of evidence that I'm carrying at least some of my rules with me. Now, everyone hold still and be quiet for a minute."

This time the spell went off without difficulty, and she saw a quick glow of more mundanely golden light. "There!"

Mick gave a sour grimace. "How *far* in that direction?"

"About... half a mile, I think."

His face relaxed slightly. "Shouldn't be too bad, but let's not dawdle."

Looking in that direction, Urelle saw that the blue sky gave way to a dark, dangerous storm-filled appearance — one that didn't seem to change in size or location as they began walking. "What is *that*?"

"Unseelie territory," he answered. "The Seelie Court's bad enough — tricksters, manipulators, all that hooey's second-nature to us. But the Unseelie, well... It ain't entirely accurate if you just figure everything about 'em is *evil,* but with the time we've got, it's probably best you think that way. Not at all the kinda company you have over for a drink and a chin-wag. Some of 'em would think *you* were the drink. Lucky us, we ain't goin' that far."

As they entered a real forest, this one with immense trees that rivaled some of those in the Forest Sea, she began to understand the importance of Mick's warnings. Some of the bushes and trees were laden with fruit whose pure colors and piercingly sweet smells cried out to her to stop, smell, taste, eat. She saw Ingram start to reach out a hand, almost unconsciously, as he passed a tree with beautiful scarlet spheres, then snatch his hand back as though he'd been burned.

"By the *Lady*," he said, hand shaking. "Without your warning…"

"Yeah. That's why most who stumble their way here don't ever get back," Mick said. "Even with a warning, it ain't easy for mortals to grasp just how hard it'll be to follow the rules until they're here."

"I presume it does not affect you the same way?" Victoria asked.

"Nah. The human world? It hurts. Too much technology, too much cold iron. Here I can relax, I'm more *myself*. This is home, be it ever so horrible. It'd be easy to stay forever; except I walked away from that a long time ago. I don't much like the mortal world, especially lately, but it beats Elphame."

Urelle nodded, hearing more behind his words. She wondered what kind of terrible thing could drive someone to not only abandon the place they called home, but to prefer to live in a place that literally hurt them.

Then she caught sight of a golden glow. "There! Up ahead!"

"I can sense it," Mick said after a minute. "Holy mackerel, that's impressive."

They pushed through into a clearing, where Urelle could see the cycling golden structure of the Seal.

"Okay, swell. Get your doorway open and scram," Mick said. "Kinda power this thing's putting out, no way *somebody* hasn't felt it already. Pretty near a miracle they ain't already here, tryin' to steal it or gum it up." He stared into the otherwise-empty air. "Is this thing gonna *stay* this obvious?"

"I… don't know? I don't *think* so. I hope not. See, what we're doing is shoving our way through each link, and I think each time I do that I'm disturbing the one in our arrival location, and it should settle down when we leave."

He shook his head. "If not, you'll be leavin' me in some serious dutch. Ain't a soul I know who I'd want playin' with *this* little toy."

"I don't have *any* idea what would happen if someone tried to make *use* of the Seal, though," Urelle said, trying to imagine what a cross-reality barrier like that might do if someone tried to do anything other than what she was doing — passing through on a specific course. "Anyway, let's see..."

It was a matter of a few minutes to prepare. "Mick, step back. Once I finish the spell, it'll take everyone touching me — or touching someone who's touching me." She caught his eye. "Unless you want to come with us."

"I... Sorry, I musta been listening with my *bad* nostril. Say that again?"

"Well... you say the mortal world hurts you here, and you can't stay in your home any more, so I just thought maybe you could find a better place where we're going. Not *safe*... but not one that hurts you."

Mick stared at her, and suddenly a bright grin flashed across his face — one without a trace, for once, of his constant cynicism. "Kid, that's the sweetest offer I've heard in a long while. But... No, thank you. I've got a few friends here still, and a job that sometimes actually needs doing, and a buncha bastards in Elphame who'd get way too much satisfaction outa me leavin'. But I sure appreciate the thought." He waved his hands. "Now dust already. You got things to do."

She nodded and flashed him one more smile. "Grab on, everyone!"

And once more, the bottom fell out of the world and they fell through light...

Chapter 19
Worlds-Weary

"By the Mothers, I am absolutely *weary* of this endless journey to world after world," Quester buzzed, trying to scrunch himself farther under the little overhang of rock that currently protected them from the downpour of chill rain. Lightning flashed in the distance, and a grumble of thunder followed a few seconds later.

"We *all* are, Quester," Victoria snapped. Then she sighed. "My apologies. But yes, I am sure we all are. Yet we have no choice. As I understand it, even if we wished to, we cannot go back."

Urelle, sheltered in the farthest corner of the overhang, nodded, dark circles under her eyes visible against her earthwood-colored skin. "It's a one-way jump through each part of the Seal. The only way to get back to any of the ones we've been to before would be to get back home and start again." Then she frowned. "Well... no. Maybe not. I've *been* to those worlds, and I have some feel for their natures, and there are at least parts of them I became familiar with, so it might be possible to..."

"I don't think any of us *want* to go back. Certainly not to most of them," Ingram said.

That is definitely an understatement, Quester thought to himself. The first world had been bad enough, then they'd found themselves in a colder wasteland, dominated in the distance by a massive palace or perhaps small hill with more than a passing resemblance to a skull, and other hostile creatures hunting them. Then the beautiful world with the cheerfully murderous blonde demon-girl, Mick's world... well, the latter hadn't been *so* bad... but the others! A forest deep and primeval where even the *bushes* had tried to attack them; a great desert, with flat, red-brown sand broken by towering mesas, where two beings battled with such unspeakable power that the mesas shattered and the ground rippled like water; a dusty, sterile plain before a black-walled city, whose dust began to rise up into armies of the dead; a rolling prairie, green and gold and harmless, whose night gave birth to floating, barely-discernable monstrosities like gigantic mantles of darkness concealing crystal teeth and blades.

The latter they had only escaped with the help of one of Ingram's two remaining Extreme Luminance Flares; the incredible brilliance of the flare had kept the things at bay until Urelle could open the next Seal... at which point they had found themselves in a storm-tossed sea..."I have lost track, even, of how *many* we have passed through," he finally said aloud.

"Forty-seven," Urelle said. "Forty-seven different worlds so far." She pointed slowly. "And the way out of *this* one is over that way, about four hundred yards." She was, of course, pointing out into the storm, where visibility was currently about ten yards. Water was now pouring in sheets off the top of their overhang — fortunately they were on a small raised section of the ground, so it wasn't getting wet there... yet.

Ingram squinted into the storm, then pulled out a set of goggles and put them on. "Ugh. Not a good idea right now, even ignoring the rain. Ground drops off fast in that direction, and I'll bet you there's some real flash flooding going on."

She nodded. "I'm going to try to rest, then." Ingram put one of their camp blankets around her, and the younger Vantage fell asleep in moments, despite the rocky ground, the chill, and the storm.

He saw Ingram's concern mirrored in Victoria's eyes. "She is weakening," he said after a moment.

"We haven't had a chance for decent rest for at least two or three days, and she's the only one of us who can open the Seal," Victoria said in agreement. "She needs to rest, and not just under a blanket in a rainstorm."

So does Ingram, he thought to her, as he simply nodded, letting his antennae bob assent.

I noticed. He is wearing himself out trying to watch out for all of us. Why?

Quester thought back on the traces of thought he occasionally got from his friend. *Lingering guilt, I believe. He still feels we would not be here, in this danger, without his personal mission having dragged us here. A foolish belief, of course — if we are right, you or Urelle, or possibly both, were already targets of Ares. But,* he gave a sensation of scent and pose that he knew she would see as a fond smile, *young and earnest humans seem to often be prey to such noble foolishness.*

Victoria hid a quick smile, gazing at Ingram as he sat watching over Urelle. *Yes, you have that much understanding of us. But even you and I are in need of some rest. We cannot keep moving at this pace much longer.*

Then we must hope the next world will offer us some form of respite. This one seems to favor drastic shifts of climate — chaotic and potentially deadly.

As if the thought had been a trigger, the rain ceased sheeting down; there was no slow diminution of the rainfall, but an absolute and instant cessation, and late-afternoon sunshine streamed across the landscape.

Ingram's description had been accurate; the bank they were on turned to an extremely sharp declivity only a few yards from the path they had followed to their current refuge. In the distance they could see hills and cliffs; they were clearly on the side of a valley or canyon, perhaps half a mile wide. In the absence of rainfall, they could hear the roar of a river below.

Quester ventured out to take a better look. Rank, tough grass covered the banks, with low bushes or stunted, wind-shaped trees also clinging stubbornly to the earth and rock. *Anything that lives here would have to be adaptable and extremely resilient*, he thought.

Below, the slope became a cliff-face, dropping a hundred and fifty feet to end in foaming white and red-brown water. Glancing upstream, he could take in the expanse of the rugged landscape and guess that this canyon drained quite a large area. "It will not subside for at least a few hours, I would think," he said, glancing back at Victoria. He focused more elements of each of his faceted eyes in the direction outward from their shelter. *Four hundred yards...*

At about that distance, there was an island in the middle of the roaring torrent, one about fifty yards across and a few hundred long. *That, most likely, is where the Seal is.*

"The question," Victoria said quietly, "is whether we let Urelle sleep, and risk some other drastic change to the weather that will hinder us, or force her to act now, and find some way to cross the river."

"I hate to wake her up," Ingram said, coming up behind them, "but... I don't know. It was a howling blizzard when we first arrived, then it switched to a tropical storm in half a second, now it's calm and sunny. I wasn't measuring intervals, but I'm guessing both of those were about two hours between changes."

"If that holds, I do not believe the water will have subsided nearly enough in that time," Quester said, knowing his scent would emphasize his belief. "We could not tell due to visibility, of course, but if the same torrential rain fell over a wide range, then it may be six hours before the surge from the distant parts of the mountains reaches us, and of course, that from the progressively nearer parts of the watershed will reach here that much earlier."

Victoria, lips tight as a ruled line, stared narrowly down at the water. "I cannot argue. I think we should at least let Urelle rest for a bit longer, but we cannot wait too long."

Ingram nodded. "Then let's at least clean up a bit, get ready to move."

Quester scouted up the mountain slope and found a stone catch basin that held fresh rainwater, filled their water containers from it, and came back down. By the time he was done with that chore, the others had finished their own.

Ingram leaned down, gently touched Urelle on the shoulder. "Urelle, sorry — but we've got to get moving."

The young woman blinked, eyes barely opening, then forced herself upright. "What... It's sunny. How long did I sleep?"

"A total of an hour," Victoria said. "I'm sorry, child, but the changes seem to be about two hours apart —"

Urelle yawned widely, but nodded. "I understand. No telling what the next change will be. It was the same? The rain just stopped without warning, like the blizzard shifted to rain?"

"Yes," Quester said.

"All right." She followed them to the edge of the cliff, looked down. "So that little island?"

"It had *better* be," Ingram said, "because otherwise it's somewhere in the middle of that torrent."

"I can fly myself out there," she said, obviously thinking out loud, "And maybe I can carry Auntie or Ingram, but I couldn't do both."

"And I believe I could fly or, to be more accurate, glide myself there from one of the higher points here," Quester added, "but I cannot carry more than my own gear without my glide becoming very precipitous."

"Aunt Victoria? You don't have anything to fly with, do you?"

"I might. Let me see..." She opened up her pack and began digging through it, pulled out a large case that she opened, showing an assortment of bottles and paper packets that Quester assumed were magical scrolls or sheets. There were quite a few empty spaces, however.

"Oh, *Balance*." She shook her head, gazing at the empty spaces, one in particular. "That's what happens when you retire; you stop keeping up the stores as much as you might. I remember now, I used my last flight enchantment... oh, it must be many months ago, before we left, when the workmen had to repair a hole near the peak of the roof. So alas, no, I don't."

"Could you ferry Victoria over and then come back and pick me up?" Ingram asked.

Urelle hesitated. "I... *guess* I could..."

"Maintaining the airwing enchantment is not easy, is it?" Victoria asked. "And it must be far harder to do so when carrying a passenger. If you did that, would you have enough strength left to safely open the Seal and be ready in case the next world is also hostile?"

The answer was so plain on Urelle's face that even Quester needed no words to interpret it. "No," Urelle admitted. "I would have to rest for a while. It will be touch and go even doing the trip once, carrying someone."

"And we can't afford to rest long," Ingram murmured. "If the weather shifts back to rain again, that island may be submerged in minutes."

Quester found himself gazing at Victoria as she carefully closed the large wooden case and stuffed it back into the bag that seemed far too small to hold it. "Victoria... Ingram... could you not, perhaps, go into one of our neverfull packs?"

Victoria's eyebrows rose in wing-like arches of surprise, while Ingram just blinked. Then the two of them burst out laughing.

"Oh, now, that's so brilliant. Obvious, yet we were missing it!" Ingram said, still chuckling. "We can't bring our own neverfulls into the others with us, of course; can't overlap the manufactured spaces that way. But sure, then you and Urelle only have to carry a couple extra bags which don't weigh *nearly* as much as even me, let alone Victoria!"

Victoria nodded her approval. "It will be a bit tight for me — none of us have so little in our bags — but I can manage. Let us hurry, then."

Quester noted that Victoria not only divested herself of her own bag, but of a few other items, which also had to be kept outside of the neverfull packs; he verified this with her bracelet, finding that attempting to put it into his pack met with resistance, as though he were trying to push through a sheet of slightly stretchy steel.

With the other two members of their party packed invisibly away, Urelle and Quester were able to make it to the little island — although the updrafts and downdrafts were quite tricky, and Quester was glad to find himself on the solid ground again.

Victoria popped out of Quester's pack, once opened, and sighed as she stretched. "That was the tightest I've had to fold myself in years. I think the last time must have been when we were smuggling ourselves into Yaniltan, packed into shipping crates."

"I don't think you've told me *that* one, Auntie," Urelle said. "Oh! There it is! The Seal's right here!"

"Thank Myrionar for that. I suppose I haven't told that one, now that I think of it. Perhaps later."

"We look forward to it," Ingram said. "You and your friends got into some... interesting adventures."

"Yes," Quester agreed. "The one about the wizard who duplicated himself, especially."

"Later!" Urelle said sharply. "Let's get this over with!"

Quester jumped at her tone, as did the other two. Seeing how she stood, arms hanging just a touch too heavily, he realized the young mage was even more tired than she had admitted. "Of course," he said, and they gathered around her.

Once more the subliminal feel of tension, a sense through the link of the invisible gold-fire beauty, then the wrenching dislocation as the Seal hurled them across to the next destination...

***

Quester half-carried Urelle forward through the metallic corridors as Victoria and Ingram tried to slow the advance of the multi-winged woman who had simply materialized before them, proclaiming that they were offenses against the Creator, anomalies and abominations to be cleansed. Though her face held a distant, disinterested expression of peace, she radiated utter lethal determination.

And that shockwave of green energy she radiated nearly killed us all.

"A... little farther..." gasped Urelle. "The seal... just through the door...

"Understood," Quester said, trying to sound calm and certain as always. Privately, he was terrified. *I do not know if she even has the strength to* open *the Seal once more.*

This made the *fourth* universe they had been forced to flee as swiftly as they had arrived; first it had been another blizzard, but this one so fiercely cold and savage that they could barely see each other and the damp remaining from the prior world had turned almost instantly to frost; they had been fortunate to be able to reach the seal, despite their climate-spelled clothing.

From that to a desert, all-encompassing, filled with red-gold-gray sand as far as the eye could see, and beneath those sands monstrous *things* so huge that they rivaled the tales Quester had heard of the Great Dragons themselves.

The last had been perhaps the worst, a place where they'd gasped for breath within a wrecked vessel of alien design, air leaking into a black, star-speckled void as a gigantic ship loomed ever nearer, projecting a barely-visible beam that turned other drifting hulks into a red-shimmering liquid that was drawn inside, a beam that was eating away their own ship before Urelle had found and wrenched open the way through the Seal.

The metal door slid open before them, revealing a circular room with no other obvious exits. But Urelle sighed with relief. "There! Put me down, Quester, I have to start!"

Ingram, Victoria, fall back as quickly as you may. I will seal the door behind you and hope it will at least slow our adversary.

Coming! The distant sound of explosions. *Lady's* Name, *this thing is tough, but I think that slowed it a bit!*

Victoria and Ingram dove through the door and Quester hit the controls to shut it; Mother's Memories suddenly crystallized, told him which control would lock the portal. *Yet these memories tell me nothing of what our foe is, or even where we are. Why? Why are they so arbitrary?*

"There!" gasped Urelle. "Almost ready..."

A tremendous blow struck the solid metal barrier, denting it inward. Then a golden shimmer appeared in the room.

Nest and Mother, it's coming in!

"NOW!"

The four of them lunged together, and even as the passionless destroying shape fully materialized, the world once more dissolved in light and distortion...

... and tumbled out into a dim-lit alleyway, high brick walls on either side, dented metal bins of unfamiliar design mostly filled with trash and odd black bags spaced along its length, each not far from a metal door set into the nearby wall. Quester winced at an onslaught of smells ranging from those of garbage in various states of decay to strange, metallic-chemical tangs and the odor of many, many people.

"Are you all right, Urelle?" Ingram asked.

There was a pause that made all of them gather around the girl, but after a moment she forced herself to sit up. "I'm... not hurt. But... I can't do that again, Auntie, I just *can't* until I rest!" Tears spilled down Urelle's face, a shocking loss of her usual cheerful or determined control. She sounded years younger, a child who had reached her absolute limit of exhaustion.

"Then you won't have to," Ingram said emphatically. "We'll find somewhere you can rest. Somehow."

Victoria looked around slowly. "Not perhaps the most attractive setting... but I must say, I appreciate not having been either assaulted or endangered by the very environment in the first moments. The temperature is moderate, at least."

Quester thought it was a bit chilly, but it was certainly far superior to the places they had visited most recently.

A distant humming, whirring sound abruptly grew louder, and something flashed by the entrance to the alley. Quester got the brief impression of an enclosed metal-and-glass vehicle, running on wheels but with no immediately visible means of propulsion — magical, perhaps.

Victoria stared at that as well, and Quester became aware that the low background murmur and rumble he had been ignoring was the sound of many, many of those vehicles, as well as people. Victoria glanced around, nodded, and resettled her battle coat. "Quester, could you scout forward, if you would?"

"Of course," he said.

Cautiously he moved towards the end of the alley, trying to keep himself as inconspicuous as possible; in the dim lighting, his dark exoskeleton would help.

Finally, he reached the end and was able to get a good look up and around.

For a moment, he could do nothing *but* stare. This was a city — but a city he had never *imagined*. In every direction there were buildings, towers, seemingly faceted on every side with glass, or faced with polished stone or metal, rearing up hundreds of feet, perhaps a thousand feet or more in some cases, making the roadways beneath them into rivers of stone in canyons of glass and steel. Perhaps the Dragon's Castle stood higher than any of these... yet all of Zarathanton would be lost within the immensity of this city.

But more: the dim light came not from the sun or moon, but from lamps spaced evenly along the roadways and, in an omnipresent and majestic shimmering from nearly every one of those titanic structures. Luminance shone from within thousands, tens of thousands of those glass-facet windows, shimmered on the roadways from brilliant lamps at the front of every one of the moving vehicles, blinked and skipped and sparkled from signs and symbols on storefronts, hanging on posts, or displayed on great rectangular boards.

The people seemed to all be human — or nearly all. The mode and style of dress was wildly variable. Some wore outfits that would not have seemed out of place on Zarathan, some even wearing weapons of designs that ranged from the spare and practical to the grotesquely impractical — and the wearers, he also noted with puzzlement, also ranged from those who moved as experts in combat to individuals so obviously indolent that just walking caused them to sweat, even in the cool of the evening.

Other people wore clothing that covered the entire spectrum from odd but unobtrusive to ridiculously complex. A few inhuman figures moved here and there, one a gigantic, somewhat attenuated shape nine feet tall, wearing black, spiky armor with a full-sealed helm of intimidating design, with a huge black mace on one side and a sword on the other. Despite the forbidding appearance, people did not seem perturbed by the figure's presence; indeed, Quester saw it stopped at least twice by people, who would raise small rectangular objects towards it that would then emit their own brilliant sparks of light.

There *were* a few people, in what appeared to be uniforms, who had some sort of authority, directing traffic. After a few moments, he did notice that most of the more outlandish and peculiar figures were all either coming from or going to a particular direction.

He backed up into the alley again, sending the others the images of what he had seen. "I am... unable to say what this all means. I did not see anything that looked vaguely like my people, however."

"Indeed," Victoria said, looking quite puzzled. "And from what you saw, I incline to believe that there are only human beings in this area. The way that very tall figure moved appeared to involve stilts. I think it was a costume, but for what purpose, I could only guess. Perhaps there is a theater nearby and the costume serves as advertisement?"

"Perhaps. But if there *are* only humans on this world, that will pose a problem for me. Even on Zarathan there are those uncomfortable around the Iriistiik, and we know some of the other worlds we have encountered have people with a great aversion or fear towards beings who have insectoid features."

Victoria and Ingram nodded. "But we can't stay here," Ingram said. "Sooner or later, someone's going to open one of those doors and see us. Probably sooner; from the smell I think these might be inns or restaurants, and this is their rubbish area."

Quester stiffened as he became aware of something else: two new, stronger scents, closer than others... approaching the alley, with a touch of the smell he associated with determination and caution in humans. *Someone approaches! Two someones, to be exact!*

Even as he thought that to his friends, a figure appeared in the alleyway's mouth — a figure outlined against the light at the end of the alley and strangely smaller than he had expected. It was female, that much he was certain of, and from the silhouette was wearing one of the more peculiar outfits he had seen.

But that is only one *person...*

The problem with scent was that it was often hard to get direction. But now he realized the other smell was from *behind* them — the dead-end part of the alley, where it had not been before.

I don't see anything, Ingram thought. *At least, nothing more than a couple of rats. One of them's white, though.*

The scent is touched by that of rat... perhaps —

"Holy *crap*, Silvertail, that's not a costume!" the female figure said suddenly.

"No," said a man's voice from the rear, and Ingram cursed. Now there *was* a man there, a tall, dark-haired man, regarding them with great trepidation. "It most definitely is not... and these people are not from this world. Identify yourselves and your purpose, please," the man said. "For if you are enemies, I must call upon you to surrender; and if you are not foes of this world, you are in very great danger!"

Chapter 20
Princess Holy Aura... And Friends

Victoria spread her hands to indicate that she was no threat; the others copied her. "We are hardly enemies, sir," she said, "Or at least I would *hope* not, as we have not the least idea of where we are, and have little enough energy left for argument, let alone fighting. My niece," she gestured to Urelle, "is exhausted and in need of rest. Now might I ask who you are, and why we would be in danger?"

The man — who appeared to be, now that Victoria got a better look at him, of roughly her own age, with silver well-worked through his hair, and was wearing a suit of unfamiliar but attractive design — tilted his head, studying them.

The girl hastened down the alley from the other side. "Silvertail, we won't have much time..."

Victoria felt her eyebrows once more climbing skyward, and Ingram's arms dropped to his sides as he stared, open-mouthed.

The word *beautiful* was not, Victoria decided, adequate to describe the girl, or young woman, before her. She was supernaturally perfect, something Victoria would have expected of a goddess or a servitor of a deity. *Perhaps that is what she is.*

Her clothing echoed her mystical appearance, somehow combining ethereal cloth with crystal-and-metal armor to make something that still said *warrior* to Victoria's senses. The way she moved also emphasized that. *This young woman is exceedingly dangerous.*

"I am aware of that, Holy Aura," Silvertail answered. "Where are the other Maidens?"

"Watching; we'll get a little warning, but not much."

"What is the problem?" Victoria asked, nettled at being talked past.

"The problem is that there are some, shall we say, overzealous protectors of this world who will likely have detected your arrival as we did, and they prefer to assume the worst rather than the best of people." Silvertail frowned. "We need to get you somewhere safe, but you will stand out. How..."

The girl called "Holy Aura" suddenly giggled. "No, I don't think it'll be a problem." She turned to Quester. "Um... sir? Ma'am?"

"Call me Quester."

"Quester, then — do you think you could pretend to be, umm, some kind of automaton, a drone, a robot?"

Victoria wasn't familiar with the precise words, but the idea immediately struck a chord. If the strange costumes were accepted here, then surely...

"I believe I could make my movements imitate a golem or similar construct, yes."

"Then let's go!" Holy Aura gave an impish grin. "ComicCon's in town!"

***

You do that too *well,* Ingram's thoughtvoice came, clearly directed to Quester. *And it makes me shudder.*

Victoria could not disagree. Walking along in the little group, Quester made his movements just a hair too stiff, hesitant, mechanical, for everything from his strides to the way his antennae swiveled from side to side. Had she not known otherwise, she would have assumed him to be some dangerous alchemical clockwork construct.

It did not seem to bother the crowds of people around them, however — except for one or two for whom the realism of his appearance seemed to strike too close to home. They had to stop several times for passers-by to take "selfies" with them, specifically with Quester. More often, however, it was young, or not-so-young, men asking to "take pictures" of their escorts.

For they were now being guided by no fewer than four young ladies in outlandish costumes, along with the elegantly-attired man previously called Silvertail, but whose actual name was Trayne Owen. The former "Holy Aura", now calling herself "Holly Owen" had undergone some kind of transformation, and was now only mortally beautiful rather than transcendently so; her outfit had not changed much, but appeared... homemade, rather than created by supernal artisans.

The other three girls — Seika, Tierra, and Cordy — wore costumes of similar homemade design, from which she deduced that when they, too, took on their "Maiden" forms they would have equally perfect appearances and costumes.

Urelle was trying, with the last of her strength, to emulate the other girls' cheerful, casual walk and smiles, pretending to appreciate the other costumed individuals going by, but it was clear she was exhausted to anyone who spent more than a casual glance on her. *Ingram is not much less drained, but he is far more used to playing a part, I think.*

"How much farther?" she inquired of Trayne, who was walking next to her — giving the appearance, she was sure, of two parents with their child and her friends, lending legitimacy to their presence.

"Not far; two blocks — we have, fortunately, a large hotel suite." He indicated one of the tall buildings some distance ahead. "Just play along with our behavior, follow our lead, and we should be all right."

"And if we aren't?"

His lips quirked up in a grim smile. "Then they shall have to go through us to get to you, Lady Vantage."

"Fair enough. Though we shall protect ourselves —"

"Do not, if it comes to that. We have... standing here. Citizenship, identities, and perhaps a few useful connections. You have none of these, and if the OSC comes for you, it will go far better if you do not resist. We will find a way to get you out of their hands, if that happens, and it will be *much* easier to do that if they haven't decided you are such a threat that you need to be sealed away in a maximum-security holding cell. Or killed outright."

"I do not think I like this 'OSC' of yours," she said bluntly. She conveyed the warning to the others. Urelle was too tired to argue, thank goodness, and both Quester and Ingram accepted the instruction to not fight with stoicism if not enthusiasm.

"We don't either," Trayne said, his chuckle dry and cynical. "There are certain agents who are not so bad, but the organization itself... no, we do not like them."

Despite the presence of this looming threat, they made it to the hotel Trayne had pointed out, and after a tense ride in a vertical transportation room called an 'elevator', they followed Trayne down a short corridor and into his suite.

"Thank Myrionar and all the gods," Victoria said, and sank down without invitation into a nearby chair.

"Holly, show Miss Urelle to Devika's room," Trayne said.

"Won't... Devika... need it?" Urelle asked, eyelids drooping.

"No, she had to cancel out at the last moment," Cordy said. "Family issues, I think. Lucky, I guess, now we have an extra room!"

Victoria glanced into the room, seeing that it was not terribly roomy but did have a comfortable-looking bed. Ingram followed her glance. "I'll take the floor," he said. "You can share with Urelle."

"Very well. Quester?"

The Iriistiik exuded a sweetly spiced scent. "I could sleep anywhere. May I use a corner of this... sitting room? Leave my friends a little space to move."

"Certainly," Trayne said. "We still have some events we were going to attend, and while your presence is certainly of more actual significance, if you all need rest I see no reason that we should not leave you to it. We can speak once you are rested."

"I'll stay with them, just in case," Cordy said.

"I thought you wanted to see that panel —" Seika began.

"Well, sure, but not *that* much. *Tomorrow* I'm signed up for the meet-and-greet with Evangeline Joliet from *Telzey*, and nothing but Maiden business will keep me out of that. But *someone's* got to be here in case something happens. Or if it turns out they've got us fooled and they're not so nice." She ducked into the room obviously reserved for her use.

Trayne smiled. "You are, of course, correct," he said to the doorway. "Thank you for volunteering, Cordelia." He bowed to Victoria. "We leave you in capable hands."

"Of that, I have no doubt. I presume all of these girls have another... face, as did Holly?"

"Precisely. But we shall wait on the explanations — from you, and for you — until you are rested." He gave a brief bow. "Rest well, all of you."

"Thank you, Trayne." Victoria heard the others leave as she and Ingram went into the other room and prepared, finally, to rest. *We are safe for the moment*, she thought wearily. *Let us hope that the moment will be long enough.*

Chapter 21
Overenthusiastic Monster

He divested himself of the constricting ceremonial armor with a sigh of pleasure. Of all the minor annoyances of pretending to be the General, Ares Incarnate, it was perhaps that armor that was the worst. Not only was it an impediment to the flowing free movement he preferred, it also incorporated, rather unavoidably, a significant percentage of silver in its ornamentation.

That didn't *hurt* him, precisely, but it did make it uncomfortable — rather, he thought from various conversations, in the same manner as wearing underwear soaked in seawater and sand as it slowly dried. Silver alone would never kill him, but it would always be at the least an irritant and distraction to any descended of the King.

And he'd had to be the fine, dynamic, courageous General-Ares for several days, spreading encouragement and advice throughout the cities they had captured... and leaving subtly different influences in each one. The vise had to be tightened carefully, so that in the end the people would welcome, or at the least not fight, the forging of Aegeia into a nation of warfare, blood, and glory, a nation that would naturally, once the Seal dropped, be ready for a mighty destiny of conquest and rulership.

With a Chaoswar imminent — already underway, in fact — and events already weakening the previously invincible State of the Dragon King and Empire of the Mountain, vast opportunities awaited those who could seize the initiative. The whispered hints, the implications, the suggestions dropped in the proper ears would make it inevitable that, once the time was right, all the Cities would join with the "great General" to bring order and wisdom to the rest of the world... whether they wanted it or not.

Whether Aegeia managed to actually conquer anything was beside the point, naturally; the important thing was that by making Aegeia turn *outward* at the time it should be completing the Great Play, by focusing everything on his new and quite blasphemous version of Ares, he would ensure the shattering of the Cycle entirely. The true Ares would be unable to be reborn with such damage done,

Athena would never incarnate, and in all likelihood Aegeia itself would never recover from the damage.

But this had forced him to be traveling and mostly incommunicado to prevent any unexpected behavior on his part; he knew too well his own problems with self-control when under tension, and manipulating so many human beings was tension indeed.

Raiagamor assumed his true form, rather like a man stretching luxuriously after divesting himself of a tight suit, and touched his claws to key objects laid out on a table nearby. *I have returned. What news?*

There was no immediate answer. By itself, that was no terrible surprise; if his allies were engaged in conversation or combat, they would wish to disengage, find a safe location in which to deliver reports, or at least to prepare to maintain a normal façade while carrying on two actions at once. At that, he reluctantly returned to his disguise. Even Deimos and Phobos did not know exactly what he was, and there was no reason to give them any more chance to deduce that.

But when the pause became a minute, and the minute became fifteen, and he found himself pacing, he knew it was something else. *I grow impatient! Report immediately, or if you be in situations so perilous that you dare not leave, I require at least an acknowledgement!*

For nearly a minute there was *still* no answer, and he felt his fists tightening, claws beginning to dig into his palms. *Something is not right.*

A shimmer above the table, and Deimos' face appeared, with Phobos standing somewhat behind. "Greetings, Lord."

"It's *that* bad, is it?" he asked from between gritted teeth halfway gone to fangs.

Deimos flinched, but tried to smile. "It is far from *all* bad, sir."

"Convince me, then, for the delays and your faces tell me a very different tale."

"Amoni Agapis has finally fallen, despite a far stronger and more in-depth resistance than we had expected," Deimos said quickly. "The city is entirely ours; no resistance remains."

He raised an eyebrow. That *was* pleasantly unexpected. Even if his allies had managed to beat down the city of Hephaestus and Aphrodite, resistance would be expected to continue for weeks, as it had in the other cities. "How was this achieved, then?"

A fractional pause. "Once they had demonstrated a greater resistance than expected, other tactics were considered. Our ally offered to assist. Athena gave it leave to do what it might to eliminate said resistance."

The *crunch* noise, Raiagamor discovered, was his fist closing on a part of the table and crushing it like splintering paper. "She did not give it *specific instructions*? Just in effect said to do what it would?"

Deimos' face was rigidly controlled. "Yes, sir."

"It was sent *into Amoni Agapis* with *no restraints on its mission*?"

"Yes, sir."

"By my Father's kills," he growled. "So, indeed, there is no remaining resistance. There's not a living thing *left in the city*, is there?"

In a whisper, "No, sir."

He let out a roar and whirled away from the table, knowing that otherwise he might destroy something of value, and instead tore the door from its hinges and reduced it to splinters and crumpled, torn metal fragments. Only when he had vented enough of the rage did he turn back to his frozen-faced allies. "So instead of a city of angry but beaten humans I can use in my plan, I have a *graveyard*. A graveyard, yet, that hasn't even bodies to bury, those having fed your little monster. This is *your* failing. Did you fail to instruct *Athena* in the nature of your ally?"

Phobos spoke. "Sir, we did summarize the nature of it to her, but I am afraid she did not sufficiently grasp," at his glare he hurriedly shifted his words,"... that *we* did not sufficiently emphasize to her its... absolute nature."

"Well. So rather than another fine base of operations for the plan, I have a ghost town. I suppose it's living there for now?"

"Yes, sir." Phobos and Deimos stood straight and silent again.

He turned away, took deep breaths, slowly reasserted full control. Finally, he sighed and looked back. "Very well, let it stay there. In fact, *order* it to stay there; I have no other targets for it yet, and no need to risk its... excessive enthusiasm yet. Now, let me have the rest. Have your targets arrived while you were distracted and passed your guard?"

"No, sir! Our guardians assure us the Seal remains unbreached here!"

"Then what has you standing as though I might sever your souls from your bodies at any moment?"

"We have... been unable to complete our action against the Camp-Bels," Deimos managed to say, after a moment.

He twitched, but said only, "Go on. Why not?"

"When Amoni Agapis fell —"

"Was *consumed*, I believe you mean."

"Sir. When that happened, there were a few who escaped. One in particular made her way to the hidden stronghold. Perhaps she already knew its location, or her own abilities revealed it to her, but she found it, and two of our agents escorted her in. Once she had entered, she suddenly killed the agents and ordered a systematic search for others."

"Ordered? Killed the agents? But who could..." He would have smacked his head with a boulder if one had been handy. "You wiped out all of the city... *leaving one of the God-Warriors on the loose?*"

"The Mirror of Aphrodite, sir."

"GRGGGH!" He could not speak for a few moments, just growl. At last, he managed to get himself under control, at least for the moment. "So the *one* God-Warrior whose focus is on reflecting the truth in oneself — and thus *ideal* for seeing through disguises — is the one you let *go?*"

"We did not *let* her go, sir!" Phobos said, finally showing some spirit in his defense. "You know the power of the true God-Warriors. She evaded even our ally's attacks and saw through our traps, fought her way past Deimos directly."

"Not without help!" Deimos pointed out quickly. "Her entire honor guard was with her. None of *them* escaped."

Surprisingly, the rage began to die down on its own. *Perhaps I am learning, becoming better.* "So the Camp-Bels now have a God-Warrior in their midst, one who can see to one's heart?"

"Yes, sir."

"Hm. Did she succeed in finding and eliminating all of your agents?"

Finally, a smile. "No, sir. You had treated four of them prior to your departure. We believe she has not detected anything amiss with them."

"Then we must go with one of the older plans. Continue to attempt infiltration, but far more cautiously; we cannot afford to be caught at this point, not with a God-Warrior and the remaining Camp-Bels already on the alert. And if our targets arrive, his parents must be killed, even if our assassin is to die in the same moment."

"As you command, sir."

Indeed, as I command. "What God-Warriors remain to me?"

Phobos raised an eyebrow, but answered, "Besides myself and Deimos, sir? The Sun of Apollo, the Anvil and Hammer of Hephaestus, and the Scythe of Demeter."

He nodded. That fit his recollections; the Harp of Apollo had fallen in the assault on Talaria, and most of the others had died fighting on the other side. Athena's Spear, Berenike, was of course the wild card — if that little group of heroes *did* make it through the Seal, it was possible she, too, would arrive.

"Excellent. Deimos, Phobos, I require you here. The secondary barrier will require both of you to assist us in its placement, and the Hammer and Anvil to assist in the crafting. Your Shadow-Queen Athena has done her part of the work; I can complete it with your help."

"And the Shadow-Queen?"

Raiagamor grinned. "She, along with the Sun and the Scythe, will go to await the coming of our expected guests from outside, who should arrive not far from your current location — though I admit, the exact location cannot be determined. But even if Berenike arrives with them, she will find herself at a great disadvantage against one who can successfully play a god, and two God-Warriors!"

The two bowed, and, with no further instructions forthcoming, disappeared from the image.

Raiagamor smiled. Yes, this was the right direction. He could feel it. Even if — against all odds — Ingram Camp-Bel's little party managed to defeat Athena and two God-Warriors, they would surely be badly weakened.

And then, in need of aid, they would arrive at the trap already baited for them... and have their hope torn from their grasp even as they reached to take it.

Chapter 22
Comparative Magical Study

"Absolutely fascinating," Trayne Owen said finally, studying their group with new respect. The four girls with him — Holly, Seika, Tierra, and Cordy — stared at them with shining eyes.

"Oh my *God*," Seika finally said, "you're like *epic fantasy* heroes!"

"What?" Ingram asked. Urelle thought she almost grasped what the girls meant, but not quite.

"It is not *that* surprising," Trayne said. "True, their story is certainly epic, but the fact that it conforms to some of your society's expectations is not entirely coincidence — any more than your conformance to the *mahou shoujo* or magical girl genre conventions is an accident. Such epics *happened* in the distant past, after all."

Holly, the girl with straight black hair whose alternate form, "Princess Holy Aura", had been the one to first meet them, nodded. "I guess... yeah. Your own backstory, right?"

"And that of Lemuria and its predecessors and contemporaries, yes. And with magic now returning to this world in force, the same mystic and dramatic imperatives may return here as well." His gaze rested, with uncomfortable intensity, on Urelle. "But *I* am most interested in your descriptions of magic. I believe there may be much to learn from you — and much that I might teach you."

Urelle had covertly examined the five people, and the sight had nearly blinded her; the power wielded by the so-called "Apocalypse Maidens" was immense, and if brute power wasn't Trayne's forte, he was so ancient that sheer depth of knowledge more than compensated for that lack of essential force. The thought of being instructed by *another* being of ancient knowledge was fantastically tempting.

But..." Sir, I would like nothing more than to study with you, but as our story must show you, we have little time to spare."

"Alas, yes. And the fact that your world lies far from this one does not, in any way, mean that it is not our concern. As I believe we all believe your rather startling tale... ?" he glanced at his young charges and allies, "... yes, as we believe you, it is now clearly part of our mission to ensure you can continue onward."

"You're okay to go on, Urelle?"

"Of course I am—"

"Do not *of course* us, Urelle Vantage!" Aunt Victoria's voice was affectionate yet somehow iron-hard. "You were pushing yourself beyond all bounds towards the end. We all recall the Wanderer's cautions about your power. How badly — and I require an *honest* answer — how badly are you strained?"

"If you will allow me," Trayne said, "I believe I can ascertain how injured she may actually be. Assessing one's own condition, especially in regards to spiritual injuries, is difficult."

Victoria glanced at Quester and Ingram, and then at Urelle. Urelle nodded. "I... already took a look at all of you, to make sure you were what you seemed to be."

Trayne laughed. "I sensed a bit of such magic from you, yes. And quite appropriate that you should have; as they say in this world, 'trust... but verify'. I have your permission, then?"

"You do," Victoria said.

Trayne instantly disappeared, replaced by the form of a white rat wearing a small golden crown. "I have far better access to my magic when not maintaining the human form," he explained, a trace of embarrassment in his voice.

"Wait, then you aren't actually human?" Ingram said in surprise.

"I... *was* human. Still am in my heart. This is the result of... well, we can discuss it later."

Urelle studied every gesture, memorized every word, as the little rodent bounced from point to point around her, muttering invocations in a language she had never heard before. Still, parts of his work *were* familiar. Trayne-Silvertail's movements created a five-pointed star about her, and while some of the symbols he inscribed were not identical to those she knew, she could make out clear connections to the Five Great Elements — called, rather inadequately but conveniently, Earth, Air, Fire, Water, and Spirit. There were other magical traditions and conceptualizations of the powers, but that was one of the more common, most often used by people such as the Guardians of Nature.

As he completed his ritual, Urelle felt something sweep through her, a touch of crisp, cold air, a hint of coldmint, a subliminal sound of running water and crackling fire, a scent of earth in rain.

Trayne reappeared in human form. "You are not badly injured, but *strained*," he said. "There are signs — scars, one might say — of a prior serious injury, some months before, but it has healed well. I would not recommend you do anything of significance with your magic for at least a day or two, however, and if your tale of your travels is accurate, you would very much like to have your full strength available before you transition either to an unknown world, or your own — since your enemies may be waiting there."

"Then we shall wait here a day or two," Quester said firmly.

Urelle felt a twist of guilt. "I *hate* slowing us down. This is the *third* time we've had to delay because of me! I didn't think I was so, so, *delicate!*"

"You're not delicate at all!" Ingram said.

"No, you're not," Cordelia said, to her surprise. The tall girl, whose amazingly pale coloring and gold hair reminded her somewhat of the Wanderer, gestured at the others. "Your friends are basically fighting types, right?"

"Some kind of monk," Seika said, pointing to Victoria, "Straight-up fighter with two-weapon fighting," that being a nod to Quester, "and a higher-tech fighter-monk type. Yeah, they're the beatdown squad."

"Well... true enough, for the most part," Urelle agreed cautiously. "So...?"

"*So*, if *they've* overstrained themselves or gotten bad hurt, you can *tell*, right away. And more than that, that stuff can be *healed* pretty easy — both from your story, and from my own experience." She winked, and for an instant blue-green power flickered around her. "I'm the main healer in our little group, and it's not hard to put bodies back together as long as they're not dead. But if the *spirit* is hurt? You can't *see* if anything's wrong unless you can see the soul, and there's pretty much nothing except time and rest that'll heal it."

"And *one* of those three times," Ingram said, taking her hand, "was when you'd gone through that Ares-damned *Crucible* and been beaten down soul *and* body over a couple of days by yourself. So no, you're not delicate at all."

"It is decided, then," Victoria said. "We will stay here until our hosts are prepared to leave. You said this 'New York City ComicCon' lasts through tomorrow, correct?"

"Correct. This is a wise decision, Lady Victoria," said Trayne.

"What of these adversaries you mentioned? Will they be able to find us here?"

"It is my hope that they will not. These rooms are covered by concealment charms, and as long as we use only minimal magical power it should not be detectable from outside. If they detected your arrival, the search will be concentrated in that alleyway — but I very much doubt that they will be able to find much of interest, as the existence of ComicCon and the vast number of costumed individuals of all descriptions will render you rather less memorable than in almost any other circumstance. Quester would be the only possible exception, and he played a very convincing part. They may eventually analyze video footage and determine he is a target of interest, but I would think this will take them more than a day or two."

Urelle shook her head and smiled. "Well, then, if I'm going to be stuck here resting, Mr. Owen, could we get in a little comparative magical study?"

Trayne smiled brilliantly. "I would be honored, Miss Urelle Vantage!"

***

"By the *Balance*," Urelle said, absently eating another of the tasty potato slices called "French fries" and tapping her notes, "the powers are at once so much the same, and so different!"

"Indeed." Trayne was re-reading some of his own notes. "Your mages — for the most part — draw from energies around them. You yourself appear to literally *interface* with the fabric of the universe to perform what you call 'shaping'. The power *strains* you, yes, but more because you are... hm, a *support structure*, a channel for energies that you can guide and control."

"While *you* have to literally *burn up* part of your own material substance to... what, *catalyze*, I guess, the connection, to allow you to get the universe to go along with your attempt to change things." Urelle let out a long breath. "That must be a strong limit on how powerful a wizard can *be* in your world. I mean, even if you could cheat it a bit — gain a lot of weight that you didn't really need — that'd be good only for a few big shots, and then you'd have to spend weeks or months stuffing yourself to try it again."

"Ha! Yes, although the power *accessible* can be exponentially increased both by the amount of mass sacrificed *and* the skill of the mage."

"Oh, of course, that word... 'sacrifice', as in willingly giving something up for the sake of your goal or magic, that covers the mass thing as well as things like giving up something less tangible but just as important." She flipped through some of her older notes. "On Zarathan, *unwilling* sacrifice is used by some of the nastier types."

"Oh, that is *certainly* part of the way our adversaries can operate," Trayne said. "Willing and conscious sacrifice, however, is much more powerful for those wielding the lighter magics. Is this not true on Zarathan?"

"I'm... not sure." She paged through more of her original notes, some on the more popular stories and myths. "Well, under the right circumstances, personal heroic sacrifice is certainly seen as a fine thing, but I don't see it as being something that directly drives magical power. You mean that literally, right?"

"He really does," Holly said, coming in and fiddling with one of her costume clasps that was being stubborn. "We were *way* more powerful than previous incarnations of the Maidens because we did some new and pretty important personal sacrifices along the way. Which was a good thing, since it let us end the Cycle by killing off Azathoth of the Nine Arms for real."

"So you people had a Cycle too," Ingram said in a pensive voice. "That's interesting."

"Parallels across worlds," Seika interjected, looking excited. "Maybe it's not coincidence! I mean, we've had theories that there's infinite universes out there, some just a *tiny* bit different than the one we're in..."

"Likely not coincidence... but the connections are likely to be hard to see. Seika, Holly, Cordelia, if you're bringing Ingram with you, you are *responsible* for him."

"Don't worry, Silvertail," Cordy said. "He's removed all the items Holly says were 'active' magic and you agreed the passive ones shouldn't be detectable."

"As have I," Victoria said. "I will keep an eye on all of them. It *is* a slight risk... but in all honesty, when will we have an opportunity to see such a world as this again?"

"I admit," Trayne said with a quick grin, "I would find it exceedingly difficult to resist the temptation myself. And who knows? Perhaps you will see or learn something of use. Just be cautious."

"Oh, I shall."

As they left, Urelle bent back over their notes. "I wonder... could either of us use the other's techniques?"

Trayne's eyebrows shot up. "You mean... use magic whose principles lie in another reality entirely? My initial reaction is that it's a ridiculous idea. Yet... there are many similarities between our magics, as well. The correspondence of the elements, the mechanics of spell design you have articulated, the nature of the interaction between spirit and magic, these are all very similar. Do you have reason to believe it could be done?"

Urelle reached into a pouch, touched a certain metallic book. "Maybe. The Wanderer that we mentioned in our story... he's said to come from a completely different world, one without magic at all. And he can do things that other mages simply can't do. I saw a vision... connected with him," she went on carefully, trying to avoid any truly dangerous knowledge, "that showed a city very much like this one. So maybe he even came from *this* world, before your victory over this 'Azathoth'?"

"I cannot say it is impossible; how he would have done so, however, is beyond me. Still... perhaps we could attempt it. You and I are well-trained beyond the basics of our knowledge; it would not be a waste of time to see if following the instructions of the other will yield any results."

Urelle smiled. "Then let's start!"

"One moment," he said, with a smile that acknowledged her eagerness with his own interest. "I must strengthen the wards first; as we do not know exactly what the results of our experimentation will be, it is best to assume that they may be obvious if not shielded against."

He made a circuit of the entire room, sketching symbols on the ceiling and floor, muttering phrases in a language Urelle did not know. Finally, however, he came back, and sat. "*Now,*" he said, "we can begin."

Chapter 23
The Final World

Ingram gripped his *anai-k'ota* tighter. "You ready, Urelle?"

"Almost." She held up her hands, gazing through a triangle made between them. "Ah! There's the Seal!"

"Good," Silvertail said — in his rat form, sitting on the radiantly beautiful Princess Holy Aura's right shoulder. Cold rain did nothing to dim either Ingram's spirits or the glory of the four Apocalypse Maidens. He felt somewhat guilty for staring, but he'd seen Urelle having a hard time not looking too, and since they *were* leaving it wouldn't matter much. "We will guard while you open the way and depart. Hopefully, nothing will interfere. At least this rain discourages casual wandering through Central Park."

I would have preferred one of the more nearby alleys," Quester thought candidly. *Limited access, more easily defensible. This copse may be out of an immediate line of sight, but trouble could come from any direction.*

Victoria shrugged. *True enough, but it should take only a few minutes, and I am reasonably confident of our allies' abilities to protect us.*

Given that Urelle says the four of them have a power level at least equal to Berenike? *By the Lady, I'd* hope *they could defend us for a few minutes!*

Ingram saw through Urelle's eyes for an instant, glimpsing the eternally-in-flux yet forever-fixed Seal as she prepared to wrench it open.

"Ready!" she called.

"Trayne, it was an honor to meet you and work with both you and your... protégés," Victoria said.

"Likewise, Victoria. It may be unlikely, but if ever you find yourself in our reality again, please look us up."

"I assure you, I will."

A quick round of handshakes and goodbyes followed. Ingram found himself somewhat glassy-eyed after receiving an emphatic hug from the six-foot tall Princess Radiance Blaze, who reminded Ingram in some ways of Urelle's big sister

Kyri. He noticed Urelle also looked similarly dazed after her own hug from Tsunami Reflection, the perfected vision that was the Maiden form of Cordelia Ingemar.

But she shook it off and gestured to the now-visible glow. "Now, let's go!"

Literally as the Seal began to open, three distant, emphatic *thump!* noises reached Ingram's ears, and three canisters dropped in the center of their circle, passing through the Seal's immaterial substance; even as they landed, the canisters began spewing a thin white mist everywhere.

A touch of a sharp, astringent smell tickled Ingram's nose, and even as he thought *poison!*, the world tilted up beneath him. Distantly he heard shouts and a flash of light, but even that faded away...

***

Slowly he blinked his way back to consciousness, feeling Quester's own confused, dulled perceptions gradually sharpening. For a moment he didn't move, assessing his own sensations. *Where am I? Am I tied up?*

Feeling nothing but warmth from what he presumed was the sun, grass and earth beneath him, and no sign of any restraints, he took a deeper breath and carefully levered himself up to a sitting position.

"Good! You're finally up!" Urelle said.

His head felt like someone had inserted a wooden wedge between his temples, but otherwise he didn't feel too bad. Raising his eyes, he saw Victoria and Urelle seated on some nearby rocks, a small fire before them heating up a pot of something that smelled more than merely edible, despite a touch of nausea. "What happened?"

"Someone — I would guess this 'OSC' they told us about — ambushed us just as we were leaving," Urelle said. "Like we'd discussed with Silvertail, he and the Maidens had a much better chance to deal with the OSC, and if they were after *us*, well, best not to be there, so I got Aunt Vicky to grab you two up and then finished opening the Seal. Ended up here and we've been waiting a few hours for you to wake up."

"Wait, why didn't you and Victoria fall to their poison vapors?"

"After the time that Ares' thugs took us down that way?" Urelle demanded. "I've had an air-purity spell on conditional ever since. And I guess something like that is an old story for Aunt Vicky."

"Oh, certainly," Victoria said. "One of my little bangles is specifically made to prevent that sort of attack from working."

"Fortunate indeed," Quester stood with careful precision. "Perhaps we should look into such things, Ingram."

"When we get the chance, I guarantee it. Twice is two times too many." He glanced into a pouch. "I have a mask that *would* work, but I can't wear it all the time, and that stuff worked *fast*."

Victoria mimed something dropping from her hands. "Indeed; you fell like stones. But all's well, in any event. I'm sure our friends could deal with the threat; I did not see any of them falling when we left."

"Nothing's bothered us since arrival? That's promising," Ingram stretched, and glanced toward the pot. "Mmm, that's the leftovers of that stew we had a while back."

"Yes, I thought it was a good time to unseal it. It's almost ready," Victoria said, giving it a quick stir. "Why don't you go over there and take a look at the view? It's well worth a few moments."

Looking around, Ingram could see they were in a small, sheltered circle of stone, with a mostly grassy floor to the circle and a few patches of pretty flowers. Following Victoria's indicated direction, he and Quester exited the dell and found themselves not more than ten feet from the edge of a... cliff?

Then he looked up and around. "By the Founder and the Lady..." he breathed.

Illumined by a golden sun in a clear blue sky, beautiful, towering mountains, slopes covered with greenery, and with sparkles of distant towers and domes just visible near their bases, drifted like clouds. Beneath, the immense floating islands tapered off in irregular cones of rock and earth, as though they had been roughly cut from the ground of the native world. Dazzling glitters and plumes showed where rivers and streams plunged off into the airy abyss.

Ingram cautiously stepped to the cliff edge and looked down. Perhaps, far below, there was a hint of some surface, or perhaps it was merely a darkening of distance. But in all other directions were the great floating mountains, some barely the size of hillocks, others so huge that Ingram could not even guess at their size — they seemed to be entire sections of a mighty mountain range.

Flocks of gorgeously-plumed birds streaked out over the edge of the floating mountain they stood upon, and streamed onward towards one of their neighbors. Other creatures, some birdlike, others more sinuous, swam or flew through the air, and in the distance, Ingram thought he could see something of less organic, more solid lines, a vessel that somehow flew across the immensity of the aerial ocean.

"You were right, Aunt Victoria," he said. "That's well worth seeing."

"Astounding, isn't it? But Urelle has something even more astounding."

He trotted back to the little circular dell. "What is it?"

Urelle's smile was filled with relief. "This is *it*, Ingram! The Seal's *different* here, I can feel it! This is the end of the world-sheaf!"

"Wh... Ares and Athena! You mean this is really the end — we can get *home* now?"

"And," she said, "if I haven't just been leading us on a tail-chase, not just home. We'll come out *inside* Aegeia!"

"Then let's open the Seal and get —"

"Wait and calm yourself, young man," Victoria said, and Quester indicated his agreement by seating himself nearby. "We have no idea what may await us in Aegeia... but it seems exceedingly unlikely that another hour or so will make a difference. So why not first have a meal, now that you are awake, and all of us prepare as though we go to a great battle before passing through?"

Ingram restrained his own worry and urgency. Victoria was — as usual — correct. Being fed and then fully prepared before emerging into whatever Aegeia was like now? That was the smartest thing he'd heard anyone say in a while.

So he sat down, accepted a plate, and ate two servings of Victoria's stew. Then he took out his full battle gear — the hidden armor, his weapons, additional protection for arms and legs, the more useful technological devices — and made sure he was ready. Urelle was layering on spells of protection — not just for herself, but for the rest — and Victoria and Quester were ensuring all their defenses and weapons were prepared.

Finally, Ingram looked around, and nodded. "We're ready as we'll ever be," he said. "Urelle?"

"Grab on for the last of these rides," she said, no longer nervous, but confident through the experience of fifty trips across different worlds, "we're going home!"

The Seal yawned wide and they plummeted one last time into a spinning abyss...

Chapter 24
Amoni Agapis

Victoria only stumbled slightly this time, feeling her feet strike a flat and solid surface and instantly adjusting to her new position. The others, too, did not fall.

She experienced a momentary sense of *déjà-vu*, recognizing that they were once more standing in an alleyway. However, unlike their visit to New York City, it was daytime, the alley was cleaner, and the architecture was very different. The pavement, too, was not the strange black, tarry material she had seen before, but was carefully fitted stone blocks — marble, she thought, which was a striking and surprising choice for what seemed an ordinary side street. "Are we... home, Urelle?"

"I think so... but I can check. If we're not..." Her niece focused and ran through a now-familiar ritual. Her smile broadened. "*Yes!* There's no sense of the Seal anywhere at all within my range — that's *miles* — and that means we *have* to be back on Zarathan!"

"Back on Zarathan is wonderful," Quester said dryly, though his scent was filled with a quiet pleasure, "but can we be sure we are now *inside* Aegeia?"

"Yes, we can," Ingram said, another slowly-growing smile lighting up his face as he pointed down the alley.

Framed between the straight, simple walls of the alley were two statues. The one on their right was that of a man, immensely broad of shoulder and mighty of arm but whose figure was bent, somewhat hunched of shoulder, with one leg in a golden brace. His face was square, seamed not with age but with focus and concentration and determination — not a *handsome* face, but one that would still hold the attention of any who looked upon it, and he wore a leather workman's apron. Golden eyes glittered in his ebony face — for the statue was carven of pure, polished black marble — and he stood before a great anvil, one hand gripping a great hammer, the other holding the hand of the statue beside him.

That second statue was of a woman, tall and straight and proud of figure, dressed in a flowing gown of white and gold; she herself was carven of gold-brown marble, with a face so flawlessly beautiful that even Victoria had to look twice to assure herself that it was real. She, too, was smiling, her hand gripping that of the man next to her. Before her on the anvil was a bouquet of roses, flowers of ruby with emerald stems, and her hand held a polished mirror of purest silver.

"Aphrodite and Hephaestus," Ingram said, his smile trembling, eyes shimmering with tears of joy. "Welcome to Aegeia, all of you... welcome to Amoni Agapis, the Anvil of Perfect Love!" He turned to Urelle and hugged her, lifting her up and spinning her around despite his slight form. "You did it, you *did* it, Urelle!"

Urelle laughed and hugged him back. "I did! By Myrionar, I guess I really *did!*"

"You did indeed, and we are all very proud of you, and grateful. And what fortune, to have come out in one of the cities. I was thinking we might have to hike miles just to discover where we were." She tried to recall the maps Ingram had shown them. "We are still far in the north of Aegeia, yes?"

"Oh, definitely. Several hundred miles still to Aegis, which is where Ares is going to be now. But if the war's not too far along we might be able to take a boat down the rivers, straight to Aegis itself." Ingram reached into his pack and got out his Camp-Bel sigils, and also affixed two little tabs or symbols to his collar — a pair of open books.

"What are those?" Victoria asked. She remembered seeing the same tabs on one or two of the other Camp-Bels — the Captain before he'd died, certainly, and the one — Kerridan — that they had found dead in the jungle.

He glanced down, realized she was looking at his collar and touched the tabs. "These? They represent a member of the Captain's Crew. I don't know if I *quite* qualify, really, but Pennon said I should keep the Lieutenant's; until I found someone who could say, for sure, I had the right to wear them. And if we run into any Camp-Bels, this will make them listen hard, even if they remember me as the 'failure'."

He turned. "Let's go! If we can make contact with Clan representatives here, we could be on our way in just a few hours."

As they started out of the alley, Urelle asked, "But your Clan fled or hid, right? Will there *be* any of them... well, here?"

"They'll have left marks, traces for other Camp-Bels and no one else. I can read them." He touched the scanning device called an ISNDAU. "Some of the marks will be only detectable with this, or magic of a *really* specific sort."

Victoria stopped as they exited the alley, and felt her stomach tightening. "Ingram... this is the central square of the city. So... where are all the *people?*"

Ingram froze, and then glanced around with increasing concern. "Lady's *Wisdom*. I don't know. This place should be *crowded* at this hour. A siege, maybe? Nonessential personnel would be staying in their homes if a battle was underway. Everyone else would be at the walls, or barracks near the Palace of the Hammer and Rose."

Victoria gestured for silence and then turned slowly, very slowly, listening.

The tension increased, accompanied by a tingling, creeping feeling of dread. She heard... *nothing*. Not distant cries of battle, not shouted orders; no movement, large or small.

And the silence was more profound than the mere absence of the citizens. As she listened, sharpening her senses as much as possible, and as her friends's faces began to show their own awareness of something terribly wrong, she realized that the *only* sounds she heard were those of the wind — a whisper of cloth rippling in gentle motion, the creak of a door far away, and perhaps, just barely at the limit of sensing, a trickling of water.

But no cries of birds, no flapping of wings; no sound of dogs or horses or riding-lizards; no scuttling of rats; not even the buzzing and humming of flies and bees and beetles.

"Great *Mothers*," Quester buzzed in quiet horror. "This place is *dead*."

"But how?" Urelle asked, her hands now poised to grip and control the fabric of reality. "I don't see any blood, no bodies, no signs of struggle!"

Ingram and Quester looked at each other. "I think —"

"Wait." Victoria knew her voice sounded terribly off even as she spoke, but in this case that was good; the others paused instantly. "Quietly, everyone. Just in case something *else* is listening." *Communicate only through the link for now*, she added.

Understood, Quester replied instantly. *Ingram, what were you saying?*

I think we should check a few of the houses around the square. There may be clues as to what happened.

An excellent idea, Victoria thought. *Together. No one goes* anywhere *alone*.

Yes. Quester's mental voice was too controlled, showing his own tension. *Let us not make ourselves vulnerable.*

They surveyed the buildings, all of them lit with an incongruous cheerfulness in the brilliant sunshine. Victoria was aware of the intensity of the sunlight, the pressure of heat on her face, the trickle of a drop of sweat being absorbed, for the moment, in the roots of her hair. Something about the situation had already awakened all her instincts, and her senses were hyperaware, making everything she sensed more intense.

We have to do some talking, or our assumed observers will guess that we have a way to communicate outside of talking, Urelle pointed out.

You're right, of course, Victoria responded.

"Let's check this house," Ingram said quietly. "Maybe we'll learn something."

Yes. We can speak the obvious words, but anything we guess or deduce that is non-obvious, we keep to ourselves, Quester said.

The "house" was a mansion, obviously a dwelling for someone rich, highly placed, or both. "Ingram, you've been here before," Victoria said, keeping her voice low. "Whose home is this?"

"It was a few years ago... but last I knew, this was Sideras' home. He's... call him the boss of the armorers for the city."

Set back from the square itself under a stone awning supported by white marble pillars, the door was a large, polished red-brown wood with silver inlay and an elaborate silver handle. Ingram tried it, found the door locked, but that was little impediment to people of their experience. The door swung open.

The interior was very dimly lit, mostly by light from the open door, but there was no sign of anyone, or anything, inside. Senses as on-edge as they were, Victoria strained her hearing; nothing at all, save — perhaps — a momentary, nearly inaudible sigh or hiss.

"Stay alert, everyone," Urelle murmured. She gestured, and a sphere of pure white light floated up, hovering over them.

With the additional illumination, they could see that the door opened on a broad entrance hall, floor inlaid with some symbol — perhaps the personal family crest — a spiral staircase straight ahead, and three other exits, one left, one right, and one beyond the staircase.

The archway to the right opened into a sitting room. Victoria felt a tap on her shoulder, followed Ingram's pointing finger.

She knelt down, looking at the cracked goblet on the floor. A deep burgundy stain formed a graceful arc across the carpet, with a curlicue at the end nearest the goblet. An overturned chair and small table were nearby, along with a scattering of papers.

"Someone was sitting here. Something startled them and they jumped to their feet, upsetting the table, sending the glass flying," Ingram muttered, echoing her own thoughts. "I don't see much other sign of struggle, though, do you?"

"No," she said slowly. *No bloodstains. No broken furniture. No damage to walls, or the window to the side there. Nothing knocked off the shelves or other tables.*

I do not like this. Quester's thoughts were so controlled as to be mechanical.

"This way," Ingram whispered, leading them back to the hall and through the central exit, which led to a hallway. His face was drawn and grim.

Victoria was aware of a vibration within her own chest. *By the Balance*, she thought to herself in astonishment, *I am* terrified *already*.

Ingram paused by the next door. *Dining room here. Let's... look.*

A creeping cold chill washed over Victoria, for she was suddenly absolutely certain of what she would see.

The dining room had a circular table in the center, with places for nine people. Five of the places were set in a close-spaced arc, clearly for a family or close friends dining together. The scene was illuminated in soft colors by a beautiful, broad stained-glass picture window spanning most of the far wall.

Food lay on the plates — gravelseed rolls, pingrain with vegetable mix, skewers of marinated and grilled meat, fruit pastries — and not as though waiting for the diners. Bites had been taken of various dishes; glasses were half-full, one of them with clear lip-marks from someone whose lipshine was wearing off; utensils lay scattered, out of place, as though dropped suddenly. It had not happened recently — decay had already well-advanced on much of the food — but it had happened with terrible suddenness.

"Great Balance," she said, making it half a prayer. *Dear Myrionar, this cannot be what it seems. Please, Myrionar, Chromaias, great Terian, do not* allow *it to be!*

Ingram and Quester stood frozen, staring, and then looking around, gripping their weapons.

Something chuckled.

Victoria whirled around, but saw nothing, just the empty doorway.

Another snicker, and the four of them turned, seeking the source; once more, there seemed to be nothing there, no possible location for the sound.

"Not *that* easy to hide," Urelle said, sounding unsettled as well. Her fingers danced across the air in time to whispered words, and a glow pulsed out through the room and beyond.

This garnered a laugh, a laugh that came from all around them. "Not *that* easy to find."

The voice was deep, unsettling, gelid, *gurgling*; not a sound ever made by human or even Iriistiik, and it spoke with palpable malice and vicious amusement.

And Victoria's heart stuttered, a stab of agonized panic, for she *knew that voice*.

"Victoria *Vantage*," it said, and an edge of spiteful eagerness was now clear in that rippling bass, "how *lovely* to see you again!"

Chapter 25
The Darkness That Devours

Quester had felt his own limbs lock in unreasoning fear when the Voice had spoken, and could both see and sense the shock and horror in Ingram.

Out! Out that window, now!

Victoria's terrified thought brooked no pause or argument. As one, the four adventurers sprinted and leapt out the window, covering their faces with their arms to protect against shards of metal and glass.

Even that speed had *barely* been enough; there was a hissing sigh of displaced air and something black surged behind them, missing Quester's feet by mere inches. They tumbled to a halt amid a rainbow shower of glass shards.

"What?" Urelle's voice was shaking, but not just from the eerie confrontation; she was staring at Victoria, whose skin had lost its warm undertone; the older woman was on one knee, panting, looking like someone very near to death. "What *was* that, Auntie? What?"

Ingram opened his mouth to answer, but Victoria cut him off with a desperate thought. *No! Do not reveal what you know!*

He snapped his mouth closed, angry with himself for failing to think.

"Something that I thought was dead. Something that *should* be dead," Victoria said, still kneeling and staring with revulsion and horror into the dark opening of the shattered window. "An abomination that calls itself the Darkness That Devours."

Ingram looked at her. "Tell us." *We know what we saw, but you went through the entirety of the adventure.*

"So glad you remember, little adventurer," the Darkness' voice said, before Victoria could speak. "And now you travel with children and an insect. A gift this is, that you would come here into my new city, and lack the ones who saved you before. Where *are* the lizard and the singer? Nearby? Or far away?"

"Perhaps nearer than you think," Victoria said. She gestured for them to move up the street, back to the central square.

"Far, far away, then. That pleases me. Do not worry, Victoria Vantage. You won't die first. I'll take your companions instead. I promised you that, remember."

"I remember," she whispered, hatred hot and cold in her voice. Then she turned to them, beckoned them to the statues. Once there, she sank down to the pavement. "It can undoubtedly hear anything we say. Fortunately, I wrote an account of those adventures." *I will give you one of my notebooks. I don't have that one, but I will tell you what you must know via the link. Pretend to read it as we talk this way.* "Here it is. Read swiftly. We have little enough time."

Thank your Mothers and you for this link, Quester, Urelle thought.

You are more than welcome.

Ingram grimaced. "Thanks," he said. He, Quester, and Urelle bent their heads over the black-covered volume with its weathered and stained pages.

Ingram, you and Quester know what this thing is, too? How?

He flashed her a mental smile. *The Guild can use magical records of other people's adventures as a framework to test candidates. Victoria's experience was the basis of our Guild examination.* He shifted his mental focus. *How accurate would the simulation be?*

Extremely accurate. Having fought the Darkness there would be effectively the same as having fought it in this world.

Ah, Quester thought. *So that is what you mean about* time. *It abhors light, so we are safe outside... as long as the sun is up.*

Ingram glanced up reflexively. The sun had passed its zenith already, and the midafternoon heat was reaching its peak. *We've got less than six hours. Probably five.*

I can make light, Urelle said. *We can keep it at bay. I think I could weave a spell that would maintain bright light around us all night, even.*

Victoria sighed; she looked somewhat better, but still off-color and her hands trembled. *Not good enough, child. Oh, I am sure you could make a barrier it could not pass, but it is not stupid. It has magics of its own; it might be able to batter down your barrier, and certainly could use indirect means to attack us.*

Yes, but if the light is bright *enough it will hurt it. We could harm it, drive it off.*

Ingram shook his head. *This... monster wiped out all of Amoni Agapis. That can't be a coincidence or accident; Ares or his forces* brought *it here. If we don't destroy it, it's a weapon Ares will be able to use again and again — against any enemy, including us.*

And I had thought it had *been destroyed,* Victoria pointed out. *Cillerion Somari, Toron, Suwaka, and I trapped it and thought it destroyed.*

"You thought you destroyed me, Victoria," the voice said, and for a heartstopping moment Ingram thought the thing could *hear* their link, had the ability to read minds, and that would surely doom them. But it went on, "You finished off the Nest, spent a fine time in Mirror's Valley, then went off."

"How did you *survive?*" Victoria ground out. "I was sure not one fragment of you escaped the light of song and dragon!"

A bubbling laughter, like boiling mud. "None of me *did* survive, little Adventurer. None, that is, save a tiny piece kept in the Temple of Kerlamion."

Victoria cursed.

"Yes, of course, having slain me and wiped out the Xiilistiin, your demolishing of that temple was just the last, what is the term, *cleanup* task. But it *was* underground, and it *was* dark, and when you broke the altar, I was not foolish enough to attempt to attack you, with you in your strength and I in my weakness; I flowed away, a shadow within shadow, and fled."

"Myrionar damn me for a fool," she murmured, and Ingram bit his lip at the intensity of the self-recrimination in her voice. "Suwaka *said* she sensed some evil that peaked and receded, and we simply attributed it to the breaking of the altar — to Kerlamion's presence resisting and then fading."

"Yes, the little Toad-priest's words brought me closest to pure terror as I had ever felt," the thick voice said smugly. "Followed by such joy as you dismissed them."

I already hate this thing, Urelle thought. *But since it* is *light out, couldn't we just leave? I mean, it has to be killed sometime but we've got your mission, Ingram. If we can —*

No. Ingram felt her surprise at the iron in his thought. *I am a Camp-Bel of Aegeia. I am in one of the great cities and its destroyer waits here, taunting us. I cannot leave this be. I cannot give it a chance to destroy more lives and souls, nor allow it to remain here, squatting on the graves of those it killed.*

Victoria looked at him and nodded. *And I... well, this is a job I didn't finish. We can't let this thing escape.*

I understand both of these points, Quester put in quietly, his scent neutral, controlled. *And I think Urelle does as well, even though she — fortunately — lacks the personal context. But we should also be practical.* Can *we expect to defeat such a monster? I remember it well from our experience, Ingram, as do you; you harmed it badly indeed, but I do not believe you destroyed it, even with the ELF.*

"And you have reaffirmed your bond with Kerlamion, I suppose?" Victoria said. "Bound to his darkness, once more within his temple?"

A gurgling of laughter like sewage rumbling through a pipe. "No, my creator and I have parted ways, indeed. I am my own and my own alone, though the Xiilistiin and I have come to an understanding."

"You work for the false Ares, then?"

"I work for *myself*, little adventurer. But I benefit from these false gods, and I watch, and I hear many things. 'False Ares' indeed, but you know nothing of it. Better far that you die in my embrace, Victoria Vantage, than that you meet your end by his will."

The cruel yet absolute *sincerity* in those monstrous words left a leaden, frozen ball of ice in Ingram's guts. The Darkness That Devours was — despite all the adventures they had had since — still the most monstrous foe Ingram had ever faced, and from these words Ingram found himself shuddering at the thought of what the false Ares must be, to leave even the Darkness with such a grim view of his nature.

You're right, Quester. If we can't figure out a plan that holds a chance of success, we'd be fools not to move on. But...

But yes, we must see if we can formulate such a plan. You are correct that, if at all possible, we must not leave such a monstrous thing free to act, especially as it is allied with our enemies; a failure to face it now may mean we must face it later, with our other enemies aiding it.

"I would prefer not to meet my end at all, and rather to witness yours and his," Victoria said. Her color had nearly returned to normal, and her voice was stronger. "And I intend to."

She took out a piece of paper, wrote on it, and passed it to Ingram. On it was written "And here is how we will truly annoy it."

Ha! We can scribble randomly while planning much more in detail via the link. It will assume we are communicating slowly using notes.

Do you think there is *a way we can defeat this monster, Auntie? How big is it? What can it do?*

A grimace. *It is huge — gathered together, it is a living pool of black... not flesh, exactly, but something animate and of a texture like hot tar, approximately a hundred yards across and twenty deep.*

By Myrionar... A sense of mental calculations faster than Ingram could follow. *By the* Balance, Urelle went on, *that's larger than anything I've heard of other than the Greatest Dragons.*

Yes. You cannot defeat it by main force. It is simply too huge. It can split itself into pieces, shaping them however it desires, although the pieces must remain connected to the main body, if only by a tiny strand of its substance; disconnected, they collapse into lifeless pools that slowly evaporate if the creature does not reabsorb them.

So it must have a... brain, a core, a nucleus that is vulnerable? Quester scribbled meaningless symbols on paper, passed them around the group. The Darkness continued to talk, but slowly stopped as it apparently realized they were ignoring it.

No, I do not believe so. I believe it can... focus *its consciousness into any given part of itself. Thus, how it survived; its consciousness retreated to the most distant remaining portion of itself, even as it burned, and then severed the connection to ensure what we did could not catch it.*

What did *you do?* Urelle asked.

A simple description would be that Cillerion wove a song that... resonated with the creature's essence, its material, and Toron summoned dragon-fire to follow that resonance, with Suwaka's help. It resents me *because I was the one who gave them the idea, and managed to keep it at bay until the combined enchantment began to work.*

Urelle was quiet for a moment. Then, *So that's how it can speak all around us. In the house, it was in the pipes and the vents. It's able to extend parts of itself through caves or pipes or interiors of walls, so it can see and hear everywhere.*

Correct.

A slow smile glimmered on Urelle's face, and Ingram felt his heart leap. *Ingram, you have one more of those Extreme Luminance Flares, right?*

Yes. But only one, and unless we can get it all to come to the flare —

No. The smile was becoming dangerously sharp. *No, we can't do that.*

But maybe, she went on, *just maybe I can get the flare to come to all of* it.

And, exchanging meaningless pieces of paper, Urelle began to outline a plan.

Chapter 26
Light Versus Darkness

Sun's going down, Ingram's voice said in her head. *Last chance. Are you sure you want to do this, Urelle?*

Truth? She was absolutely sure she *didn't* want to do this at all. If her idea didn't work, or if one of her friends couldn't quite do their part, they were all dead, and Ingram's journey ended here. Their whole story ended here.

But "want" didn't enter into it. The dead city, beautiful as a perfectly mummified corpse, demanded she try to avenge it. The terror she had heard in her imperturbable Aunt Vicky called to her to protect the woman who had become her mother. The fear from both Ingram and Quester told her that it was something she *had* to do.

Yes, she answered. *Are all of you ready?*

We are, Quester thought. *Multiple light sources ready. We stand just outside your circle, but within the area you believe will stay illuminated. I have my weapons all prepared, as do Ingram and Victoria.*

A reminder to you all: it did not take my group seriously the prior time we fought it. It did not believe anyone could harm it so badly. Thus, its attacks were measured to terrify, not to kill. I do not think it will make that mistake again if it realizes we have formulated an effective plan. Her aunt's thoughtvoice was calm, though all of them could still sense the underlying fear.

She could see Victoria before her, eyes closed as she focused on the Eight Winds. *Please, Myrionar... don't let me fail. Don't let me kill my aunt, don't let me be Quester or Ingram's death.* She thought, again, how strange it was to be praying to the Balanced Sword when the God of Justice and Vengeance was, somehow, her own older sister.

But then, I always did know I could trust Kyri. She took a deep breath. *And that means I have blood of Myrionar in my veins, and I am also the apprentice of the Wanderer himself. If I fail... I will fail in a way that would make him proud.*

The light of evening faded, the stars began to gleam, and the silence become a waiting, threatening and profound as darkness flowed across the land.

Pure living blackness fountained from a dozen points around the square, streaking with monstrous speed for the four people, one sitting on the solid stone of the pavement before the Anvil, the others ranged about her. There was no subtlety in this assault, no reluctance or caution, no touch of finesse; this was a brutal, massive attack to either test their defenses to the limit — or wipe them out in a single instant.

In the moment she saw the first hint of motion, Urelle made the final gesture that sealed the circle and activated the spells therein. Blue-white light flared out and the abyssal flood halted as though it had struck a wall. With an effort, it drove its way inward towards the three surrounding figures, forming daggers and claws and mouths and insectoid striking arms, but most boiled and smoked away before reaching their targets; the few that did were cut down by the flashing weapons of her friends, the remains evaporating like water drops on a red-hot forge.

She allowed herself a tight smile as she saw that the Darkness That Devours had paid no attention to the *second* circle, one surrounding her friends at just a short distance outward from the first — just far enough away to be in shade, safely away from the destroying light, the closest approach the Darkness could make. *That* circle did not glow, did not call attention to itself at all. But that did not mean it was inert.

That's exactly right, monster. You want to keep the closest eye you can on us. You have to. For all your bragging, you are afraid of Auntie, and you should be. Old adventurers get to be old because they beat everything that tried to kill them.

The initial assault having failed, the tide of pitch receded, leaving only a rippling verge barely visible in the light, lapping over her second circle.

The second assault was a blast of power, darkness distilled into magic, something to wipe out all other enchantments. Had she not expected something like this, it might have overwhelmed her, broken the central circle, dispelled the light... and they would all have died an instant later.

But Victoria had warned her the Darkness That Devours was no mere thug, physical threat and no more; it was either a mage on its own, or one gifted by its maker or another with power to channel to its own needs. She shored up her defenses, drew on the strength that had come to her over the last year and more, and though the light flickered for an instant, the circle held. For long minutes the

Darkness continued its assault, but at last she sensed it accept that for now, at least, her will and her power outmatched its own in the realm of the arcane.

Be ready, she thought to the others. *The third phase of attack begins, and I'm pretty sure it's going to continue for a long time.*

It had better, Ingram thought grimly. *You need it to go on a while. And somehow, we need to survive it.*

Abruptly, a hail of missiles — stones, sticks, twisted metal pieces that had been decorations or armor — shot from the darkness.

Ingram spun his staff, deflecting many of the attacks; Quester simply shielded his eyes and the mundane attacks bounced harmlessly from his exoskeleton. Holding the broad blade of Twin-Edged Fate before her, Victoria also weathered the storm unscathed. The few that passed were bent aside by her dome.

Have to trust they can hold off whatever it throws, large or small. My shield will catch strays, but it can't withstand a large assault by itself — not when I have something far more important to do.

The word "resonance" was the key. Once before, according to Victoria, they had sought to destroy it by finding a way to trace it, to send fire through its own substance. And it had *nearly* worked, reducing the Darkness by its own admission to the tiniest fraction of its former self.

But Urelle knew *why* it had failed; she suspected the legendary music-mage Cillerion Somari had eventually figured it out himself. The fire from an Ancient Sauran had to FOLLOW the resonance, had to make its way from Toron *through* the substance of the Darkness. It could do so swiftly — swift as flame following a trail of naptha — but not instantaneously. And the Darkness had *sensed* the implacable wave of incineration screaming its way through its alien flesh, had had time to withdraw its *self* into the farthest reaches of that flesh and — just in time — cut off its connections, letting the fire burn out just short of absolute destruction.

But there was *another* way to make use of the resonance... if you also had the understanding she had gained, through all the universes and her training, of location and distance.

And if you had a friend with an unexpected weapon; a weapon tested in battle against this very foe... yet never seen by that foe, here.

She focused on the second circle, on the contact she had with something dark and hostile and alien, born of the malice of the King of All Hells and his mastery of pure light-consuming hatred. With exquisite care, she let herself expand her consciousness out, touching the Darkness That Devours as lightly as dew settling onto a flower. In the focus and fury of the battle, it did not sense her. Why should it? The magic she used was weak, barely the light of a single distant star compared to the bonfire of her shield and the flaring brilliance of her companions' defenses. There were thousands of stars, and none were a threat even to its light-sensitive substance.

But with that touch of mystical luminance, she could feel a response, a vibration, that came from the aversion of the Darkness to purity and light. And that vibration *rippled* outward, to her senses like the concentric circles created by a stone cast into a still pond. And just as those tiny wavelets would themselves make *more* wavelets striking any edge or obstacle, she could see the ripples flickering, extending, tracing the edge of the monster surrounding them.

She followed, her will resting lightly on the veriest surface of the creature, a breath of the softest wind — something beneath notice, when Ingram had just thrown a brilliant chemical flare into its seething mass. The ripple and light expanded outward, took on form and structure.

It was like the Seal in a way, Urelle realized. The Darkness That Devours was *living magic*, bound to an infinitely flexible form. Its essence consumed anything it could overpower, added not just mass but energy, perhaps knowledge, to the Darkness as it did so. But that structure was something Urelle *understood*, destructive and evil though it was; she knew how to follow the structure of a spell, living or not.

Her vision expanded, and she could see the thing spread across the square; with a vague shock of fear she sensed massive pieces of it, linked to the others with tiny wires or webs of the rest, dragging massive weapons — arbalests, trebuchets, mystical projectors — from the armories towards the square. *Soon they will be throwing boulders — or worse — at my friends.*

She suppressed the worry. Either she could do this in time, or she would have to rely on her friends finding some way to deal even with siege weapons. There was no turning back, no alternative to success but death.

Now her mind was beginning to feel the strain of keeping all the components of the Darkness in mind — but she *had* to. Now she could see the dark glittering of the creature spread through the neighboring buildings, tiny strands ending in eyes peering through a thousand cracks. And those, too, attached to things *below* ground, and she was suddenly *intensely* glad that they had verified how solid and thick was the stone immediately beneath the central plaza, for there were caverns and pipes and tiny cracks that became holes and eventually passages, and throughout each and every one of them, *thousands* of them, the black-glinting essence of the Darkness That Devours trailed, sometimes a puddle one could step across, at other moments a thread scarce thicker than a spider's web, now a cable thicker than her arm.

She focused all her soul now, the sound of battle fading to nothing, engraving in magic and will the almost impossibly complex network of the monster's extent, infiltrating pipes and walls and wells, caverns below and hidden passages in buildings above, and following it, ever outward, ever downward, until at last she found it, the central mass, still nearly fifty yards across despite the immensity of its network.

A concussion vibrated the stone, and a spray of splinters tore through her surrounding shield; one carved a bleeding trail across her cheek, and the pain nearly undid her. She wavered for the merest instant. *Seige weapons are already starting to fire.*

But the next missile was met by Twin-Edged Fate, carved in twain, passing harmlessly to the side. And Urelle somehow found her balance.

One last pass over the immensity of the Darkness' structure, and even then she nearly missed it — a faerie-trail of light, the merest hint of sparks, leading away from the central body to a tunnel that let out into the ever-dark depths of Lake Cathrefti, and thence to a small mass, barely the size of her own head, lurking there as a watcher and final escape.

Not this time!

Ingram had out his *hedri'at*, and the weapon spat a series of flaming discs, carrying fire and light to a misshapen monstrosity even as it aimed a trebuchet; the weapon slewed sideways as the creature reflexively flinched from the light, and fired uselessly to the side.

With the very last of her concentration, she reached into her lap, touched the rune-covered cylinder, and detonated the Extreme Luminance Flare.

The warnings on the canister were clear: *User should maintain a minimum safe distance of thirty meters.* Closer than that, the fierce light of the ELF could burn skin and clothes; at short range, it would vaporize almost anything. Yet now, activated, it barely glowed, a shadowy, almost imperceptible flicker from the canister sitting on her armored skirt.

But there were intolerable blazes of light all around them. At the edge of the second circle, the night-black ooze flared white and exploded into noisome steam. On the rooftops above, the distorted creations of the Darkness turned momentarily to miniature suns and exploded, their lethal cargo tumbling down to shatter, useless, on the marble pavement below. Windows sent out momentary beams of harsh luminance, blue-white stars shone out of cracks in earth and building, a column of starfire erupted from three deep wells, and the very depths of Aphrodite's Mirror were lit for one brief instant as though the Sun itself had come to rest in the shadowed depths beneath its rippling surface.

All simultaneous, she thought, even as the others shielded their faces from the surrounding radiance. *Like a teleport of the sort the Wanderer described, bending one point to meet another, crossing boundaries like the transitions through the seal. I found all the points, the area touching on every single portion of the Darkness That Devours... and linked it, through rune, will, and power, to the surface of Ingram's last Extreme Luminance Flare. All the light that could burn things within a sphere two hundred feet in diameter was transferred* directly *from the casing as it ignited to the Darkness.*

The monster had had, literally, no time at all to react. There was no retreat, even if it *had* had warning, because every part of it was set ablaze at the same instant.

However, as the last fragment of the Darkness That Devours vanished, Urelle had to switch her concentration from maintaining a connection that no longer existed... to protecting herself. For without that connection, the incendiary fury of the Extreme Luminance Flare must now be unleashed from where it actually was.

She could not possibly restrain that energy; at best she could *redirect* it. She let herself drop flat onto her back as she did the only thing she could imagine working: making beneath and surrounding it in a curved wall a perfect mystical mirror, *keeping* it perfect, reflecting not just ordinary light but *heat*, what Ingram called "infra-red", for if she did not, the thing would burn through even her enchanted armor and thence through her body.

A column of pure argent touched with aqua blasted up from her, and even the nimbus of reflected light *from* the beam was like the open door of a furnace, prickling her skin with its heat. "Urelle!" Ingram shouted, but though they tried, none of them could come close. And she could not help them, or even reassure them, because her every faculty was focused on maintaining that perfect reflection.

The heat rose, the prickling becoming actively painful, as it would if she'd kept her face close to that furnace's open door, but she could not spare even a thought for the pain. She screwed her eyes shut against the unbearable light and shored the mirror up with will and focus, counting off the unending seconds as the ELF lit up all of Amoni Agapis with its near-silent incendiary fury.

"Perfect" was not, in fact, achievable, she realized, as she felt heat radiating through the skirt. *Once it really starts burning, I won't be able to focus — and then I'll die!*

The others heard that, her thought intense enough to pass through the link even without her meaning to send it.

Urelle! That mirror-shield, is it solid?

She managed to respond. *No! It's... just a field of energy that reflects!*

Good. A sense of confidence along with worry from Ingram. *Then don't move, but keep that field up — no matter what!*

I... okay. But hurry!

On my way.

A few burning seconds passed, and the heat through the skirt was becoming painful; she could not even make out the others' discussion over the link, for all her mind was focused on not letting her last defense drop. But then something slid along her skirt, slid *under* the ELF, and lifted it up.

She opened her eyes, trying to keep the mirror shield active, and saw Ingram raising the *anai-k'ota* slowly over his head, blade and shaft held completely flat and parallel to the ground, the crescent-shaped blade underneath the mirrored parabola that concealed the ELF. "I can't hold that long if you move it away from me!"

"Don't have to. *Quester!*" he shouted as he now held the ELF fully overhead, over six feet in the air.

The Iriistiik lunged forward, his great crystalline sword held flat, swinging in an arc from low to high as Ingram gave the blade the slightest flip upward and dropped flat. There was a *crack* and an instant of intolerable light, scorching body and clothing and hair alike — and then it was daylight for a moment as the Extreme Luminance Flare arced up and away, now a hundred feet and more away, farther, at the peak of its arc, coming down... and falling on the far side of the wall. A blast of brillant steam showed that it had landed in Aphrodite's Mirror.

In a few moments, light and steam faded away. Their eyes slowly adjusted, and there was nothing but the dark and the stars. For a few moments, the adventurers simply lay or stood where they were, in the silence of the city.

In the distance, at last, the song of cricket and nightbird began.

Chapter 27
Approach of Heroes

Raiagamor stood at the top of the Aegeian Path and looked down. Below, wreathed in early-morning fog, was Aegis, soon to be the center of a new empire. Not, of course, that *empire* was his goal. It would be the *result* of his goal, the breaking of the Cycle and the Aegei themselves, and a tool and path to his next goal, perhaps. That sea of fog was like the future — indistinct, but soon to reveal what was to come.

There were just a few last loose ends to be tied off before he could truly declare the reign of Ares and the end of the other gods' power. The question was *when* those loose ends would be dealt with. It had been a while since he had heard anything, and that was disturbing. How long until Berenike's favored party returned to Aegeia? How long before the Camp-Bels could be ended?

Neither question was an 'if'. He had no evidence, but he was nonetheless certain that the Camp-Bel renegade, his Iriistiik friend, and the two Vantage women *would* find their way through the Seal; the King had been certain of it too, and only a fool bet against the King. And that meant, with equal near-certainty, that Berenike would come with them.

He ground his teeth, then enforced tediously-learned discipline onto himself. *Berenike.* Her very existence still bothered him — more than ever, in fact. The more he had thought on it, the more certain he was that it *had* been the would-be Spear of Athena who had been buried. But if that was the case, there were only two possibilities. The first, and most straightforward, was that, somehow, Berenike had been resurrected.

But resurrection of the truly dead — rather than reviving those who were only minutes from their last breath — was a mighty and rare feat indeed. It happened — certainly, on a world with a thousand gods it happened — but perhaps once a year, once every five, perhaps every ten, and that usually required the direct intercession — the *requested* intercession — of the god who held dominion over the soul of the one to be raised. It also required the consent of the soul itself, and most would choose the afterlife rather than the mortal life.

Admittedly, Berenike was exactly the sort of person who *would* choose to return, out of a sense of obligation and honor if nothing else. But there had been none of the Aegei incarnate and active at the time, and had an intercession been prayed for at any of the temples, he would have known. As Aegeia had not been Sealed at the time, it was possible that another of the gods had intervened, with Athena's blessing... but by the *King*, Raiagamor was certain he would have sensed such vast powers moving so near to him.

The alternative, unfortunately, was just as difficult to believe; that someone was *pretending* to be Berenike, for what reason he could not easily imagine. The imposture would have to be extraordinarily accurate to any level of detail, to have fooled both Deimos and the young Camp-Bel, who had known Berenike personally. And the *power* needed for the imposture? If it wasn't a god or god-warrior, it would require a mage of surpassing power, or at least the ability to channel a vast amount of energy for a short time.

He shook his head, still staring at the shining fog-bank. This mystery was impossible to resolve through mere *thinking*. The truth would be known once the current Berenike, whether escaped, revived, or impersonated, returned to Aegeia and could be examined. And that would be — must be — soon.

Unfortunately, by the nature of the Seal and dimension-spanning travel, there was a very wide area in which the Adventurers might appear, far larger than could be easily monitored. Was the silence because they had not yet returned, or because they *had* but had evaded detection?

He had done everything he could here. The defenses of the Aegeian Path were ready now, bound into the two great columns at the beginning of the Path. The Hammer and Anvil of Hephaestus — or, more accurately, formerly of Hephaestus — had reinforced the columns to withstand even battering rams or other ordinary, or even extraordinary, forces. If he activated them, there would be no way to reach him at the top of the Aegeian Path. And once the last of his potential adversaries was dead...

But he was getting ahead of himself. He dug a claw into his thigh, making the pain clear and sharp, to remind himself that anticipation was not an aid to success once it stopped being a motive and drive and became a distraction.

He returned to his own chambers, and once more he brought out the crystals and laid his hands upon them. "What news?" he asked, and drove the same question through the crystals with his will.

Once more there was a delay in response... one that dragged on much longer than mere distraction might easily explain. At last, the face of Artemisia-Athena appeared. "Lord Ares."

"Who else, pray tell? What has happened?"

"We believe your Adventurers have arrived."

A spark of eagerness tempered with caution. "Ah! Excellent." Then he frowned. "Wait. How do you mean, you *believe* they have arrived?"

"The Guardians are certain the Seal was disturbed. *Something* has almost certainly come through. Despite this, none of us have *seen* anyone yet. However..."

He growled. "Do not hesitate!"

"However, something has happened in Amoni Agapis."

It is like trying to drag the mountain, pulling information out of these fools! "What do you *mean*? Stop this obfuscation!"

"It appears..." She took a deep breath. "Sir, it appears that the Darkness has been destroyed."

He blinked incredulously at her for long moments. *Destroyed? That abomination?* It was almost inconceivable. The creature's very *nature* made it almost impossible to kill; it would never come into light if it could avoid light, would never uncover nearly the totality of its substance, and after its one defeat, it had learned even greater caution.

Oh, certainly, *he* could have killed it — the thing had but one soul, after all, no matter how huge it was. But there were not many others outside of the King's people he would have imagined able to kill the Darkness That Devours. "How sure are you?"

"There were great flares of light from the city — literally lit up the entire sky at one point — and it has failed to make its check-in rendezvous, which it could do with the tiniest portion of itself."

Well, *light* was certainly a good indicator of someone fighting that monster, but the Darkness would hardly have exposed itself easily. But failing to make what should be a routine check-in? No, that indicated, difficult though it was to believe, that the Darkness was either destroyed, or so badly injured that it had fled without even bothering to warn its allies. The latter was possible, but amounted to the same thing as far as Raiagamor was concerned. "Then in all likelihood that is where the Adventurers are. Yes?"

"We... believe so, sir."

"Then watch the gates and the river. They'll leave shortly, perhaps once it is full-light, and we would *much* rather they get no farther." He thought a moment. "If I accept that they *did* destroy the Darkness, then there is only one good candidate for the killer. Make sure you are ready to deal with an extremely formidable mage; the girl Urelle Vantage is likely the most dangerous of the group."

The false Athena raised one eyebrow. "The girl? But what of Berenike?"

"Oh, she could have — in fact, almost certainly, did — have *something* to do with it, but like most of the God-Warriors, she is designed to face opponents that can be killed by direct strikes. I cannot, offhand, imagine a way in which she could have used her god-light on *all* of the Darkness, without shattering the city itself in order to spread light throughout all the spaces beneath — and that, you would surely have seen. No, it is a mage we need concern ourselves with."

"Understood, sir. Anything else?"

"Not at the moment. But I want a report *immediately* when anything happens, from now on. Understood?"

"Yes, sir."

Raiagamor stood a while, staring unseeing into the distance. He was strongly tempted to join Athena and the two God-Warriors; then he could confront the little adventuring group and their protector immediately, wipe them out.

But...

Yes, but. What do they know? What is the real meaning of what the Cards told me? The Cards always spoke truly, so regardless of the details in which he had been misled, the core truth remained: at least one of the travelers was the final true obstacle between him and total victory. The problem was that he still knew nothing of the actual *form* of the threat they posed. Would they somehow, through perhaps supernatural force of personality, rally every city to their cause, break his grip of fear and threat? Would they directly attack his forces, break the power he was building? Would they somehow cause the true Athena to manifest?

Or would they somehow have gained knowledge of how to slay *him*?

That last, naturally, was the one that gave him the most pause. On the one hand, he could not see how anyone could have given them that information; of all the beings in the cosmos, there were three, and *only* three, who knew the way in which he might be slain: Raiagamor himself, his Mother, and the King.

But there *were* the gods, and a few other powers, who often could uncover secrets, who might have heard hints, gathered enough clues, and through inspired instinct or shrewd analysis hit upon the truth. And Raiagamor did not wish to expose himself to anyone who knew how he could die; not unless he knew for certain that he could prevent it.

No. I will stay here, and reinforce both my physical and political power. I doubt they can win past my false but truly mighty goddess and two god-warriors. And if they do... well, then I will have more information to apply to the problem.

Decision made, he turned to the doorway. There was much to do, if he were to complete the debasement of a country.

Chapter 28
Deific Ambush

"That was an *awfully* impressive spell you... well, basically *invented*, Urelle," Ingram said, eyes focused on the ISNDAU. "Are you okay? I mean, you've been pushed a *lot* lately."

She peeked over his shoulder and saw that the ISNDAU was displaying images of the city they were passing through, as though it had its own eyes and was showing them what it saw. "I'm constantly amazed by that thing," she murmured. "Okay? Oh, you mean my soul, my spirit? Yes. It was healed a long time ago, and nothing we've met since has quite pushed me as far as that..." she shuddered as she remembered the carnage she had wrought. "... as that one time," she finished. "I'm pretty sure I'm a lot stronger than I was a few months ago."

"Certainly you are," Victoria said. "It is the nature of an Adventurer; we die, or we become stronger."

"And it's not like *I* am the only one who's been pushed. All of us — you, Auntie, Quester — have met and survived things that tested every limit we had." Urelle smiled, but she felt a tired edge to the expression. With an effort, she went on, "I think we're all so much stronger. Maybe enough to take on a God-Warrior or two."

Ingram shook his head, and Quester's buzz-flap was accompanied by the smell of camphor and oil. "Do not go so far," Quester said. "Remember that we have yet to face a God-Warrior without our own, and we have never seen what one of Ares' warriors can do. I am unsure if we could defeat Berenike; I must therefore assume the chance of defeating any God-Warrior is not good."

Ingram glanced at her. "I feel it too, you know."

I thought I was hiding it. "The... well, *tiredness*?"

"We have had Ares-damned few breaks," he said. "Since that day we left your estate, I think we've been traveling with hardly a pause for... must be a year by now? More? Quite a bit more, I think. Kinda lost track going between all those other worlds. It *wears* on you. Quester and I used to take breaks between every major adventure — even if we were still traveling, we'd be looking for something *fun* to do instead of fighting things or chasing something hostile."

"Adventurers become battle-weary, yes," Victoria agreed, "which is one reason that the end of a grand adventure often involves a party; time for rest, relaxation, a loosening of the tensions of constantly fearing for your life, or the lives of your companions. Alas, I cannot think we can spare the time here."

"No," Ingram said. "Even if they have no way of contacting the Darkness, that huge flare of light might as well have been a giant arrow pointing down at us saying *Look here!*. And time's got to be running out for us. At some point, Ares will have gained a strong enough control of the country that he'll have effectively broken the Cycle, especially if he really does have a false Athena. But once this is done... well, I'll have to show you all what real Aegeian hospitality is like."

She grinned at him, and then with only a touch of self-consciousness leaned over and kissed him on the cheek. "It's a deal!"

He smiled back and gave her a quick hug; out of the corner of her eye she saw Aunt Victoria smiling fondly at both of them. *It's... okay?* she sent to her aunt through the link.

He cares for you, and you for him, and both of you have shown yourselves well during these adventures, Victoria's thought-voice replied, warm and affectionate. *What could I possibly object to? If you'd just run off after him because you were infatuated, I would have had strong words for the both of you, but it was more than that, and you showed your judgment to be sound. Yes, you're both young... but one grows up fast on Adventure.*

"Ha!" Ingram's triumphant shout startled her. "Found them!"

They gathered around, seeing a blank marble wall in front of them... but in the display-window of the ISNDAU, strange symbols glowed brilliantly. "What does it say?" Urelle asked; the symbology was like no language she was familiar with.

"The first line summarizes the decoy-and-hide plan," Ingram said slowly, running his finger along the display, zooming in occasionally to look more carefully at a particular symbol. "The second... Oh, excellent! The rest of the Clan's not far away at all!"

"Truly? This is a long way from what you said was the main base near Aegis, Ingram," Quester said.

"I think that was the point. If they were going to abandon..." his voice caught, "abandon the Compound, the assumption would be that anyplace in the area would be too close to the scrutiny of the enemy. Oh, there's going to still be some way to keep an eye on the Aegis region, but the Clan would have moved as far away as practical. I didn't know we had a base this close to Amoni Agapis, though." He tapped the pins at his throat. "Wasn't cleared to until now, I guess."

"So how far is it?"

He squinted at the display, enlarged the last line and looked over it several more times before shutting the device off. "Maybe a day's travel off to the west."

Her spirits rose at the thought of being able to reach a group of allies — skilled and resourceful allies — so nearby. "Then let's get going!"

"We should go, yes," Victoria said, "but let us consider exactly *how*. We assume our enemies have seen the light of our victory; they have not entered the city with an army yet, nor have we seen or sensed any of them. I think we should therefore assume that they will be watching any exits from Amoni Agapis and be ready to ambush us upon our emergence."

Ingram frowned, then chuckled. "Not *that* easy. There are several hidden exits from the city. I don't know all of them — only the rulers did, probably — but I know a couple."

Urelle shook her head, and she couldn't keep her disappointment from showing in her voice. "Ingram, think for just one second. Can you even *imagine* a secret passage that the Darkness That Devours wouldn't have found?"

His gold-brown cheeks flushed dark. "Um... no. I guess not."

"Neither can I. That thing stretched itself throughout the whole city, and it was here for, I guess, a couple of weeks, based on the condition of the food and such."

"An excellent point, Urelle." Victoria leaned on her axe and looked around.

Urelle felt her chest tighten, looking at Aunt Victoria. The older woman looked just a touch older, leaned more heavily on Twin-Edged Fate than usual; her dark skin still had the faintest off-color tone. It dawned on her that Auntie hadn't really looked quite the same since their first horrific encounter with the Darkness. "Auntie," she finally said, "are you... all right?"

"Of course I..." Victoria trailed off, glancing around at the others. She sighed. "Not entirely, child. I have been feeling a bit overtired recently."

Ingram's eyes narrowed. "How do you mean 'overtired'?"

"Oh, more easily out of breath, a bit of cramping in my chest, that sort of thing — perhaps I have a touch of something."

Urelle saw the boy's mouth tighten. "Sit down," Ingram said, in such a sharp tone that Victoria actually *did* sit down in surprise.

What is it, Ingram?

I hope... nothing. But I'm afraid it isn't. The ISNDAU was in his hands once more, and he advanced to point it at Victoria. After a few moments, he shook his head. "Take off the armored coat — it's interfering."

"What are you looking for?" Victoria asked. "I see you are concerned, but I am accustomed to knowing *why* people are worried." Despite her words, Victoria quickly divested herself of the coat — and Urelle thought she *was* breathing more quickly than she should.

"I am checking your heart function," Ingram said. "The ISNDAU will give me a lot of data on how your heart's functioning, if I can tune it right."

Victoria looked suddenly far more grim, and Urelle swallowed. "You think these are symptoms of my heart... failing?" Victoria asked after a moment.

Ingram studied the readings, put the ISNDAU near Victoria's chest, adjusted the controls. "They *could* be. I read up on this kind of thing as part of my studies."

"If it *is*, what can we do?" Urelle asked, trying not to let her voice waver.

"If the damage is recent and minor, a healing draught would fix it," Ingram said, still fiddling with the ISNDAU. "But that's not going to address whatever underlying problem is causing it. On the positive side, with half the Clan just a day off, there will be people there with both the old tech and the magical and medical training to help."

A few tense minutes went by, then Ingram sat back. "Drink a healing draught *now*," he said. "It *is* a heart attack, and it started recently. Didn't kill you, thank Athena and Zeus the Lost himself, but it must have been a near thing."

Victoria obediently drank one of their healing draughts; her underlying color immediately looked better. "Yes, I think you are right," she said slowly. "Thinking back on it, I felt a pain in my chest, and a great deal of weakness, in those first moments when we realized the Darkness was here."

Ingram nodded. "Makes sense. A great shock that caused your heart to have to suddenly *lunge* into action — you were lucky."

"Twice-lucky, young Ingram," Victoria said, rising to her feet and shrugging her armored coat back on. "First not to have died, and second to have had you to recognize the danger. I assume that traveling a full day through the usual jungle would not have been good for me."

"No, it wouldn't; a fair chance of triggering a fatal incident. *Now* you should be back to what you were before — which means you could still have one, but probably not in the next day or three."

"Thank you, Ingram."

"Thank you so much, Ingram," Urelle said. "I knew Auntie looked a little peaked, but I would never have guessed..."

"You're welcome, of course. Let's just get her to the Retreat so she can be tended to right — we can't afford to lose our actually *experienced* member!"

"I can't afford to lose me, either," Victoria replied. "But now we are faced with the same problem: how are we going to leave this city without being followed?"

Urelle saw the most obvious solution. "Over the walls?"

"Can you just take us *through* the walls?" Ingram asked. "The walls are pretty high, and if someone's watching there's a good chance they'll see us silhouetted against the sky when we go over. Go through at ground level, though, far away from any of the known gates or exits? No one will see us."

"I... might?" She thought about it. "It's not *impossible*. The Wanderer's book calls it 'phasing' — passing through material without damaging it or you. But... well, let's go find the right part of the wall. Over or through, we still want to do it to the West, and far from any exits we know of."

"Do *you* know where all the secret exits were?" Victoria asked. "You did, after all, see the entire extent of the Darkness, and I would presume it was observing any possible entrance."

"I wish I could remember the details, Auntie, but I just barely held it all together for a few seconds. I can remember a few probable exits, but the ones I remember were on the north and east sides."

"Ah, well, it was worth a question, anyway."

With Ingram to guide them, it wasn't long before the four of them were standing at the base of the high wall, a hundred yards or so north of the main western gate. Urelle studied the smooth, polished stone of the wall, then laid her hand on it.

Pain lashed up her arm and into her brain, and she staggered back. "Ow! Ow ow ow ow!" She reflexively shook her hand as though trying to get hot oil off it, but the pain just slowly subsided. "Well, that means the answer is *no*. The wall's like those back at Zarathanton — maybe not as strong, but there's a *lot* of warding magic to keep anyone from affecting it in any way. Bet you can't dig through the foundations either. When the city was under siege, there were probably anchored air-shield charms to prevent aerial attack, and I'm sure the outer side's warded to prevent climbing."

Ingram frowned, as did Victoria. "Does that mean that we can't go over the wall either?"

"I think we probably can; the enchantments wouldn't be designed to keep people *in*, just out; after all, you'd want to be able to shoot outward, or even escape or send out sallies, and maybe you'd do that over the walls where people weren't watching — just like we want to. So if we just go out-and-down, they shouldn't give us trouble."

"Can you be *sure*?" Quester asked. "I would not want to have an unpleasant surprise as we tried to go over a sixty-foot wall."

"Analyzing these spells... sure, I *could*, but it'd take hours, probably. There's a *lot* of them and some of them are touched with godspower; I don't think they'd want to make it easy to take them apart."

"Undoubtedly," Victoria agreed. "Then we will try it. Our alternative is to exit through gates we are almost certain are watched."

It took only a few minutes to climb the stairs and reach the top of the wall; the four crouched behind the battlements, peeking cautiously out and down. For about fifty yards out from the walls, the jungle had been mostly cleared, though low brush and scrub remained or had regrown since the last clearing; the road leading out of the western gate was visible, vanishing into the forest. *Not many farms or anything on this side,* Urelle thought.

No, Ingram replied. *That's all along the sides of the lake, so to the east, northeast, and southeast for the most part. This part of the Iron Forest — that's what the jungle around here is called — is left mostly intact, for hunting and other reasons.*

I do not see any people waiting, Victoria's thought-voice said, *but of course that means little; from this angle we cannot see directly in front of the western gate, and they could be well concealed in nearby brush, or using blending or invisibility charms to cloak them from detection.*

A quick open-closed flap of wingcases and an ambivalent scent from Quester. *Then no point in hesitation. I will glide with you to the forest, and Urelle can do the same with her airwing charm and Ingram.*

And both pairs at the same time, to minimize any chance to be seen, Victoria confirmed.

Quester took a strong hold of Victoria, and Urelle did the same with Ingram after casting her airwing spell and feeling herself lighten. *Ready?*

On three. One, two, three!

Quester leapt out from the battlement and spread his wings wide. They could not keep both aloft, of course, but he could manage a reasonable glide to a safe landing. The same was true of her airwing; as she and Ingram jumped off, all his weight dragged slightly at her arms, but far more on the flight enchantment that was meant to support only the caster. Instead of flying level or rising, they were inexorably dropping despite her willing every ounce of lift possible into the spell.

Nonetheless, they made it to the thick edge of the jungle, and in a few moments, more had found a trail and plunged deeper into the less-overgrown area beneath the great trees. *Did we make it?*

No telling yet, Victoria answered. *We were not shot out of the air, which is a good sign, but as our opponents are not amateurs, they would presumably not do us the kindness of alerting us to their presence by shouting "there they are!" or anything of the sort.* Her attention shifted, something that Urelle could sense in the mindlink through a sensation she could not describe. *Ingram, you can lead us to your people, yes?*

I can get us to the right general area. The response was confident. *After that, the patrols will find us. If they don't, I can eventually locate the entryway myself, it might just take a few hours; I know how to tell when I've found it, but it's going to be* very well hidden.

The four moved as quickly as they could, following a dim trail that led almost due west. Ingram led the way, followed by Urelle, Victoria, and then Quester. As they were passing the center of a clearing, Urelle staggered, disoriented and confused; it felt as though someone had struck her head with a weighted pillow and then dumped a thousand pounds of sand on her, yet there was nothing visible — and in fact, nothing had touched her; even her hair felt undisturbed.

But still, something's wrong!

Even as she thought that, even as her stumble alerted the others, three figures flickered into visibility, spaced evenly about the clearing's edge, and Ingram gave a wordless, incredulous, terrified snarl as his gaze flicked from one to the next.

Directly in front of them, arm extended, pointing an imperious finger at them, night-black hair curled in tight ringlets that cascaded down her back and over her shoulders, deep brown eyes amused and cold, was a woman taller even than her sister Kyri, with the same powerful, smooth musculature visible beneath the glittering golden plate-and-mail armor she wore. Her face was severely beautiful, dark olive skin smooth and unblemished on a high-cheekboned face with a faintly hawklike nose lending it a deadly predatory air. The robe-like overgarment on her armor, and the symbol of shield and spear on the chest, left no doubt as to who this was: the false Athena herself.

The other two figures were dressed in stylized armor whose basic design was all too familiar to Urelle, calling up memories of the first time she had seen a true God-Warrior. The first was a man, tall and slender and more startlingly beautiful than Athena; even in the dappled sunlight of the jungle clearing, a faint aura shone from his golden hair and skin, as well as the gold-and-silver armor he wore and the silver-and-emerald chaplet of laurel leaves on his brow. Unlike Athena, who bore no visible weapon, he held a great bow of gold, with a crystalline string, and arrows of diamond and gold-leaf glittered in the quiver on his back.

The third was another woman, of average height, ordinary in appearance other than her well-defined muscles showing long and strenuous training. Her armor was green and brown and touched with gold and silver, and the helm from which flowed her curly brown hair had the form of a wood-carven skull. In both her hands she grasped an immense scythe, and her dark brown eyes showed no expression.

Athena, the Sun of Apollo, and the Scythe of Demeter! Ingram's mind-voice jangled and vibrated with his anger and fear. Despite all their prior encounters, Urelle realized that Ingram could not throw off all his prior life's training so easily; two God-Warriors and an incarnate Goddess — real or not — were intimidating enough for her, Victoria, and Quester; for Ingram, they were invincible legends who were supposed to be on *his* side, not seeking his destruction.

That strange *weight* was still on her, too, but she ignored that for the moment. *What can they do, Ingram? Do you know anything about them?*

His mind steadied a bit, but tension and fear still filled the underlying edges. *They're all powerful warrior types — not like Deimos or Phobos who rely on some of their other powers more than their fighting prowess. Athena... well, whatever's playing her has to be at least powerful enough to pretend to be a god, but I have no idea what she's going to be able to do. The Sun of Apollo loves his arrows, but he can fight close up. He's also able to heal his allies, so we might want to take him out first. The Scythe is the aspect of nature that ends* life, *so in some ways she might be the worst, but I don't know the details.* She sensed a grimace. *We didn't study the God-Warriors as enemies very often, sorry to say.*

"Surrender, Ingram Camp-Bel, Quester of the Iriistiik, and Victoria and Urelle Vantage," Athena said, in a firm and unwavering contralto. "Your opposition to Us ceases in this moment; you may only choose whether it ends in life or death."

Ingram swallowed, but didn't seem able to speak. Quester, however, had no such problems. "We offer you the same choice. You serve a false Ares, all of you. This we know from the words of gods and others. Surrender to us, join *our* cause, and it may not be too late for Ingram's Aegeia."

Urelle knew all Quester was doing was playing for time, giving Ingram a chance to regain his own focus. *Quester, are these...*

Xiilistiin? Almost certainly, I would think. Surrender is not an option.

The three figures laughed. "Well we know it," said the Sun of Apollo, "which is of course *why* you must either die or be captured. What say you? Is it not better to live and see the day, than to be sent down into the darkness only Hades knows?"

Quester and Ingram exchanged glances, and she sensed with relief that the young Camp-Bel was fully back to himself. "Not in the hands of the Xiilistiin," Ingram said, and the two sprinted directly towards the Sun of Apollo.

Sensing that action, Urelle whirled on Athena, fingers stretching out, mind focused to shape the air itself into a shield —

And her mind and fingers and soul caught *nothing*.

She gasped, tried again, even as Victoria — momentarily unaware of her plight — charged the Scythe of Demeter. *Nothing!*

Athena loomed over her, a deadly cold smile on her lips, and a great Spear materialized from nowhere in her long-fingered hand. "Magic, little Vantage? I have forbidden it. Within a hundred paces of me, no magic will function!"

Urelle dove aside barely in time as the Spear drove two feet into the earth where she had been. Athena's Spear was a long, vicious weapon, leaf-shaped tip glittering sharp silver, a crossbar three feet up the shaft to prevent victims — animals or otherwise — from driving themselves all the way to the wielder. Urelle tumbled away, trying to escape, but the false Goddess paced after her, waiting for a pause or failure to shift that would provide an opening.

Ingram tumbled away in her peripheral vision, a single backhanded blow from the Sun casting him aside like a toy, while Quester's every blow was caught by the golden bow and deflected; a single gesture and Quester, too, was thrown down. The bow rose, an arrow was nocked in the moment, and Urelle realized the mocking eyes were looking at *her*...

Agony ripped through her leg and her tumbling was halted instantaneously; a diamond-gold arrow had pierced entirely through her calf and pinned her to the ground. The false Athena smiled, and raised the Spear.

But a slight, lavender-haired missile streaked in from the side and knocked the strike *just* off course, Athena's spear impaling the ground once more. And in the anger and fear filling Ingram's mind, she heard and felt that focused tension, and a cry that he shouted both with mind and body:

"BERENIKE!"

Instantly their three opponents whirled, came on guard, eyes searching the skies, knowing what was to come.

Silence.

Ingram's eyes grew wider, filling with shocked disbelief, as seconds ticked by. No flash of living gold streaked from the sky, no clarion voice announced the arrival of the infinitely confident Spear of Athena. The clearing was as still and silent as the dead city of Amoni Agapis in the grip of the Darkness.

And as the full horror of that inexplicable failure reached them, Athena laughed and turned, and cast her spear straight for Urelle. Frozen at this second impossibility, Urelle found herself unable to move a muscle.

But once more Ingram was there, shoving her aside — and screaming as the deadly silver leaf-blade impaled him entirely through.

Chapter 29
Power of a Queen

Quester fought desperately to find some hesitation, some error of technique, *any* chink in the defenses of the Sun of Apollo, but nothing worked; the God-Warrior brushed his javelins from the air, took the impact of longmace on his vambrace, parried Quester's sword casually with his bow.

What is wrong? Urelle has not cast a single spell yet! And —

"BERENIKE!"

He had felt the spike of desperate determination, knew that Ingram had correctly judged they had not a prayer without the help of his childhood friend, and felt, for an instant, the tiniest sense of relief. With Berenike's shining indomitable power they would surely have a way to prevail.

But Berenike did not come, and a moment later a scream pierced his tympani, his mind, and his soul as Athena's great Spear ripped through Ingram's gut.

Everything froze to Quester's perceptions; all he could think, all he could *feel* was the terrified, shocked, despairing agony from his first and best friend in the human world, the incomprehending fear from Urelle, the furious impotent fury of Victoria, a fury with a painful tightness growing in her chest.

My Nestmate is dying!

Something *snapped* inside him, something that had waited in the depths of the mysteries within, in the heart of all the memories that had been denied or obscured. Quester of the Iriistiik whirled, scarcely conscious of Apollo's attention turning back to him, and *screamed* rage and hatred at the cold-sneering face of Athena.

Athena was blown backwards, crashing into and *through* the mighty trunks of one, two, three forest giants; as she skidded to a halt on her back, the last of the three trees toppled with awful majesty onto her.

Apollo leapt back and fired, his diamond-tipped arrow a streak of sunlight through the air — a streak that stopped an inch from Quester and dropped, useless, to the ground. Even in that moment, Quester felt the memories of the Mothers crowding in and around him... around *her,* and *understood.*

That was why he... now *she*... existed. Why the Gray Warriors existed. A hidden Mother, a Mother in potential, a chance for rebirth when the Nest was threatened, a chance hidden away in isolation, away from the Nest, for once less vulnerable alone than together. *That* was why the Mother had not recalled Quester, why the *memories* of the Mothers had been fogged. That was why Quester had been told that "he" was the proper form of address, despite the inherently female structure of the body. And it was why, in desperation, Quester had found that the thoughts of one *not* yet a Nestmate, Victoria Vantage, were open and readable.

Because Quester had been born to be one of the Queen-Mothers. Because *she* was the last Mother of the Iriistiik.

The second pulse of power exploded from her, a shockwave that drove the Sun of Apollo and the Scythe of Demeter back fifty yards and more, only their superhuman strength keeping them upright. Disbelief and shock were written on both the God-Warriors' faces. "Impossible!" the Scythe of Demeter gasped. "Magic is *banished* from this place!"

The distant fallen tree quivered, and then was shoved aside. The false Athena rose, blood that was not the hue of human trickling down her face, but still she smiled, a feral, savage expression. "Not magic, oh, no," she said, and there was a buzzing tone to her voice now, one Quester knew all too well. "*Psionics*, the powers of the mind. We had *suspected* the Gray Warriors were hidden Queens, needing only the right circumstance to awaken, but now it is certain!"

Quester focused, the still-vague memories enough to guide her, and sent a wave of mind-crushing force at Athena.

The false god winced, but Athena's mind withstood the force, and Quester felt something resisting her newfound power.

"But not a true Queen are you, not yet, perhaps not ever," Athena said. "Not without that which only a Nest could provide, to complete your transformation. Power you have, yes. But long days and weeks and months you will need to fully control it, to learn its ins and outs, the complexities of a power so great and subtle." She smiled, and there were traces of something terribly inhuman in that smile. "While we already know them."

A screaming chorus of hatred drove against Quester's newly-formed mindscreens, and she heard herself buzzing in pain. *I must resist. I must! Ingram is down, Urelle's bereft of her magic and injured, and Victoria cannot defeat one of these by herself!*

Keeping most of her strength focused on protecting her mind, Quester found that she still had some to spare, her mind's capacity for focus and attention expanding far beyond prior limits. She sent a telekinetic spiral of force out, grabbing and tearing at everything Not-Nest in range, and stones and dirt and even entire *trees* raged around and out, tearing at the Sun of Apollo and the Scythe of Demeter, dragging them from their braced stances and then hurling them out and away. With precise force, she also broke the crystal-gold arrow pinning Urelle to the ground, yanked the shaft out, freeing the girl to move.

Quester held no false hope that that assault had finished either God-Warrior, but it gave her a breathing-space, a chance to focus, and she drove everything she could at the false Athena. *If I can but fell* that *one, I think all else will be possible!*

The other two are already getting up, I can hear them! Urelle's mindvoice was panicked. *Ingram's in bad shape!*

I will do what I can, Victoria thought, *but I fear I am no match for any of them.* Beneath those thoughts, Quester could sense the hints of pain, a tightening in the old Adventurer's chest. Stress was not Victoria's ally in this.

I will stop them. Somehow.

But Athena merely defended herself, evading the largest missiles Quester could throw, until the Sun and Scythe joined her. And then all three of them attacked.

The impact of the Xiilistiin-Athena's mental thrust was so great that Quester nearly fainted on the spot. Only sheer willpower and the links to her friends, her Nestmates, kept her conscious enough to throw up a defense as the two God-Warriors slammed into her.

She tumbled backwards, grappling with the God-Warriors, trying to throw them off or damage them. Clawed hands and chitinous legs dueled with armored fists and twisting arms, and somehow, she was free for an instant that let her seize the shaft of the God-Warrior's Scythe, ignoring the burning agony of the weapon rejecting any but its chosen wielder, spun and hurled the Scythe of Demeter and her weapon high into the trees.

A tremor in Quester's new senses sent her diving, crystal-gold arrows hissing through the air she had just occupied. She cast off the Xiilistiin mental attack for an instant, riposted with all the strength her revulsion and desperation could give, and as Athena staggered, Quester turned her anger on the Sun of Apollo; all the

God-Warrior's speed and skill meant nothing when insubstantial telekinetic power grasped his entire body and hammered it once, twice, thrice into a granite boulder, until the boulder crumbled under the assault.

But the Scythe was back, the God-Warrior's weapon cutting through air and tree alike as it spun through the air towards Quester, and Athena's mental assault was redoubled. Quester felt herself *wilt* under the pressure, took a cut across her chest that was scant inches from carving into her vitals.

This is desperate enough! Quester could sense Urelle reaching into the pouch at her waist.

But there's no magic, Urelle, came Ingram's pain-filled thought. *Even that can't help if...*

I think it can. I think I can. If I can just do this right, if I just have enough time...

Quester caught the Scythe's strike on her sword, put psionic power into her parry, forced the God-Warrior of Demeter to stumble directly into the path of the Sun of Apollo. *I will give you the time!*

Dancing a line between risk and death, Quester fought to keep all three adversaries engaged, concentrating only on her, as she saw/heard/felt Urelle gripping the Lens of the Wanderer in her hand.

I'm still alive, Urelle's thoughts came to Quester. *The magic of life — the godspower that lies in us all — can't be turned off.*

A sense of a smile from Victoria. *And a bit* more *of that in us. But how...?*

Trayne Owen — Silvertail Heartseeker — showed me the way.

And with that, even as yet another mind-crushing attack fell upon Quester like an avalanche, Urelle Vantage reached into her own soul, her *self*, and somehow, in a way Quester could not grasp, set it afire. Within the forbiddance of magic, still eldritch power rose within Urelle, flowing through her, into her hand.

And the Lens of the Wanderer ignited in a flame of rainbow light that shamed the sun, the light expanding to match that of the ELF, and then *detonating*, the Lens exploding into dust.

Even their attackers were caught unawares, dazzled by the mystic light that should not have been, blinking desperately to clear their vision, to see what had happened.

To see, along with Quester, a new figure, with a black-and-silver cloak streaming from his shoulders, the Staff of Stars in his hand.

Chapter 30
Wanderer's Wrath

Urelle stared up, spots still drifting before her eyes, but she finally felt a moment of hope, because the Wanderer stood over her. The ice-blue gaze flicked from one to the other, narrowing in concern at Ingram's injury, and then turning to glare at their adversaries, who had paused at the unexpected new arrival, Athena in particular staring in shock at the impossible use of magic within her forbiddance.

"Which of you is the one stupid enough to be attacking *my apprentice?*"

The Sun of Apollo raised his bow. "Who are *you?*"

The Wanderer gave an exaggerated expression of shock. "Oh, now that *hurts.* You don't know who I am? What *do* they teach them in these schools?"

"Wanderer," Urelle whispered urgently, "they've shut off almost all magic here! Be careful!"

Athena caught the first word, at least, and stepped back. "The *Wanderer?*"

"The one and only," he answered. "Thanks for the warning, Urelle."

He jabbed the Staff of Stars into the ground, and a pulse of the same multicolored light blasted outward; Urelle felt that indescribable pressure fade and disappear. Athena's brows lowered. "Hold, now, how?"

"Do you think you're the only one who's ever come up with that trick? Magic-negation is an old idea, and I've got my own ways of dealing with it." The sharp smile she'd learned to expect during her training, whenever he was challenging her. "Not that I'm going to actually explain *how* to you."

The false Athena gave a snarl that had the faint buzzing undertone of the Xiilistiin hidden within. "Oh, you *will* explain how. Alive or dead."

With her reawakened senses, Urelle barely caught a hint of power unleashed — not magical, but the same power Quester had suddenly manifested. The Wanderer winced, but the Staff flared blue-white, and Athena blinked. "You are a mage, not a master of mind!" she snarled.

"True," the Wanderer said, grinning through gritted teeth, eyes narrowed. "But if you know the *right* magic you can play that game just fine — and you have *no* idea how very much of that magic I've got. Right back at you, you Xiilistiin imitation god!"

Athena staggered, white and green light spitting off her like a crackling firework. But the two God-Warriors caught her, and she instantly straightened. "Then let us see how well your legend can withstand a *Swarm*, Wanderer."

Lethal intent made manifest crisscrossed the air between the Wanderer and their three adversaries, invisible to others but ghostly clear to Urelle. She shrank back, then backpedaled away as burning, screaming agony lanced into her brain from the smallest *backwash* of what the Xiilistiin were directing at the Wanderer.

The blond wizard stood rigid, polychromatic light shimmering around him, teeth clenched, every muscle tensed as he pitted his own will and mystic power against the psionic might of a Swarm of the Xiilistiin, channeled through a false god. Between them, the lush grasses and small bushes of the clearing wilted, turning dead-brown in moments.

Ingram cough-gasped in pained shock as the spear through him simply *vanished*, gone back to wherever the false Athena had called it from, unable to be maintained in the face of that mythic assault. Victoria was next to him, trying to compress the wound, and Urelle wanted to join her... but she could not turn her gaze and senses away from that terrible, silent duel.

The Wanderer took one step forward. Athena and her two companions swayed, but then they gave a trilling, inhuman snarl and leaned forward. An invisible shockwave echoed from between the dueling parties, almost knocking Urelle and the others to the ground. The Wanderer wavered, but then planted the Staff of Stars solidly before him and began to mutter something in a language Urelle did not know.

The great gem atop the Staff blazed brighter, and now it was not a shockwave, but winds blasting outward from the combatants, as though the air itself was attempting to flee. The Wanderer raised the Staff, and took another step forward. Then another, and she could see a determined, sharp smile on his face as he took a *third* step, and the faces of his opponents were growing pale.

And then the Wanderer's eyes blinked, distracted, as though he heard a distant call that he could not entirely ignore.

There was no time to warn her teacher — no time for anything except the realization that he was, for some reason, for this moment, vulnerable.

A realization Athena had as well. With a triple shriek of triumph, the three thrust their arms forward.

The deadly mind-attack *ripped* outward, combined with a massive telekinetic blow; the Wanderer *screamed* and flew, convulsing, into a tree, bouncing off of it and tumbling, twitching uncontrollably, to the ground.

"*NO!*" Urelle heard her own cry of disbelieving horror echo around the clearing. *The Wanderer, down? No, it can't be!*

But it *was*, and now the false Athena smiled, recovering already from the strain. The Sun of Apollo also smiled as he stretched his arms in preparation for the final fight, and the Scythe of Demeter drew her weapon back with her own sneer.

Myrionar send you all *to the Hells!* She remembered what she'd done the last time she'd felt this much rage, focused, reached out, *smaller, not so large, just under them...*

The ground detonated beneath two God-Warriors and a false God with enough force to send all three hurtling skyward. Praying that would keep them busy for a few moments, she ran to the fallen wizard. "Wanderer! *Wanderer!* Are you...?"

He wasn't *breathing*. She sagged to the ground, feeling utter despair. The Wanderer had failed. Ingram was down, maybe dying. And now she saw their enemies, rising from where they had fallen, brushing away the dust of the explosion as though it had been the slightest inconvenience.

"He *was* powerful," Athena said. "But now he is dead." A smile, this one *wrong*, the smile of something that may wear a human face but no longer needs to hide itself. "As you all shall soon be, all but one."

Quester intercepted her blast of golden fire with his newfound power — but Urelle saw Quester wilting under the pressure almost as swiftly as the grasses between the false Athena and the Wanderer had. Apollo's Sun was drawing his bow, and the Scythe was now pacing towards Victoria and the wounded Ingram with a swift and unswerving stride.

Then she heard a shuddering, gasping breath, and the Wanderer's eyes snapped open.

For an instant, she recoiled; there was a cold and vicious *rage* in those eyes unlike anything she had ever seen, nothing like the rapier-sharp, warm and humorous man she had known.

But that gaze snapped sideways, towards Athena and her allies, and she heard a faint chuckle. "Fine," the Wanderer breathed. "No more Mr. Nice Guy."

Without warning, he rolled forward and came to his feet, one hand flinging something straight for Athena.

Her power caught the object, a cylindrical thing not terribly different from Ingram's ELF, and shattered it in a blast of smoke and vapor and flying metal fragments before it had covered half the distance, even as Quester's defenses failed and he, too, was hurled far across the clearing. "Do you think I will permit you to strike me with anything?"

"It was worth a try. Do you want a rematch?"

"I think... not." Pure golden godspower roared towards the Wanderer.

The Wanderer vanished, reappearing behind Athena; she barely parried the Staff with her own Spear, newly-materialized in the instant. Her riposte met only air, but the other two had turned to assist, and the Wanderer found himself between all three. A geometric cage of pure light surrounded him just as all three lunged to the attack, and sent their assaults rebounding from it.

But the light had wavered, and Athena knew just as well as did Urelle that against the powers they wielded, ordinary magic simply could not prevail. They struck again, and again, and now the shield around the Wanderer was flickering, weakened. *It will take another hit, maybe two, and then --!*

Athena raised her Spear, then hesitated. Her hand went to her throat, and she coughed.

The Sun of Apollo's handsome face twisted, and he coughed too, then gasped, face twitching, as Demeter's Scythe began to do the same.

The Wanderer lowered his Staff and watched.

"What... did you..."

"That canister was never *meant* to hit you," he said, and his smile was savage. "I *expected* you to blast it. You dispersed it very well indeed. And the timing was just right; the only other who might have been peculiarly vulnerable you happened to knock out of the area of effect."

Athena was on her knees now, face taut, showing something inhuman underneath, straining, coughing. She vomited and began shaking. "W-w-whattt..." she buzzed.

"A somewhat enhanced and tailored version of malathion," he said. "Not that that *means* anything to you. Might to the Camp-Bels, if they ever hear about it. The important point: it's a poison that affects arthropods — even magical ones — very much more than humans. Basically, nerve gas, and as we can see," the Sun began keening in gasping agony, "a very unpleasant way to die. Congratulations, I've been saving that stuff for hundreds of years."

Urelle felt gooseflesh springing out all over her body. This was *cruel*. It wasn't like the Wanderer at all.

As though he'd sensed her thought, he glanced back at her. Then he blinked, shook his head, and raised the Staff. Lightning flashed and thunder roared, and when she could see again, their enemies lay still and smoking beneath the sky.

"Sorry you saw that," he said to Urelle. "But... they nearly destroyed my *mind*, almost turned me to a vegetable or a puppet. Of all the fears I have... *that* is the worst. By far. I was not quite rational for a few minutes." The warm smile was back. "Seeing you... that reminded me of myself. Thank you."

She breathed a sigh of relief. "I'm glad." She looked over. "Can you help Ingram?"

"Of course." He knelt by the injured Camp-Bel, whose face was going grey; Ingram was half-conscious. "Oh, not good. Gut wounds are very bad." He pursed his lips. "I can't do that trick I did to save Victoria now, either; I was in the middle of something that I *have* to get back to, very shortly, and I can't be so drained." The Staff flickered, and she could see the Wanderer gazing at Ingram for a long moment; then he nodded. "I can do a sort of patch job, get him on his feet, but you will have to get him real healing soon."

"A powerful healing draught won't do it?" Quester asked. "They heal so many things, and this isn't like Victoria, who has a long-standing issue."

"Well it's — wait, what is this about Victoria?"

"It appears," Victoria answered, as she knelt by Urelle, "that my heart is not in the best of shape." She rummaged in her pack, and Urelle gratefully accepted a small healing draught for her leg.

The Wanderer winced. "Seen that all too often. Anyway, in this case, Quester, the problem is that while a powerful healing drink or spell could fix all the *damage*, what it won't do is clean out the abdominal cavity — and you *do not* want half-digested food and literal crap inside that. Infection will absolutely invariably follow. That's going to need either surgery or high-class healing magic from an active practitioner."

"Ingram believed the Camp-Bels had the technology to treat Aunt Vicky," Urelle said. "Does that mean they could help Ingram?"

The Wanderer raised one eyebrow. "From what I know of the Camp-Bels, yes, but they're several hundred miles away in Aegis. My quick fix will not last nearly long enough for you to travel *that* distance."

"Ah, so you are not entirely up to date," Victoria said. "The Camp-Bels did not go into hiding anywhere near Aegis; they are, according to Ingram, only a day's walk or less from here."

The Wanderer's expression lightened. "Well, now, that's a horse of a different color." Once more, Urelle heard a faint shift of accent and emphasis that indicated he was making one of those obscure personal jokes. "Let's get Ingram to swallow this; it's a powerful restorative made by a friend of mine."

With a little resistance from the half-conscious and confused Ingram, Urelle managed to get the lavender-haired boy to swallow the faintly-glowing liquid.

Bright white light, with a faint chiming of associated music, danced around Ingram's injury, literally singing it closed. The gray tone faded, replaced by Ingram's more usual gold-olive wood tone, and the violet eyes snapped open. "Ugh... *Wanderer?*"

"Yes. Things were pretty dicey there for a while, but you'll be okay if you can reach your people. Tell them you had a wound that penetrated the intestine and that you need to have prophylactic irrigation and cleansing of the peritoneal cavity to prevent peritonitis."

Ingram nodded. "I will." Then his expression darkened. "Berenike... she never appeared?"

"No," Quester answered. "Perhaps something about that magic-dampening field interfered."

"I... guess? Last time we saw her she was in one of those other universes, so the combination might..." Ingram gave his body a shake, as though to dismiss the issue, but Urelle could feel that he was still very worried.

"I think I've done what I could here," the Wanderer said. "So —"

"Before you go, sir," Urelle interrupted, "can I ask... what happened? Something distracted you in that fight, and almost got you killed."

A wry smile curved his lips. "Turns out *two* groups really needed my help at the same time. The other? Your sister and her friends."

Victoria straightened, and Urelle grabbed the Wanderer's hands. "Kyri? *Friends?* Needed your help? What *happened?*"

"Hold on, hold on," he said, laughing. "I can't give you details of what was going on there — just got a vague impression. I know *how*, and I *did* meet her friends earlier. She's traveling with a Prince of Skysand, named Tobimar Silverun, and a really pretty adorable little Toad named Poplock Duckweed. Poplock's the real brains of the operation, though — not that your sis or Tobimar are stupid, but when you measure about six inches long you learn to use brains over brawn a *lot*. Anyhoo, I gave Poplock a crystal I mined years ago, and he used it in a *really* clever way; someone taught him Gemcalling, I guess, because I felt the call to my spirit all the way here."

"Where... I mean, do you know *anything* about what happened after she left?"

"I know the outlines. I really have to go quick, but to summarize, your sister was right, she found the Spiritsmith and got her armor — the armor of the Phoenix, as that's her name now — and she, Poplock, Tobimar, and a kid from my own homeworld faced down and defeated Thornfalcon, who was the rottenest apple in the Justiciar's barrel — except for whatever is their secret boss, the one that let them hide from Myrionar. They had some clues on that, and went to Moonshade Hollow to follow them."

"Great *Balance*," Victoria whispered. "Moonshade Hollow? No one has ever returned from that place."

"Well, judging by the timing, they've survived quite a time there and were facing down something really badass. Might be they've finished her quest, but I can't tell." He stepped back. "If I had more time, I'd tell you more, but I *really* have to be going." He bowed. "You used my Lens well, Urelle. Now... you will be on your own. But," he grinned, "if you could figure out how to summon me from *inside* a dead-magic zone? You'll do *just* fine."

He vanished in a flare of light.

Ingram stood, looking superficially himself, though Urelle could still sense controlled turmoil within. He looked at Quester. "What *happened* to you, Quester?"

The Iriistiik looked uncomfortable... and also a bit different. There were faint touches of gold on parts of his — *no*, Urelle corrected herself, remembering the dialogue during the battle, *her* exoskeleton. "I discovered... I, myself, am a Mother."

Ingram blinked. "Oh." A pause. "*Oh*, that makes so much sense."

"Out of many things, yes. There are two ways to make a new Mother, it appears, and the Grey Warriors are a survival-oriented method." Quester's tone was amazed. "Hide a potential new Mother from others, send 'him' away in a very non-Mother guise, until they can find even a few new Iriistiik to bond with. Then they can work as a nascent Nest, eventually make Mother's Meal so that the Grey Warrior will become a full Mother, and a Nest is now fully reborn."

"It also helps explain the Coin's confusion," Urelle said. "Whatever they were looking for, *you* must have also been a close match."

"Indeed," Victoria said. "And that was what the false Athena meant about you needing something only a Nest could provide."

"Yes." A bittersweet wave of cinnamon and burning. "I have some of the powers of the Mother, but I cannot truly become one without a Nest and the Mother's Meal." A deep breath that expanded her thorax and abdomen. "But it is still a blessing. I have more of the Mother's knowledge, and powers I did not have. We will all be stronger for this."

"We will," Ingram said, and gripped his friend's clawed hand.

"Now," Urelle looked to the west, "let's go. You and Auntie need to get to the Camp-Bels — and so do we."

Ingram nodded emphatically. "This way."

They entered the jungle, and the last Urelle saw of the false Athena was a final wisp of smoke.

Chapter 31
The Camp-Bels' Refuge

"We must be getting close," Ingram said, squinting into the slowly-darkening jungle. Realizing he really couldn't see that well now, he pulled out his nightviewer goggles and put them on. An enhanced view of the jungle appeared, low-light imagery with infrared superimposed. He could see scuttling little bright dots where the smaller denizens of the forest were moving in the underbrush; just at the edge of detectability, a vast glowing shimmer moved away — a grazing beast, Ingram hoped, although it could be one of the larger predators like a *halkyor*.

"Then we must watch carefully for a sign of presence," Quester said. "How do you feel?"

Ingram shrugged. "Maybe a little cramped? Problem is that a lot of the early symptoms of the infection are ones I can convince myself I'm feeling. If it has started, it's not bad yet. Victoria?"

"I admit I felt not entirely well at the worst part of our prior battle," Victoria conceded, "but I have not felt notably unwell since."

We still need to find my people soon, Ingram thought to Quester. *Next time her heart has trouble, it could just take her right out.*

I believe we are all in agreement, Quester thought. A sense of hesitation, then, *Are you... unbothered by my change?*

If it hadn't been for the nervous seriousness beneath the question, Ingram would have laughed. Instead, he replied with equal gravity, *Not bothered a bit. You're still* you, *aren't you? We always knew there was more to who you were, and this makes sense of it all. We're still friends, all of us, right? Then that's all there is to it.* There was no way, Ingram thought to himself, that someone like him — denied most real friendships for years because of some secret plan — would *ever* betray a friendship on his own.

Thank you, Ingram. It was perhaps a foolish question, but I needed to ask it. Her thoughtvoice hadn't changed at all to Ingram's perceptions, except maybe to have become even more clear and precise.

You put up with learning I had run away from my people and stole stuff on the way; this is nothing. I mean, it's something, for sure, but it doesn't change us.

A psychic laugh. *No. No, it does not.* The mental impression of an antennae-touch combined with a human hug. *Thank you again, though.*

You're welcome.

The problem, Ingram decided, wasn't that his Clan didn't leave good directions, but that *following* directions in a huge jungle at night was really tough — even with aids like his goggles or the spells Urelle had just put on herself and Victoria to let them see more clearly. One mighty forest giant looked pretty much like another, and the Clan had to be understandably cautious about putting obvious signs on the route. The ISNDAU could make out certain invisible markings, but you had to get close enough to do so. And if you deviated too far from the course, well, you'd never get close enough.

They could have left the specific coordinates, but it wouldn't do any good to anyone who didn't have an ISNDAU. And since there's only a few of them (one of which I stole) most people wouldn't be helped that way; they could find the markings with goggles, spells, or other tricks, but only an ISNDAU would really track the coordinates well.

"It's getting late," Victoria said. "Perhaps we should stop and resume the search when it is light?"

"We *could*," Ingram conceded, "but if I *do* have an infection starting, it could get very bad, very fast. We won't have a chance of finding anything if I end up collapsing."

"Hm. True enough. Perhaps we —"

A whipcrack of sound, both rare and familiar, echoed through the jungle, and dirt and leaves fountained from a spot ten feet in front of them; Ingram froze, as did the others, looking around for the source of the sound.

"Freeze! Identify yourselves!" came a sharp, high voice from somewhere in the trees.

With the hint of sound, Ingram could just make out a diffuse glow ahead and to the left; he transmitted that through the link. "Ingram Camp-Bel and party," he shouted back.

A pause, then, "*Ingram?* Thank the Founder, if that's true. Advance so we can see you clearly."

Ingram led his friends about twenty feet into a less-brush-filled area; a brilliant light suddenly played upon them from above. "By the Lady, I think it is. Please stay still a few more minutes."

A man's figure, wearing full-coverage camouflage, showing the almost-faceted shape of combat armor underneath, emerged from the jungle. A *hedri'at* was slung over his shoulder, and he had a shortsword on one hip and a combat knife on the other. "If you are truly Ingram Camp-Bel, prove it."

Ingram reached — very slowly and deliberately, so as to not provoke an unfortunate response — into his pack, and withdrew the same case he had received all that time ago, at the Vantage estate. "Then see here, the Captain's Insignia. Called, I return. And here," he indicated his collar, "the insignia of the Crew and of Rank, given me by those who left as both distraction and emissaries."

The newcomer drew out a wand, somewhat similar in appearance to those used to verify Guild Patches, and passed it across the Insignia; the wand's transparent shaft turned a pure green. "Verified!" The camouflage mask was yanked off, showing a grinning face as seamed as black driftwood, topped with short, tightly-curled, grizzled hair. "By the Founder, *welcome*, Ingram!"

"Sergeant-Armory Valery!" Ingram was startled. "You're *here*?"

"And where else would I be, with that foul impostor having driven every virtuous soul from the Cities? Nothing for us to protect now, Ingram, not until you returned."

"*Me?* I know there's something important about me, but —"

"Words of the Captain himself, that if things got to this point, we had to await your return. Don't ask *me* why, I don't have the answers, but it's good to see you now — maybe now I *will* find out why the one they called a failure is the one we had to wait for!" The Sergeant waved his hand in a quick pattern. "They're clear, we're going in!"

"Lady's Wisdom," came the voice from the trees, descending quickly, "you mean we'll finally get the mysteries answered?"

"Looks like," the Sergeant agreed, as the speaker came up to him, pulling off her own mask and revealing a woman about halfway between Victoria's and Urelle's age, but with red-orange hair that contrasted with polished obsidian skin. "Ingram, you know Guardian Chelle, yes?"

He kept from grimacing. "We've... met."

Chelle bit her lip. "It appears...," she said, with an air of embarrassed reluctance, "... I have long-overdue apologies to make. But let's do that inside, if we can."

"Sure," agreed Ingram. "This is Quester, who's been my friend and companion since only a few months after I left, and Victoria and Urelle Vantage."

"Welcome," Sergeant Valery said. "We can use all the allies we can get, right now. Follow me."

Ingram noted that despite the acceptance of his symbol, Chelle followed behind at alert, and he could see two other forms shadowing them, one at each side. "Problems with infiltration?" he guessed.

"And bad. We lost a lot of good people, and it would've been more if the Mirror of Aphrodite hadn't been with us. Still not sure we've rooted them all out — at least one seemed normal to the Mirror, but was betrayed by its attempt to aid its allies in the combat."

Xiilistiin? Ingram thought.

Almost certainly, Quester agreed. *But the thought that they could hide from a God-Warrior's sight is disturbing. Especially the Mirror. One of her powers is seeing truth, just as a Mirror reflects what is truly before it. I'm worried now.* He swallowed, then asked the question that he hadn't dared before. "My parents... are they...?"

"Neither of them hurt, son. Rastus and Ianthe are both fine, and I have no doubt eager to see you. They were *terribly* worried when you left, you know."

I guess I do, now. "I'm sorry for that."

"Tell it to them — which will be shortly. Ahh, here we go!"

The low hillside before them looked like any other — overgrown with brush and gnarled tree-roots around slowly crumbling mossy boulders. But when the Sergeant presented his fist (and a particular ring thereon) to one boulder, it rolled aside, moss, brush, roots and all — to reveal a lighted, metal-walled tunnel going straight into the hillside. Once their party passed inside, the boulder rolled back — revealing that on its rear side it was covered with what Ingram was pretty sure was battle-plating from one of the original landing shuttles of *Rhyme and Reason*.

A short distance down the corridor, they reached another sealed door with, Ingram recognized, an intercom next to it, along with another ID sensor. "Sergeant

Valery reporting in," the Sergeant said to the intercom, "with the best news. Our runaway's come home, and brought friends with him!"

"What? By the Ship and the Founder, that's wonderful!" came another voice that Ingram vaguely remembered from his childhood. "I'll let everyone know! This is something for an immediate Council!"

"That it is. We'll head right along to the conference room, then."

"Yes, Sergeant!"

As he led them inside the second door, and into a broad corridor with well-spaced ceiling lighting, Ingram mustered up his courage to speak. "Sergeant, you should be aware that two of us are in pretty urgent need of medical help."

The Sergeant paused, looked around. "What's this? You all look healthy enough, Ingram."

"I took a gut wound that's been sort of healed, but I'm not cleaned up inside. Victoria has a heart condition that needs to be looked at."

The grizzled head nodded. "Ah, understood. Well, neither of those are killers in the next few minutes, eh? So we should at least get the first meeting out of the way. Obviously, tell us if things get bad for either of you."

"All right."

Truth be told, Ingram had no intention of putting off *this* meeting. He'd been traveling for more than a year with this ahead of him, the chance to finally see his parents and demand the answers they owed — why he had been raised to think he was a failure, trained at the same time alongside Berenike, the Candidate for God-Warrior, kept secret and obscure.

He calmed himself through wonder, just studying the smooth, metal-walled corridor, so different from that of any structures he had seen from Aegeia to Zarathanton, a deliberate and direct echo of the halls of *Rhyme and Reason*.

Are you ready, Ingram? Urelle asked.

Yes. I mean... I'm nervous, I'm worried, I'm tense, but I'm excited and I'm sure. This is it. This is when we'll all have the answers, and maybe we'll know how to defeat the false Ares after this!

Well, Victoria responded, *I am sure it will at least clarify many things and help start a strategy in that direction.*

A larger door to the side opened, and the Sergeant led them in.

There were already quite a few people gathered there, with more coming in by one of three doors every minute. "How many of the Clan are there left here?" Ingram asked.

"More than you might think, Ingram," the Sergeant answered. "Even after the one fight, there's two hundred seventy-nine of us here. More than we generally gather in one place ever... but these are unusual times." He looked concerned. "The refugees, the ones who left us, how many are left?"

He couldn't hold that intense gaze, and let his eyes look away. "Not... many. The Captain and the Lieutenant fell. So did a lot of the others, both during the sea battle and then after. But they're trying to rebuild in Zarathanton."

"Ah. A tale, there, but we will talk of it later," the Sergeant said after a moment.

The far door opened, and two people entered, followed by a stream of others. But those others did not matter, because the two were a tall, spare man with straight black hair, a severe, narrow face now lit up with unexpected relief, and a shorter, slightly plump woman with wavy brown hair and a cheerful face that was shining with relief and joy; Rastus and Ianthe.

His parents.

A surge of guilt, relief, and heartbreaking longing exploded through him and he began to run forward. "Mother! Father!"

The two also ran forward. "Ingram! Oh, thank the Founder —"

Without so much as a pause or a change in expression, smiling Sergeant Valery lunged from behind Ingram and impaled Rastus Camp-Bel entirely through his chest with his shortsword. At the same time, one of the women behind Ianthe whipped out a *hedri'at* and sprayed edged death in an arc that crossed straight through Ianthe's back; his mother's blood exploded out, splashing Ingram's chest and face with warm, salty horror.

The room erupted in chaos; his three friends bulled forward, surrounding him in an unbreakable guard as he scrambled to his mother, screaming and crying. Rastus' eyes had already gone blank — the false Sergeant's strike had pierced his heart — but Ianthe's were still open, fixed with unwavering intensity on Ingram's.

There were shouts and screams all around, and Ingram vaguely recognized wavering screeches of Xiilistiin unmasked. He reached his mother, tears streaming down his face, even as a blaze of pure white light announced the arrival of the Mirror of Aphrodite, and felt Ianthe's hand grasp his with convulsive tightness.

His other hand was already in his neverfull pack, and he grasped the bottle he was seeking. "Here, drink, drink!"

His mother snatched the healing draught from him and drained it in three swallows. Color returned to her face, the dreadful wounds closing, the blood flow ceasing.

And then the wounds burst open again, and Ianthe gasped in agonized shock.

What? Ingram stared, mind frozen for an instant. *She was* healing*!*

Then his brain caught up with the situation. *Founder and Athena, no — a curse on the* hedri'at *discs, or a magical poison, something that prevents ordinary healing from working!* He caught Ianthe as she sagged back to the ground. "Mother! Oh, Founder, *no*, Mother, Mother, I..."

"Hush, Ingram!" Her voice was harsh with agony, and she was already pale. "I have no time." He saw her eyes shift, dancing around, and realized with a crushing pain in his heart that she *dared not* tell him the secrets — not when any of those who seemed allies might be enemies, spies controlling their actions to catch a hint of secrets long denied them.

Quester! Quester, can you link with my mother, please? *She... she has what we need to know —*

Quester's horrified regret was tinged with unjustified shame. *No, I cannot, now — I must concentrate to link to one I have never met, and —* Quester parried two strikes at her head *— I cannot pause now, or we all may die!*

Oh, by the absent Father and the Lady, no, no... Somehow, he regained control of his voice. "I need to know... oh, *Lady's Wisdom*, Mommy," his voice broke, "I'm sorry, I need to tell you how, tell you why —"

"I know, we know. We were *so* sorry, Ingram." Ianthe's jaw tightened. "And we are *so very, very proud* of you, Ingram, do you know that?"

The words pierced him like icy, joyful, terrible swords, and all he could answer was with a sob and a nod.

"Then listen, and... somehow, understand." Her gaze caught and held his again. "The statistics, Ingram. The analysis." She coughed, a spray of red, and her breath rattled. "The killer, the day you were rescued. Find that data. Read it. *Understand* it. I wish..." another cough, "I wish I could tell you more..."

"I know, I know." He glanced around himself, seeing half-transformed Xiilistiin and Camp-Bels and even the Mirror still in battle, smashing through the walls, causing the base itself to quiver, and realizing that the only faces he *knew* he could trust were the three guarding him, and the Mirror of Aphrodite. "I know." *The data. Where can I find it?* But even that question would be too dangerous. His mother was trusting him to find a way. She had told him all she dared, and she would be gone, gone in seconds, seconds after he had finally found her.

He wrapped his arms around her. "I... I love you. I'm sorry I ran away."

"Don't... be," she said, gasping. "We both love you, Ingram, and... *Lady*, it hurts... and I think your running away... saved your life." Her arm reached up and hugged him tight. "Now... who are your friends?"

He was almost blind with tears, the shapes around him wavering as through moving glass, but he pointed. "Quester, she's an Iriistiik, she's been my best friend... Urelle, she's an awesome wizard, and I think I love her, and that's her aunt Victoria," as the wobbling shadow that was Victoria swung Twin-Edged Fate to strike down a lunging form, "who's just incredible..."

"I... see that," Mother whispered. "and this..." she touched the patch on his shoulder.

"I'm Zarathanton Guilded, Mother. We've had so many adventures — we met the *Wanderer*, Mother, would you believe," his throat was tight and he forced the words out cheerfully, through sobs.

The fight subsided around him, the room going quiet, until the only sounds were faint moans of pain and breathing, and his own voice continuing, "... and then we left Thologondoreave — they threw such a party for us, I think just because we gave them an excuse..."

In his arms, his mother lay still, without breathing, without pulse; but despite the blood pooling about her and Ingram, there was a smile along with the drying tears on her face.

Chapter 32
Acceptable Losses

"These rules are for your *protection*," Raiagamor said, looking gravely at the gathered citizens of Aegis through the mask of Ares. "I understand that curfews and such disrupt some of your daily business, and certainly we will make exceptions for those who can show their work after the curfews is essential, but we have to be able to work efficiently against the seditious forces that seek to undo the unification we have accomplished."

"I've heard — pardon my boldness, Lord Ares — that we *wiped out* Amoni Agapis!" That was Leonidas Koukouva, the Kyverni of Aegis. Raiagamor was mildly impressed; he'd adjuged Leonidas as easily led, venal and possibly a coward, given the known corruption in his regime and several quite questionable activities that Raiagamor could trace directly to him. It seemed that the Kyverni was at least *somewhat* a ruler after all.

He put on a pained expression. "Where did you hear that?" It was actually a rather important question — as it had been only a short time since the Darkness had consumed everyone in the city, the fact that the event was known in even vague outline indicated very quick lines of communication. But for these purposes, it wasn't so vital — he would discover the truth later. "Never mind. I can guess. Kyverni — Leonidas, I assure you, *we* — the forces under my command — most certainly did *not* 'wipe out' Amoni Agapis. We may have been *fighting* them, as we have the others, but I assure you, I had no reason whatsoever to wipe out the entirety of the city."

And that much of course was nothing but truth; he was *still* mildly peeved that his subordinates had allowed the Darkness to slip its leash so badly, but in the end, it had paid its own price for *that* little venture. Tonight, he would see if his allies had managed to pick up the trail of the adventurers from outside. For now, he had other things on his mind. "Our initial intelligence, to the contrary, indicates it was the *insurgents* who did this." Truth and falsehood would be the best course. "They had a... creature, a terrible being unlike any I have ever seen before or since, a thing of living darkness. They unleashed this upon Amoni Agapis, and..." he bowed his head.

Leonidas looked pale under his bronzed skin. "Truly? What of this thing? How can we defend ourselves from it?"

"When I heard of it, the Lady Athena and I agreed it must be stopped, and she met it in the empty streets of Amoni Agapis; in a battle that truly must be made an epic to be repeated, she dueled it for seven hours, and in the end destroyed it." He nodded at the applause, then held up his hand. "Save your plaudits for the Lady. That, of course, does not assure us our enemies do not have other terrible weapons, and for that reason we *must* maintain controlled order. We must be able to move swiftly and to distinguish legitimate business from that of our adversaries. Do you understand, Kyverni?"

Leonidas pursed his lips, then nodded reluctantly. "Yes, Lord Ares. We understand." There was an assenting murmur through the crowd.

"Excellent. I sincerely hope we will be able to relax these rules and return to normal; with the Lady Athena's victory over their secret weapon, that time may be quite soon, once we are assured that there is no longer any significant organized remnant of the insurgent forces."

With a few more exchanges of meaningless assurances and platitudes, Raiagamor managed to extricate himself from the crowd.

This has been a day to test my patience indeed, he thought. The loss of the Darkness was somewhat two-sided — at least he didn't need to worry about that uncontrolled monster's caprices anymore — but knowing the party that contained his potential nemesis was here and uncontained was a different matter.

He was now reaching near-certainty that it was the young wizard, Urelle, who was his final obstacle. How that was, he did not yet understand — powerful or no, magic should be little hindrance to him. But she fit very well all of the known characteristics, from the indications of the coin to being well-trained yet unaware of her full power. The others... well, *Victoria* Vantage was also a possibility, if the gods-blood in her was a hidden power she could learn to activate.

Still... that, also, did not explain the *how* of the threat. He had already *eaten* one god, and could eat any number of others foolish enough to present themselves to his claws and Hunger. Even if Urelle Vantage were to combine magic and godspower, it would be little more effective. They had no way of knowing his one true weakness (at least, the one weakness that mortals or even most immortals could exploit), and without that, the most they could do would be to try and disrupt his control of Aegeia.

And *that* seemed also very doubtful. There were only four of them, and five cities — six, if one counted the now-empty Amoni Agapis — separated by hundreds of miles. Each of the cities, again aside from Amoni Agapis, was held by troops loyal to him and guided by Xiilistiin impostors — and visited frequently by one or the other of the God-Warriors under his control.

He shrugged, dismissing the concerns. Allowing himself to brood on those problems was one of the things that could build into the uncontrolled rage, and control was *the* paramount characteristic he needed, especially now. He had deliberately sealed off his aura and mind during this day to prevent any distractions as he toured Aegis, set up the various measures that, under the guise of added security, would lead to resentment and restiveness. He could not risk any uncharacteristic behaviors to lead to any doubt that he *was*, in fact, Ares. That was essential

Eventually — and not too long from now — the cities would come to resent the gods. And once those of Aegeia *rejected* the gods, oh, *then* the Cycle would end, indeed. And wearing a new face — whoever became the natural leader of the rebellion — Raiagamor would turn the former bastion of self-contained wisdom into the next scourge of the world.

In the darkness of full night, he finally made his way up the stairs of the Aegeian Path, shedding the lesser guardians along the way. Only when he approached the main Temple and his chambers did he relax and allow his senses to expand outward.

And instantly, insistent thoughts beat in on him. *Lord Ares! Lord Ares, ANSWER!*

That was Deimos' mindvoice — and one filled with angry desperation. Raiaga took a very firm grip on himself before answering; clearly *something* had gone badly wrong. He entered his chambers and touched the crystals. "What is it?"

"Where have you *been*?" Deimos demanded.

He allowed a flicker of incandescent rage to strike out over the distant connection; Deimos flinched. "Do *not* speak to me in that fashion. Ever. I was conducting careful arrangements in the city, ones I could not risk being interrupted at. Now tell me, what happens?"

"*Everything*. It is a disaster." Deimos shook visibly with anger and frustration before he managed to get his demonic-Xiilistiin nature under control. "First, Athena, the Sun, and the Scythe reported they had discovered the intruders. Neither of the God-Warriors has since made contact, and the Swarm has sensed the ending of Athena."

By my King's claws. "They are all three dead? With no hint as to the cause of their demise?"

Deimos' smile was bitter. "Oh, there is a hint, *Lord Ares*," he hissed. "See here, the image granted to the Swarm when they were asked for its full power to be directed to Athena."

Into his mind came the first direct picture he had seen of his adversaries: the tiny lavender-haired Ingram, the towering Iriistiik Quester, the tall, aged figure of Victoria Vantage, and the smaller, delicate shape of Urelle Vantage.

But in the center, standing over Urelle and between the others and Athena, was a tall, blond, startlingly pale-skinned man wearing a black-and-silver cape and strange, alien armor, and holding a seven-foot Staff capped by a brilliantly blazing crystal.

A chill swept through Raiagamor, defying even the native arrogance of his species and that which he had cultivated for centuries out of mind. "The *Wanderer*?"

"So it would seem. Though he also appears to have departed shortly thereafter."

"The *Wanderer*," he repeated. "By my Ancestor, what is the relationship between him and my adversaries?"

"He referred to the girl as his apprentice."

That was the last piece to the puzzle. *Oh, yes, my enemy* is *Urelle Vantage. The apprentice of the Wanderer, the mage for whom destinies have no hold, for whom the laws bend and prophecy breaks. If she has learned* his *secrets, then cautious, indeed, I must be.*

He knew that even the King regarded the Wanderer with some wariness; not *fear*, of course, but definite caution. Raiagamor, then, would have to be doubly cautious. "Go on."

"The four arrived at the Camp-Bel's hidden fortress this evening. Per the instructions, most of our remaining hidden forces struck to silence Ingram Camp-Bel's parents. It is *believed* this was successful, but our only remaining spy could not be absolutely certain. It is possible that, despite mortal wounds, they managed to convey some vital piece of intelligence to Ingram."

"And the remaining spy?" he asked, weighing possible actions.

"Was discovered as he reported. His report was not completed. We assume he is dead."

Now the rage was leaking out despite his control. "Do you," he snarled, "have any *useful* information to give me?"

Deimos looked satisfied, perhaps because he at last saw the same frustration on Raiaga's face as he had felt. "Our spy *did* report that Ingram Camp-Bel and Victoria Vantage had some injuries or illnesses that may take time to treat. They are not likely to move swiftly for a while."

"Very well. Then here is my command. You, Deimos, will take control of our forces near Amoni Agapis, replacing Athena, and lead them to the Camp-Bel refuge. I want it surrounded, seiged, and broken. Bring me the four Adventurers — alive or dead. If your Swarm still has a use for the Iriistiik, well and good — as long as capturing him does not impede your capture or destruction of the other three!"

Deimos bowed. "As you command." The vision went blank.

Raiaga managed to maintain control until he reached the room he had set aside for his rages.

But afterward, as his shaking body recovered from the devastation of emotion, he felt calmer, more at peace. It would take, perhaps, two days for Deimos to reach Amoni Agapis, and a day to coordinate the assault. If Ingram Camp-Bel was nearly so ill as indicated, that would be too short a time for them to recover and flee.

He had lost much — and the loss of Athena would be the hardest loss to cover — but in the end, his enemies would lose all.

Chapter 33
Necessities of the Clan

What can I do for him? Urelle sat slumped in a chair, feeling as though her head were stuffed with drug-soaked cotton. It wasn't just the physical exhaustion, or the injuries recently treated, or her suppressed terror at knowing Aunt Victoria was now in the Camp-Bel "operating room".

No, it was seeing the devastated, blank expression on Ingram's face after the battle, feeling the black ache of anger and guilt and tearing loss radiating from the boy, and knowing there were no words, not now, to help him. *I lost my family too... but neither Auntie nor I had our parents die in* front *of us.*

Kyri might know the loss Ingram had suffered; she had been *there*, had seen Rion struck down, had held his hand as he passed. But Kyri wasn't here.

Urelle looked down at the bed in front of her. Ingram's face, paler than usual, should be relaxed, sleeping in the recovery from whatever drugs or devices had been used to keep him asleep through the surgery the Camp-Bels had performed to cleanse his insides and save his life. But it wasn't; even in unconsciousness there was a tension, the hint of a wrinkle between the brows, a downturn of the lips, that showed that he knew something terrible awaited his awakening.

Across from her, Quester sat, squatting so her abdomen formed a tripod with her legs. Urelle had learned that this was a normal way for Iriistiik to sleep, but it still looked uncomfortable. Either way, Quester was finally sleeping, next to her best friend's bedside.

When they let Auntie out, I'll go to her. By then, Quester would have had at least some rest.

She felt the hand in hers tighten its grip, and the violet eyes opened, met hers. There was a moment in which he relaxed — the incipient frown disappeared, his lips turned up, as he met her gaze. "Urelle?" he whispered. Then the terrible, devastated blankness returned. "Mother... Father..."

Urelle just squeezed his hand tighter. After a few moments, she ventured, "I'm so sorry, Ingram."

He nodded. "I... can't believe it. I ran away, then I was running *towards* them, and then..." His voice caught and he looked away.

Following another pause, he said, "I... don't remember much. What happened? I remember," he winced, "Father getting killed, then Mother dying, and after that it's a blur until I realized they'd gotten me to the operating theater." A very wan smile. "Don't remember after *that*, of course."

At least he's asking; he's not... dead, like I thought he might be. "Well, there turned out to be at least seven or eight Xiilistiin infiltrators, and they were all the... what do you call them, advanced? enhanced? types. So in those close quarters it was deadly." She shuddered at the memory. "Auntie, Quester, and I kept everyone and everything away from you until the battle was over."

"Did any of them hear what... what Mother said to me?"

"I don't see how they *could*," she said after a moment of thought. "The shouts and screams and weapons clashing and others being discharged everywhere? I'll bet *you* had to listen carefully to hear her." She stopped, fearful that saying that would bring the moment back to him.

It did — at least, she could see he went paler and closed his eyes. But all he said was, "Yes. Yes, I did. It *was* noisy." He looked to the side, saw Quester's sleeping form, and his face's tension softened. "We'll ask Quester later, when she's awake; if anyone would know if the Xiilistiin could sort out quiet sounds from that noise, she will."

She nodded.

"Where's Victoria?"

"She's in the same operating room — did you say 'theater'? Anyway, the same one you were in."

He tried to sit up, winced, and — thank the Balance — let her help instead of just forcing his way through. She touched the controls she'd been shown and the bed folded up on the head end, supporting him. "She is? Now?"

"You had a high priority because of your rank *and* the infection that they didn't dare let get farther. But there were a lot of other wounded, and Auntie wasn't in immediate danger." She frowned. "I'm actually surprised they didn't wait a day or two."

"Didn't think we could afford the wait," came a rough voice from the doorway.

Despite his condition, Ingram tried to straighten and salute. "Officer-Medical Tisfotias!"

The "Officer-Medical" was a man of average height, with mostly straight dark hair cut short and combed back from his face. His eyes were intense, with a look of focus she associated somehow with priests — though she thought this man's passion was healing, judging by how he'd been driving himself and his people after the battle. His face was lined, and she thought he was maybe only a few years younger than Victoria.

He also, Urelle noted, had the collar-symbols that indicated he was one of the "Captain's Crew".

Tisfotias waved him down. "Don't strain yourself. Lots of careful work had to be done on you. Infection'd already started. That," he pointed to the clear, soft bag hanging from the bedside, with tubes somehow leading *into* Ingram, "is helping make sure it doesn't come back."

"If I gave him a healing draught, would it help?" Urelle asked.

"How many do you have?"

"Ummm..." she checked her pack. "Three? I think Quester has one or two left, Auntie had two or three, and Ingram —"

"One," Ingram said. "After the one that... that didn't work."

"So less than ten for the four of you? And you the linchpin, somehow, of what's going on?"

"Well, I'd thought we could pick up some more here, or in one of the cities..." Ingram trailed off as the Officer-Medical shook his head.

"Son... all of Aegeia's been at war in the last year. The Camp-Bels, well, you know we had to flee, and then there were the attacks by these Xiilistiin monsters... Healing draughts are hard to come by, right now. *We* aren't so bad off — we still have some technology of the Founder, thank Athena — but right now those draughts you've got are worth a hundred times what they might be normally. I'd be Ares-damned careful about using them."

"Myrionar's Balance," Urelle whispered. "I didn't know. Do you *need* these? I mean, if there are people worse off than us —"

Tisfotias' mouth tightened. "I couldn't deny we could use them —"

"—but the Clan believes you should keep everything you can," said a new voice. "Leontari, you were *supposed* to alert me when Ingram was awake."

"Hmph. You obviously were watching the telltales, or you wouldn't have been here to bother my patient so fast."

The newcomer was a little taller than the Officer-Medical, bronze-touched brown hair pulled tight back by a ponytail, with two small braids hanging in front of the ears. She was, Urelle guessed, around thirty or so, in very good shape judging from the muscular arms in their short sleeves, and had a square, friendly face with shrewd black eyes. She, too, wore the insignia of the Captain's Crew. "Ingram Camp-Bel, I don't think we ever met directly. Lieutenant-Commander Eklisia. No, don't bother with the salute, please, I don't want Leontari any more annoyed at me than he has to be."

Urelle was now getting annoyed, herself, at the intrusions, and saw that Quester's antennae were starting to twitch. *She doesn't need to be awakened yet!* "Ma'am, meaning no offense, I don't think Ingram's ready for much talking right now."

The eyes were sympathetic, but also unmoved. "He is a Camp-Bel, and the Clan needs him now."

"The Clan never needed him *before!*" she snapped.

"Urelle, wait," Ingram said, weakly.

"Sorry, Ingram. But after all the years they spent telling you you weren't even *good enough*, they could give you a few hours to *rest* after... after everything that just happened!"

"Adventurer Urelle Vantage," the Lieutenant-Commander said, "I recognize your points — and your passion — and I cannot argue them. Whatever our reasons, the Clan treated Ingram abominably, and we do not deserve the fact that he nonetheless has remained *of* us, and proud to be so.

"But because he *is* Camp-Bel, we must call upon him when we must — and we have no time to spare now."

Ingram closed his eyes. "Lieutenant-Commander... I... I appreciate your words. I wish I could *fully* appreciate them. But I am..." he shook his head, swallowed, and let his voice waver into a near-sob. "... I am *done* for now, Ma'am. I don't know what you think I could do, but I'm hurt and so is our friend Victoria and I just lost my *parents* right after I *found* them, and, and..." he trailed off, crying. Urelle put her arm around him and stared daggers at the two older people.

"You heard the boy," Leontari Tisfotias said to the Lieutenant-Commander. "Stop bothering my patient for a while. He's in no shape —"

A sigh, and then Eklisia took two quick steps forward and her hand flashed out, so quickly Urelle couldn't react. The ringing slap echoed through the room.

At Ingram's half-stunned, half-furious glare, Lieutenant-Commander Eklisia straightened. "The Clan *requires* you, Ingram Camp-Bel, and we *have no time*. Are you of the Clan? Do you honor the lives that have fallen and the lives that even now await our protection? *Do you?*" She gave a savage, cutting gesture with one hand that caused even Tisfotias to freeze. "I am sorry for your losses and I wish I *could* give you the time, Ingram Camp-Bel, but I cannot. If you are a true Camp-Bel, I need you *now.*"

Ingram's jaw had been tightening throughout the short speech, and Urelle felt the tension rising throughout his body. Quester stirred and then sat up; she sensed a quick interchange between the Iriiistiik and Ingram.

Then Ingram closed his eyes, drew a long, shuddering breath, and straightened, showing no sign of the pain he must be in. "What do you need me for then, Lieutenant-Commander?"

To Urelle's surprise, Eklisia's shoulders sagged visibly in relief. *She must not be exaggerating. She really* does *need Ingram for something.*

The Camp-Bel woman glanced around. "This is Clan business. I apologize, but could you —"

"Eklisia." Ingram's voice was colder than she had *ever* heard it. "Understand this: my companions are closer to me than even the Clan can imagine. There is absolutely *nothing* that you can say to me that I will be keeping from them. If you trust *me*, you trust them. Whatever missions you have for me, they will be by my side, as I would be by theirs." His hand gripped hers tightly. "They stay."

The Officer-Medical had a probably-insubordinate grin on his face; Lieutenant-Commander Eklisia stood still for a moment, then bowed. "As you wish."

She drew up a chair and sat down. "We now are reasonably certain that we have dealt with all the infiltrators — though I wish we had a way to test people."

Urelle remembered the Wanderer's last attack. "Does the word... *malathion* mean anything to you? Or the term 'nerve gas'?"

Eklisia shook her head, but Tisfotias' eyes narrowed. "Think so. Nasty, nasty stuff."

"The Wanderer said that this 'malathion' affected beings like the Xiilistiin — and probably Iriistiik — far worse than human beings. If you can find or make any of that material, I presume exposing people to it would..."

"Huh. Might work. I'd have to have antidotes on hand, of course, the stuff'd kill human beings too, and not in a nice way, but..."

"Look into it, Leontari. If we can do it while the Clan's all gathered together that would be best."

As the Officer-Medical turned to go, Quester rose, showing she had been awakened despite Urelle's efforts. "Of course, at the moment we cannot be certain *you* are not Xiilistiin."

"True enough," conceded Eklisia. "But I see no —"

"I have a way," Quester said. "Likely easier and safer than this poison. It will take a bit of time to check *everyone*, but I have discovered... that I am, or should become, a Mother or a Queen of my people. This has given me the telepathic gifts of my people —"

"Ah. And thus, if we allow you to look into our minds, you would know what we are."

"Yes. I would endeavor to look no deeper than necessary, but I would certainly pick up any immediately important thoughts — and a spy such as a Xiilistiin would have numerous thoughts that a true Camp-Bel would not."

Eklisia and Leontari looked at each other, and then the Officer-Medical shrugged. "Used enough of my patients as emergency test subjects, I suppose, might as well be one myself." He came forward and stood before Quester. "Won't hurt, will it?"

"No," Quester said. "As long as you do not try to fight too hard. I expect *some* resistance — those who are not naturally able to speak mind-to-mind find it disturbing, as I learned from my friends — but none ever reported pain."

"All right, go ahead."

Quester touched the Officer-Medical on the forehead with her antennae, and Urelle sensed the focus of concentration. Several long moments passed. Leontari Tisfotias' eyes suddenly widened, but though he tensed, he did not step back. A few seconds later, Quester's antennae lifted. "My apologies for any intrusion. You are most definitely human."

"Is that how long it will take for each person?" the Lieutenant-Commander asked.

"Roughly," Quester said after a pause for thought. "Some a bit longer, some perhaps more swiftly as I become more practiced, but that seems an appropriate interval."

Quester... Quester was right, Ingram's mindvoice said to her sadly. *She really could not have stopped to read Mother's mind in battle. It would have gotten Quester killed.*

Urelle smiled sadly. *I am sure she was hoping you would see that and understand. You could tell how guilty Quester feels about —*

Yes, and now I feel even worse about that. Wasn't her fault.

"Then let's get this over with. Assuming I pass," Eklisia said with a wry grin, "we can probably forget the poison approach and — if you're willing, Quester — just arrange that all the Clan be tested this way."

"I am certainly willing. I recall the false Sergeant saying there were two hundred seventy-nine of you then...?"

The Lieutenant-Commander grimaced. "Two hundred thirty-one now. Total of ten traitors, and then thirty-eight people killed in that fiasco in the conference room."

"Ten?" Urelle said in surprise. "I'm sure there were only eight in the battle!"

"Ten. One was caught during the fighting, trying to access sealed records, and we caught and killed the last while it was reporting back through some kind of scrying or mind-magic. And *that* is the problem."

"Hold until Quester's checked, Lieutenant-Commander," Ingram said, but his face had gone grim. "I think I'm already getting the idea."

"Agreed."

Urelle found herself tense as Quester performed her mental examination again, but to Urelle's relief this, too, ended with the Iriistiik declaring the Camp-Bel to be as human as she appeared.

"Good enough. Quester, would you go with Leontari? He'll set up your examination of the crew."

"Of course. I would suggest that we first clear a few of your best fighters, and then they will stand guard as I examine the rest."

"A good idea. See to it, Leontari. And *you* keep a sharp eye out for the first few."

The Officer-Medical nodded. "Will do, sir. Guess I'd better see to my weapons first. Come on, Quester."

Eklisia sat back down. "So. Their last spy — that we know of — was killed reporting back, as I said."

"And we don't know exactly what it said, so we have to assume it got pretty much all the information out," Ingram said. "So... how do you see things happening?"

Eklisia gave a snort. "Obvious, isn't it? Not only did you people somehow get past everything and find us — and I'll need a full report on all of this, especially as you mentioned the Wanderer! — but we also now have wiped out their spy network and as far as I know they did not learn what they really needed to learn — *why* you were so vital that your very nature was concealed for all these years. Their only reasonable option, since they know our base and most if not all of its exits — is to send overwhelming forces to take it and wipe us all out."

"Ares' *Balls*," Ingram hissed. "How long will it take them to deploy here?"

"I'm half-surprised they're not here now. Surely their so-called Athena would be in direct contact with the false Ares."

Ingram laughed, and that sound lightened the room and warmed Urelle's heart. "Not when she's dead, she isn't."

"Dead? You *saw* this?"

"That," Urelle said, "was the Wanderer's doing. He wiped out their fake Athena *and* the Sun of Apollo and Scythe of Demeter."

Lieutenant-Commander Eklisia stared, then gave a glad curse. "Ha! So their most powerful representatives here are dispensed with. Though," her face darkened, "there remains whatever monstrous force they used to destroy Amoni-Agapis."

Urelle could not restrain a giggle. "Um, *actually*, no, that thing's gone too."

"Athena's Ti... .Er, I mean, are you *sure*?"

"Sure she is," Ingram said, proudly. "Since she's the one who *killed* it."

"Not by myself!"

"No, but none of the rest of us could've even *tried* what you did. Take your credit."

Eklisia stared at the two, then leaned slowly back. "By the Aegi themselves, I think we are more fortunate than we knew." She toyed with the braid near her right ear. "All right, with that information, I am guessing it will take two to three days for them to mobilize and deploy their forces here. But that means that we have to be out of here before then, and preferably *well* before then."

"But this place is fortified! If you change access routines —"

"Even with all of our advantages, Ingram, there are only two hundred thirty-five of us, including the four of you. They have well-trained and powerful armies numbering many thousands. If they can find no way to breach the perimeter, they could starve us out. And even if we could somehow hold out indefinitely, we cannot afford to. The real *heart* of this war, the final conflict, will happen in Aegis, where the false Ares has his headquarters atop the Aegeian Path. Time is running out."

Ingram bit his lip thoughtfully. "I can't argue that we don't need to get to Aegis eventually, but what's the time pressure from?"

"Several things. First, we are certain that whatever plans Ares has are beginning to approach fruition; according to Information-Analyst Meresti, Ares may specifically intend to break *all* faith in the Aegi. That would seem insane, since that means the people would have no more faith in him, but as he isn't really Ares, yet has managed to convincingly play him, that implies he could simply drop that role and play another that fits his needs."

"That implies he's not just powerful but really, *really* good at hiding his nature. Great Wolf is the first thing that comes to mind."

"Not a bad guess, but we have no way of knowing. No one's managed to get close enough to try shooting him with a silver arrow. According to our intelligence, Artemisia Igemon had a god-slaying arrow made, before she became the new Athena, which would certainly have had silver in it, but whether she got to use it or not we don't know. If she did, it didn't work." Eklisia went back to toying with her braid. "In any event, that's two of the major urgencies: Ares' plan is nearing completion, and the faith of the people is swiftly weakening. Ares and his delegated overseers have been increasingly restricting the population in every one of the major cities, in manners that make us suspect they really *do* want a revolution against their oppressors and the gods they believe support them."

"Athena protect us. And there's *more?*"

"I'm afraid so. With his effectively unstoppable conquest completed, most of the possible support for resistance was scattered. The Camp-Bels have been providing the only means of communication to keep something of a coordinated resistance going. But some of our recent actions will undoubtedly reveal to the false Ares that something extremely odd is going on, and we have to assume that once he directs his godly powers against our network, he will find a way to break it, and possibly worse."

"Worse?"

Eklisia nodded, looking out into the invisible distance. "We have instantaneous communication between our various locations, thanks to the Founder's technology, but it cannot work without the central node -- which could not be moved."

Urelle understood. "You mean... it's back where your original Camp-Bel compound was. Near Aegis."

"Exactly. And if they realize that *that* was hidden there, they will enter the ruins of the compound and tear everything apart in order to discover what else we might have kept them from seeing. With a god, or even false god, aiding them, I am not sure all the tricks we have will be enough to keep them from finding what is hidden."

"Wait. What *is* hidden?" Ingram demanded. "I knew where the Armory was, and other places we had the Founders' relics, but..."

"But there are deeper secrets, spoken of only among the Captain's Crew," Eklisia said. Another glance at Urelle. "Might I ask... did your mother tell you what the secret about you was?"

Ingram looked at Eklisia for a long moment, then sighed. "Not... exactly. She didn't know who else she dared trust, or whose ears might hear during the battle. So instead of a straight answer, I got a riddle." He met Eklisia's gaze. "Would I right in guessing that if I needed access to the data and analyses that led to... well, to my adoption, that such data is also in the old compound?"

Lieutenant-Commander Eklisia's eyebrows rose. "Ah. So that is the clue she gave you? Yes. That part of the records is kept in the safest place possible, and we had no need of such records here in the retreat."

"All right. Then we will go with you."

The woman's mouth quirked in a wry smile. "No," she said. "No, it is we who will go with you."

"What?"

She rose, and touched the collar of Ingram's clothes, hanging near his bed. "You wear the insignia of the Crew, but I believe you had no others of the Crew to teach you. Yet... yet every indication, Ingram Camp-Bel, is that you are *vital*, to Aegeia and to the Clan, and now your mother Ianthe's words tell us that even the most oblique direction to understanding your destiny will require that you enter into the most central of our secrets. The Camp-Bels have waited fourteen years to know the truth. In those fourteen years, we have learned only that you — and now your companions — will guide us to any hope of victory that remains."

She picked up the case that lay on the desk nearby. "Too, you passed through the Great Seal itself, to return the Insignia. The Captain's Crew must direct you, if you are to reach the heart of the mysteries, and there is only one way in which that can be allowed."

She opened the case, bowed over it, and removed the glittering emblem, the rising bird of prey. "This that you carried shall be yours in truth, Ingram Camp-Bel. Duty passes. The Crew must have a Captain."

Chapter 34
Captain Ingram Camp-Bel

Ingram heard the last few words as though in a fevered dream. They carried with them a heart-deep, stabbing joy, the awestruck wonder of a secret childhood fantasy become real, and immediately behind them, the terror, both of his inadequacy and of the implications — of the desperation of the Camp-Bels that any of them could consider this, or of the horrifying possibility that this was the *proper* choice — that he, Ingram Camp-Bel, *should* be the Captain.

"No!" he said, and pushed the Insignia — the *Captain's* Insignia — aside. "There is already a Captain. The Captain passed his Insignia on in his death, and now Captain Pennon is the Captain. I was *there*. I passed that duty on, as the Captain wished. Duty has passed. I... may be not the hopeless incompetent I thought, but am no Captain."

"Are you people *crazy?*" demanded Urelle. "Ingram's just lost his parents, he's just coming to terms with what your clan *did* to him, and now you hit him with *this?*"

Lieutenant-Commander Eklisia bowed her head. "I cannot argue that this must seem... extreme. Yet the new Captain — Pennon — I recall her. A good woman, well on her way to great things. She might have become one of the Crew in time. But she was not, and if she was the one succeeding... I assume there were none of the Crew left alive on the outside?"

Ingram shook his head, still trying to grasp what had just happened. "No. The only two members of the Crew in that group that I know of were killed."

"So. That means that the current Captain, Captain Pennon, does not know the secrets of the Captain's Crew, and has no one there to tell her. Moreover, even if she did — she is not here. She cannot command the Crew, only that part of the Clan that remains on the outside." She looked at them both gravely. "That is not to disparage her, you understand. She has been given a terrible responsibility, and I have every reason to believe she will carry it out to the very best of her ability. But we need a Captain *here*, and we also *must* follow you — support you to every limit of our ability. We do not, yet, know why. It is possible that, in the end, you must leave us.

"But for the time that you remain with us, Ingram Camp-Bel, there is only one way we can be assured of unity in performance and purpose: that the one who commands the Clan be the one who must *direct* the Clan, that the one who we must follow and support must have the *authority* to do so. I have my own suspicions... but enough. Until you are part of the Captain's Crew, I can explain no more. And without a Captain, we cannot be commanded to reveal certain secrets. Access to the records you wish may, in fact, be under Captain's Seal — which means that without a Captain, we can never reach them."

She extended the Insignia again. "Duty passes. *Command* passes."

His fingers were cold. His gut ached where it had been operated on. But he finally reached up and took the Insignia. "I... I assume command of the Ship and Crew," he said slowly, disbelief giving way to a fearsome weight of truth. "Command has passed. I am... the Captain." *Dear Athena, Mother, did you know what would happen?*

Without a single trace of irony or doubt, Lieutenant-Commander Eklisia gave the double armed salute and held it until Ingram forced himself, painfully, to return it. "All right... Lieutenant-Commander," he said after a moment, "first, I think you need to let everyone know about this decision. I need to know if there is anyone in the Clan who *doesn't* agree with you. So far, I've been traveling fast and light with my friends; none of us need an argument to slow us down."

"Agreed, Captain. I will attend to that immediately." Eklisia turned to go.

"Also, Eklisia — Officer-Medical Tisfotias indicated that healing draughts were very dear at the moment," Ingram said, straining to speak in as professional a fashion as he could manage. "In my opinion, if I am to command and lead, I should be healed as swiftly as possible. This would also extend to my companion Victoria Vantage. Would you concur?"

"Sir, I would, especially since I understand that you would not be using Clan, but personal, resources for this. I would recommend, however, that you reserve your remaining healing as much as possible; the Officer-Medical is correct that it will be extremely hard to come by any more."

"Agreed."

Eklisia saluted once more, and disappeared out the door.

For a few long moments he simply stared at the Insignia, trying to grasp that it was *his*. He was Captain Ingram Camp-Bel, leader of Clan Camp-Bel. Ingram the laughed-at, Ingram the pitied, Ingram the always-last... was the Captain.

He became aware that something was being held in front of him when it was finally interposed between him and the Insignia: a small bottle, held by an equally small hand.

"Drink it, Ingram," Urelle said when he looked up. "You asked, you got agreement, so..."

"Oh. Right, of course." He popped the seal on the bottle and drank the sharp-tasting healing draught down.

Instantly the room sprang into a sharper focus, a dull fog cleared from his mind, his pains vanished. "*Wow*. I don't think I'll ever get used to that. That's the best kind of magic." A thought occurred to him. "Can you make those?"

"No," Urelle said, real regret in her tones. "I mean, in *theory* I could — a Shaper should be able to do pretty much anything — but making something that good at fixing people is really specialized stuff, and usually done by those who can cheat by getting the gods or other powerful beings to do most of the work."

"That's too bad." With the clarity of mind, the recent losses struck him again. He could *feel* his face droop from interest and cheer to gloom.

Without a word, Urelle caught his hand and squeezed gently. The warmth of her skin echoed the concern and equal warmth radiating from her thoughts, saying without words *I am here for you*.

He squeezed back and made an effort to recapture... well, himself. He forced himself to remember Mother's words and her smile. She'd given him a clue. She *trusted* him to understand it. And she and father had been *happy* to see him — overjoyed.

"They didn't think I was a failure," he whispered finally.

"Of course they didn't," Urelle said. "I saw them for a few moments... and what I saw were a mother and a father *heartbreakingly* happy to see their son again."

Captain or not, Ingram found that hearing Urelle put that into words was too much; he turned to her and let himself cry into her shoulder, the shoulder that was as small as his own but so very much stronger, a warm bulwark that would hold him up when he felt he couldn't stand on his own.

And brushing against his mind, the other presence he relied upon, calm and inhuman and no less a beloved friend for that. For a few minutes, he just allowed the loss and pain to flow out of him, and felt it absorbed, understood, and returned to him as sympathy and love.

Finally, he straightened up and wiped his eyes, feeling lighter. This wouldn't be the last time he cried over his parents — he was sure of that — but for now, he could let it go long enough to do what he must.

He stood up and went over to change into his clothes. "Pardon me, Urelle."

She turned away as he undressed. "Are you all right?"

"Better. I mean, it's probably going to hit me every so often for weeks, months, maybe even years. But I think it'd have been worse if they'd died *before* I got here."

She nodded, though her face showed uncertainty. "I suppose so, for you. You had so much... *open* between you and your parents. You needed to see them, find out what all of that meant." She shivered momentarily. "I didn't have that problem with either my parents or Rion; last thing I'd said to all of them was that I loved them. I don't think I would have wanted to sit there with Rion covered in blood, dying..." She closed her eyes. "Like Kyri did."

"Well, I'm like her in one way," Ingram said, and heard a new, hard edge in his voice that startled him. "I'm by the *Founder* going to kill the monster that ordered all of this."

"I think we're *all* with you on that," Urelle said firmly, and he could sense Quester's agreement. She played absently with a long strand of black hair. "Do you think there will be a problem with you being Captain?"

Ingram felt a sharp pang of tension, pushed it away. "I... hope not. Getting people to acknowledge me was probably harder with the first group. From what Eklisia said, this branch of the Camp-Bels were told *months* ago that my 'incompetence' had been a big smokescreen, even if it wasn't clear how or why it had been done, so they've had time to accept it and to recognize what their orders require." He laughed quietly. "If there's one thing Camp-Bels do really well, it's follow orders."

"So," Urelle said after a moment, "you are the Captain. How does that feel?"

Ingram stared down at the Insignia again. "Like... like I could shout to the sky and be heard. Like my dreams have come down from Athena's hand to warm my heart, even in this moment where I lost so much." He felt his expression waver.

"And like someone's just dropped all the weight of Wisdom's Fortress on my back."

Good, Quester's thoughtvoice said. *Then you were ready for this.*

"I don't think you could *ever* be 'ready' for this. But... more than I thought I would be. Because of all of you."

That, his best friend told him, *is what companions are for.*

Ingram nodded, radiating his thankfulness to his partner, and reached out and gripped Urelle's hand.

Then he took a deep breath and brought the Insignia up, fastened it to the upper right side of his shirt. As the Captain's Insignia gripped the material, becoming a part of it, he truly felt the weight — and the joy — become one and a part of him.

"How do we get to your people's old compound?" Urelle asked.

"Well... I have some sort-of-ideas, but I think I want to wait on that until we can talk to the whole Clan. This has to happen as fast as possible. If Eklisia's right — and I think she probably is — we've got a day, two or three at the outside, before our enemies surround us. None of us can make good plans, though, until we know what we've got to work with."

The door opened and Officer-Medical Tisfotias entered with Quester behind him — then stopped short, staring at Ingram's chest. "Good gods, so she's gone and done it."

Ingram waited — holding his breath, he realized — to see what the Officer-Medical would do now.

Tisfotias straightened and gave the Aegeian salute. "Captain. I have some reports for you."

Ingram let his breath out with a *whoosh*, feeling a cold thrill of awe and dread go through him at the deadly serious tone of the word *Captain*. "Please continue, Officer-Medical."

"First, we're just about set up for testing the Clan. We'll do the Captain's Crew first; worst-case possible is that one of the Crew's suborned. If we can at least avoid *that* disaster, so much the better.

"Second," he looked at Urelle, "your aunt's out of the surgery. Indications are all good so far. I'm guessing all four of you will be informed on her condition, right?"

"None of us would be hiding anything, so yes."

"Hmph. All right, then you all get it straight. We fixed the blockages that were giving her trouble, and once she's healed from that, she should be fine. But this wasn't the first time. There's some long-term damage that we don't have the tech to fix; maybe the Founder did back when the Ship flew, but we don't have it now, and the best healers of the Clan, the ones who were touched by Athena's grace, got killed early, so no magical way to fix it. She *could* end up having more trouble." He shook his head. "Not that I expect it'll slow her down until it really hits her. I know those types."

"But... she *is* going to be better?" Urelle asked.

"Oh, sure. But you're going into dangerous and high-stress situations, girl, and she's no kid any more. Older'n me, and she's been exposed to things that should've killed her more than once. I know I can't *stop* her, but I'm saying don't just assume she's going to keep up with you forever."

"We'll keep that in mind," Ingram said, "but as you said, I don't think there's much we can do about it. Anything else?"

"Did a quick search on that malathion stuff. We can put together a few spray or bomb items with it, but making it in larger quantities would take equipment that's back at the Compound. Still, it might be a good weapon to have in reserve."

"I agree, though Quester has to stay far away from it."

"Understood. Any orders at this time, Captain?"

"Besides getting the interviews underway?" Ingram almost said "no", then remembered. "As soon as she wakes up, give Victoria one of her healing draughts so she's ready to move. The Lieutenant-Commander and I both agree that my party must be in top shape."

"Yes, sir. Quester, are you ready for the testing of the Clan?"

"Yes," buzzed Quester. "As soon as we can."

"Then let's get to it," Tisfotias said. "We need to get out of here... without any Ares-damned spies."

As they left, Ingram stood up. "Let's go, Urelle."

"Where?"

Ingram began putting on his equipment. "To find a meeting room. As soon as the Captain's Crew is cleared, we'd better start making plans." He felt the weight of command, insubstantial yet crushingly real. "Time is running out."

Chapter 35
Captain and Crew

Balance preserve us, that poor boy. Victoria could see the pressure of responsibility in the straight line of Ingram's pose, in the tension of his face, all radiating from that rising-bird Insignia.

With Quester's screening of the Clan complete, it was finally possible to have this meeting. They were seated in a conference room, oval in shape, with the same polished-steel-and-stone look that dominated the entire hidden Camp-Bel fortress. It was a strange and alien aesthetic, one that spoke of calculations and analysis and duty and perhaps less of passion — appropriate for a group dedicated to the Goddess of Wisdom.

Besides the four of their party, there were seven others sitting about the table, all looking to Ingram. Lieutenant-Commander Eklisia and Officer-Medical Tisfotias were already familiar to her.

Of the others, Information-Analyst Meresti's gaze was dispassionate, dark eyes standing out against skin that had the underlying pallor of someone who spent most of their time far from sunlight; he had one of the ISNDAU devices before him. Officer-Communications Eletheria was a very dark woman of slightly over average height; her sharp-cheekboned face reminded Victoria of her own when she was much younger. Security Chief Koragio Theros was a man with close-cropped, graying, brown hair and a round face that showed lines of both cheer and pain; despite his seeming age, his body was clearly hard-trained.

Officer-Navigation Tsechos was younger than anyone else in the room except Ingram and her niece; straight, sleek black hair brushed back framed a normally-cheerful face and brown eyes that showed lingering shock and nervousness; he had been *Second* Officer-Navigation until the bloodbath... not even one day ago?

Next to Tsechos sat Officer-Technical Actina, the only member of the Captain's Crew to show clearly non-human origins; the delicacy of her face, the curved points of the ears, and other features indicated there was a strong trace of *Artan* or *Rohila* in her ancestry; given that Ingram had mentioned that the *Rohila* lived in the mountains of Wisdom's Fortress, Victoria was inclined to the latter guess. In front of Actina was a panel that glowed like the ISNDAU, but was larger and apparently anchored to the conference table; Actina's fingers rested on a panel composed of numerous studs whose purpose Victoria could not guess.

"This is it?" Ingram asked, and his expression echoed the shock she could feel through the link. "The entirety of the Crew? I thought there were twenty or thirty in the Crew!"

"This is all that remains, Captain," Eklisia said with a heavy sigh. "Before this... *mess* started, before you left a few years ago, there were twenty-seven members of the Captain's Crew. Three went with the expedition that left Aegeia, and you know the fate of two; from your report, I assume the third died during the ship-to-ship conflict. Two others were stationed elsewhere in Aegeia and are known dead. The remaining twenty-two were with us when we retreated, but fifteen of them were killed in the two recent conflicts with Ares' spies."

She flashed a humorless smile. "I find it extremely likely that the Crew were all targeted by our enemy."

"As your 'Crew' apparently hold many secrets," Victoria said, "were any of the Crew... used by our enemies?"

"You mean, did any of them turn out to be Xiilistiin? No, thank the Lady and the Founder both," Koragio Theros said. "My guess it was a thrice-damned near thing, though; one of the spies was living with our former Officer-Navigation."

Ingram's face became a hair less tense. "So as far as we know, they have not yet discovered the Clan secrets known only to the Crew?"

"Yes," Koragio agreed. "It's bad enough, though." His glance around the table was filled with grim exhaustion. "Of the twenty secure refuges we constructed over the years, sixteen of them are almost certainly compromised, including, of course, this one. We have four left we can use for safe refuge and clandestine operations."

"Information channels have been similarly affected," Meresti said; even his cultivated higher-Aegis accent could not conceal his own strain and cold anger. "Captain, five of nine relays are likely now known to the enemy. They are still in operation, but I expect they and their operators are in extreme danger. I need your permission to abandon them and to destroy the relays themselves, to prevent any of our communications equipment from falling into Ares' hands."

Victoria gripped her hands together to keep from moving or saying anything, as she watched the lavender-haired boy-become-Captain close his eyes, purse his lips, and then look to Officer-Technical Actina. "Are these relays replaceable, or are we destroying more of the Founder's legacy?"

Actina looked at the panel before her and her hands moved swiftly over the array of studs or buttons. "Hm. *Most* of each relay is replaceable, albeit with considerable effort. There are, however, components in each which either cannot be replicated or would require unreasonable effort to do so."

"Can those specific components be removed easily, and are they portable?"

"Removal can be achieved with moderate effort, Captain. The three relevant components weigh approximately... converting now... fifty pounds in total and maximum dimensions of two feet three inches."

Ingram nodded. *He is asking the right questions,* Victoria thought.

"And how many personnel for each relay?"

"Between three and five, sir."

"Then I want immediate action to remove the irreplaceable components, which will be distributed among the personnel. The relays will then be evacuated and destroyed. However, if for any reason they think they will not have time to remove the key components before enemy forces could take the relay, I give full permission to destroy the entire relay." Ingram betrayed his uncertainty by flicking a quick glance to both Victoria and Eklisia.

Eklisia's nod was small but clear; Victoria sent her approval directly. *I believe that was exactly correct, Ingram. You can do this. And if you want me to advise you —*

Of course I do! There was more than a hint of panic. *Even... even if I should have been the Captain, that would have been years from now! I should be, I don't know, an Officer-Trainee.*

That's as may be, Ingram, but I would point out that — rigorous though your people's training may be — years of Adventuring has likely taught you much more than you know. We are all here to advise you — but you are *the Captain,* and she let a wash of affection suffuse her next thoughts, *and I think they have chosen better than they know.* Urelle and Quester said nothing, but radiated the same confidence and affection.

Ingram managed to somehow both visibly relax and straighten at the same time. His next words held less strain and more certainty. "As I understand it, our goal now is to reach Aegis, or, more accurately, our home compound just outside of the city; we've already been told that the information Mother told me to seek out is hidden there, likely under Captain's Seal, and naturally Ares' headquarters are there in Aegis. What other *substantiative* information do you have for us about why we need to go there, and what we will need to do?"

Eklisia gestured to Meresti. "Information-Analyst?"

"The most important point is that while we have every reason to believe that Ares is approaching his endgame — and I must emphasize that we only call him 'Ares' because we do not know who or what he really is — we also have information, some from old data and some from god-connected sources, that Athena is not entirely out of the picture." Meresti raised a finger. "I know you claim that Berenike is active, despite our prior information on her death, and for the moment I will accept that as a given. It would be very useful, however, if she would join us and allow us to plan some of our strategies around her.

"Leaving that aside, however, all indications are that there remains one route for Athena to manifest, one that can occur only at the summit of the Aegeian Path. We do not have the details, but it is *believed* that an appropriate candidate need merely reach the Statue and open themselves to the Goddess. Under the current circumstances, I expect she is eager for any such candidate to appear."

"But what about the Temple Trainees?" Ingram asked. "That's the usual route for —"

"There was a terrible 'accident' that brought down the trainee hall. There were no survivors," Eklisia said, with icy sarcasm on *accident*. "We have no proof, of course, but we are certain that Ares' agents arranged that accident, and its universal lethality. Similarly, her Sword and Shield were removed from display some years ago on a pretext of cleaning or some such, and no one seems to know where they went."

Ingram blew out a breath. "That was a long time ago. Do we have any idea when Ares stopped being Ares?"

"No direct evidence," answered Meresti, "but my best guess would be just before the embodiment; as you know, there are often little hints of the Cycle to come, and one of them indicated that in this Cycle, Phobos would be an outsider — specifically, a woman of the Odinsyrnen."

"Ah," Quester buzzed, her antennae bobbing, "which means that the current Phobos must have been chosen between that hint and the actual manifestation.

Thus, presumably, the false Ares usurped the position of the true god just shortly before."

"That is how we read it."

"To get back to your main question, sir," Eklisia said, "it appears that even the last route to ascension is effectively cut off. One of our sources witnessed the testing of a barrier that, when activated, appears to enclose the entirety of the Aegeian Path, from the obelisks that mark its beginning to the very top. We have not yet gotten any analysis of the enchantment, but we assume it is powerful, indeed."

"If I can get close enough to *see* it, I can probably get an analysis of it," Urelle said.

"That is one of our hopes," Eklisia said. "Our magical resources are small; we relied on mostly external support for that purpose, aside from our in-house artificers."

"All right," Ingram said. "So, we return home. Information-Analyst, including our remaining safe refuges and known allies, what is our best-time *secure* route to Aegis? I don't want to get to our base with a thousand of Ares' troops on our heels; we'll need some time."

Meresti nodded to Actina. "Officer-Technical, if you please?"

A few taps on the device near her, and Actina caused a map of Aegeia to manifest in the air above the table. *That... is quite impressive. Is that purely technology? I have seen mages such as Urelle do that...*

It's definitely pure technology, Auntie, Urelle responded. *I'm not sensing a trace of magic from that.*

Meresti gestured. "Based on our current intelligence, our best route would be to strike directly southward until we reach the Ludusi River, here." A streak of green light followed his gestures. "We have allies in the small village who are already arranging for river-worthy boats. Then we travel down the Ludusi to the fork where it merges with the Tachys to become the Kentrikosa."

The line dropped southward again. "We will have to stop before we reach the point where the Kentrikosa and Iliyos merge, however; Ares' people in Talaria have a blockade at the intersection. Across country to the west — heavily forested but lightly patrolled — here, then turn south where some of our sympathizers run a ferry across the Iliyos. At that point we can cut diagonally through here, with a care to avoid Lyra itself, and come out here, at our original stronghold."

Three bright white dots of light appeared on the path, one at the confluence of the Ludusi and Tachys, one inland and west of Talaria, and one not far from Lyra. "Luckily, three of our four remaining safe refuges are along this route. We will also reduce our exposure by leaving a garrison at each of the refuges; I would recommend fifty or so at each, leaving us about eighty or so for when we reach our main objective." He looked up.

"Sounds straightforward," Ingram said after a moment. "Commander Eklisia — consider that an official promotion, by the way — Commander, how are preparations for departure going?"

"Well enough, sir. We have always been aware that we might need to move swiftly. We can depart within hours."

"Officer-Medical? How about our injured?"

Tisfotias grimaced. "Eight people who really can't move well under their own power. We'll have rotating squads of carriers for them, I guess. Most people are in shape to take a turn carrying the litters. Shouldn't slow us down much, though I hate having to drag my patients through this." He shrugged. "Better than what'll happen if they stay, though."

"Officer-Technical, will we have to leave anything valuable behind?"

The narrow face and delicate eyebrows emphasized Actina's pained expression. "A fair amount of the infrastructure and support equipment is not easily or quickly removed, Captain."

"Then I would like the traps placed before we leave, and prepare the best demolition we can in the remaining time. When our enemies invade, I want them to break into a deathtrap." Ingram's anger at the people hunting his Clan was no longer hidden.

Actina bared her teeth in a savage smile. "Yes, *sir!*"

Ingram glanced at his own ISNDAU. "I want to depart in six hours — before there's any good chance their forces can reach us. With luck we can maintain at least a few days' lead. Any questions?"

After a pause, Eklisia nodded. "You have not yet asked about the details of some of the secrets of the Crew."

"If the details are relevant *now*, for the decisions I have to make *now*, then I'd better hear them," Ingram said. "But if I guess right, it won't make any *real* difference until we get where we're going, correct?"

Commander Eklisia considered for a moment. "Correct, sir."

"Then we don't need to be distracted by that information. It's been kept secure by being cautious, I see no reason to change that. I of course *command* you to tell me anything and everything you feel I need to know *when* I need it, but if I don't need it or ask for it, we'll leave it for now."

"I have no more questions, sir."

"Then meeting adjourned," Ingram said, not without a note of surprised relief that people were *listening* to him this way. "Crew, make it all happen."

Ingram didn't sag down in his seat until the rest of the crew had left. "Oh, *Founder*, I feel so terrified and half like a fraud at the same time!"

Victoria nodded. "It's rather like being a parent, from what I understand. You're doing quite well, Ingram."

"*I* thought you did *wonderfully*," Urelle said.

"I agree," Quester said. "What do you want *us* to do?"

"*You* go get some rest, Quester," Ingram said. "You finished doing the screenings just before we held this meeting; you must be absolutely exhausted. I don't know if *I* can sleep right now, but I'm sure going to try. We'll be driving as hard as we can from now on, and once we *reach* Aegis…"

"Yes," Victoria mused, "once we get there it will become challenging."

Quester rose from her sitting position and headed for the door; Victoria could see from the Iriistiik's posture and wingcases that Ingram had been correct; Quester was near the end of her strength.

"Come along, Urelle," she said. "Captain Ingram's advice is very sound. We'd best get our rest now; gods only know when we will get any again."

Chapter 36
Intercepting Messages

Urelle walked as quietly as she could in the group of Camp-Bels. *And I'm still too noisy.*

Being fair with herself, she *was* much better than she had been back when she'd first chased down Ingram and Quester. Passable, perhaps quite good by now.

But even the archivists, even the few *children* still with the Camp-Bel group, were quiet as mist stealing through the trees. The whole mass of over two hundred people passed through the forest like a sussuration of a mere dozen people whispering. Lacking the telepathic link that Urelle now shared with her three companions, they still almost never needed words to convey instructions; quick, precise hand gestures could send out or retrieve scouts, convey information as to new hazards or directions, even, apparently, occasionally convey jokes, as evidenced by occasional grins on the otherwise-solemn faces surrounding them.

Urelle could sense Ingram's impatience, echoed by the rest of the four of them, at being surrounded. The Camp-Bels were protecting their Captain, as was their duty, but it still felt terribly restrictive when you were used to moving at your own pace, in your own way, through the jungles of Zarathan.

With an effort, she dismissed these concerns. There were spells to focus on, spells that she wanted easily known, practiced in her mind to be unleashed on a moment's notice.

Since they *were* in the center, and thus not likely to be surprised from any direction, she had taken the opportunity of the last few days to study the Wanderer's Book carefully, with an especial focus on the things she had seen him do. He had displayed a deadly economy of action during his battle against the false Athena and her companions — an efficiency that showed that his often-florid conversational style was merely a mask for a mind with a clear and dangerous understanding of the battlefield.

Urelle had recognized that the Wanderer had actually applied several self-enhancement spells, and the ones she had been able to derive using the Book now were poised for use, on her or her friends, waiting in the antechamber of her mind.

Right now, though, she was trying to understand the lightning-fast teleportation, that his book called "lightning step", that he'd used during that fight.

Long-range teleportation was... unreliable, though apparently the Wanderer himself had a trick to allow him to get away with it. But short-range transference was not nearly so dangerous, and as the Wanderer had shown, could be a truly awesome power on the battlefield if you could use it in the whirl and press of combat. The lightning step, according to the book, was actually not quite teleportation, but an absolutely *incredible* acceleration of motion from one point to another... that was survivable because the body was temporarily turned into its component particles, which streamed to the new position and reformed at a speed that even Urelle couldn't quite believe.

This is one of the things that could take a long time to master. I think he's probably got a separate formula for the dissolve-reform trick that you have to derive first, *and then add the acceleration between the dissolve and the reform.*

But the Wanderer had shown her a couple of *other* methods of transferring from one point to the other, and she *really* liked the one that bent the so-called fabric of the world. She thought she could pull that one off.

But moving an object from point A to point B was *hard* using that technique; it would exhaust her, because there was something that the Wanderer called *energy of potential and position* involved. She didn't quite get the mathematics involved, but it seemed that if you had an object of a given size in a given location and transferred it to another location, there was an inevitable change in energy associated with the object, because there had not been an object in the new location, and there had been one in the old, and now that situation was reversed.

Wait, reversed? she thought with a startled moment of insight. *What if...*

She was suddenly aware the whole troop had paused, her own body having halted when those around her did. Not a muscle twitched.

What's happening?

Getting a report from the field now, Ingram answered. A few moments of that silent hand-language, and Ingram continued, *Not good. Looks like some of Ares' patrols are in Katasarion — the village where our allies are supposed to have boats for us.*

Could they have anticipated us? Quester asked.

They certainly could have, Ingram replied. *If they know as much as we think, they could anticipate our travel in broad strokes — if they guess that we intend to return to our original home. I don't think they would guess that, though.*

Scouts? Can you infiltrate, find out if it is *targeted?* Victoria's thoughts were precise and focused. *If these are just passing patrols, we could simply withdraw a bit, leave a watcher or two, and continue on once they leave.*

We're discussing that, Ingram said, continuing the silent conversation with the rest of his Crew. *The real problem is the time element. With Urelle and Quester helping, we probably left no easily followed trail from the refuge, but our adversaries are both determined and skilled. Once they realize we left the retreat before they even got there, they'll certainly pick up our trail. So, we don't know if we have hours, days, or even a week to spare. We have to assume hours. Waiting is not something we can afford.*

A few more moments were spent in silent conference — hand-signals for the Camp-Bels, and telepathic discussion for their own group. Finally, Ingram sighed, both audibly and telepathically. *No real help for it. There's no possible way to sneak over two hundred people into that little village without being noticed. We'll have to find a way to take out the patrols — and do it in a way that will keep them from raising an alarm to anyone else nearby.*

We're not near enough for them to hear us, let's not keep doing this two-sided conversation. "Do we know how they might send the alarm?" Urelle asked, keeping her voice low and looking both at Ingram and the rest of the Captain's Crew. "They don't have your devices, so it would be magic, yes?"

"Hm," Meresti grunted. "Yes, magical. They don't have access to any technology like ours, and... no, wait. Those Ares-damned Xiilistiin. They could use mindpowers."

Ingram cursed. "And no way to tell if there are any of the monsters in this patrol, either."

"I may be able to," Quester said after a moment. "I had direct mental contact with the false Athena and, through her, the Swarm. The sensation was... distinctive."

Ingram's face lit. "That would definitely help," he said, then, more cautiously, "if you could do it without them *noticing*, that is."

A quick scent of cinnamon mixed with grass. "Unless they are actively *looking* for me with their minds — something that would be very difficult to maintain all the time — no, they would not notice."

Ingram hesitated only for an instant. "All right. Go to the front. The scouts will get you as close as they can."

As the tall Iriistik bounded off, Ingram's gaze switched to Urelle. "If there aren't any Xiilistiin in the group, it's going to be magic. Can you keep them from getting out a message?"

Urelle wished she could answer that one easily. "If I know *how* they were going to... probably. Without knowing how, probably not. The *best* way would be to hit them so hard they never get a chance to send one. Do we have *any* information on their likely message methods?"

"Meresti? Sounds like your field."

"It's always risky to assume the past holds your answers," Meresti said slowly, his drawling upper-Aegis accent even more pronounced than usual. "But on the other hand, organizations rarely change things that work. We're not far from the edge of Talaria's territory, and their patron, Hermes, had shown them how to craft speaking-stones that worked over long distances. Not cheap, not easy, but they made them for patrols like this — one of their major advantages in the wars. With Ares having conquered them... yes, I'd bet they're using the stones."

"One per patrol? Or more?"

"One. Maybe only one per two patrols. If Ares is using this as a standard for his forces, they'll be spread thin. But remote patrols like these would definitely have one. He'd probably given his top officers different ways to communicate — or maybe they were all Xiilistiin. But for these kinds of patrols, the stones would work fine."

Urelle nodded. She had some idea of what kind of enchantments would be necessary to make such a device. "Have you ever seen one of these stones?"

"Yes. Worked in Talaria for a while as a bodyguard myself, you know, back before all this mess started. They're a bit fancier than just stones; they're carved geodes — hollow stones — hinged together. Inside there's the real speaking stone, held in the crystal network that makes up the geode's core. To use it, you unlock a catch on the stone, open it, and then focus on the speaking stone itself. Usually takes only a few seconds to establish the link, then it's just like talking to someone else."

Meresti looked at her, eyebrow raised. "Does that help?"

Crystal network, he called it. It's definitely a structure that could be used to guide and focus magical energy... to resonate with the right type of stone placed inside...

As she thought about it, she found herself starting to smile. "Yes, Information-Analyst," she said. "Yes, I think it helps a great deal. Tell me, these geodes — what type? That is, what kind of crystals?"

"I'm... not entirely sure. They were purple? Very hard stone, did not scratch easily, sometimes transparent at the base and then darkening towards the tips?"

She gestured, showing an array of lavender-to-deep-violet, six-sided crystals. "Like that?"

"That's it exactly!" Meresti said, without hesitation.

"Amethyst," she murmured, the smile broadening. "Colored quartz. Yes, Ingram," she said, meeting his amethyst-colored gaze, "I think I *can* do something about that!"

At that moment, Quester dropped back down among them. "No Xiilistiin," she reported positively.

"Oh, excellent," Ingram said, and she could sense his tentative relief. "Urelle thinks she has a handle on their magical communications. What is it, Urelle?"

"Quartz," she said. "It's one of the best crystals for magical resonance around, which makes it ideal for this kind of communication."

"Interesting," Officer-Technical Actina said. "In a sense, the same is true for technology; quartz has some very interesting properties. But please go on."

"Really? We'll have to talk about that later. Anyway, the really important point is that quartz is actually one of the most *common* materials in the world. A lot of rocks are a high proportion of quartz, *sand* is quartz, and so on. Knowing the basic kind of structure they're using, what I can do is... well, make *all* the quartz around try to resonate with such a structure. The effect will be like trying to shout to someone across a hall and finding that every single part of the hall's making an echo that's just a *tiny* bit off in timing from all the others." She looked to Ingram, her raised eyebrows asking if he understood.

Ingram nodded, delight obvious on his face. "Oh, that's perfect! To anyone at any distance it would be just noise!"

"And better — because a smart design for such a communication spell would screen out noise, so that you could use the communication stone even in a windstorm, or near a waterfall."

"Again, a fascinating and accurate parallel with our communications technology," Actina mused. "And since the noise produced is a direct, if distorted, duplication of the message being sent... the message *itself* will be filtered out as well. A receiver will hear, effectively, nothing. It may not even know the stone was in use."

A very clever idea — as I expect from my neice. Victoria's pride was evident in the thought.

"Perfect," Ingram said. "Then — if everyone agrees — here's what we'll do..."

***

Urelle stood behind concealing brush, peering out at Katasarion. The village was indeed small, no bigger than Gharis back home, although very different in appearance — houses high on stilts, connected by walkways to each other and to the docks that extended out nearby. Ingram had pointed out how those walkways were constructed so that if the docks rose with the water, the walkway would rise with them.

She surveyed the area around them, trying to imagine what it must look like with water ten feet higher, the river spreading wider, tearing at everything in its path. *But these people have lived here for centuries; I guess they know how to build to survive it.* Nonetheless, traces remained; the undergrowth below the pilings was much shorter than that in the more elevated jungle they had left, showing it had all been stripped away not long ago, and there were stones ranging from pebbles to boulders piled against and around each support for the houses — possibly debris washed down, possibly protective bracing *against* debris.

Fortunately, while the patrol's members looked very much like the residents, they were making no effort to be stealthy; they wore uniforms that echoed the groups that had stalked Urelle's party for hundreds of miles through the Forest Sea.

Ingram's scouts had gotten one more vital piece of information: that the patrols were following a pattern. One would walk through the town itself, sticking to the walkways, and the other would work its way through the area *under* the town. They would meet at the base of the dock ramp closest to where Urelle stood, and then the topside patrol would go down under the town and those who had previously taken the low patrol would go high.

It was everyone's best guess that it was at *that* point — where the two patrols met — that they would use their speaking-stone to deliver a report. "We will hit them *immediately* after that," Ingram had said. "Urelle does her quartz-echo trick, we target the one with the stone, take him down first, then we finish it."

"Capture the stone, if possible," Meresti had added. "If we can hear their routine communication before we strike," he glanced at Quester, who bobbed her antennae, "we could imitate it periodically, gain us some time before there's any suspicion."

"Perhaps even gain other information," agreed Commander Eklisia.

"Agreed. But the primary goal is just to take them out without them getting off a warning."

She could see the first patrol of twenty men coming down the ramp now, led by an older man wearing three plumes on his armored helmet; just coming into view beneath was the second patrol, a similar three-plumed helmet adorning a younger, taller man who was also leading his group, which was the same size as the first.

She was momentarily disoriented as she found herself abruptly seeing the first man at much closer range, so close it seemed she could reach out and touch him. *That's... amazing, Ingram, but* warn *us next time!*

By the Balance, yes, Victoria thought tartly. *I nearly fell over when my eyes started seeing things through yours.*

Sorry, Ingram responded. *But I think it's got to be one of those two that does the report, so I'm keeping my farseers focused on them when they meet. You'll be able to see it as clear as me. You think you'll be able to hear them, Quester?*

A sense of amused confidence. *If you all stay quiet, yes. The wind favors us, coming in my direction, and my senses are sharper than yours.*

The two groups met and saluted each other with the same two-motion salute the Camp-Bels used. Then, through Quester's link, she heard sounds to go with Ingram's image:

"Anything to report?" the older man asked.

The younger one gave a wry smile. "Exactly as much as the last five times, sir. My men are starting to get tired, and so are yours. How much longer do we keep this up?"

"Until nightfall, son. The Ares-damned cowards can't launch boats at night. And the alert says they'll be here today or tomorrow, maybe day after at the latest, so we just have to put up with this a few days."

The younger man nodded. "What if they try to take the boats at night?"

"Ha! Then they'll have a bitter surprise, because your patrol's going to be on one boat, and mine on the other." The older man looked around; for a moment, vertigo struck Urelle as she saw the action through her own eyes, felt for a moment as though he could see her. She decided to keep her eyes closed until Ingram's transmitted vision ended.

"Well, time to report."

True to Ingram's expectations, the older man drew out a stone that fit Meresti's description exactly, pressed his hand to it, flipped a catch, and the stone opened, showing the glittering crystal set in a geode, with mystical runes inscribed around it. He closed his eyes, took a breath, and then spoke. "Hail to Ares and Aegeia! Patrols seventeen and eighteen, reporting in. No activity to report; Katasarion's quiet. Will bivouac in suspected transports in case of night infiltration."

The responding voice was very faint but still audible. "Understood, seventeen, eighteen. Will expect your next report in one hour. Hail to Ares!"

"Hail!" The older man closed the speaking-stone and thrust it into an inner pocket.

Ingram's visual sending stopped, and Urelle unleashed the spell she had prepared and held ready.

Magical energy *surged* out of her, saturating the area around the two patrols, sensitizing every piece of quartz from the tiniest grain of sand to a huge crystal buried a foot below the ground to the crystal whose location Urelle now knew exactly. She gasped as she felt the power running out of her like water from a badly-cracked barrel. *I can't hold this spell long!*

But they had known that. In the instant she finished the spell, there was the whisper-twang-hiss of four bows fired at once.

The patrol should have been taken by utter surprise; there was no visible sign of Urelle's enchantment, and had they even guessed the Camp-Bels were so close they would not have been so casual. They had suspected nothing.

Despite that, *something* alerted the older commander and others — perhaps a small but crucial sensitivity to magic that told them someone was casting a powerful spell nearby. The commander whirled and crouched, and two arrows meant for his head passed through air, and those meant for lower down ricocheted off his armored shoulders.

That had merely been the first split-second of the assault, unfortunately for the patrol; they were forty men in total, but *two hundred* Camp-Bel warriors exploded from the forest verge, some firing their ancient weapons that tore through armor and flesh with beams of pure light and thunder, others with weapons for more close quarters.

The commander went down as one of Quester's throwing-spears transfixed him through the neck, just as he was drawing the speaking-stone out again. He spun half around and tumbled to the base of the ramp, stone rattling to the ground ahead of him.

He's down! Urelle let up on the spell with a sense of immense relief, letting her strength flow slowly back. The commander hadn't had a chance to get a message off — but it had been close.

Still, the two patrols were organized, trained, and competent. They formed up into a defensive square, holding up shields that proved their enchanted nature by repelling fire from those thundering technological weapons. The two forces collided and Urelle winced at the clash of weapon, shield, and flesh. She didn't dare cast much magic in that mess, and the four of them had been effectively *ordered* to stay out of the main battle, despite Ingram being Captain.

The Camp-Bels had strung out their line, a core of their fighters focused on engaging the enemy, and a larger group reaching outward, to ensure that there could be no escape. The only direction in which the enemy could flee at all would be along the waterline... and that would be no escape at all, given how slowly a man might swim compared to those who would follow him on the shore.

Urelle thought that tactic made sense, but the orderly defense of the two patrols fell backwards and sideways, towards the pilings under the houses. She wasn't sure *that* made sense. They might be weakening their opposition on one side temporarily, but even if they *ran* in that direction, they would just be caught by the extended Camp-Bel line; they might gain twenty or thirty seconds, but no more. Yet that seemed to be what they were trying to do.

Then a flash of anothers' sight, this a strange prismatic layering of many images into one that could be no one else's sight other than Quester. A small group of the guards — four or five — had fought free for an instant at that end.

And from that group one *sprinted,* his companions throwing themselves bodily against any who might pursue. Urelle recognized the second commander, the younger man. As arrows and bolts of energy spattered around him, the man skidded around behind one of the pilings — and in Quester's sight, she could see he was pulling something from his pocket, something that looked all too familiar.

Two! They had two *speaking-stones!*

Urelle realized they had only a very few seconds before the surviving commander could open the speaking-stone and attune himself to speak. She had dropped the echo-screen and couldn't hold it at that distance anyway.

And there was no one close enough to get him.

Unless...

She looked across to where the young patrol commander hid, saw the column with its scattering of stones...

She reached out, *stretched,* felt the very fabric of *existence* beneath the world, held out her hand in front of her, as though bidding someone to stop.

Reversed, she remembered. She didn't have the strength to move herself from *here* to *there*; the energy of potential and position change would be too great.

But what if she only changed which object *held* the energy of each position?

There, at the base of the column, a stone, a stone that must weigh almost as much as *she* did. She envisioned her hand like a mirror, reflecting the stone on one side, herself on the other; she *bound* that vision into the fabric of the world, that *this* side of her hand was *here* and *that* side was *there*...

... and then she flipped her hand around and *wrenched* at the essence of the world.

There was a shock through her entire body, and she stumbled — and caught herself against the support column. The young patrol leader goggled up at her, the speaking-stone open but his concentration utterly disrupted.

Then she grabbed for his hand.

The young soldier was strong, trained, and tough. But he hesitated, the shock of her arrival and of the unexpected ambush combining with her slender and harmless appearance to give her one split second more.

And she had the Vantage strength.

By the time the others arrived, the soldier was unconscious at her feet, and the speaking stone was in her hand.

Chapter 37
Logic of Command

"That was a Wisdom-blessed close call," Eklisia said. "I've never seen that trick you used, wizard, and you thought *fast*."

Ingram smiled as he saw Urelle's gratified and slightly embarrassed expression at the compliment. "I'd been thinking about how to do that earlier today, so I had it prepared, in a way. And thank Quester — she was the one who showed me the man getting away."

"Speaking of that," Koragio Theros said, "what do you want us to do with the captives, Captain? Besides this guy," he gestured at the now-groggily-awake second commander, "we've got three others alive, only one of them critically injured. Healers think they can save him, though."

Ingram was about to say *what do you think?*, but Victoria's mindvoice intruded. *Your intention to be considerate of others' feelings and to take advantage of the wisdom around you is commendable, Ingram,* she thought, *but you* must *phrase your words like a commander, not like a friend or adventurer in a small group of equals.*

She was right. If he was going to be Captain, he had to be *Captain*. That didn't mean ignoring all the resources he had around him... but there were proper ways to go about it, especially now. "Bring the able-bodied ones here."

"Sir!" It took Security Chief Theros only a few minutes to get the other two captives.

Able-bodied was something of an exaggeration, Ingram noted; they'd been heavily beaten down before surrendering, one of them with his arm in a cast and the other showing darkening bruises all the way up one side of his body. The younger commander had a bandage tied around his head, but otherwise looked in better shape than his comrades.

Ingram nerved himself to appear cool and in control — something that would be hard to do when the prisoners noted that Ingram was barely taller than they would be on their knees. "Urelle, are they under any enchantments? I don't want to waste my time trying to talk with people who are under compulsion or control."

She made a few gestures; once more, Ingram thought he could faintly *see* what she was doing, even though such magic *should* be invisible. The ghost-light flew out, echoed through the three men before him, and returned to her.

Urelle shook her head. "No, they're not under any kind of enchantment. They *were* exposed to some pretty powerful... um, glamours? Mind-influencing auras? And not too long ago. But there's no *active* magic left on them."

"All right." He turned to the commander. "Sir, I am presented with a major dilemma, and I hope you can help me resolve it."

The man stared at Ingram, then looked up at the Security Chief. "You jest with me? Call this child your *Captain*?"

"This is no jest, sir," Ingram said, holding his hand up to keep Theros from speaking. "I am Ingram Camp-Bel, currently Captain of Ship and Clan Camp-Bel." He touched his shoulder. "Also, Guilded Adventurer, Zarathanton. If you wish, I can prove my competence on your body, before these your men, but I will have to make it swift; we have only so much time. I would rather not kill you or maim you." He set his jaw and paused before speaking. "But rest assured, I *will* have you killed if I must."

The commander's gaze had gone from being amused and offended to surprise, and finally a wary acceptance — better than Ingram had hoped. "I... see. Guilded Adventurer?"

"I and my companions. My being Captain is... unexpected, but I assure you, very real. What is your name, sir?"

"Sub-commander Geraki, squad eighteen under Commander Lycosa."

"Thank you, sub-commander Geraki. I believe you can understand my dilemma. We must move swiftly to avoid pursuit. I cannot leave you in the hands of the villagers, since being kept prisoner here could rebound upon the village. We cannot safely keep you four with us if we cannot trust you; I would have to detail multiple people to keep you under control at all times, and this would slow us. If we did not gag you, you could easily alert others to our presence." He took another breath, steeling himself. "You see, therefore, that killing you appears the most rational choice. I would prefer another. Have you anything to say for yourself and your companions?"

Good, Victoria said. *Mentioning his companions will force him to consider others. It is much easier to contemplate martyrdom if one can avoid involving one's allies.*

Geraki's mouth twisted in a sour smile. "You could surrender."

Ingram laughed in startlement. "Well, that *is* a different suggestion. But no, that's not possible. Let me put it another way: you serve Ares, yes?"

"Hail Ares!" he said emphatically, and the other two echoed him.

"No, don't hail him. Because he's not the true Ares. He's an impostor, and so was his Athena."

"*Captain* Camp-Bel, I was hoping for a better story than *that*. I have *seen* them, and felt their power."

"Oh, don't mistake me. I am not saying they do not have the *power* of gods. They simply are not the gods they're claiming to be; they're impostors trying to destroy us from the inside. Well, *Ares* is. His Athena is dead, and he's going to have a time and a half trying to figure out how to hide *that*."

"And how exactly do you expect me to believe *that*?"

"Because I think you are an intelligent man. You know the Cycles as well as I do — better, yes? You're older than me, you've studied them longer. Look at what *this* Ares is doing. Look at it *without* the glamour you recall, without his shining power, and think about what he's *done*. What he sent you to do here. Do you really believe that after *Cycles* of absolute loyalty, the Clan Camp-Bel would be wholesale traitors?"

The other two looked uncomfortable; Geraki frowned, looking around. "You're *all* Camp-Bel?"

Quester buzzed with amusement. "Not *quite*. I, Victoria, and her daughter... er, niece... are not of the Clan, merely friends and allies of Ingram. The rest... yes."

Geraki hesitated. "I knew a few Camp-Bels, in Talaria. Is Manuwell or Lepida Camp-Bel among you?"

Ingram looked to Commander Eklisia. "Commander?"

"Manuwell was killed, I know that because I had to write the report. Hold a moment."

There were some calls and shouts, and a few minutes later a tall woman, squat in build with a mass of curly hair about her head, approached. "Lepida Camp-Bel reporting, sir! What do you need of —"

"*Lepida!*" Geraki straightened up, trying to stand. "Is that really you?"

"Hold — *Geraki?*" With scarcely a pause, she went on, "yes, of course it's me, do you think anyone else would want this mop on their head?" Ingram thought that was an unfair characterization of what was obviously a well-tended head of hair, and her grin confirmed it was some kind of joke between the two.

"They say that Ares... isn't Ares."

Lepida Camp-Bel nodded. "Hard to believe, but if you've seen some of the things we have... kid, Amoni Agapis is *dead*. There's nothing left but buildings. And they had these... *things*, Xiilistiin, that infiltrated us. Killed an Ares-damned lot of our people. They've been trying to wipe the Clan out for months."

"Sub-Commander," one of the other two prisoners said, "You really know this person?"

"Lepida? Served with her for months in Talaria. Yes, I know her. And... I trust her word." He looked up to Ingram. "What do you want of me?"

That was a small stroke of luck. "All I ask is your word, and that of your men, that you will travel with us without resistance. We will not force you to join our cause, or fight for us, and if there comes a battle and you see a *harmless* way to escape, I will not deny it to you; but you will make all efforts *not* to draw attention to us."

The sub-commander was silent for a few moments. "Lepida, you give me your word as a Camp-Bel and an old comrade that all of these things are true?"

"I do, Geraki. Sorry, but it's all true, and we're all in trouble past our necks."

"Then I agree. Peristeri, Koraki, I can't make you do this, but..."

The other two looked at each other, then shrugged. "Sub-commander, you've been good to us over the last year or so; we'll take your course for our own," Koraki said.

"Excellent," Ingram said, feeling a deep sense of utter relief flooding him, now that he knew he didn't have to order cold-blooded murder. "When your companion awakes, it will be your job to convince him of the necessity for cooperation. But we will now begin moving. Lepida, since you know the sub-commander, I want you heading the detail that takes care of their fourth member and does overwatch on them."

"Yes, sir!"

"Good. Choose eight people for the job — one medic among them until the fourth one is on his feet. Dismissed!"

"Sir!"

A few minutes later the prisoners and their watch had departed. Ingram sat down and blew out a long breath.

"Well-said," Eklisia said, and sat next to him. "A stroke of luck there. If you don't mind me asking, what would you have done if he refused to cooperate?"

"Challenged him to single combat, and hoped I could beat some sense into him."

"No, you would not," Security Chief Theros snapped. "That's an idiotic choice, given how important you are. Yes, I know you're good in a fight — what kind of Camp-Bel would you *be* if you weren't? You could still end up dead, and *you are not replaceable*. If you *insisted* on that response, it'd be up to me or someone else to be the challenger. But it'd be a better choice to just kill 'em."

His dark eyes bored into Ingram's. "And you knew it, just from what you said at the start. You *can't* bluff that kind of thing, Captain."

Ingram thrust back his protests. *This... this is the worst price of war.* "Yes, Chief," he said quietly. "But let's hope it never comes to that. But if it does, I'll give the command. I'd do it myself, if I have to. I won't put that burden on anyone else."

He could feel the aching sympathy of his friends, and tried not to let it rip his heart in two.

Theros held his gaze for a few more moments, then nodded. "Good enough."

Ingram nodded once more, then turned to the Commander. "All right, Commander; let's get to those boats now." He looked at speaking-stone, still in Urelle's hand. "Can we fool them with false reports?"

Urelle smiled, and he felt her cheerful confidence. "We overheard their contact pattern, and I can use just a touch of magic to make Tisfotias, whose voice is closest to that of the dead commander, sound just like him."

"Then do it; we're getting close to an hour now." He looked at the sun, filtering through the trees. "And we need all the time we can get."

Chapter 38
Picking Up a Lost Trail

My forces are becoming limited.

This wasn't true, of course, for his ordinary army — there were enough and more than enough mortal warriors for his current needs. However, he *had* lost the single most powerful warrior in his command — Athena — and with her two of the contenders for the second place, the Sun of Apollo and the Scythe of Demeter.

Two God-Warriors and one who had been but a breath from being a true god, wiped out in a single battle — but a day after the most deadly monster in his arsenal, the Darkness That Devours, had been destroyed.

He looked down, contemplating the circle he had laid out on the stone. It was certainly sufficient for the planned use — summoning a powerful demon, the being whose name translated to Shadow of Nightmare, one of the first children of Kerlamion. It would not *hold* such a being long, of course, but that wasn't necessary; Shadow of Nightmare, deadly though she was, would not have the chance of a shadow against the noonday sun of opposing Raiagamor.

What she *did* have to offer was a shapeshifting talent that came close to matching Raiagamor's own — something rare indeed in anything not Great Wolf. That, combined with sufficient godspower, would make Shadow of Nightmare a more than acceptable replacement Athena, once she absorbed the soul-record that Raiaga had of the prior one.

But 'sufficient godspower', ah, there was the rub. Raiagamor considered his reserves of that power. Godspower was not, strictly speaking, the same as a glass of water; given time and focus, the power of the gods grew of its own accord, concentrating the worship of a thousand spirits into new, pure, sparkling drops of the essence of creation and destruction. The problem was that he had been using what he stole from Ares far, far faster than it replenished. The creation of the false Athena and the Seal had been intended to be the last major uses of Ares' energies outside of his own needs.

Raiagamor snarled half-heartedly. He *needed* a large reserve of the energies of the gods to maintain his imposture and have the ability to deal with any, shall we say, unexpected events — the kinds of events Adventurers seemed to trigger as a matter of course. The question was whether he also *needed* the false Athena.

It would certainly make things *easier*. The duality of Ares and Athena was ingrained in the Aegeian pyche; having Ares appear first was normal, but having Athena up and disappear in the middle of the Cycle, especially the way they had been... changing the script, so to speak? Not expected, not artistic, and potentially disruptive.

But... no. He did not *need* the false Athena any more. Breaking the belief in the gods was the current goal, and so disrupting the pattern could be just as easily turned to his advantage as against it. Regretfully, he gestured, and the circle was blown away, the valuable powders re-sorted and returned to their vials. No, he had lost three valuable pieces, and he was just going to have to play the game without them.

Still, he could not complain overmuch; Deimos and Phobos, the Demon-Xiilistiin God-Warriors, had served him extremely well so far, and the Swarm had proven its overall worth many times. He was *most* relieved, truth be told, by the destruction of the Darkness That Devours. The creature had been vastly powerful, but also a nearly uncontrollable random factor.

The only things left to mar his approach to final victory, alas, were the same annoyances he had been dealing with for months: Clan Camp-Bel, the party of four led by Ingram Camp-Bel, and the mystery of where and when Berenike would reappear.

That last concerned him most. Where *was* Berenike? All prior indications had been that the Spear of Athena was closely connected to the little band of Adventurers, and it truly surpassed belief that those four could have found their way through the Seal but Berenike had not.

Yet if she *were* here..., what was she *doing*? Her known character ought to have her finding Ares and doing her best to beat him into the ground. Failing that, she would surely be doing *something* straightforward and obvious. Despite this, she wasn't. There hadn't been a sighting of Berenike since the day the Seal had gone up.

He shook his head. *Perhaps, seeing the extent of the changes I have wrought, she has decided on more subtlety.* No one would have called Berenike stupid, even before she became the Spear; as a living representative of the Lady of Wisdom, she would have more than her share of common sense.

This implied that all of his problems would have a common nexus now: the Camp-Bel clan had thrown in its lot with the four Adventurers, and so Berenike must not be far away from them.

But if things were going well, they should be captured or killed very soon; he had been able to arrange squads to intercept them along any of the likely routes. He should —

A quick series of raps on the outer door, and before he could even bid the knocker to enter, the door opened and both Deimos and Phobos came in — wearing dark expressions that brought a foreboding to Raiaga's heart. "Lord Ares?"

"You *will* wait in future to be told to enter," he said, with a venomous sweetness. "For had my choices this hour been just *slightly* different, you would have interrupted a summoning, and *that* would have been... costly, to say the least."

"Yes, sir. Apologies, sir. It's urgent, sir."

That many *sirs* from Phobos amounted to a triple danger signal. "What is it, then?"

The two exchanged glances, then took identical deep breaths and spoke. "We've... lost them."

Raiaga stared narrow-eyed at both of them, and he saw the faces before him pale. "What do you *mean*, precisely? Lost them *how*? As I recall, we had multiple squads in the area, equipped to communicate swiftly and coordinate action!"

"Yes, sir," Phobos said, standing rigidly at attention. "Sir, the squads at the most likely target remained on station for two additional days, and saw nothing. They were then told to rendezvous with the others at a specific checkpoint. They reported that they were approaching... but never arrived."

"Which checkpoint?"

"The intermediate one, nearer Amoni Agapis."

"What?" If the retreating Camp-Bels had gone in that direction — seeking allies, perhaps, in Velos — they might have passed near that checkpoint, but they should have done so *long* before now, given when they knew the Camp-Bels had abandoned their compound. "What were our enemies doing anywhere *near* there at that time?"

Deimos gave a twisted smile. "They weren't. Tracking back showed that despite their reports, units seventeen and eighteen had never approached the checkpoint. Took us a while to be sure, but as far as we can tell someone's been feeding us false reports from them since the second day they had on station. The Camp-Bels arrived in town, somehow took out both patrol groups without either of them being able to get out a warning, and — presumably — took boats downriver. They must have guessed or been warned about the blockade, though, because they were never sighted there, either. Best guess is that they're now somewhere in the forests around Talaria, but that's *only* a guess."

Phobos tossed him a set of papers. "All our report."

Raiagamor gritted his teeth, counted to one hundred and then backward, before he trusted himself to take the report and read through it.

They are right, by my King's claws. Those soul-damned Camp-Bels walked right *through our cordon and on their way, and we now have no idea where they've gone, or what their destination truly is.*

Oh, *eventually* their destination would have to be Aegis and Ares himself... but what they intended to do *en route* was a major concern, and one he could not...

Wait. He leafed back, studied the report of the village more carefully.

"Phobos, see this section? Is it *correct*?"

Phobos read the indicated section. "Yes. The bodies were found in a mass grave, probably dug by magic, and —"

"I mean the *list* here."

"Certainly."

"Then," he said, smiling tightly, "there are *four missing bodies*."

From the narrowing and widening of their own eyes, he was pretty sure they were making the connections.

"No reason for them to have buried just those four separately," Raiagamor said. "So they *have* to have taken them prisoner. Perhaps convinced them of the rightness of their cause, or just dragging them along because they surrendered." That *would* fit the attitude of someone like the young Camp-Bel or his young mage friend. He wouldn't kill people in cold blood, even if it *really* would make more sense.

Raiagamor grinned. "I think I see a remedy for this error." He crossed to the strategy table, found the listing of their forces, and noted down the names of the four missing soldiers. "Yes. Yes, indeed. We know these two very well, do we not?" He indicated two of the names.

Phobos squinted at the paper, and then suddenly laughed. "We do indeed, sir!"

"Then here is what must be done," he said, and outlined a simple, if widespread, course of action. "The chances of contact at *some* point are high — they will have to arrange for provisions, or else pause for hunting, at some point along the way. Once any contact has been made... I expect we will find out what we want to know."

He grinned savagely. "Young Camp-Bel's mercy will be the death of him!"

Chapter 39
Breaths of Relief

"We're in the final stretch," Commander Eklisia said, as they finished crossing the small stream.

Victoria nodded, shaking a bit of mud from her boots. "So I gather, from the fact that we departed the vicinity of Lyra yesterday. How much farther, do you think, until we reach the Camp-Bel compound and Aegis?"

Eklisia squinted ahead; the brilliant emerald green of leaves and crimson, blue, gold, and violet of flowers were scarcely muted under the canopy, with the sun above unclouded and making the semi-clear areas under the trees seem near to open pathways. "Not *terribly* far, but not a short distance. A hundred thirty to a hundred fifty miles, I think. Important thing is that we know this territory fairly well, and we've left a hundred and fifty of our people at the other locations, so we can move faster. Say three, four weeks." She grimaced. "Jungle like this is always a challenge. We'll know we're very close when we cross the Syvia."

It took Victoria a moment to recall where she'd heard that name before, then it came to her; that was the stream that the young Berenike had fallen into and been rescued by Ingram. Likely the crossing would be an important moment for the boy-turned-Captain.

She looked ahead, where Ingram and Urelle were walking together; from the gestures and occasional quiet words that reached her, they were discussing magic and some of Urelle's newest revelations. The four of them had been working on unique tactics each night, some distance from camp. These tactics were based on their link and particular abilities, exploiting how Quester's lightning-fast mental interconnections allowed them to coordinate actions in the midst of combat without giving an adversary a clue as to what they intended.

She saw Quester emerge from the jungle ahead — she had been in the vangard — and frowned. She knew that tense pose, and the quiet of the link was also a warning that Quester felt she had unwelcome news to impart.

Abruptly, the forest *lightened*. Despite the momentary foreboding, Victoria felt as though a veil of despair had been drawn back, a weight she had forgotten she carried had been lifted from her. The colors of the jungle were more brilliant, the scent of life about her stronger, surer, more *real* than it had been for a long time indeed. The entire world took a breath, and awakened, and smiled, knowing that there was now nothing to fear; that darkness had passed, and hope had returned.

"Myrionar's *Balance*," she breathed. "What *is* that?"

The answer came to her as Ingram spoke, his eyes wide with joy and renewed belief. "Kerlamion's been *defeated*," he said, and the rest of the Camp-Bels about them paused, to hear the words and understand. "The Black City has been driven from the face of our world, and it is ours once more." He turned to the others. "You hear that, Clan? Even the King of All Hells has fallen; our enemy will fall as well!"

There was no great cheer — the Clan was more disciplined than that — but a whisper of joy and prayers of thanks rippled throughout the ranks from one side of the expedition to the other.

My apologies, but I fear I may have to spoil some of this good news, Quester thought to them.

Ingram's grimace was visible as he turned to face his friend. *Somehow, I am not surprised. Is it something to be discussed this way, or should we speak?*

Our bond is by far the best way at first. As Captain, you will decide who to tell afterward, of course.

The tiny head bowed, the long lavender hair that had escaped his ponytail momentarily screening his face. *I suppose. Urelle, Victoria, you hear this?*

Yes, Ingram. We are both aware. What is the problem, Quester?

Geraki and his subordinate Koraki — two of our former prisoners.

She sensed Ingram restrain a curse. *What? I was sure their repentance was genuine, especially over the last couple of months. Even* Theros *agreed with us about stopping a constant watch, and he's the sort who normally checks the man looking out of his own mirror for suspicious behavior.*

Quester's antennae dipped, and as she approached, Victoria could smell contrition in the pine and vinegar scent. *And I agree. Everything I could sense told me that they had come to believe our version of events.*

So what changed? Urelle asked.

As you know, my sense of scent is far superior to yours — or indeed, that of any in this company. Externally, they show no change, but in the last day or so I have scented increasing tension in both of them, with considerable admixtures of guilt and shame. Quester overlaid the thoughts with his own sense-impressions, and even with her minimal understanding of Iriistiik scent-interpretation the sharp-musk smell of shame and the earthy undertone of guilt were clear.

"Ares *Balls*," Ingram murmured aloud. "All right. It's a Camp-Bel matter for sure, though. Commander!" he called out. "A word with you, please."

Eklisia moved up to Ingram. "Captain."

"I am very much afraid that our former prisoners have some kind of secret, and given the circumstances, probably a dangerous one." He frowned, then continued, "Quester reports the change occurred only the past day or so. Find out — before we speak with either Geraki or Koraki — whether either or both of them were ever *out of sight* during our close approach and reconnoiter of Lyra, and if so, for how long."

Eklisia's mouth was a thin line. "*Those* two? Hades and Persephone *take* it, I was sure-"

"So were we. That's why I want to know fast and quiet."

Eklisia saluted. "Right away, Captain."

Do you think we're in immediate danger? Victoria asked Quester.

I did not scent... well, the immediacy of fear I would expect if it were an ambush expected shortly. So no, I do not believe so.

Ingram's thoughts showed a touch of relief. *Hope you're right, Quester.*

I think I can put a sensing screen around us, about a mile out, Urelle offered. *I can't hold it for all that long, but it should give warning if anything really dangerous is approaching.*

What if it's already closer than a mile? Ingram asked.

A mental smile. *The screen moves out from me to its farthest point; if there's something between me and there that we need to know about, it'll sense it.*

Do it, then. Thanks, Urelle.

The flicker of affection was close to a kiss, and Victoria smiled. Ingram relied on all of them, but it was clear that Urelle was the one he cared for most.

To everyone's relief, Urelle sensed nothing of great significance in the area (a nest of flame ants off to one side, and a forestfisher in the canopy above, but nothing worse). Less than an hour passed, however, before Victoria saw Commander Eklisia moving towards them.

Eklisia saluted Ingram. "Captain!"

"Report, Commander."

"Sir, it's pretty clear that both our friends were out of sight of anyone else for approximately an hour to an hour and a half at our closest approach to Lyra. Each group spoken to was not given a hint that we had any specific suspicions. It also seems that different groups each had the impression of Koraki and/or Geraki being 'just over there' in another group. Probably based on seeing Peristeri or Numismus elsewhere and assuming all four were together."

Victoria had never heard Ingram *growl* before, but he sounded almost like a jungle cat for a moment. "That's pretty clear, then. Get Chief Theros, have him pull both of them from their unit and bring them here. Try to keep it quiet until we figure out what's going on. Something happened that we missed, and I don't want anyone making a false jump before we've figured out what it is."

"Sir."

It was a tense fifteen minutes before Security Chief Theros appeared with four of his men leading Geraki and Koraki. "Here they are, Captain."

As she had expected, Ingram did not waste time. "What have you *done*, Geraki? Koraki?"

Victoria thought she could smell guilt herself, for a moment. The two men's faces were so wooden that there wasn't the slightest possibility they were innocent.

"What do you mean, Captain?" Geraki said after a moment. His voice was too artificially casual to be believed.

"I mean that you disappeared — both of you — somewhere near Lyra for about an hour. And you both *stink* of subterfuge — literally." He nodded to Quester.

The Iriistiik bowed. "My apologies," she said, "but... it so happens that while humans can conceal their thoughts and words, their scents tend to betray them. I can smell that you are both ashamed and guilty of what you have done. And more so now, that you are caught."

Geraki exchanged a glance with his subordinate, then buried his face in his hands; Koraki simply stared down at the ground. Ingram waited.

At last, Geraki lifted his head. "They have our families. Back in Aegis."

"You tried to *contact* your families?" Theros' voice was very nearly a snarl.

Both men shrank back. "No! No, sir! We're not fools. They contacted *us*. There was someone watching; they saw the scouts, followed them back, and called us out."

"What did they want, and what did they promise you?" Ingram asked, his voice low.

"What do you think, Captain?" Geraki gave a bitter grimace. "They promised us our families' safety in exchange for telling them what you were up to. Specifically, they wanted to know your destination and any details of your intentions."

"And what did you tell them?"

"That you were headed for Aegis, by way of the old compound." Geraki shrugged. "They weren't happy that we didn't have details as to *why* you were going there, given that we'd pretty much emptied the place, but we both convinced them of the truth — that only the Captain's Crew really knew the details, and none of them were talking."

Koraki lifted his head at last, and to Victoria's surprise there was the faintest smile on his lips. "We did, however, mention that we were pretty sure you were going to use the hidden tunnels from the southern approach to get in."

Theros blinked. "But there are no..." He, Ingram, and Eklisia smiled abruptly at the same time. "There *are* no hidden tunnels on the southern approach," Theros finished, his voice now appreciative.

"But they'll have one demon's hell of a time proving it," Geraki said, with his own frail smile. He glanced at Victoria, Urelle, and Quester. "South of the compound, the land drops steeply away in a series of gullies and heavily tangled jungle brush almost all the way to the sea. If they're searching there for tunnels hidden by magic or Camp-Bel technology, they'll be spending half a lifetime doing it."

Ingram nodded, then said, "Stay there, both of you." Chief Theros' men closed in a bit tighter, as Ingram led the rest of the group to a little distance away.

"What do you think?" he asked.

The Security Chief looked as though he'd bitten into a bitterbug. "This operation's just gotten ten times harder," he said.

"Not *that* bad, surely," Victoria said. "Yes, they know we are heading for your compound, which is not good. Yet this misinformation the two gave our adversaries should assist us, should it not?"

Theros did not look convinced, but Commander Eklisia had a thoughtful expression. "Some, certainly. As Geraki said, the terrain to the south is truly rugged. The only reasonable approach to intercept us, since they do not know where these purported tunnels are, is to spread their forces to detect our approach and then follow us to the tunnels — allowing them to not only catch us, but perhaps to discover any hidden surprises we wished to conceal via said tunnels. Thus, a large portion of their forces will be stationed there."

"But not all of them, unless their commander *and* Ares are fools, and they aren't," Theros said. "They'll have to assume it's possible Geraki and Koraki were either lying or misled, so they'll have at least some kind of cordon around the whole compound. Maybe alarm enchantments or watchspells, too."

"I can probably get us through anything like that," Urelle said. "Also... some of us should just go straight to the Capital. I'd say Auntie and me, and whichever people you choose who won't be instantly recognized there."

"Wait," Ingram said. "Why do you need to go to Aegis, before we even find out the secrets under Captain's Seal? Why not wait?"

"Because no matter *what* the secrets are, you still need someone to get up close to this new barrier, close enough to figure out what it's like and how to get through. That won't change. And neither you or Quester should go — you're pretty instantly recognizable and they've *got* to have people watching for you. Me and Auntie look more like, well, a lot of other people. And Quester, of course..."

"... is unquestionably unable to hide," Quester agreed. "Ares and his Xiilistiin were hunting my people; they must be primed to detect and capture or destroy any Iriistiik they meet. No, I believe Urelle is correct. Not only will it mean we are addressing two of our mission objectives at once, but also it will mean that if they *do* get a hint of Urelle's group being present, they may believe that the entire story told by Geraki was a lie — that the capital was our objective."

"Do you believe their current story?" Victoria asked. "It makes *sense*, of course, but any well-thought-out lie would."

Ingram immediately looked to Quester.

"They are absolutely telling the truth," Quester said promptly. "They were quite relieved, truly, when they finally spoke. As those hiding things often are, upon the revelation. They may fear punishment, but the subterfuge is over."

"And I can't really justify punishing them," Ingram said after a moment. "If someone were holding my parents hostage... well, Camp-Bels may be taught to never give in to hostage situations, but I doubt I could convince myself to just ignore the threat. Neither of them are Camp-Bel, so I certainly don't expect them to follow that bitter calculation to its end. They *did* increase our risk, but they did what they thought they could to mitigate it."

"I.. suppose." Commander Eklisia conceded. "My bigger concern is how they knew to look for the two of them. They were *targeted*."

There was a pause, then Security Chief Theros cursed. "Only one explanation; they're being more thorough than I thought. Someone dug up the grave we buried the bodies in, counted 'em, then went back over the records to figure out who *wasn't* in the grave. Then they made a good guess that they'd been turned to our side, made sure to get their families in hand, and set up a bunch of watchers in the cities on our path. They knew that we'd have to at least take a look in each city, to see how things were. Rather than try to position multiple assault forces along our path, they figured they could figure out our destination and then hit us hard there."

"I *suppose* they could also have done some sort of divination," Ingram said, "but that sounds a lot simpler as an explanation." He looked to Urelle. "Urelle, you can't pull two duties in two different places. We need to get to the compound *first*, because you're the most skilled wizard we have, by a long way. You have to stay with us until we're past any traps or sense-screens or ward-spells they might have put up. Once we reach... well, whatever entrance the Commander has in mind... then you and Victoria can head to Aegis, but first we need to get to the destination."

Urelle nodded. Victoria smiled. *Very good, Ingram.*

The young man did not entirely succeed in hiding his gratified expression, but then turned and walked back to the prisoners.

"Geraki, Koraki, you're free to return to your unit."

The two rose and saluted, with startled expressions. "You are... sure, sir?" Geraki asked.

"Very. I couldn't expect people to ignore threats to their families, and you weren't in a position to ask me or anyone else what to do. And your additional misinformation should make it possible for us to evade their trap. But if you *are* contacted by them again, I want you to come to me *immediately* as soon as you're clear. Same for anyone else," he said with a glance to Eklisia, who nodded. "I'd rather talk than execute my potential allies. Make sure that's clear to everyone."

The grateful looks both of the men gave as they saluted again and left showed no trace of the doubts they had had a few months before, when they first met the diminutive Captain of the Clan.

And as Ingram turned back, Victoria saw there were hints of lines on the young face that did not belong on a boy not even a third her age. She suddenly felt the weight of her own years, more heavily than she ever had. *May the Balance damn this Ares, or whoever he is. For all the wonders we would have missed, I still would wish that my daughter and this boy had been spared this.*

But Ingram was smiling, despite the weight she could see upon him. "All right," he said, "let's move.

"We don't want to keep Ares waiting, after all."

Chapter 40
Aegis

Urelle teased the strands of magic apart, inch by inch, controlling her breathing and making it a calm rhythm by which she could let time and urgency pass, leaving her only the task before her.

Finally, the warden spell-wall — that appeared to circle the entire compound along its original fence — was fully parted, a gap twenty feet wide and fifteen high clear through its insubstantial yet sensitive matrix. With a casual gesture, she summoned an oval of light that exactly fitted the open space, then, to provide a margin of safety, shrank it by a foot on all sides.

"There," she said to the waiting Clan. "Cut the fence there and you can just walk through."

"*Well* done," said Theigo Camp-Bel; his rugged dark-brown face showed his amazement mainly through the wide hazel eyes. "By the Founder, I would never have believed it had I not seen it; I've been studying magic for four decades, child, and that's a task I could never have assayed. Not in such swift time, anyway." He chuckled. "Should've spent less time in the library and more in the field, I see."

"You're far too kind, sir," Urelle said, embarrassed.

"No, he's right," Ingram said. "Commander, how are we doing on the perimeter?"

"Five scouts neutralized along the way. We've got maybe an hour, maybe less, before the enemy realizes we're here and on the northwest side."

"How about inside the fence?"

"Observers say there's only two guards on the inside. They haven't any idea what to guard, anyway. One of them will be passing this area in about five minutes." He gestured two of the men forward; they held specialized metal-snips. "We'll have this part of the fence down in a few moments; Urelle, can you make it look like the fence is still intact?"

"Sure. If Theigo can help me, I can make it so that they won't even see us standing on this side, as long as we all stand close."

"Perfect. Then when I give the signal, we take the guard fast and quiet."

As predicted, a lone guard, wearing Ares' colors, strolled quietly and with apparent alertness through the deserted compound. He reached, then passed the open gap... then paused, sniffing.

He is not human! Xiilistiin!

Quester leapt straight through the gap, and even before his hurtling body reached the guard, his psionic abilities hammered the patrolling man-shaped being to the ground; before it could even attempt to escape, Quester's longmace smashed down on its head.

"Founder help us," muttered Ingram. "Did he get a warning off, Quester?"

"I... do not believe so. He was not quite sure of what he was sensing, and then I struck him very quickly. But we will not be so lucky a second time."

"Hide the body," Theros said. "If they can't determine when or where he was killed, it'll help."

"Won't the hole in the fence rather betray that?" Commander Eklisia pointed out.

Theros grinned. "Only if our resident mage here can't fix it."

"I can definitely do that!" Urelle said. "Just get everyone through and then stand the original back in the right place."

The remaining Camp-Bels filed through the wide opening swiftly, and Urelle then caused the hole in the fence to close. A moment later, she let the hole in the warden spell-wall reduce and fade away.

"All right, let's move! The entrance we're looking for is about a thousand yards this direction!" Eklisia strode ahead, the others following.

Urelle noticed with a bit of a shudder that they were now passing through a small graveyard that had been hidden behind a low building nearby. Ingram slowed and stopped.

"What is it?" she whispered.

He pointed, with a faint smile. The headstone gave readable dates, showing that someone young had died and been buried here, but the name was inscribed in an alien script she did not know; glancing around, she saw a large number of the nearby stones were also written with the same unknown alphabet. "What does it say?"

"It says 'Berenike'," Ingram said. "This is where the false body was put, after they moved it out. No one outside of the clan could read it." He gestured to the fence a short distance away. "I wonder if she knew, even then. Maybe they'd told her. Anyway, this was the last place I saw her, until the day *you* first saw her. She stood right there," he pointed to a location just to the right of the headstone, "and told me she'd always be with me in one way or another."

The others continued to move farther in. "Thanks for showing me," she said. Then, before she could let her reluctance stop her again, she asked, privately, *Ingram... are you in love with her?*

Ingram twitched, but kept control of his face otherwise. *I... In a way. Yes. But somehow, I know it's not something that could ever happen. I don't know why. I know she cares about me, too, and now that I know that I wasn't a failure...* He shrugged. "Yes. I love Berenike," he said aloud, quiet but clear. "I think I was in love with her for a long, long time. Still am, maybe I always will be."

He looked up and met her gaze. "But she isn't you," he said, and there was a world of meaning in those four words. "And I don't want you to be her. Just yourself. If you... I mean, if I'm the person you..."

"You are," she said. A flash of self-consciousness made her add, "I mean, as much as I can be sure of anything. It's not like we're as old as Aunt Vicky."

Ingram tentatively took her hand. "No. And we could be wrong, I guess. But I don't think so."

It was a *strange* first kiss, she thought dizzily, as their lips met for the first time. Standing in an old graveyard, with the Clan Camp-Bel streaming around them, deliberately ignoring their Captain and the young wizard with him. At the same time, it was achingly sweet and sent a tingle straight from her lips all the way through her body to her toes, and she leaned in, wrapped her arms around the delicate-looking body, and *really* kissed him.

They pulled apart at the same moment, and smiled — she was sure — identically star-struck, foolishly amazed, smiles. Then with an obvious effort, Ingram forced himself back to seriousness. "I've got to... um, Captain some things."

"I know. And Vicky and I are going to have to do some things of our own, as soon as you've found the right place." She gripped his hand again. "But I'm glad we took a few minutes."

"So am I," he said, and their mental link echoed both their sentiments to their very core.

So are we, Quester's mind-voice said with a wry humor, reflected by Victoria's fond affection.

Now Ingram did blush. *It's hard to hide from this audience, I guess.*

I will contrive to find a way, Quester said, answering Ingram's unspoken question. *I understand your need for... private moments, even if an Iriistiik has a hard time understanding many of them.*

Ingram moved swiftly forward, Urelle at his side, catchin up with Commander Eklisia in a few minutes. "Found anything, Commander?"

Eklisia looked at the two of them and gave a smile of her own, then nodded. "See that building there? The ruined one?"

"That was the west storage unit," Ingram said after studying the area. "They took down several buildings, I see," he added, looking farther out. "Not all of them. I wonder why?"

"Likely someone pointed out that there was nothing wrong with the *buildings,*" Chief Theros said. "No point in what they did here otherwise."

"All right. So what about the storage unit, Commander?"

"There's an entrance to *actual* secret tunnels there, hidden under the floor. We'll have to clear the rubble from the northwest corner, though."

"This sounds like something I might assist in," Quester said.

The Commander raised her eyebrows. "Ah, yes! Your telekinetic abilities; they will not register on magical senses, and may be much more quiet. If you have sufficient control... ?"

"I am not quite ready to perform surgery without either set of hands," Quester said, dipping her antennae in a smile, "but I believe I can be acceptably precise when moving larger masses, yes."

"Good," Urelle said. "Commander, if that's your objective, then I think Auntie, I, and our assigned guard force should be departing."

"Agreed," the Commander said.

Ingram showed no sign of concern outwardly, but she could feel that he was worried for her — as she was for him. Instead, he looked to Theros. "Chief, you and your men take care of them."

"Begging your pardon, sir," Commander Eklisia said, "but we'll be needing all the Crew for this." The Chief's eyes narrowed, but then widened, showing he understood whatever Eklisia was getting at. "And if I understand the nature of Quester's... connection to the three of you, neither Urelle nor Victoria will need our technology to communicate their findings. Yes?"

"Quite so," Victoria answered. "In point of fact, I would prefer *none* of you came with us, upon reflection. The fewer to be spotted means fewer chances we *are* spotted."

The muscles in Ingram's jaw bunched visibly, but she heard him take a breath before speaking. *You know Auntie's right, Ingram,* she thought.

A mental sigh. *Of course she is. She's got more experience at this Adventuring game than the rest of us put together.* "Agreed. I don't *like* it, but I can't argue your points... and if we draw attention here, we'll need all the help we can get." He gestured towards the low mountain or tall hill that was visible in the distance. "Get going. We need to know about that defensive barrier as soon as possible."

"Count on us!" Urelle said, trying to radiate confidence. It wasn't *entirely* an imposture.

The two of them left the compound toward the northeast, farthest from expected patrols. It didn't take long to unweave the ward from within. "All right, Auntie, now we have to really move."

The beloved face looked down at her with a smile. "And you have a plan for that, do you?"

"This spur of forest goes down most of the way to the city, so we shouldn't be noticed if we keep to it. Then, according to Ingram, we'll be near a busy intersection, so we *should* be able to enter the streets without a problem." She concentrated, bringing up her mystical focus. "I think I can make us both *much* faster."

"Enhancement spells? Very good, Urelle. Yes, if you can speed us up and give us the needed endurance, it will take relatively few minutes to run the miles to Aegis."

These enhancement spells were pretty basic, although the speed one — an air-fire linked channel to the body — would require a *lot* of her power to maintain. On the positive side, her strength should come back quickly once she dropped that enhancement. Endurance was much easier, as it was an earth-spirit linked enhancement, and could be supported directly by the earth they were running over.

She focused on Victoria. Slowly, her vision of the supernatural replaced the mundane, and her aunt glowed before her, a racing fountain of sparkling gold and sapphire and argent that yet stood still and solid. She attuned herself to that indomitable, still-young spirit, and brought that resonance forward, the *song* of the spirit calling to a deeper sound, one nigh below the threshold of hearing, that echoed from the stone and earth below. The spirit called to the earth and the earth spoke to the spirit, and suddenly emerald light rose from the ground and mingled with the other fountaining colors, wrapping them in its power and spreading to outline all of Victoria, a green-glowing woman with tri-colored fire at her heart.

Great! That's the endurance enhancement, and it's working fine! She copied the process on herself — no point in exhausting herself *before* getting the reinforcement. Then she once more focused on her aunt, calling on the swiftness of the air and the power of the fire that dwelt within the center of the soul, and with a final twist hooking them to the power welling up from the earth; it would still put a strain on the spirit through which it all flowed, and the body that was driven faster, but for a short time it would be all right.

She made sure the same enchantment was complete on herself, and then nodded. "Let's go, Auntie!"

Victoria leapt away, and Urelle followed. She found herself laughing with delight as the ground *flowed* away beneath them, streaming past on either side without effort, the two of them running lightly faster than a sithigorn at full sprint — and the riding birds were known to be able to outpace hunting cats for short distances.

"By the *Balance*, Urelle, this is magnificent!" Victoria said, eyes shining. "I haven't felt this *lightness* for years, since I retired!" She hurdled a fallen forest giant, four feet across, as though it were a curb.

She smiled at her aunt's startling enthusiasm. "It's one of the things the Wanderer taught me — he called them 'buffing spells', though I don't know why. They don't polish anything." She bounded from the top of a ten-foot boulder, came down thirty-five feet away, kept moving. "To be fair, a lot of his conversations were like that. You knew what he *meant*, but it never made sense the way he said it."

"He *is* far older than any of us truly understand," Victoria said, "and the context for his words may come from another world entirely. I daresay I could make a few references you would never understand, either."

"I guess so. It was strange. But I really learned a *lot*." They leapt over an eight-foot stream without preparation or hesitation. "My big worry now is if we'll be able to see this barrier. If they don't have it up, I might not be able to analyze it at all."

Victoria gave a smile that actually reminded her momentarily of the Wanderer; it had the same sharp, knowing quality his smiles often did. "Oh, I don't think we need worry about *that*. It will be active soon enough."

"How do you know?"

"There isn't the slightest possibility that those watching and searching near the Camp-Bel compound will fail to notice their arrival very shortly. And I would be *very* surprised if Ares did not immediately prepare for the worst once he gets that news. The Camp-Bel reputation is not unearned, after all."

Urelle had to agree. It made sense. If you went to the trouble of making a shield to seal off your final approach, there was no point in giving your enemies a chance to sneak in *before* you activated it. So, once you knew they were close... on it went.

It was only a few more minutes before they saw the trees thinning out; the two slowed to ordinary human speeds and Urelle dropped the enhancements. "Now, we just get a look at what the regular people on the streets look like right now, and we can either change from our packs, or if I have to, I'll tweak our appearance magically. I'd rather *not*, though, because any magic I use for that could be obvious to people looking for disguises."

Peering from the brush, the thing that first struck Urelle was that there were a lot fewer people in the streets than she had expected. It was the time of day that markets were normally open — and indeed, there were some open stalls visible at this broad intersection of two streets of well-fitted pavement stone — sort of a town square without the square, so to speak. But it wasn't as *busy* as she would have thought.

Still, there were people, and they had some general similarities — loose clothing of lighter colors, often robe-like in appearance, of varying hues. This matched the buildings, built mostly of stone that ranged from white to pale pink to pale golden yellow; the roofs were of what looked like curved sections of clay tile, or sometimes of wood, though that was less frequent.

In general appearance, most of the people looked not much different from those at home. Neither she nor Victoria would stand out — well, aside from Aunt Vicky being awfully tall for a woman, but there wasn't much she could do about that.

Urelle? Ingram's mind-voice reached her. *We've found the entrance, we're going in. How are you?*

Well, at least he was making progress. But... *We've reached the edge of the forest. I don't like what we're seeing.* She sent him an image of the scene before her.

Ingram's returning thoughtvoice was worried. *By the Lady, no, that's bad. I know that market, we traded there quite a bit. It's usually ten, fifteen times that busy. Watch yourselves.*

We will. You, too.

Guards patrolled the street — more of them than would be normal. *They are on alert.*

Yes, Victoria thought back. *More importantly, look at their faces. I've seen this before.*

Urelle studied the people she could see, and slowly she began to see what Victoria meant. *They all look... nervous, even when they're just doing ordinary things, like buying food. And they watch the guards whenever they think the guards aren't looking at them, and try to avoid getting too close... without* looking *like they're avoiding them.*

Precisely. They are terrified of these patrolling guards, something surely not normal. Victoria's gaze narrowed, searching the visible area. *And a few of the visible houses are empty; that one appears to have had its door broken in. We will have to be* extremely *careful, Urelle.*

Victoria didn't have to explain any more. Whatever Ares was doing, it obviously included crushing any resistance at all in the capital, and he didn't care what anyone thought about him anymore. *He must be close to whatever endgame he envisions.*

Changing clothes, fortunately, was easy. They didn't look identical to the locals, but close enough that no one would be likely to remark on it... unless they drew attention to themselves some other way.

They slipped around the side of a nearby house and waited until there were no obvious watchers, then walked casually into the street, following it towards the center of Aegis and the towering hill with the broad stairway Ingram called the Aegeian Path, that led to the very summit - the place where, if their information was right, they could call Athena.

Somehow.

It wasn't *far* to the Path — a mile or so now — but the streets seemed to stretch before them forever. Their footsteps sounded unnaturally loud, when so few people were on the streets. A guard approached, and they imitated the others — subtly avoiding while in no way being confrontational, or too obviously frightened.

The entire *city*, Urelle realized with a creeping shudder, was too quiet. Not quite the dead silence of most of Salandaras, evacuated in the face of war, but far, far too subdued for a living, dynamic city. This was the faint sound of fear, of dry-mouthed caution watching from a window, of slow-burning, inescapable, wearing terror. *And it's happened only in a few years; when Ingram left there couldn't have been a hint of this, or he'd have mentioned it!*

Victoria's voice spoke again in her head. *Well, now, that's inconvenient.*

Following Victoria's gaze, she saw that ahead of them — near the entrance to the large square that lay before the Aegeian Path — the street was blocked off, large sawhorses dragged into position across the street and several guardsmen standing, watching anyone trying to enter. *I suspect we will find that there is no easy approach to the Path. How close will you need to be in order to analyze the spell?*

She could see the Path going up, visualized a spell that could envelop the entire area. *Not too close. One of the rooftops overlooking the square would probably be close enough.*

Then let us do that.

Victoria immediately led them up a side road, out of sight of the guards. After a few moments, she found an opportunity to draw Urelle into a narrow alleyway. *Now, if you could...?*

It required only a few moments to use the airwing spell to bring them to the rooftop. This was one of the ones made of wood — solid and only slightly pitched. There were five buildings between them and the edge of the square; the last one, on the edge of the square, was also wooden, and the slope looked manageable.

Had they been able to just sprint, it would have been a matter of a few moments to get from that beginning point to the target rooftop. But before crossing from one to the next, they had to be cautious — make sure no one was below to see the movement as two figures made a magic-assisted leap from one roof to the next. Sometimes that meant waiting several minutes for a safe moment.

Two roofs away — and suddenly Urelle's magical senses screamed at her. She looked up.

A wavering, pearlescent shimmer suddenly enclosed the Aegeian Path from base to peak.

You were right, Auntie, she thought. Inwardly, she tensed. *That means they've noticed Ingram's people.*

As long as they don't notice us, Victoria thought.

A few more minutes, and they came to a very light landing atop the roof at the edge of the square. There was a laundry line strung across it, currently empty of clothing, and a door in the roof for access, but there was no sign of anyone there. *I'll only need a few minutes,* Urelle thought.

She brought up her hands, focused through them, studying the vast magical construct above her.

It was not as immense as the great Seal around all of Aegeia; nor was it nearly as complex. It *was* powerful, though, a simple, three-dimensional repeating, symmetrical structure that would resist any form of force. But having done this multiple times now, Urelle knew what she was looking for; the perfect structure *had* to have a node, a nexus at which it was assembled, brought together...

Victoria pulled her back, gently. *You were leaning too far out, Urelle. Someone could have seen you.*

Sorry, Auntie.

She focused again. Where was this gigantic structure *anchored?* She hoped it wasn't at the peak; climbing the extremely steep cliffs on the rear of that peak would be a huge challenge.

The door rattled behind them.

Before Victoria could reach it, it popped open, and one of the guards, dressed in a breastplate, crested helmet, and armored skirt, rose into view, sword drawn. "Who are you, and what are you doing on this roof?" he asked.

At that moment, Ingram's voice reached her mind again. *Urelle, they've found us! We need that information* fast!

Acid burned in her stomach as she answered. *They've found us too, Ingram,* she thought. She turned to focus on the column. *But I'll get it to you. Somehow.*

Victoria stepped a bit forward, holding her hands spread wide to appear nonthreatening. But the man's eyes narrowed... and then a terrible and fearsome smile spread across his features.

"Oh, We remember *you*," he said, and there was a chill and alien undertone to his words. "You killed the Swarmfather, one of those sent to the Outside."

Great Myrionar, no! It's a Xiilistiin!

Chapter 41
The Secrets of the Clan

Quester watched the two women disappear in the distance, and could sense Ingram's grim, resolute focus as he banished the worry about them to a separate corner of his mind.

To Quester, the desolation of the abandoned Camp-Bel compound was even sharper than to her comrades; she could smell the lingering scent of hundreds of people clinging to every wall, every door, every path... and the newer, sharper smell of those who had come after, contemptuous of the history of this home, this *Nest*, that had been the center of an entire people. She could see, emphasized in the spectra beyond human perception, the remnants of the violent search, not merely in the grossly obvious detritus of shattered locks and broken doors, but the scrapes of dislodged earth, the scratches where even walls had been subjected to focused violence to test them, to see if they hid secrets not obvious to the simple eye.

And more; her antennae returned the residue of covetousness, hatred, hunger, and frustration of the searchers, a psychic trace burned into the areas where they had most hoped to find survivors or secrets. Quester shivered, her wingcases giving a sussuration of her discomfort, as she recognized the physical and psionic odor of the ancient enemy. *Xiilistiin were here. Perhaps leading the search.*

Not surprising, Ingram responded. *Ares trusts them with a lot of his dirty work, and they have senses like yours. The combination of human and Xillistiin searchers would have uncovered pretty much anything.* She could sense his worry that this meant that the secrets they sought here had been destroyed — or, worse, discovered and read.

"Are we ready, Commander?" Ingram asked aloud.

"If Quester is, yes. How large a mass can you lift, Quester?"

"In truth," she responded, "I am not entirely sure. Many hundreds of pounds, at the least."

"We need that corner cleared — to a space at least ten feet on a side, more by preference. The door we seek is not that large, but we will want the area around it clear and able to be protected."

"Understood. I will assay this task."

Quester surveyed the ruin's northwest corner. It had been constructed of stone and steel, sheathed with wood inside and out; a combination of fire and some sort of greater force, perhaps magical, had brought it all down. It was a daunting obstacle; the rubble towered almost ten feet over her head.

Yet I did stand, if for only a few moments, against a false god and her warriors. Perhaps this is not beyond me.

She reached out with still-new senses, feeling the caress of steel and the rough scrape of stone and the sharp edges of glass, the bitter tang and squeak of charcoal, the stinging rasp of burned dirt and paper, the crackling vibration and stench of the dead, buried but unmarked, within the wreckage. Too, she felt the traces of lost determination, unmoored anger, unrestrained despair, indiscriminate shame and fury, hovering about this and other buildings.

"There are... shades here," she said in a low voice. "There was no effort made to help them pass, not through sympathy nor ritual nor banishment. Their anger and confusion is strong here."

Eklisia cursed. "Monsters. Just left the place to become a ruin haunted by shades and revenants, maybe worse?"

"Well, that's one way to reduce the chances of anyone casually poking around," Ingram said, his light wording belied by the tense grimace on his face. He shook his head. "We don't want to touch that wreckage, or anything here, if we might trigger a revenant. What can we do for these spirits?" he asked, looking at the other members of the Crew.

"We're of the Clan," Officer-Medical Tisfotias said after a moment. "You're the Captain. If we can assure them we're here to reclaim what was lost, that their sacrifices weren't in vain? That should work."

A swirl of leaves danced around the corner, though there was no wind. Quester found herself drawing back; there was something menacing about that otherwise innocent motion. "Do your prayers or whatever you must do swiftly; I think as I have noticed them, they have now sensed us."

The Crew gathered about Ingram, making a wedge with the tiny lavender-haired boy at its head. Ingram turned to face the building, and the swirling leaves that had now been joined by another tiny swirl of dust, and gave the crossed arms-going-to-upright salute, echoed by the rest of the Crew.

"I, the Captain, have returned!" Ingram's tenor voice was loud in the deathly silence of the compound. He reached up, detached the Insignia, and held it out. "The Captain and Crew return, and we thank you, the fallen, for the gift of all you had, for the lives you lost to safeguard the secrets of the Clan and the people of the Clan as they fled. Know that your sacrifice was not in vain. The Clan lives — some beyond Wisdom's Fortress, and others throughout Aegeia. And we, the Crew, have come to reclaim the secrets you have guarded. Go to your rest with Athena and the true Gods, and know that you are honored and remembered."

The twin swirls circled each other, and had become three, the third black with charcoal dust. They were taller now, and the hiss of the wind was audible. They vibrated with the words, swayed back and forth, but they did not disperse. As the last echoes of Ingram's voice died away, the three rose higher, ten-foot dust-devils beginning to spin faster, guarding the fallen rubble.

"Athena's *Spear*, they're not listening!"

"I was afraid of that," Tisfotias growled. "You've got a good turn of speech, boy, but you're no priest. They can't sense you clear, and they're too angry and confused and half-there to know what you're saying."

"But we don't *have* any priests with us," Ingram said. "I can try the prayers to send on the spirits of the dead, but it's been *months*."

"You're right; that won't work now," Security Chief Theros said grimly. "Been too long. But if we can't figure out a way to get through to them *quick*, this is going to turn into a fight against our own dead."

As if to emphasize this, vague, hostile glows like eyes appeared, floating as if projected against the dusty swirl of the columns, and a board — studded with rusted nails — whipped through the air, flying over the heads of the Crew. They drew weapons — except for Ingram.

"No!" Ingram snapped. "We can't fight our own people, the ones who died to let the Clan escape."

"We'll *all* have died in vain if we can't fight back," Eklisia pointed out mildly.

"We need..." his head snapped up. "Quester! Quester, you could sense them — can you talk to them? Send them something, let them know who we are?"

"I do not know. I will try."

Quester reached toward her sense of the spirits, the embodied heartache and fear and abandonment and rising rage and fractured sense of duty. *You face the Crew*, she thought, projecting it at that psychic trace. *The Captain and Crew have come for you. Lay down your anger, know you are no longer alone, you are not forgotten.*

The rage and fear lashed back, a sting of agony in a part of Quester she had barely known existed, but Quester ignored it, did not let a sense of her own uncertainty and pain reach the thoughts she sent. *I am not of them, but I am a bridge. Hear the words of your Captain.* She sent Ingram's speech, intertwining the words with the earnestness that was the boy's strongest essence. *The Clan has returned for you. See them. Hear them.*

The lashing was stronger, yet less focused, like a crying child beating against her, striking as hard as they might but with no idea of how and where to hurt her, or even true intent to do so. It hurt — especially inside, where she had no armor and dared not defend herself as she would against a true foe. These were the remains of those who had defended the compound at the last, those who had known they would die, for the sake of a few hours more of freedom and misdirection. She would not fight against their terrified, confused rage. She linked more strongly with Ingram. *Tell them yourself, Ingram. Speak through me.*

She felt a surge of his determination, his faith in her and his belief in his people painfully pure, and she became a conduit of his thoughts and hopes. *I am Ingram Camp-Bel, now Captain, and I say to you that we are here to reclaim what you defended! Your tasks were well-done, and* better *than well-done, and we give you all honor for your work! Now let go of this place, and go to that awaiting you in Elysium!*

Confusion rose, became ascendant over rage. The whirling funnels wavered, then collapsed slowly, becoming misty half-visible figures. One — a woman in the strange blocky armor of the Camp-Bels, with a huge hole through her chest — stepped forward. "Captain...?" she asked, her voice as distant as thunder from a clear sky. "You... failure... Captain?"

Eklisia stood forward. "I am Lieutenant-Commander Eklisia of the Crew, now promoted to Commander. Ingram was no failure, but a deception — a victory within a cloak. He stands for us all now, and he bids you lay down your arms and rest. Guardian Maenea, you and your people have done enough."

The ghostly eyes sharpened, moved their gaze across the entirety of the crew. Then her shoulders sagged, and phantom blades dropped from her hands. "The Clan... endures? The secrets are safe?"

"We endure," answered Ingram, "and the secrets we have come to claim, as you have made them safe. Go now to your rest, and know we salute you."

Once more the Crew gave that Aegeian salute, but this time the shades before them returned the gesture. For an instant, Quester saw others — dozens, perhaps a hundred or more, barely-visible figures who stood rigid, holding a salute to the living. Then they all turned, and walked away, towards a Light that Quester glimpsed only for the smallest fraction of that instant.

The compound was quiet, but there was now no menace in the silence, no sense of pain or fear or loss. It was merely an assemblage of partially-ruined buildings.

Quester did not need to be asked to try her main task again. She extended those psychic senses, grasped once more every element of the rubble, and braced herself, as though ready to lift a massive weight, psionic power echoing by her body. Her claws clenched, gripping the immensity she sensed, and she *heaved*.

With a scraping rattle and a grinding sound of crushing stone, half the ruined building rose into the air, not merely the northwest corner but a rectangular block of jumbled granite and metal and detritus sixty feet by seventy-five and reaching heights of twenty feet, uncountable tons of mass floating as though it were smoke. Quester was barely aware of the gasps of those around her, merely of the immensity of the pressure building on her mind and body. She drifted it to the side, unaware precisely of what she had done, but looking, sensing for when what she held had passed again over another pile of wreckage, something that would not be further harmed, and with infinite care lowered her burden.

Even with all the care in the world, the unbalanced wreckage, freed of the constraints of Quester's will, could not be entirely silent nor balanced; metal screeched and protested, masonry shifted and cascaded down the sides of the new and higher pile of rubble. But even after the readjustment settled, over sixty feet of the length of the building's foundation was as clear as though swept by a Titan's broom. Quester straightened, looking around — and her own antennae froze as she realized what she had done.

"By the Missing Father," whispered Eklisia. "I would never have believed it."

I had no idea you could do anything *like that!* Ingram thought.

She let him smell cinnamon and wine. *No more had I. It was a strain... but I had not the slightest conception that being a Mother, even* half *a Mother, made me so powerful.*

Ingram shook himself. "We can stand around and gape later," he said. "Find this door and get it open!"

Commander Eklisia moved forward, surveying the northwest corner of the smooth stone slab that had been the foundation. After a moment, she pointed a wand that somehow reminded Quester of the ISNDAU, with its inlaid lights on a smooth surface, and abruptly an eight-foot section of the floor dropped away, leaving a broad set of stairs leading down into darkness — a darkness relieved in a moment by a soft white glow. "Here, Captain!"

"By the... that's impressive." Ingram moved forward with Quester. She studied the revealed doorway as they entered, saw that the edges were not straight but had resembled natural faint cracks expected in such stonework. Even one trained in locating secret doorways would have been hard-pressed to find it. A sense of subtle magic, combined with a trace of the scent of a thunderstorm, touched her antennae as they passed inward.

Urelle? she heard Ingram send. *We've found the entrance, we're going in. How are you?*

We've reached the edge of the forest. I don't like what we're seeing.

A quick flash, roads and markets strangely deserted.

By the Lady, no, that's bad. I know that market, we traded there quite a bit. It's usually ten, fifteen times that busy. Watch yourselves.

The procession of eighty descended the stairs and followed Eklisia down a long hallway, paneled in wood but, to Quester's scent, reinforced with metal throughout. They passed several doorways, the hallway lit by small objects fastened to the wall at intervals, before turning through another doorway and descending again. There was no mistaking, now, the scent of eager anticipation and amazement from Ingram... nor a subtler but equal anticipation and hope that she could scent from the rest of the Crew.

Finally, they came to a more massive doorway than the others, this one with a strange glowing panel set into the wall. Eklisia moved forward and spoke. "Commander Eklisia, with the Crew, for admittance."

A sheet of green light sprang into existence, startling both Quester and Ingram, and passed down Eklisia's body. "Recognized," said a new, feminine voice, calm contralto, even, clear, and precise. "Promotion of Eklisia to Commander is now logged. Identify new members."

"Holder of the Insignia, Captain Ingram Camp-Bel," Eklisia said.

"Confirm, Officer-Medical and Security Chief?"

"We confirm," Tisfotias and Theros said. "Ingram Camp-Bel is appointed and acknowledged as Captain."

The green light played over Ingram. "Recognized," the voice said, "Captain Ingram Camp-Bel. Full security authority delegated. Command has passed. Orders, Captain?"

Ingram blinked, then gestured to Quester. "This is Quester. She is a... friend of mine who should be given Crew status. I am unsure of procedure."

"Understood. Level of access?"

"Er... The same as Eklisia?"

"Please confirm appointment of Quester to Commander-level access?"

"I confirm," Ingram said, looking at Eklisia.

"Confirmed," Eklisia said, with a tiny smile at Ingram's uncertainty. "The Crew now requires entrance to the Archives. The remainder of the Clan will stay out as rearguard."

"Opening Archive Doors."

The massive door slid aside into the wall, revealing a short corridor that opened into another room. Quester and Ingram paused in that doorway to stare.

The Archive room was entirely made of metal, painted white and gray with splashes of other colors for various half-familiar symbols. Against the far wall were a set of... cabinets? Blocky metallic objects with lights winking from their surface, bracketing a line of three seats. Each seat was before a broad oblong of dark polished glass, with a set of studs or buttons beneath it — dozens of these studs, many nearly identical except for symbols on each, some others of different colors and sizes. The whole room had a stronger scent of that lightning-like smell, and a faint, alien hum pervaded the air.

"Welcome to the Archive, Captain," Eklisia said. "Here is where we will get our answers, and where we are closest to the true secrets of the Clan."

Ingram shook his head slowly in amazement. "These... I saw things like these in some of the ancient records and stories. 'Computers', yes?"

"Exactly," Security Chief Theros said. "Ancient thinking machines — these are called the 'portable auxiliary data archive' in the oldest documents. Apparently, the Wanderer, among others, helped get it set up and running, Cycles ago. He helped a *lot* with our work in the early days."

Quester remembered a certain incident. *Well, that explains, at least partially, how he had those materials of your Clan, yes?*

I guess. If he helped with this, *his help must have been worth a lot. Strange that there doesn't seem to be much if any magic involved, though, since he's a wizard.* "How do I access it?" Ingram asked. "We need to —"

A buzz came from the doorway. "Intercom active. Accept transmission from outside?" the feminine voice asked.

"Yes!" Eklisia said, her eyes narrowing in concern.

"Commander! Captain! Do you hear me?" The voice was that of Geraki.

"We hear you, Geraki," Ingram said.

"We're in trouble. Aegeian troops coming in force."

"Hades *damn* them," Eklisia said. "Someone was watching, saw us clear the rubble."

Ingram's eyes were wide, and Quester felt a shock of fear as well. "Commander... we're trapped in here. There was only one entrance to the Archives. And our people outside... most of them haven't anywhere to go, either."

Urelle, they've found us! We need that information fast! Quester noted how Ingram did not bother to address how they might be able to make *use* of the information.

They've found us *too, Ingram,* came Urelle's answer. *But I'll get it to you. Somehow.*

"They're alerted to Urelle and Victoria," Quester said quietly, trying to repress a sense of hopeless desperation. "If they get us the information, we will have to be able to act on it in moments. I admit... I do not see how."

He could sense the same helpless anger rising in Ingram. They were miles from Aegis, and even if Urelle told them of some weakness in the defenses, how could they strike fast enough to matter?

Commander Eklisia's mouth tightened. She glanced at Theros and Tisfotias; the latter just gave a cynical grin. "Ekli, he needs to know now. No way around it." The Camp-Bel healer gestured to the blank wall on one side of the Archive.

"Right," Eklisia said. "Theros, set the destruct. We'll need to admit the rest of the Clan, too. We'll need them."

"Got it."

"Wait, what?" Ingram said sharply. "Destruct? We haven't even *got* the information we came for! And we can't fit eighty people in this room, and even if we *could*, we can't hold out in a siege!" He glared at the Commander and Officer-Medical. "And what do I need to know now?"

"What you need to know is that this isn't the true Archive," Theros said, as he tapped something on the array of buttons before the central oblong of glass — an oblong that was now lit and displaying complex diagrams and images of multiple colors. "As the ancients said, it's just a backup. Now you'll have to consult the original." He turned away. "Because there's one last secret the Clan has."

The far wall slid aside, revealing another wall of metal, with a broad circular door inset into it. As it opened, swinging out to reveal a chamber filled with brilliant daylight even so far underground, the Commander nodded. "The Crew is *not* merely a tradition, and the position of Captain is not merely symbolic. For *this* is our final and greatest secret.

"We have *Rhyme and Reason*."

Chapter 42
Berenike's Farewell

Ingram stared with utter disbelief at the circular door — an *airlock!* — that had just opened before him. He was seized with a sense of pure unreality, and repeated dumbly, *"Rhyme and Reason??"*

"Indeed, that's the first reaction of every new member of the Crew, when finally, it is determined they are ready and are shown here for the first time," Commander Eklisia said. Her face was abruptly creased with her own wondering smile. "I remember it well."

"You have to give the order, Captain," Theros said, his rough voice tense. "Or delegate to us — that'd be faster."

Still stunned by the implications — RHYME AND REASON? — he held onto the so-new authority he'd been given. *I have to* act *like a Captain.* "Give the order, and I'll approve it. I'm not delegating until I *understand* what's going on."

A glint from both Eklisia's and Theros' eyes showed approval. "You will, Captain," Eklisia said. *"Rhyme and Reason,* orders pending Captain's approval: approximately eighty new recruits, members of Clan Camp-Bel, will be entering. Open Archive doors, only allow Clan members inside. Archive destruct is set."

"Purpose of such large numbers of recruits?"

"Security," Theron said. "The Clan has been under attack and there is now an attempt to gain the Archives. We are retreating to the final defensible position."

"Understood. Captain, will you confirm?"

The orders seemed reasonable. "I confirm these orders. Make it so." He'd heard the prior Captain use that phrase a few times.

There was the faintest suggestion of a chuckle before the feminine voice said "Acknowledged."

"Now, inside, Captain," Eklisia said. "The rest will—"

Echoing faintly through the now-open doorway — open to allow the retreating Clan to enter — came trilling screeches that were all too familiar.

"You get inside — you, everyone else. Quester and I are going to make sure everyone makes it." He began to sprint for the doorway.

Theros went to grab him. "No, Ingram! You cannot —"

"Am I the *Captain* or am I not? Because if I *am* I have just given an *order*, Chief Theros, and if I'm *not* then I'm going anyway!" He shook off the hand that had touched him. "And there's something *I* can do that no one else can, but I have to get close enough!"

He sprinted onward, Quester close on his heels.

Berenike? came the questioning thought.

Yes. I can't just call her by... telepathy. They slipped easily through the retreating Clan, heading for the shouts and shrieks of the invaders and the rearguard. *I have to be in danger, I have to* know *I'm in danger, I have to* believe *it.*

They burst out into the cross-corridor and turned to the clamor of battle.

I think you should find it believable, thought Quester after a shattered-second pause.

Fifty yards away, the corridor was *filled* with Xiilistiin — crawling along the metal ceiling, marching along the floor, darting along the walls. Many were the main insectoid form, others vaguely or more humanoid. A few ranks back, a taller, darker figure moved — a Swarmfather.

As Quester came into view, the entire swarm of the soul-stealing creatures let out a trill of savage hunger and lunged forward, surging past and over three Camp-Bels despite the lethal chattering of their ancient weapons. The Clanspeople shrieked in all-too-human agony, and blood *fountained* as bladed legs decapitated all three.

Ingram screamed his own horror and rage back at the oncoming swarm, and concentrated. *They're coming, Berenike! They're coming and nothing can stop them!*

For an instant he thought nothing would happen — that whatever had stopped her appearance in the battle against the false Athena would stop her again, or that — far worse — there was no one left to answer.

But then golden light burst out from *behind* him, and with a clarion laugh of trumpets and bells, Berenike, a golden stroke of lightning, flashed above and between them, and detonated in the center of the swarm with gilded fire.

Xiilistiin were blown away from her arrival, ants before a boot. The surviving Camp-Bels were untouched by the power of the Spear of Athena, and immediately retreated at full speed. "Go! Go!" Ingram urged them, gesturing down the corridor. "There is a final safehold! Go!"

"A safehold for them, but not for you," the Swarmfather buzzed, and he was surrounded by a strangely pearlescent-gray bubble that — for the moment — was holding off even Berenike's fusillade of auric-blazing fists. The half-human face twisted with a frightening grin. "And we recall Athena's advice on the matter."

The Swarmfather raised a staff of twisted, dead branches and brought it down.

Gray light howled through the corridor — and Berenike *staggered*. Her golden glow blew out like a candle in a hurricane, and before Ingram's stunned, disbelieving eyes she *faded*, becoming paler, translucent, an *outline* that looked down at itself in shock as great as Ingram's own. Quester gave a rasping buzz of incomprehension, and the Swarmfather *laughed*.

The laugh sparked rage in Ingram's terrified, confused heart — and, it seemed, in Berenike's as well. The transparent girl's head came up and color *rushed* back into her, flaring brighter than before. "You will need more than *that*, monster!" she said. "*Storm of Spears!*"

The barrage that had taken down Deimos bludgeoned the pearl-gray shield, strained it, shattered it, sent the Swarmfather careening back into more of the Swarm. "Ingram, *go!* I will hold them here, but *you must get to your ship!*"

"I—"

"By Athena and our friendship, *go!*"

He vaguely realized he had to flee, that she was right, but it was so hard to do.

Then Quester's hand gripped his upper arm and the two of them were running, running as fast as they could, as gold and grey battled in a blaze of energies that slew everything around them, shook the steel-lined corridors, sent blasts of hot and cold air surging, staggering them.

They were nearly to the Archive when Ingram felt something... *break*.

He fell bonelessly to the floor, barely aware that his cheek was bruised and scraped as he skidded towards the Archive on his face. Quester was screaming something at him, but it didn't matter, because he was so broken inside.

Goodbye, Ingram. The golden smile was sad.

Goodbye? No, Berenike! I can't... I can't lose you!

She shook her head. *Oh, Ingram. I'm so sorry. But it's time. It's* past *time. You don't need me any more.*

He gasped, both at the wrenching pain of the statement and the treacherous, horrifying part of him that seemed to be *agreeing* with her, saying *no, I don't, not any more.*

He was barely aware that Quester had dragged him through the Archive door and was shutting it, sealing it behind them, but the awareness of physical safety meant nothing, not with the terror of a loss he had always feared now present.

I'll always need you, Berenike, I'm not... not...

He could *see* her now, standing at the edge of the cliff, smiling in that moment that he had begun his fall. *Not strong enough?* She laughed. *You've faced so many things now, Ingram. You've made friends who awe me. You've found someone who loves you, who will stay by you forever, I think. You can let me go now.*

A glacier-cold chill of denial and remorseless understanding froze him as she smiled.

As he fell.

As she was impaled by one of their pursuers, the smile of benediction still on her face as he plummeted towards the waiting sea.

And suddenly she was gone. He sat up on the floor, tears pouring down his face, shuddering in the wake of the revelation.

"What is it, Ingram?" Quester's voice finally penetrated. "What does it mean? What happened? Is Berenike hurt?"

"Berenike's *dead*," he whispered.

"*Dead*? The Swarmfather was more powerful than *Deimos*?"

"No," his voice still a whisper, a breath of air forced from lungs that could barely breathe against the pressure that crushed his chest with grief and confusion and understanding. "She... she died *years* ago. She's been dead ever since that day on Kyriarcnis."

"Dead since..." Quester stared at him, huge faceted eyes whirling internally with his own confusion. "But then *who was that?*"

"I... I don't know how. Or why. No. I know why, just not *how*. Because I couldn't bear to lose her, I couldn't *accept* that she'd died for pathetic little Ingram. She'd *never* die. Ever."

Quester froze. "Ahhh." The wash of scent from him was so complex that, experienced as he was in his friend's scent-language, Ingram couldn't begin to sort it all out. "I understand. It makes sense of so very many things now, Ingram."

"What? It makes *sense*? I... *how*?"

"I believe... yes, I believe I *can* answer that." Ingram could sense Quester's thoughts, assembling understanding from dozens of little hints. "There was, of course, the certainty on the part of Deimos — one who should have known — that she was dead. There was the... oddity of the way in which she departed. Now that I know your story and think on it, she did not fly away in an ordinary fashion, but would depart as though falling into the sky... or as though *you* were falling away from her."

Ingram heard himself choke on a sob.

"Similarly, there were her appearances. As Urelle and others have often noted, teleportation is severely limited. How was she able to sense your danger and arrive essentially instantly, no matter where you were — even literal worlds away? It would make more sense, would it not, that it was because she was *already* nearby?

"Then there were the peculiarities both Victoria and I noted when she would appear. You would be... distracted, less effective. And when something distracted *you*, it seemed also to affect her. We thought that perhaps there was some kind of curse or other enchantment meant to inhibit those from Aegeia who were adherents of Athena, but then why were you *only* affected when Berenike was present? Her power level also varied in... interesting ways.

"Another clue was that she failed to appear when in the magic negation field. Yes. Urelle had the answer, although she applied it to the wrong question."

"Wrong question?"

"Do you not recall? When I — at the time, inexplicably — read Victoria's mind, during the one battle with the Xiilistiin? Urelle mentioned that 'subconscious magic' under stress was a real and well-known phenomenon, and that that was how Victoria had momentarily linked my mind to hers. And she has mentioned more than once that you seemed to have a powerful mystical aura of your own. You have shown sensitivity to magical effects."

The great faceted eyes looked down, and Ingram shivered as she finished, "You *created* Berenike. From your own magic, magic that you never suspected existed, pent up within you by your own lack of confidence and certainty of your inadequacy, and from your own belief in Berenike as everything you wanted to be, everything you wanted to *see* in the world.

"When Berenike died, you focused everything you had — all of your will, all your emotions, your hopes, your dreams — into denying it. And... in a way... you brought her back. Perhaps her spirit heard you; there has seemed to be a touch of something more than ordinary magic in Berenike's appearances. But *that* is why you were never quite yourself when she was fighting; most of your mind, your subconscious mind, had to be *playing* Berenike, maintaining her personality and powers for those watching."

"I... made her," he repeated, half-questioning, half-accepting a truth he had known for a long time.

"It makes sense." Quester suddenly burst out in the buzzing laugh of her kind. "Oh, by the *Mothers*, how much you have confused the trail! Our adversaries have been forced to devote so much effort to the mystery of her survival, to suspecting that *she* was the true adversary, to trying to locate her within and without Aegeia."

Ingram forced himself to stand, shaking, still barely able to grasp the truth — for that part of him was nodding, firmly in agreement, *knowing* that Quester had answered all questions. "A false trail we never expected... that we never *planned*." With another effort, he managed a smile for his friend; she deserved it. "Even though she was never here."

Quester shook her head. "Oh no, Ingram, she has *always* been here." She touched his forehead and then his chest. "And I am sure she always shall be."

Chapter 43
Rhyme and Reason

As Ingram accepted Quester's newest — and, he thought, truest insight, he became suddenly aware of clamour elsewhere in his mind. *Ingram! Ingram, are you all right?*

I... yes. I had a shock. A big shock. But what about you?

A flash of vision: Victoria holding an entryway against Xiilistiin in the uniforms and faces of the *Astyn*, the guards and enforcers of Aegis. *We're okay for now, they're stuck trying to get through that doorway — one at a time or two at a time Aunt Vicky will keep them down. But if any of them can climb these walls...* her mental shrug was clear. *I have my own job to do. But you'd better be ready to act when I get it, because we won't have much time here!*

I will be. I promise.

He and Quester ran to the airlock, trailing the last of the Crew. Eklisia, casting a worried glance at Ingram, was speaking with the Security Chief.

"Theros, join the rest of the Clan, you know where they'll be needed."

Security Chief Theros grinned a deadly grin. "The armory. I'll see to it."

"The rest of the Crew, with us." The Crew, Ingram saw, had stayed behind; it was, he supposed, only fitting that if the Captain led from the front, they had to be willing to stay to the end, too.

The airlock (*airlock*!) could have held up to twenty people; with only seven - Ingram, Quester, Commander Eklisia, Officer-Medical Tisfotias, Information-Analyst Meresti, Officer-Navigation Tscheos, and Officer-Technical Actina — it was roomier than Ingram would have expected.

The sense of unreality was still strong, especially after the terrible, yet somehow uplifting revelation of the truth behind Berenike. *It was all me. I don't know how, but it was me.* Atop the other impossibilities, it was almost too much; he expected to wake up from a dream, a beautiful if so obviously self-aggrandizing dream (*Me? The source of power that could duplicate the Spear of Athena? Me, the Captain? I thought I stopped dreaming of* that *ten years ago...*) any moment now.

The inner door of the airlock opened, and waiting for them were two women. Ingram felt, somehow, that he had seen them before, even though he knew that was impossible, for they were like no one he had ever seen. The two wore identical uniforms modeled after the oldest in the records (*or perhaps all ours were modeled after these*), dark jackets trim and perfectly fitted but unmarked, surprisingly, with any insignia of rank. Appearing to be in their early twenties, they were tall and slender but broad shouldered, clearly in excellent training, skin nearly as pale as the Wanderer's, hair rich earthwood brown with highlights of red; their gray-green eyes were also identical.

The twin on the left wore her hair in a short, angular cut, straight and smooth and precise; her expression was reserved, though a faint smile played about the edges of her mouth. The twin on the right smiled merrily, her eyes twinkling, and her hair tumbled in shimmering waves across her shoulders.

The two stepped forward as one and knelt, their eyes now on a level with Ingram's. "Welcome aboard, Captain." said the one with the laughing eyes. "We have been waiting for you for a long time."

"You... have? Who are you?" Even as he asked, he knew the answer, and a chill swept his entire body.

"I am Rhyme," she said, and gestured to her companion with the cooler smile, "and this is Reason."

He stared at them both. "I... I don't understand. I don't... I *can't* be Captain, not of the real —"

"Ingram Camp-Bel," Reason said levelly — though she, too, smiled, taking the edge from her words, "you *are* Captain, and we *have* been waiting for you."

He looked around, feeling the inutterable thrill of a dream becoming reality, and the terrifying feeling of that reality becoming responsibility, the lives of every Camp-Bel, perhaps of every citizen of Aegeia, now resting on the shoulders of little Ingram Camp-Bel. His gaze caught that of Eklisia. "*Explain,*" he said in a strangled tone.

***

Urelle gritted her teeth and ignored the clash of weapons behind her. *I have to trust Auntie to keep them away from me. There's no one else who can do this.*

Opening her internal eye, she *Looked*.

A tapestry of mystical light shimmered into existence before her, most of it separate little sparks of light, water-repelling cloaks or cleaning wands, enchanted weapons or tools. But above and beyond all those was a sky-spanning, rippling sheet of flowing enchantment, racing about the entirety of the Aegeian Path, sparkling with power and structure and purpose.

At first, she could make no sense of it; unlike the Coin enchantment, it was not a stable, almost crystalline structure, amenable to patient analysis; nor was it akin to the Seal about Aegeia, an ever-repeating, ever-expanding, ever-changing *pattern* that could be analyzed in its essence without having to comprehend its entirety.

This shield was almost *chaotic*, with the air of something built to showcase the sheer power of the creator. The energies making it up surged and danced and rippled, and it was *that* thought that gave her a perspective. Somehow, the barrier reminded her of a river in flood, a tumultuous, barely-contained barrier that would absorb or tear apart anything that attempted to pass it.

But a river has banks. And a river has a source. The raging cauldron of this shield must also have the equivalent — something that gave the chaos form, something that gave the shapeless strength and guidance. She struggled with her perceptions, trying to trace the flow within the whirl and crash and roil of the immense barrier — and to ignore the clangor of weapons, the hiss-snap of spells, the sounds of her aunt fighting to give her one more second, and then one second more.

Then she saw it; a faint arc in the conceptual-physical space of the magical barrier, an arc that repeated, never quite the same, never entirely disappearing. *It's not a* river; *it's a* fountain.

And with that thought, she could see the linchpins of the enchantment — two columns of stone, twenty feet across at the base, carved of solid granite into the shape of Ares and Athena, the one holding a stone sword and the other a granite spear. The two hadn't been brought there and set in place; they were pieces, she thought, of the actual bedrock that formed the small mountain before her, and reinforced with magic so that the stone itself was armor.

The seal surrounding the Aegeian Path was anchored by those two mighty columns, welling up from within the one as though the solid stone were the conduit for a spring of unlimited power, roaring out to the edges defined by that mountain slope, and then back to the other column, drawn in and channeled to the first. They formed a perfect, unbroken cycle of power, the energies hurled from one to the other and between them a nigh-impenetrable storm of energy.

Destroy those pillars, and the shield would collapse. But Urelle shook her head in dismay; she could barely imagine *anything* that could hope to achieve that. The spell she'd unleashed against the Xiilistiin, she thought, would be simply swept away in that cataract of energies, never to touch the stone itself. Aunt Vicky's Twin-Edged Fate would rebound from the enchanted stone like a pebble from armor plate.

But she had the answer they had sought. *Ingram! Quester! The columns at the start of the Aegeian Path! We have to take those down — somehow!*

That accomplished, she turned to aid Victoria, and see if they could survive long enough.

※※※

Quester was only a touch less stunned and amazed than her friend, and grasped as desperately at the explanations as Ingram.

"We only have time for the briefest explanations," Eklisia said, leading them along a broad corridor lit by daylight-colored insets in the ceiling. "Reason?"

"Yes, Commander. Captain, *Rhyme and Reason* was nearly completely incapacitated very long ago, but she was not *destroyed*, merely buried when the bluffs where she crashed collapsed on her. The original Camp-Bels dug their way out of the wreck and, as you know, became a force of importance during the Cycle in which they landed. They allowed the assumption of the ship's destruction to stand, but the Crew has always remained to learn the essentials of how to run her, if that ever came to be possible."

They entered another chamber, and to Quester's surprise, after the doors closed she could feel the entire *room* moving swiftly upwards. *It's an elevator, like the ones on the world of the Maidens.*

"A few Cycles later, the adventurer named the Wanderer made contact with the Camp-Bels, and in exchange for information the Clan could provide, he agreed to help find a way to make *Rhyme and Reason* as nearly functional as could be on Zarathan. It was..." she smiled faintly, "a labor not of a lifetime, but of *many* lifetimes."

That explains the Clan artifacts the Wanderer had. Part of his payment for... this. "But what did you mean about *me*?" Ingram demanded. "I can see that at least some of the ship is intact — more than I'd ever have imagined — but what did you mean you were waiting for me?"

Rhyme reached out and pressed a crystal chip into Ingram's hand. "That explains everything, Captain. Especially how and why the Clan did what they did to you, and why Reason and I were sure that one day you would be the one giving the orders. We do not, I am afraid, have much time. Read that after."

"And what of *you*," Quester asked. "You are not... real." It had taken a few moments, with the shock and confusion and the swirl of unfamiliar scents, but she was certain of what she was saying. "Neither you nor Reason are living beings. What are you?"

Ingram stared. "They're not?"

Reason's left eyebrow arched. "Fascinating. You are, of course, correct, although I would prefer that you say we are not *biological*, for I believe my sister and I are both *real*."

"As for what we *are*?" Rhyme laughed again. "The ship was provided with... call it a thinking machine that was made to cover both the rational and the emotional spectrum, so it could understand human decision-making and support it rather than conflict with it. The Wanderer... brought that capability out far more during his work over the centuries, by talking to it... to *us*... as we developed."

She and Reason smiled, and Reason went on, "the idea of the ship's systems being in operation for centuries had not been contemplated by the designers. Once the Wanderer realized there were two... crewmembers who had been born purely of the ship's constant operation, he found a way to let the ship give us a semblance of bodies. We can support the ship and the Crew far better this way."

The door of the chamber opened, showing a corridor subtly different from the prior one, ending in a solid double-door that opened as the group approached.

Quester was almost overwhelmed by Ingram's emotional surge as they entered the semicircular room. Spaced around the perimeter were more of those strange panels surmounted by the polished-glass plates — but these flat glass objects glowed in multiple colors, showing strange symbols and images and graphs moving across them. A faint humming filled the room, and Quester watched as the others of the Crew spread out, each choosing a seat in front of a particular panel.

In the center of this room was a chair, in some ways nearly a throne, with a peculiar design that Quester could see, after a moment, was intended to allow the chair to turn to face any of the stations. She did not need to be told; this was the Captain's position.

Ingram reached out with fingers that shook visibly, and touched the arm of the Captain's Chair. "By the *Founder*..." he murmured.

Then they both were touched by Urelle's urgent call.

***

"The Camp-Bels have been located," Deimos said without preamble, "and our fugitive visitors with them."

Raiagamor looked up sharply from his worktable. "Where?"

"The old Camp-Bel compound, as we suspected. Though we have found no trace of southern tunnels, and the group have instead entered through a previously-undiscovered access area in the compound proper."

Raiaga growled and was pleased to see Deimos wince. "You said the compound had been searched *thoroughly*."

"It was," Phobos said, entering. "This was concealed by means we do not understand. There was no magic to it, and the sensory returns from this door feel like those from solid ground when the door is closed."

It seems the Camp-Bels were able to make use of their technology in a wider variety of ways than I expected. "Very well. I presume they are being pursued?" He stood; his concentration on this minor task had been broken and he now felt the need to pace. The two demon-Xiilistiin followed him as he strode from the room.

"The Swarm has sent a large number of our people into the tunnels, yes. The Camp-Bels have tried to maintain stealth; it is assumed they seek something hidded within. They will not be allowed to leave with it."

"And our little adventurers?"

"Traveling with the Camp-Bels... hold." Phobos' eyes narrowed, the glint showing a hint of something unhuman within. "Correction; the female members separated from the others. Our patrols have just found them in Aegis."

Now it was *his* turn for narrowed eyes. *Separated? Here, where they must surely know their adversary's forces are gathered, alert, and ubiquitous?* "Show me," he said, striding out the temple doorway and to the edge of the Path, looking down over the city. "*Where* in Aegis?"

Deimos frowned, then pointed to a set of buildings near the base of the mountain. With eyes far superior to human, Raiagamor could make out the flash and sparkle of combat atop one such roof.

But that's not the important point, oh no. "The barrier. Their child-wizard is attempting to analyze my barrier!"

"Do you believe she might succeed?"

He bared suddenly-crystal teeth in a snarl. "I believe I would be a fool to think otherwise. And she would not *do* this unless she also thought she had a way to communicate what she found." He recalled electronics and other technologies from a dozen worlds. "Yes, they could have given her some such device. Send more reinforcements there, and swiftly."

He stood, rigid, staring down at the distant glitter and glint of struggle, and farther out, at the flattened area that was the Camp-Bel compound. *The ending is nearer than I had thought.*

***

Ingram saw the two columns in his mind's eye, and gritted his teeth. "Athena *curse* it!"

"What's wrong, Captain?" Eklisia asked.

"That barrier's anchored to the the two Grand Stele at the base of the Way. Bound to them. Urelle says the only way to break the barrier is to break the columns themselves."

Eklisia cursed as well. "Legend says it took fifty years to carve them, and that they were reinforced by the Father of Gods himself to make them as near eternal as anything."

"And while we're down here, Urelle and Victoria are already under attack. And there's no way *out* of this ship, even if the Xiilistiin can't find a way through the door. Unless there *is* another escape hatch?"

"Why would you want to escape?" Reason asked, and then suddenly she and Rhyme started laughing. "Oh. Oh, Captain, I am afraid we have failed to make something clear.

"Captain Ingram Camp-Bel, *Rhyme and Reason* is — aside from spacedrives — fully operational."

For a few precious instants, Ingram just *stared* at the twins. "Fully... operational?"

"Yes, sir."

He stared at the blank, shiny rectangular area at the front of the command deck. Blank, because they were buried in the earth. *But what if...*

"Rhyme, Reason... can this ship *fly*?"

Their smiles were double blades of challenge. "Yes, Captain!"

"Can she fly *out of this hillside*?"

"Yes, Captain!"

"By the Founder..."

"Sir!" Commander Eklisia saluted. "If that is your intention, I must point out that once we *do* that, our greatest secret... *isn't*, any more."

As he grasped what Rhyme and Reason meant, Ingram found himself dizzy, so lightheaded with excitement, with disbelieving awe, with hope and fear and everything else, that he felt perilously near to fainting. But he managed to sit straight in the chair. "You're right, Commander. But isn't this exactly what the Clan's kept this secret *for*? For the chance to make a final, unexpected strike against our enemies, in the name of the Clan and Athena herself?"

Commander Eklisia's salute and smile was a benediction and blessing. "Indeed, Captain."

"Then..." he took a breath, "let's make this the one that counts, Commander. Officer-Navigation!"

Tscheos straightened. "Captain!"

"*Rhyme and Reason*—LAUNCH!"

***

A quiver ran through the ground, a vibration Raiagamor felt through his feet and heard in the air. "What is *that*?" he growled.

"I have no idea," Deimos said, brow furrowing.

"It was not too nearby," Phobos said. "See there, birds have taken flight across Aegis. This was felt —"

In the distance, the entire Camp-Bel compound *shuddered*. Raiagamor froze, staring, the first intimation of impossibility entering his mind.

Even as the rumble of *that* motion reached them, louder and far clearer than the first tremor, the Camp-Bel compound crumpled, began to sag towards the sea... and then lifted upwards.

Raiagamor found himself standing atop the steps of the Aegeian Path, mouth agape in disbelief, as a titanic shape rose from the earth, stone and dirt and trees and even *buildings* falling away, showing a shining silver streamlined hull five hundred feet long, crescent-blade prow streaming the earth of its long burial. It rose farther into the sky, graceful body now showing the majestically molded curves of two huge engines, one on each side, multicolored lights marking its outline; it spun once on its long axis, casting away all the accumulated detritus of centuries. A small amount of that detritus screamed as it fell with the voices of Xiilistiin.

Behind him, the footsteps of the Hammer and Anvil of Hemphaestus slowed to stunned immobility. "What... what *is* that?" the Anvil breathed.

"*That*," Raiagmor snarled, "is a *problem*. And that is what I have God-Warriors for."

"That thing is the size of a *mountain*," the Hammer protested.

"Then you had better *get moving*," Raiagamor said. "Because I want that *thing* back on the ground — in *pieces* — faster than it just came *up*, do you understand me?"

"But—"

The rage *exploded* from Raiagamor, the disbelieving frustration at his enemies' latest gambit combining with the reluctance of his own allies breaking, for a moment, his rigidly-enforced control.

Blade-tipped fingers drove straight into the Hammer of Hephaestus and Raiagamor grasped the combined human-Xiilistiin soul and *ripped* it from the body, consumed it in a single brutal moment and cast the corpse down the stairs. "Now," he rasped, seeing the other three God-Warriors backing away from him, "get that ship *down*!"

Chapter 44
Starship Versus Godspower

Ingram felt as though he could float on will alone as the viewscreen cleared, and for the first time he saw Aegis from above, for real, not in a daydream, the entire city with the Aegeian Path looming above, spread out beneath like a tapestry of white marble, red brick, and green trees. "Tscheos," he heard himself say, sounding as calm as though this was something that happened every day, "Take us around towards the Path."

"Caution," Reason said. "Do not pass over any portion of the Path or its mountain. Doing so was what converted our original landing from a controlled glide to a crash. Nothing save ordinary birds and similarly natural flying creatures are permitted to fly above the mountain of the gods."

"A shame," Quester said. "I had been thinking that if we manage to take this barrier down that we could then reach the top of the mount in moments."

"Alas, no," Rhyme said. "If you are not one of the gods residents on the mountain, the only way up is the long way."

"Rhyme and Reason, do we have defenses? Weapons?"

"All fully operational. As your stories have told you, Ingram," Rhyme answered with a fond smile.

Embarrassment might have touched his cheeks with warmth, but he didn't mind, not now. "Raise all defenses. They're going to try to stop us."

"Shielding going active," Tscheos reported, a thrill of excitement clear in his own voice. "All systems report full coverage."

Something was nagging at Ingram's mind, and as he studied the movement of the city below him, the words "full coverage" triggered it. "If we use our weaponry on something down there, what happens to the city?"

"We should not use any of the main torpedo load-outs," Reason said. "Those are easily capable of destroying a city larger than this one. The energy weapons are far more concentrated and their damage over a wider area will be significantly less.

However, there will still be untoward consequences within a few hundred yards of the target."

"Can we extend our shields to enclose the Grand Plateia? Prevent those 'untoward consequences'? I don't want to injure any innocents in our battle."

Rhyme nodded. "The shielding can be configured in this manner. The shields are designed as overlapping independent sections, and can be projected and contoured as needed within a fairly wide radius relative to the ship." She gestured to an array of lights on one of the forward control areas. "Note, of course, that this means spreading our defenses across a much larger area, and we will be that much less defended."

And if we're taken down before we can deal with the shield, this whole thing's for nothing. Ingram knew this was the unspoken but obvious argument against weakening their defenses in any way. The coldest part of him *emphasized* that argument; hundreds, *thousands* had died already because of the false Ares and his maneuverings; if a few more lives were lost along the way, a few homes and businesses wiped out, well... it was war, was it not?

But he knew this was not the trade any true Adventurer would make. And more, he had to be able to live with himself, and look his friends in the eyes, when he was done here. "Extend the shields to protect the city. Find the optimum distance from the target columns to minimize shield extension and maximize protection for Aegis."

"Yes, Captain." The array of lights reconfigured, showing two curved sections well separated from the main set — obviously representing the ones protecting the Plateia.

Urelle? he thought. *Can you protect yourselves from an explosion? We're trying to shield the area, but —*

I can put up a barrier that should blunt any such thing. There was an undertone of awe in her mindvoice. *By the* Balance, *Ingram, that's your legacy? That's* Rhyme and Reason?

Yes. And I can't believe it myself.

Well, came Victoria's mindvoice, *it certainly saved* me *some effort; once that... vessel appeared, our assailants left. I presume they saw* that *as a far more immediate problem.*

A sparkle was visible to the side of the viewscreen. "What...?"

A chime rang out from one of the stations. "Minor attack — one of the adversary's magicians, I would guess."

"Officer-Technical, can we *speak* to people outside?"

"Yes, sir, there are powerful external speakers."

"Activate them, please." At Meresti's nod, Ingram spoke.

"This is Captain Ingram Camp-Bel of the starship *Rhyme and Reason*," he said, and how he managed to keep his voice steady through that first line he could not imagine. "People of Aegeia, a monstrous traitor has taken the face and power of Ares. Against that, even keeping our greatest secrets is no longer of importance. We are here to stop him — even if we must pit the power of the Camp-Bel legacy against that of a god. For your own safety, *get inside and stay in shelter!*"

The sound of the last word had barely faded before *Rhyme and Reason* lurched like a man colliding with a cart. "What —"

"We are under attack," Meresti said. "Three primary opponents; they appear to be God-Warriors."

"We must hurry," Rhyme said, and her face was grave. "Even starship shields will not hold long against that kind of barrage, stretched as they are."

"Get us a good angle," Ingram said, gripping the arms of his chair tightly, ignoring the harness that had automatically enclosed him. "Prepare to fire."

***

Raiaga's claws sank into the balustrade of the stairway as he watched the God-Warriors trying — and failing! — to penetrate the defenses of *Rhyme and Reason*. The great exploration ship with its open-book symbol clear on the hull staggered under the assault, but neither slowed nor retreated.

It was coming about now, in front of the Path, and suddenly two discs of the hull vanished, replaced by squat, double-barrelled turrets that Raiagamor had seen in records shown him by his Mother long ago, and he tensed anew. *Call them null-rannai, call them novaguns, call them simply blaster cannon,* he thought, *they are weapons meant for use on things a million miles away in deep space.*

Only a madman would fire one here, in atmosphere.

Only a madman, or a desperate one. And Raiaga could not argue that Ingram Camp-Bel could be more than a little of both.

Hurry! He thought with fury at the three God-Warriors. *They are near to firing!*

***

Phobos streaked upward again, wings unsheathed, no longer bothering to disguise his nature. *It does not matter if we do not win.*

Yet again, the invisible yet all too tangible barrier repulsed his assault, an attack that could have left a crater fifty feet across in solid rock. *But I felt it yield, the slightest bit. Brothers, sisters, we shall keep striking it in the same spot, stressing whatever generates it!*

The others answered with assenting screams. Only two other God-Warriors remained — Deimos and the Anvil — but the rest of the Swarm could gather, could begin to project its own attacks with range and power.

A squat, broad cylinder the size of a small house popped up out of the ship's hull, and began to swing around, bringing two long, dull-gray barrels to bear on the righthand column. At the same time, smaller doors and projections appeared, and bolts of energy and projectiles *spewed* from them, catching Phobos off-guard, sending him falling momentarily through the air.

These smaller attacks were much more effective against the ordinary Xiilistiin troops, and Phobos heard Deimos snap out a new command, withdrawing the Swarm warriors until they might have a chance.

The Anvil smashed into the barrier again, and this time there was a definite sense of weakening. Phobos smiled, an inhuman expression on his usually-human face, as he and Deimos prepared for another attack.

Almost there.

***

Ingram could see the base of the Path clearly now — and the great columns with the shimmer of energy playing about them. "Battery one, target the base of the left column. Battery two, same point on the right column. Prepare for full-power volley upon lock."

The words sounded so strange in his ears, words that he had said in private, pretending to be a starship captain going into danger, a dream that only Camp-Bels might have, and only a dreamer and a failure might indulge.

But now they were *real*, and he heard the *CHUNG-WHIRR* as the great guns swiveled to position.

Rhyme and Reason slewed sideways, and alarms clamored through the ship. "Those Ares-damned monsters hit hard!"

"Extremely so," Reason said. "One or two more concentrated strikes like that and the in-atmosphere shields will go down."

"Target one locked," Tscheos said. Another huge concussion, but *Rhyme and Reason* remained airborne, crosshairs focused now on two great granite figures. "Target two locked."

"*Rhyme and Reason* — FIRE!"

Even as he spoke, Ingram saw most of the lights for the shielding vanish, felt the ship buck beneath him. *Only the shields for the Plateia — the only ones they're* not *hitting — are still up!*

A tiny dot on the screen swelled with terrifying rapidity, the narrow, vicious face that had haunted his dreams more than once swelling to full size as Deimos himself streaked towards the now-defenseless ship.

But out of the corner of his eye, in that final split-second, he saw both Rhyme and Reason's lips curl in a deadly smile.

For that fractured instant of time, Deimos' face was abruptly illuminated by an ominous glow; his eyes widened in that moment — and then the screen went white.

Rhyme and Reason reared backwards, spinning sideways through the air, as two mighty blows struck it. But somehow Officer-Navigation Tscheos steadied her, turned the careening spin into a controlled arc, and came about.

On-screen, the blaze of light faded, and Ingram heard cheers throughout the control deck as the two great columns teetered for a moment, enveloped by a cloud of smoke and dust, tilted, and toppled with fearsome grace, their thirty-foot-thick bases entirely vaporized by the power of starship weaponry.

Of Deimos, there was no trace at all.

"Losing control, Captain," Tscheos said. "Those last two shots hurt."

"Yes," Rhyme said. "However, concentrated fire from our defensive network also managed to injure both of the remaining God-Warriors at the same time. We are clear for the moment."

Ingram shook his head to clear it, saw an image provided by Quester. *Yes, that's right!* "Put us down on the Grand Plateia. That's right in front of the Path and close enough to Urelle and Victoria so we should be able to reach them!"

"Yes, Captain."

"Captain?" Security Chief Theros' voice came from somewhere in the air.

"Yes, Security?"

"If you're going out, the Clan's ready to support."

For just an instant, his old stubborn pride tried to reassert itself, maybe with a touch of something else associated with him and Urelle. *I wanted to get there myself!*

But that *would* be stupid beyond belief. Charge out with just him and Quester... or with Theros and the whole Clan to make sure Urelle and Victoria made it out safe?

That wasn't even a question.

"As soon as we can get there, Theros. Leave enough on board to keep *Rhyme and Reason* safe."

"Got it!"

He rose from the chair, the harness retracting automatically. "Quester — this is it."

The claws gripped his hands. "It is."

With one last wondering glance around the command deck, Ingram dashed out.

Chapter 45
Setting the Stages

Even Raiagamor's eyes were momentarily blinded by the fury of *Rhyme and Reason*'s main cannon firing. But he did not need to see in order to sense the sudden collapse of the shield that prevented any intrusion onto the Aegeian Path.

At the same time, a worse shock ripped through his mind, a long-cultivated and hidden link torn away. *Deimos... Deimos is dead. The demon that motivated him has been either destroyed or banished, and either way, lies now beyond me.*

He could sense, also, that the two remaining God-Warriors were injured. They would recover... but there was very little time, now. *Swarm, how many can you send to the Path, to slay those who seek to reach the top?*

The Xiilistiin Swarm-Heart deliberated a moment. *Three hundred may be spared.*

Send them to the first landing. Do not get within line-of-sight of the Camp-Bel ship; they will not use their main weapons again, but the range and power of even their secondary weapons is nothing to be despised.

He shifted focus. *Phobos, Anvil, rendezvous with them. Let my adversaries show themselves and move beyond easy retreat,* then *fall upon them.*

Will you not join us? Phobos asked. *Your power would be most welcome.*

He chuckled darkly. *I daresay it would, but I reserve* my *power for any who can pass* you. *Make it so I do not* have *to exert myself overmuch.*

The demon-Xiilistiin's reaction at being told in subtle yet unmistakable words that he was a mere dispensable tool was amusingly intense, but the sense of rebellion and hostility was not to be tolerated. *If you wish to meet the same end as the Hammer of Hephaestus, by all means protest. Better, I think, you should make yourself indispensable by* succeeding.

Phobos' retort was pure rage combined with resignation and determination. Raiagamor smiled; if the false God-Warrior survived, the latter two would temper the first and Phobos would still be of use. If he didn't, well, it would not matter, would it?

And the simple fact was that his allies did not truly grasp the gap between their powers, formidable though they were, and his own. The Xiilistiin knew he was playing a god and used godspower in some ways — that alone should have given them pause, but they shared a similar arrogant attitude with Raiaga's own people: they were used to taking others' power and using it for themselves. Thus, a powerful ally or adversary was also viewed as a resource.

Deimos and Phobos, of course, as demons he personally had summoned and bound (with some deception as to who was bound to do what, naturally), had a somewhat better idea of just how powerful Raiagamor was... but only somewhat. They understood he was a Great Wolf — and presumably the Swarm-Heart *now* understood that, after he'd impulsively executed one of the God-Warriors. They did *not* understand just how old Raiagamor was, nor that he was not, in fact, a Great Wolf at all, but something else.

Something far more dangerous.

At that thought, there was the faintest sense of a cynical laugh. *And arrogance is very much yours as well, is it not?*

Raiagamor was startled, and truth be told, pleasantly amused at that unexpected comment. *Ah, my little tenant, you speak! You are here to observe the finale, yes?*

To watch my sister's hand end you, indeed.

Raiagamor laughed aloud, his voice echoing about him. "End me? Oh, come now, once-Ares, that is a step and another step too far, even for you. I ended *you* in your own quarters. Here? With her not even incarnate?"

The four who come for you have survived everything you sent, you abomination, Ares said coldly. *Not merely your warriors, but my Sister's own Seal that you replicated. They have slain the formless slayer, struck down your false Athena, and even brought forth* Rhyme and Reason *from the tales of legend. My sister's hand is with them.*

"Oh, of that I have no doubt. The Cards point to them in more ways than one, and who would oppose me here, save the Lady of Wisdom and War? But I have slain one god already, and I will slay another if need be."

Another touch on his mind, this one less angry, more rational; he allowed it through. *What does the Swarm wish?*

Merely an offer. If you desire, the Swarm believes we have a way to neutralize your adversaries, assuming they pass the forces you have just sent.

Given how handily their enemies had dealt with their various Xiilistiin opponents before, Raiaga felt he was justified in radiating skepticism. *Obviously, that would be gratifying, but just as obviously, you need no permission from me.*

We wish to verify that you have no use for any of them. If we claim these four Adventurers, it will not bother you?

It will be a minor disappointment, in that I had hoped to finish them myself, if they proved sufficiently formidable. But I am no impractical fool; if you have a plan that will eliminate them, I relinquish any claim. Show me your intent.

It was quick, a conceptual sketch of ten thousand words in a single concentrated image, and Raiaga was momentarily startled by the implications.

Then, as he came to grasp the full irony of the Xiilistiin plan, Raiagamor began to laugh.

Chapter 46
To the Aegeian Path

Victoria wiped dazzled tears from her eyes and stared as twin plumes of dust and fire rose from the bases of the great columns, the huge statues falling with broken majesty to the ground as the barrier they had supported flickered and vanished — followed by the honeycomb-like glow of the shield Urelle had conjured to protect them. Above, *Rhyme and Reason* banked unsteadily but leveled out, descended towards the Grand Plateia, the huge ship momentarily blocking out the sun as it passed overhead.

"Come on, Auntie!" Urelle grabbed her hand and pulled; Victoria recognized the sensation of Urelle's airwing spell and let herself be pulled over the edge, to glide swiftly but safely to the ground. They both hit the pavement running, as the Camp-Bel ship landed with a grinding *crunch* of stone-beneath-metal.

They were scarcely halfway to the vessel when a ramp dropped down from the lower hull, and Camp-Bels — wearing new green, silver, and blue armor that covered them from head to toe in shining material like porcelain and each carrying at least one of the ancient Camp-Bel weapons — streamed out in a coordinated formation, spreading into lines that faced the Aegeian Path. Five of them ran, still in coordinated movement, to meet the two Vantages and then surrounded them in a protective formation, escorting them behind the defensive line. "Lady Victoria, Miss Urelle," the slightly metallic voice of Security Chief Theros said from the one leading their guard detachment, "the Captain and Quester will be here momentarily. Please put these on — anywhere will do. They don't even have to be visible."

From his hand, Victoria took a badge, about an inch and a half across, with *Rhyme and Reason*'s emblem emblazoned across it; Urelle was handed another. "And these are...?"

"IFF beacons — Identify Friend or Foe. Our weapons won't target anyone wearing one if we have IFF targeting active — which we will. This will be real helpful if we end up in a firefight."

Victoria affixed hers to her wristguards and saw Urelle put hers next to her cloak's clasp. "It certainly sounds convenient, but what if one of our enemies steals one of these devices?"

"Not *that* easy," Theros said with a grin that was faintly visible through the tinted visor of his helmet. "When I gave them to you, they took your biometrics and coded them in. Unless we re-set them, no one but you can use that particular badge."

"Your technology seems to be at least equal to any magic I know," Urelle said, staring at the apparently solid and magically inert badge. "That kind of spell would be really hard to put together."

"These badges were hard to put together, too," came Ingram's voice, and he was suddenly embracing the two of them; Victoria could feel his body shaking with emotional reaction, and both she and Urelle put their arms around him. Quester's arms, and her warm and certain mind-touch, joined them, and for a few moments the four stood there, once more together.

I was so terrified for you, Ingram thought — more, perhaps, to Urelle than to Victoria, but that was no surprise.

And we for you, Victoria assured him. *But I had never even* imagined... she nodded towards the ship looming above them.

A shaky laugh. *Oh, I'd* imagined *it enough times, but I always knew it was just that, imagination of a useless failure. And now...* The wonder and terror of the truth washed through them all from Ingram. *Now I'm the Captain of Rhyme and Reason. The first real Captain she's had since the Founder Herself.*

Are you all right, Ingram?

I'm so very all right, and not all right, at the same time. But I guess I'd better be all right, because we have to get moving. We've sprung the biggest surprise ever on Ares and his people, but we can't give them more time to get ready.

Victoria nodded her approval. "Then we'd best be moving."

Ingram straightened, took a deep and marginally less shaky breath, and turned to Eklisia, who had just come down the ramp. "Commander, report. What is the condition of *Rhyme and Reason*?"

"Sustained notable, but not critical, damage to several systems, including flight controls, secondary engines, and some of the defensive generator grid. All of it can be repaired."

A blast of relief washed through Victoria from the young Camp-Bel. *Thank the Founder, I didn't break the ship on her first outing.* "Are the weapons systems still active?"

"Some of the point defense is out, but the main guns are still fully functional."

"All right." He looked around. "Security Chief?"

Theros gestured to the V-shaped double line of armed and armored Camp-Bels — who had somehow, to Victoria's astonishment, produced some kind of barricade from apparently nowhere while they were talking, and were crouched behind it, weapons sighted up the Aegeian Way. "Captain, the Clan will support you on your assault, as promised."

Ingram stared. "The armory had all *that*?"

"*Rhyme and Reason* was a military exploration vessel," said Reason, having materialized nearby. "Of her complement of two hundred fifteen, it was expected that one hundred eighty would be capable of serving in combat situations if required, and equipment for that complement was provided. While over the centuries, there have been occasional uses of the reserve materials in the armory, the vast majority of it has been maintained and preserved for use in the event that the ship was once more flightworthy."

"I see," Ingram said, still clearly startled, but, Victoria noted, already thinking about what he saw. "Theros, if we don't fully succeed up there, *Rhyme and Reason* is the last reserve we *have*. I want half your people to stay with the ship; you'll need it, if they send a God-Warrior after you."

"Understood, and I agree," Theros said after a moment. "I recommend setting weapons to auto-targeting and autofire with IFF; that ought to hit even things moving faster than human."

"Do it."

Victoria looked at Reason. "No sign of our attackers? I would have expected them to strike once you were on the ground."

"I believe they have decided not to risk coming in line-of-sight of *Rhyme and Reason*. Sensor records show that Deimos was caught directly in the main cannon firing path, and was completely disintegrated; this must be a cautionary event for them."

"So I would think!" Victoria looked up with new respect at the ship; to have destroyed a *God-Warrior* without godspower? A fearsome vessel this was, indeed!

Ingram saluted Theros and Eklisia. "Keep her safe," he said, looking at Reason and then the ship above.

"I thought I would —"

A quick shake of the head cut Theros off. "Absolutely not. There's not enough trained Crew left. I *have* to go. It's where I was *meant* to go. But I need you to run the ship and, if I don't come back, the Clan. Eklisia, you're in command in my absence."

Her arms came across and up in the Camp-Bel salute. "Sir!"

Ingram looked up at Victoria. "Ready?"

"I had best be, yes?" She turned and strode towards the Aegeian Path; the other three followed her.

One arm of the "V" collapsed its barricade, which proved to be a multitude of post-shaped objects, one to a soldier, that were then slung back over their shoulders. The Camp-Bels stood and without need for directions, fell in to a diamond formation, surrounding the four Adventurers as they began to ascend the Aegeian Way.

"When do you think they'll counterattack?" asked Urelle.

Victoria squinted upward. "On the first of the large landings, I would think. Once you're past the edge of that landing, the guns of *Rhyme and Reason* cannot sight on you, and you don't want to let us get any *farther* up if you can avoid it. Yes?"

Both Quester and Ingram agreed. "That makes eminent sense," the Iriistiik said.

"Agreed," said a familiar voice from the Camp-Bel nearest Ingram. "Any advice, Captain?" Sergeant Lepida went on.

"Sergeant!" Ingram bobbed his head toward the woman, whose armor made her look even more squat and powerful. "Not... sure. I haven't done a lot of larger-group tactics."

"I've done a bit," Victoria said. "If they intend to attack us on the landing, they would likely be already prepared and waiting. With, I would presume, the remaining two God-Warriors as their main forces. Yes?"

"Sounds right." A ghost of a grimace seen through the faceplate. "They're probably hurt, but who knows how fast they might heal. Best to assume both of them are ready to fight again. Any suggestions?"

Victoria exchanged some telepathic thoughts with the others, smiled. "We believe these false God-Warriors are, in their core nature, Xiilistiin," she said. "I believe some specific preparations were made...?"

There was no mistaking the grin behind the smoky-colored glassy helm. "Yes, Ma'am!"

"Then," said Ingram, "I want you ready to open with those as soon as we clear the stair. In fact," he pointed, "when we reach the third stair down — still just below any possible line of sight — I want everyone to open and link their barricade wands, then we charge the last three steps *behind* the barricade, drop and lock on the landing a few feet in. All weapons on IFF autolock and fire, active as we clear the last stair. Have we got a recognition scan from *Rhyme and Reason* on the two God-Warriors?"

"Yes, Captain. Both Phobos and the Anvil of Hephaestus were scanned multiple times."

"Then input those parameters; they're to be top-priority targets." Ingram held up his hand, testing the wind. It seemed to be mostly blowing uphill, inward from the sea. "The special weapons have to have a proximity cutoff — I don't want them fired or detonating closer than fifty, sixty feet." *That will make sure Quester doesn't get any.*

"How large are the landings?" Victoria asked.

"Oh, they're big. Not as big as the Plateia, but say three hundred feet across. Got that all, Lepida?"

"Got it and transmitted to the squads. No objections. All weapons now set for IFF autotarget and fire. Special weapons ranging limitations set." They were approaching the top. "Barrier wands *out*," Lepida said. Despite the quiet tone in which she spoke, Victoria saw that all the Camp-Bels instantly responded, reaching back and pulling the pole-shaped wands to a ready position. *Some kind of communicating link between them?*

They're called helmet coms, yes, Ingram answered. *Pure technology, so they should be pretty secure from eavesdropping, too.*

"Open and link barriers on my mark... three... two... one... *Mark!*"

Instantly, forty separate barrier wands snapped into broad shield sections which then locked together with almost no pause. They were three steps below the edge.

"Prepare to charge on my mark. Stay low and fast, people — assume you're going to be under fire from the moment the first hair on our heads clears the stairs. I want the barricade *sliding* on the landing, ten feet forward, then stop, lock, and fire." Sergeant Lepida's tone was calm, precise, and focused. "Ready?"

There was a murmur of assent. Victoria took a breath and focused herself, once more, into the Eight Winds. *And so, the final steps are begun.* She felt the faintest twinge in her chest. *None of that*, she thought to herself. *A few more hours is all I ask.* The pain receded, though she doubted it was because of her own demands.

"On my mark, people. Three... two... one... *MARK!*"

Clan Camp-Bel's warriors, forty strong, lunged forward, bellowing "*For Athena! For the Founder!*"

Chapter 47
Phobos' Finale

Quester threw up her own telekinetic screen as her antennae cleared the shelter of the top stair, reinforcing the barricade, and Urelle created her golden honeycomb-patterned barrier at the same moment, leaving tiny gaps for the Camp-Bel weapons.

Their guesses had been right.

Even as the Camp-Bel barricade crested the landing, a storm of projectiles and spells met it. Without the psionic screen of an Iriistiik Mother and Urelle Vantage's magical barrier, the entire assault force might have been killed or cast back. Instead, despite the withering assault of mystic crossbow bolts and fire beams and light spheres, the Camp-Bels plowed forward and dropped solidly behind their barricade, which threw out anchoring struts that drove firmly into the stone beneath, and in one motion raised and aimed their weapons, weapons whose names and abilities Ingram's mind-voice reviewed even in that moment.

Phobos and the Anvil were already halfway across the hundred yards' distance when the Camp-Bels' weapons took aim with the speed of the thinking machines embedded within them.

Fifteen hypersonic coilguns and twenty packeted-plasma rifles fired simultaneously, and even the reactions of a God-Warrior were inadequate. Phobos, perhaps just slightly more paranoid, threw up his arms, vambraces shielding his head, but the Anvil of Hephaestus took the entire storm of technological death head-on.

The Anvil was *halted* in his tracks, sent tumbling back, blood mingling with shards of his deific armor; even the godspower-backed metal could not entirely shrug off impacts at a dozen times the speed of sound, nor the incalculable heat and shock of a dozen detonating miniature suns. Phobos also ground to a halt and cursed in pain and shock, though he did not fall.

Quester's psionic senses were just able to detect, a split-second later, the far worse assault that followed.

Five canisters landed — three at Phobos' feet, two nearly atop the Anvil — and exploded, spraying a dense whitish mist everywhere. Quester's breathing-tubes snapped shut in sympathetic reaction.

Phobos and the Anvil shook their heads and crouched low, scuttling towards the Camp-Bel line, hands and weapons now glowing lethally gold with their stolen godspower, and projectiles and energy alike spumed harmlessly from the auric aura. Anvil brought up one hand and *smashed* it down, tearing through Urelle's barrier and cracking the barricade section behind it. Phobos did the same, and though Quester tried to drive the two back, it was clear that it would not be long before they broke the triple-layered defense.

The Anvil slammed another blow home, drew back his arm for another... and then wavered, with a surprised look. Phobos staggered, went to a knee, and hissed. "What... ?"

No one bothered to answer; with the God-Warrior's hesitation, the entire Clan unleashed a second fusillade. The canister-throwing weapons fired high now, dropping their drifting doses of death into the mass of Xiilistiin now marching forward behind the two God-Warriors.

The Anvil fell, pierced and burned in a dozen places, and began to shudder, keening loudly in an inhuman pitch. Phobos had once more managed to deflect most of the Camp-Bel weapons, but there was foam on his lips and infuriated agony writ clearly across his space. "Poison... gas? How did..."

Now Urelle answered. "The Wanderer."

"Wanderer? *Kashkt!*" The last word was spoken in a gravelly voice, neither fully human *nor* Xiilistiin, and Quester tensed, even as Phobos tried and failed to roll himself to his feet. The Camp-Bels were now firing at the main Xiilistiin forces, who were starting to stagger from their own encounter with the noxious vapor.

Phobos' eyes glowed. "You incredible mortal *vermin*. You have *killed* this body, and *he* has linked me *to* it." The glow flared brighter. "*But I will not die alone!*"

Shargamor's Mercy! Quester threw everything she had into the best shield she could imagine, pulling the very *air* into solidity before them, and sensed Urelle's panicked surge of power sealing her own barrier — one instant before Phobos *detonated*.

The explosion was not merely fire and force but *psychic*, something deeper and infinitely vicious, ripping not at the body but the soul, trying to rend the very essence of the spirits surrounding the dying demon that had been Phobos. The

Camp-Bel barricade shattered with the sound of a thousand plates beneath a hammer, and they tumbled backwards, some continuing to roll farther down the stone staircase. Quester could not maintain her shield, focused only on protecting her friends, using nothing but her own will to prevent a hideous death.

The lethal wave of fire and hatred subsided, and Quester slowly rose to her feet.

The landing was *burning*. Oh, the stone itself was mostly untouched, save for the fifteen-foot crater of boiling lava where Phobos had lain, but the forces of Ares were literally on fire, blazing with eerie green and orange flames. Looking around, she saw many of the Camp-Bels lying still, some of them burning — their *armor* burning! — as well.

Victoria stood, as did Urelle and Ingram, staring around at the horrific devastation. "That *monster*," hissed Ingram at last. "Killed as many as he could on both sides, just because he was *beaten*!"

The four of them began desperately checking the fallen Camp-Bels. Sergeant Lepida got to her knees, then managed to stand. "Great Founder. *Camp-Bels!* Sound off! Who've we got?"

It took only a few minutes to determine that out of the forty Camp-Bels who had accompanied them, only ten were in any way functional. Ten more were badly injured.

And twenty were dead, seven of them being slowly and completely consumed by the flames that refused to be extinguished.

"That's it," Ingram said, face white with rage. "That is *it*. Sergeant, you get back down the Path. Get everyone evacuated — even the dead."

He looked around, and Quester echoed his iron resolve, one duplicated by Urelle and Victoria. "No one else. We're going to finish this. And we're going to finish it *now*."

"Now," agreed Quester. "The Xiilistiin, *and* Ares. We finish them both."

"Absolutely," Victoria said, coldly. "Will they be together or separate?"

Quester tilted her head, stretched out her antennae. "Ares wants us stopped. He will be the last. Somewhere before we face him, there will be hidden the Xiilistiin."

Then she felt it — the faintest touch of a unique odor, even through the stench of burning bodies. Deeper and darker than the creatures they had already faced, but oh, so similar. "Yes," she said, and gripped her longmace tightly. "Hidden... but not from me."

"Then lead on," Ingram said, and brought the *anai-k'ota* around in a brilliant cutting arc. "We're right behind you."

Chapter 48
Past Mystery, Present Trap

Ingram followed behind Quester, trusting her and the others to keep a clear eye out. *I have to see what is in this data now. If it's going to do us any good, we need the information before we run into the fake Ares.*

Understood, Victoria sent. *We'll watch. Make it fast; It may be one or two landings up, but the Xiilistiin cannot be that far off.*

He nodded, then inserted the crystal record into the ISNDAU and sealed off his thoughts so he could concentrate on reading; an alert from his friends would penetrate, but he wouldn't be casually distracting them with his thoughts, or being distracted by theirs.

All right... First, the Seers on Kyriarcnis had predicted a dark start to the next Cycle. Seemed verified when there were a bunch of atrocities shortly after Ares appeared — they couldn't connect them to the General, though. But the big event was the murders...

He was vaguely aware that Quester was drawing away from him, and increased his pace to match.

It was an effort to keep his mind sealed as the horrific details came out. *By Athena, I hadn't realized it was so* many *children!* It had not just affected Aegis itself, but most of the villages and smaller settlements for almost fifty miles around. *Hundreds* of victims.

Another increase in speed; Quester must be hot on the trail. There, at first, seemed to be very little pattern — a concentration on the very young, but it wasn't clear if there was more to it. But then the Camp-Bels had asked *Rhyme and Reason* to analyze the data with its own "forensic database" which included something called "multivariate statistical analysis".

The thinking machines had given a terrifying answer; that while there were others being killed, those were merely a smokescreen, a deception, distractions to confuse the watchers and make them uncertain. The true targets were female infants, all between six months and one year of age.

And there were only a very few left alive.

Analysis had also shown that the killer was extraordinarily well-informed, apparently able to penetrate almost any defenses, as though it knew details of the defenses and wards of each residence. Because of that, the Camp-Bels had kept this discovery a deadly secret, and sent people to watch and intercept.

Even then, several more people were murdered, including two of the targets, the unseen assailant having somehow entered under the eyes of the Camp-Bels. *How* only became clear at the final house, when the watchers decided to wait no longer and entered without warning, to find the father in the act of murdering his own children —

INGRAM! Urelle's mindvoice broke through. *Something's wrong!*

He looked up, to see that Quester was once farther ahead, almost running. *Quester, slow down! We don't need to wear ourselves out on the stairs!*

His friend's mindsense was... *odd*. Ingram felt a peculiar urgency, an eagerness he hadn't sensed before, but also a tension. *No, Ingram, we must hurry!*

What is it, Quester? Victoria asked. *Do you sense something?*

Yes! It's urgent! We must go faster! Instead of slowing, Quester started running, the skip-bouncing stride of an Iriistiik in a hurry that pushed the other two Adventurers to their limits, and beyond Urelle's. Glancing back with concern, Ingram saw the young mage was keeping pace by using her airwing spell to allow her to leap many feet at a step.

"Seriously, Quester, *slow down!* No matter what you're sensing, we need to stick together!"

With a visible effort, Quester slackened her stride enough for Ingram to close the gap, but still moved forward at jogging pace. They had crested another of the great landings, but now Quester plunged through the doorway of a small building to one side of the landing. Her taloned feet made echoing *clack-clack-clack* noises as she trotted down the stairway within, a stairway that plunged deep under the ground.

Okay, there's definitely something wrong. Ingram shoved the ISNDAU into his pack, even as Quester broke into an all-out run. "Quester --!"

The three of them redoubled their efforts, now just trying to *catch* their friend, who slowed only the slightest bit at their entreaties — just enough to allow them to close the gap down the long hallway revealed at the base of the stairs. "Stop, Quester!" Victoria shouted. When there was no answer, she said "Quester, stop *immediately* or we will have to *force* you to stop!"

Ingram couldn't even make out Quester's thoughts any more. The link was still there, but it was all fuzzed with urgency and confusion and hunger and hope all mingled in a nauseating blend. "Okay, stop her, it is," he said, and all three of them lunged forward as Quester passed through an open doorway.

A mass of white, sticky strands *fountained* from either side of the doorway, and even from above, covering Ingram, Victoria, and Urelle. Ingram tried to tuck and roll, but the stuff dragged and pulled and tangled, sending him crashing to the floor — where he found that all his efforts were just tightening the strands' grip on him.

"Oh, *Myrionar's Mercy*," he heard Victoria breathe, horror in every syllable, and stopped fighting long enough to look up.

The three of them lay at the entrance to a huge cavern that was almost completely festooned with the strands — the *webbing* — that had captured them.

And it was crawling with Xiilistiin. There were hundreds of the creatures, some the ordinary insect-like monstrosities, but many others more or less humanoid; a few were Swarmfathers, larger, semi-human abominations made from multiple powerful victims assimilated into one.

In the center of the room was something far worse. The webbing came together, top and bottom, funneling in from all sides, and bunched into an elongated *something*, a tangled mass that bulged out like a snake that had swallowed a ball, a snake made of nothing but thousands of strands of web, and that bulging, fibrous mass pulsed and flickered green and yellow and orange, the light chasing out through the webbing and then returning to echo in that mass, that resembled nothing so much as the egg-case of a spider the size of *Rhyme and Reason*.

And Quester was still moving forward. She slowed only as she approached that glowing mass, and one of the Swarmfathers stepped before her. Ingram felt a ripple of consternation in Quester, one overridden by something else... a feeling?

No, Ingram realized with slow-dawning horror of understanding, *a scent*.

"Welcome to your new Nest," the Swarmfather said. "Your Meal is prepared... Mother."

Chapter 49
Swarm and Nest

Quester perceived everything in a strange and frightening duality. A part of her was screaming in horror and shame and guilt, that she had led her friends into this monstrous trap, and struggling — so far to no avail — to change her actions, her movements.

But the other part of her was enveloped and overwhelmed by the *Aroma*, the scent of something so sweet and savory, so deep and rich, that all other foods, all other smells and sensations in the universe, were as nothing to it. A smell emanating from an eight-sided bowl just before the one who had welcomed her.

There was a *Song*, too, a music that called to her with that waiting Aroma, that touched her mind and soul with the promise of a Nest, of a unity beyond any she had known since the horrible day when the Mother had cut her off and cast her, alone, into the world.

She reached the bowl and sat before it... and despite all her other half's efforts, reached down to take a handful of the brown, mealy substance that glittered like gold and smelled of all the Heavens.

And still she could hear...

"What have you *done* to her?" Ingram screamed. "She knows better than *this!*"

The Swarmfather turned, and the small part of Quester scraped her mandibles in rage as she heard its contemptuous tones. "*Knows*? Yes, of course, with her conscious mind, she knows. But the Iriistiik — even more, in many ways, than the Xiilistiin — are bound by their nature. The right sound, the right scent, the right motions, these can sway them, can make them look the other way, can draw them and control them."

"But you're not..." Urelle trailed off with an intake of breath, a whisper of realization, even as Quester took her first bite.

It blossomed in her mouth like joy and unity, magnifying that Nest-call, drawing her out and up. Behind it there was something else, a bitter chemical touch, a sense of corruption and decay, of something *wrong*, but only that weak and ineffectual part of herself, the conscious part, realized it.

"Indeed, young mage," the Swarmfather said. "It is what we *are*, it is our *nature* to deceive, to infiltrate, and Iriistiik are our most natural and select prey. We know them, know them better than ourselves."

Now she was *gobbling* the Mother's Meal desperately, feeling that joy, that *rightness* in front of the subtle lies swelling within her, towards the ultimate ending her very soul desired and demanded. The Song — that, too, touched with a sound not at all right, yet equally irresistible — was growing stronger, touching the part of her that had awakened, the telepathic essence that could bind her to a Nest in truth.

"But she *has* to know you aren't Iriistiik!"

"Again, a part of her. But can you keep your eyes from dilating in the darkness, from shrinking in the light?" The Swarmfather laughed, a grating, buzzing sound like a sawblade. "You cannot change your *body* so easily, and when your *body* is the one that responds, that *perceives*... it is easy. Even easier if one is a Xiilistiin Swarm-Heart with the aid of godspower."

Quester had finished more than half of what was in the bowl, and she felt tingling throughout her body, presentiments of a Change that was coming nearer with the speed of doom. Inside, she cast about, becoming desperate, searching for some way to break free from the cage her own body's reactions had made.

"It would not, of course, be *certain* to work," the Swarmfather conceded, "if there were a living Nest of *her* people — no matter how far away. The other Mother might sense, might guide her away. But we and Ares have carefully destroyed all the other Nests. Today, she will become a Xiilistiin Mother, the first born not of us but of the Iriistiik, and give to us the powers of their Mothers as well."

Quester picked up the bowl, ran her palpi around it, scavenging the final crumbs, as the tingling became a pressure, vibrating higher and higher within her, the call of the Nest (Swarm) reaching a dizzyingly seductive height.

"I don't care *what* she becomes," Ingram said. "I'll free her — *we* will free her, somehow, even if it takes the rest of my life!"

"By the *Balance* you better believe it!" Urelle's voice was tear-laden, but filled with determined fury.

"Indeed," Victoria said quietly.

"Fools," the Swarmfather said, and Quester felt his antennae brush hers, and the Song became almost the entirety of the world, reaching to connect her to all of its Singers. "You will have no such chance. Though indeed, you will be her friends again, for such as you? Your powers are *precisely* what the Mother of the Xiilistiin will need to begin the most powerful line of all." The others shouted again, but the Swarmfather's laugh drowned them out. "She is deaf to you, deaf and blind to the mere mortal world. She is hearing us now, hearing the call of the Swarm as the call of the Nest, and with Mother's Meal working in her, she has no choice. She must have a Nest, and aside from the Xiilistiin, there *is* no Nest!"

And Quester's entire world — her universe — halted, even the instinct-consumed body freezing — as she heard, as she *understood*, those words.

"But... I *have* a Nest," Quester ground out, speaking herself for the first time since the dreadful, wonderful Aroma had struck her.

The Swarmfather stiffened, a suddenly-grotesque statue. "What... ?"

"I have a Nest," she repeated. "It is small... only three," and now she was rising to her feet. "But each of them is a hundred — a thousand — *ten thousand times a hundred* greater than any of yours!"

She whirled, and as she did, opened her mind. *Ingram! Urelle! Victoria! I do not deserve it — not after leading you here, into this trap that would steal your bodies and souls and make you into monsters like them. Yet...* Even now, she hesitated, knowing what her friends were like, what *humans* were like, knowing what terrible price she was about to ask.

But was there any other choice? She could see none. The only other choice ended in worse than death. *Yet... would you trust me once more? Open yourselves to me, as never before, so that — for even a single instant — we could all four be as one?*

The Swarmfather was rearing back, coming to combat readiness, yet with a glacier-slowness. For a moment that was nonetheless an eternity, Quester heard no response from her friends, and felt despair rising to swallow her.

And then, three mindvoices spoke together:

You don't have to ask.

For one instant, Quester *Saw* her friends. Ingram, the young boy trained near to death, the child always certain of failure, yet never quite losing his dreams, and never even close to losing his courage, who loved Quester with the intensity only friends who have shared a thousand battles could, in some ways stronger than his attraction to Urelle, rivaling what he felt for Berenike. Victoria, old and weary yet indomitable, memories of loves had and lost, little secrets and terrible battles, and the suffusing tenderness and determination surrounding her love for her niece. And Urelle, youngest and still well-acquainted with loss, but still holding her faith that the good and right would triumph over the corrupt and evil, and deeper within, a girl touching a wellspring of power even she barely began to understand.

They were all her Nest.

In that instant, the power of the Mother's Meal ignited within her.

"*Impossible!*" screeched the Swarmfather, even as he threw up his arms to block the blaze of golden-green light that erupted from Quester.

"The Iriistiik may have no Nests," Quester said, hearing her voice thundering throughout the room, "But *I* do, and for their sake, I will be *their* Mother!"

Fire and ice and magic boiled through her, melting her into nothing but the single and singular awareness that she was *Quester*, and that she was bound to the newest Nest of all. She held to that awareness as the Meal rebuilt her.

The Swarmfather had recovered, and lunged forward, even as Quester's friends screamed, struggling uselessly against the webs that held them.

At the last instant, Quester's exoskeleton *split*. A black-and-green arm lashed out of the crumbling shell and seized the Swarmfather's rostrum in the moment of descent, halting the eight-foot monstrosity as though it were a ball being caught. Then, with a casual gesture, that arm cast the Swarmfather aside, sent him tumbling to fetch up, stunned, against the Swarm-Heart.

"And you will kill no more, ever again!"

Quester touched the rage and loss and cold need for justice inside her, and heard three other beloved voices, sensed three other spirits —the memories of a hundred Mothers guided her, showed her the way, and a light shone from her, a light that cast sharp-edged shadows across the entirety of the Xiilistiin Swarm — before it detonated into a shockwave that swept the cavern like the weapons of *Rhyme and Reason*.

The Swarm-Heart fought back. It had the power of hundreds of Xiilistiin, no few of them Swarmfathers and special forms who had consumed beings of might. It had its own mental skills, not at all inconsiderable; and she was there, at the center of its power.

And it all meant nothing. The webwork column bent, bulged, and then *tore*, adding a green-yellow-orange flare to the pristine white of Quester's absolute force.

The Xiilistiin were swept away, even the Swarmfathers incapable of fighting the immaterial yet implacable wave of telekinetic power. The blast swept over her friends, stripping away the webs, yet leaving them untouched, and then *smashed* into the walls, floor, and ceiling with the impact of a thousand battering rams.

The Xiilistiin *splashed*. And the pressure on her mind — *their* minds — was gone.

Chapter 50
Rebirth and Revelation

Urelle rose, weaving a bit on shaky legs, dizzy from the combination of terror, shock, relief, and amazement. She stared at Quester, and the other two joined her. "Quester... is that *you*?"

Before them was a graceful humanoid figure, standing over seven feet tall, legs and arms and back patterned with black and green that faded to a faintly verdant cream on the torso, neck, and head. The hands and feet were startlingly human in outline, though tipped with short green-black claws; the same was true of the second-hands that grew from the base of what appeared to be a ribcage. Glittering wings spread wide behind her, shimmering in the slowly-dying light of the Swarm-Heart and that of scattered fires flickering in the webbing, limning the veins of the dragonfly-like pinions with ruby and gold, with rainbow flashes from within the glassy-clear substance. The ovoid abdomen was gone; a short, spike-like protrusion was all that remained. Urelle saw Ingram turn away in confused embarrassment after a moment, for the rest of the body was undoubtedly human in design, and inarguably female in all ways.

Her face was strongly defined, shining like Quester's chitin, but mobile in a way Quester's never had been. Her eyes glittered with the facets of an Iriistiik, but were smaller, set off by what appeared to be brows in the human model; a sweep of feathery almost-hair rose above those brows, cascading down, an emerald-glinting waterfall that whispered when it moved like a handful of gems and gold. The mouth was very human, though Urelle couldn't see what it was like *inside*.

"Yes. I am Quester," she said, and even the *voice* was different, a warm contralto with only a hint of the buzzing resonance that had defined Quester's prior speech.

"What *happened*?" Ingram's tone echoed all their confusion. "And, um, put on a cloak or something."

Quester looked down at herself, and made a sound somewhere between a gasp and a laugh, turned around. "Indeed," she said. "But I confess I have no truly appropriate clothing."

"Hold a moment," Urelle said. "Auntie, let me... yes." She dug into Victoria's pack. "Can I take a few of your clothes?"

"As I don't intend to change my wardrobe in the next few hours, yes."

Urelle took two of Victoria's spare cloaks and spread them out. She glanced to where Quester stood, then extended her senses, reached out and touched the *essence* of that shape, brought it to the cloth and bade the cloth follow that shape, the two becoming one in her mind.

The cloaks rose into the air, draping an invisible form; then they began to both unravel and weave themselves together, slowly becoming a travel robe that was made for someone seven feet tall, with a small extra pair of sleeves above the waist. She then levitated that over to Quester.

"Thank you, Urelle. I knew I could count on you." In a few quick motions, Quester was dressed, and turned back to their group. "I suspect I will need other clothing later, but this will do for now."

There was a deep, brief rumble and a clattering of stones pattered down from overhead. "Let's get out of here," Ingram said. "Explanations can wait; what you did weakened this whole area, and I think there's more caverns hollowing out the entire hill."

They hastened out, through the hallway and up the stairs, until they could see the light of day from the second landing up ahead. "Now, Quester, what *happened* to you?" Urelle repeated.

The new face tilted in a familiar way, and Quester smiled. "The incalculable. The Swarmfather was correct; the Mother's Meal, or their version of it, overwhelmed my instinctive reactions, and I could not fight it; even though it *was* slightly different, I could only sense that as an... under-taste, a single note off in a symphony."

Her new face grimaced. "Fortunately for me, *that* was merely a difference in biology and taste, not a poison or anything of that nature. As a *nearly*-complete mother, the entirety of my biology is designed to demand that completion, so even those slight differences were nowhere near enough to let me break free. And, similarly, he was right in that, without any Iriistiik left, I could not bond to them rather than to the Swarm-Heart."

"But you'd already bonded to *us*," Victoria said.

"Yes." Her smile was brilliant — showing shining, clear teeth, though with something moving behind them that wasn't precisely a tongue. "Something they had not known, and — in truth — that I had not considered to be the *same*, although I had called you Nestmates. The adoption of humans to the Nest had always been done *after* a Nest was established, and they had never, quite, been connected to the Nest as the Iriistiik born to it."

She smiled again and laughed; the buzz-rasp of the old Quester was momentarily clearer in that sound. "Oh, but that was because the Nest was *based* on Iriistiik. The Mother was born of us, raised by us, brought to the edge of awakening for us, fed Mother's Meal by us, and bonded to us so that she would Become a true Mother with us." She bowed low, a fluid motion showing the flexibility that no Iriistiik had ever had. "But this time, I was born of the Iriistiik... but I *grew* with Ingram, cut off from my Nest; I came to the edge of awakening for *you*. I made my first true bonds with the four of you. I was fed Mother's Meal in your presence. And so... I became a Mother with *you*."

Ingram reached out and touched Quester's hand, which gripped his. He looked up, startled. "It's... warm. Soft."

"I am *of* you, now. I still am also Iriistiik..." She trailed off.

Urelle remembered the Swarmfather's words. "... but you are the last."

Quester took a deep breath and shrugged, her smile now obviously forced. "Well, not *truly*. We came to Zarathan from far beyond the sky; Iriistiik surely still live among the stars. And there may be a few more un-Nested Gray Warriors, and — possibly — a Nest or two far enough away that even a Mother would have a difficult time reaching them — perhaps on the other side of the world."

That's a lot of maybes, Urelle thought to herself. But it might comfort Quester to think those maybes were truths.

They emerged into the slanting sunshine on the broad landing of the Aegeian Path. "So," Ingram said with a cheer that demanded a change of subject, "it looks like becoming a Mother made you a lot stronger."

"Oh, very much so," Quester agreed eagerly. "Even with memories of Mothers before me, I am just starting to understand how much more." She looked up the Path. "I believe we have much proof that I, as well as Urelle and Victoria, was one of those their Coins, and thus their prophecy, sought."

"Are you all right? Do you need to rest? I mean, that must have been the most stressful thing *ever*," Urelle said, trying to grasp it all. *She didn't just get bonded to us, she changed her entire body design, rebuilt herself in moments to fit the people to whom she was bonded!*

The feathery hair rose along with another smile. *By the Balance... her hair* is *her antennae! She didn't lose them, she* gained.

"The Mother's Meal provides the resources for the change. While mine was very *different* from any other awakening I have heard of... the body is always rebuilt at that time. I am fully able to continue — and I do not think we have much time." Despite the changed voice, her tone was somehow *completely* Quester's as she said, "And you, Ingram, need to finish your own reading, and quickly. If we are right, only Ares remains, waiting for us above. Or he may be on his way."

Ingram started, then reached back to pull out his ISNDAU. "Founder, you're right about that."

Urelle sensed him beginning to read — starting at the terrible night he had lost his family — and damped her connection; *that* part wasn't her business, and she sensed the others also turning their mental gaze aside.

With Ingram following, the three others began to walk up the stairway. Urelle heard a faint murmuring from Victoria, the litany of the Eight Winds, and knew her Aunt was preparing. *I'd better do that, too!*

With Quester in the lead, with her newly-enlarged abilities, Urelle took the time to craft her own defenses, layering mystical armor and absorption and deflection, sense-deception and spiritual strengthening, and enhancing her own body's speed and strength and toughness. She touched the others with some of her power, shaped a bit of reality to defend them, and prepared in her mind all the other most powerful defenses and offenses... and, of course, mobility spells, for in a battle there were few things more useful than physically commanding placement of oneself and others.

A vast, echoing shock of disbelief, realization, denial — a chaotic blend of excitement and loss and anger and transcendant joy — burst in on them as they crested the next landing. But before any of them could speak, they saw they were not alone.

Before them, standing in the very center of the third landing, was a titanic figure, over seven feet in height. Though shorter than Quester, the man before them surely outweighed her by a factor of two — and that was excluding the massive, spike-protected armor with its heavy pauldrons, gauntlets of steel gripping an immense two-handed sword that made the ones her sister Kyri had practiced with look like rapiers. The blade alone was eight inches across, a ludicrously heavy shaft of steel whose sharp edges appeared superfluous; so huge a weapon would literally crush anyone struck by it at least as much as it would cut them.

But all of that was secondary to the sheer *power* the figure radiated. An aura of blood-red surrounded him, and the smile above the short, sharp, black beard was contemptuously amused. Even the false Athena had not had a presence filled with such concentrated menace. There was no doubt at all who this was.

"Heroes *do* find a way," Ares said. He wore no helm, only a crown composed of many copies of his own sigil — a chariot wheel crossed with a sword and a torch. The torch's flames were rubies, the swords were silver, the chariot wheels of gold. "So now you come before me, having bested my allies. I suppose you believe that makes you a threat?"

Urelle *had* thought that. But faced with the god himself, she was suddenly, terribly unsure whether even the Wanderer himself would have been a worse opponent.

If her aunt felt the same way, she showed not a hint of it. "Yes, as a matter of fact. And you know we are. That is why you were hunting us from before the time we even knew you existed. Save your posturing for those who will be impressed by it, counterfeit god."

The teeth were bared in a grin that was also a snarl. "Oh, such fine spirit, Lady Vantage. Yet your heart beats so swiftly, and there is a pain waiting behind that. Should you be daring death when it lies so near to you?" The eyes — which held a crimson flame within — darted to Quester. "And now the last Iriistiik has lost even the outward seeming of her race, and for what? Your people are gone, your god has done naught to protect you, and even the last Mother can no longer bring your people back!"

"Shargamor trusts that we shall carry out his will," Quester said, and there was a serenity in her voice that Urelle desperately wished she could feel. "And *my* people are here, with me."

"Yes, so you must believe, if you are not to despair. A fine refuge in sophistry and denial, Quester. Though I congratulate you on a most... *artistic* defeat of the Xiilistiin. I was extremely pleased with the Swarm's last instants of terror and dismay."

Ares' gaze shifted. "And what of the little Camp-Bel? A great surprise you gave me, yet it is already felled and plays no part in the endgame. Not a trace of the

Lady of Wisdom is to be found, your pathetic imposture of Berenike has been shattered, and you think to face *me* with naught but the pride of your clan?"

For an instant, Ingram gave no answer; Urelle was not even sure that Ingram had *heard* Ares.

And then Ingram laughed, a laugh on the edge of insanity and revelation, and his eyes came up to meet those of Ares; and, impossibly, Ares took a single step back at what he saw in those eyes, as Ingram calmly slid the ISNDAU back into his pack.

"The Lady of Wisdom and War outplayed you from the beginning, when you made the first move in this game," Ingram said, and his voice vibrated with incredulity and fear and hope. "When you arranged the murders of the children of Aegeia, already she had you outmaneuvered." His words wavered, the pitch cracked, yet the absolute *confidence* in them did not waver, despite the underlying terror and waiting ecstasy and fury.

Urelle gasped in shock as he cast aside the *anai-k'ota*, letting his signature weapon clatter unheeded down the staircase, as though casting aside a part of his life. "Her final gambit is played, and her piece stands before you."

Golden light began to radiate from within Ingram Camp-Bel. "*I am the Spear of Athena!*"

Chapter 51
The Spear of Athena

Victoria whirled as the auric radiance flared up, and saw Ingram ignite into pure gold-white fire.

Ingram's form dissolved to a sketch of a boy in pencil and flame, and the fire about him grew more intense. From the inferno condensed twin vambraces and gauntlets, which flew and bound themselves to the spectral shape with shockwaves of luminance and sound. Boots with shining greaves were also born of the singing gods-fire and fitted themselves to the outline of Ingram with the same concussion of light. A crown of golden laurel leaves touched the lines of hair as a delicately sculpted breastplate affixed itself about the nigh-invisible chest, and then an armor skirt materialized, one armored leaf after another fitting itself onto the waist.

And the white-gold flame *exploded* out, knocking Victoria, Quester, and Urelle to their knees, and even causing Ares to totter. In the center of the god-forged fire the figure stretched, shifted, and then solidified as the blaze coalesced into a quiver of javelins slung over the shoulder of a tall, violet-haired girl, a girl whose face and features and intense violet eyes were still hauntingly familiar.

Time froze. Victoria felt Ingram's mind open, saw a flash of truth, of the past and present all entertwined.

A man stood over two cradles, and before Ianthe or Rastus Camp-Bel could move, drove shadowy talons down. The wail of a baby was cut off, and the hand with its smoky claws rose again.

Before it could fall, the two Camp-Bels struck, and the battle was short and furious. They looked about at the carnage, then went to the other cradle, where cries had continued.

The cries of a baby girl.

Ares' jaw dropped. "*What?*"

In the time it took to blink, the Spear of Athena was *there*, and drove her fist forearm-deep into Ares' gut, sending the god tumbling across the hundred-yard expanse of the landing.

"It was the *girl* who survived," Urelle whispered, even as the golden-armored figure slammed into Ares again. "They called on allies — maybe even the Wanderer, he *could* have kept that from me — and *turned the girl into a boy*, and then hid the boy as an inconsequential failure, never treating him specially..."

"... so that it never occurred to any that the story of that night was a lie," Quester finished.

"And so, *Ingram* is also one of those of his prophecy," Victoria breathed, and began to laugh.

Ares blocked the next blows, struck back, but Ingram — the *Spear of Athena*! — simply spun about and delivered a kick to the face that sent Ares flying to the next landing, only one more remaining above, that one a scant hundred yards below the final temples, including the legendary Statue of Athena.

"And that explains Berenike's power," Urelle said, still putting the pieces together. "When she was using something more than ordinary magic... that must have been Athena touching the boy - the *girl* - she knew would have to become her true God-Warrior!"

They sprinted up the stairs, occasionally having to catch their balance as concussions jolted the stone beneath them.

Ares and the Spear of Athena fought back and forth across the landing, dodging, ducking, punching, kicking, firing blasts of power, all at speeds so great that the eye could only see a blur. It took all that Victoria could manage to push the perceptions of the Eight Winds to a level where she could tell for certain which combatant was which as they darted to and fro.

And as she did so, she saw that not only had the god lost his sword, but also that Ares was blocking more and more, and even the *blocked* punches from the gold-silver clad God-Warrior were driving the god backwards.

"Every movement... every blow... is faster and more powerful than the one before," Quester murmured.

Victoria nodded, a smile growing on her face. "She's still getting *stronger*."

Urelle's face shone, her eyes tracking the motion of the tall warrior girl with the aid of sorcerous speed. "Ingram... *Ingram* is going to defeat *Ares!*"

The god heard her as he skidded to a halt thirty feet away. "Defeat *me*? Fools. This *is* a God-Warrior, yes. But I am a *god* — the God of War!" He dodged back from a double-handed strike that shattered the stone where he had stood, and held out his hand; blood and ebony-colored energies flared, and a gargantuan red-black axe materialized. "So let me remind you of what that *means!*"

Ares parried the next strike and then whirled the axe around and down. *"DIE!"*

There was a concussion, as though the Camp-Bel's ship had struck the mountain, knocking all three of them from their feet. But looking up, Victoria gasped.

The great axe-blade had *stopped*, for Ingram's gauntleted hands had caught it in mid-blow. Ares' eyes were wide with disbelief as the girl raised her own to meet his; the golden fire of that gaze was visible to all three of her companions.

"*You're* not Ares," she snarled. "Everything you've done here is against everything he stands for!" She pushed, and Ares grunted, gave back a half step, his smile now a snarl of incredulity. "You have no love, you have no joy, you have no passion, save only for *yourself!*"

Sharp, metallic *pings* echoed across the marble expanse of the landing as Ares' axe began to *crack* under the pressure of the gold-clad fingers. "Who are you? What have you done with the true Ares?"

The golden fire went pure silver-white. *"SHOW ME YOUR TRUE FACE!"*

The axe shattered and the Spear of Athena blazed forward, carrying Ares irresistibly with her. Up the stairway they went, Ares plowing a trench through the stairs, his own snarl juddering like a man riding a washboard in a cart. At the penultimate landing the silver-burning God-Warrior continued in a straight line, taking Ares into the sky and smashing him with blow after blow.

The War-God's armor was *breaking*, Victoria saw with awe. The great breastplate split and fell away, clanging pitifully on the stone, the fire of the assault igniting the clothing below, leaving the broad chest bare except for a single triangular piece of armor set over the heart, seeming embedded in the skin itself. Ares tried to dodge, but the Spear of Athena caught his leg, whirled him up and over her head, and hurled him straight down.

The landing *splashed* like water, marble shards and stone dust rippling out from the impact crater along with the scattered pieces of the armor on Ares' arms and legs. The entire little mountain shuddered at the force of that blow, and then *again* as Ingram dropped from the sky like a stone onto Ares' chest, flaming with pure godspower.

Blood flew from Ares' mouth, and that shining armor chestpiece cracked and fell away, leaving only the stubs of the metal points that had secured it to Ares' chest. Before the god could recover, Ingram grabbed him and spun around, faster and faster and faster until she and Ares were a blur, emitting a whining drone with the speed of their rotation. When Ingram released Ares, the god streaked across straight into the mountainside.

The detonation sent Victoria, Quester, and Urelle flying away, and only Quester's and Urelle's reactions kept them from falling down the broken staircase. And then Quester and Urelle cursed and kept all three of them flying, for the mountain began to *collapse*.

The upper central portion of the mountain sagged and dropped straight down, not a landslide, but a complete collapse, into what Victoria realized had to be the entire complex of caverns within, including the Xiilistiin chamber. The cave-in expanded, the stone already cracked in innumerable places by the stupendous battle above. The fourth landing was gone, and the third was being consumed by the yawning pit, and then the highest landing began an inexorable slide, taking the minuscule dot that was Ares down with it as the Spear of Athena leapt clear.

But that was not the end. The highest edge continued to crumble, and mighty temples began to plummet into the abyss, followed by the statues of the gods, including proud Ares and noble Athena, sliding into the pit with a roar to shame a dragon.

A vast cloud of dust billowed from the yawning chasm, only slowly disippating. Silence reigned, broken only by the grumbling crackle of rock slowly settling, a few pebbles shifting; above, only the last temple remained, the edge of a cliff only steps from its front door.

The three of them landed at the edge of the second landing, looking across and slightly down. The shining figure of the Spear of Athena landed in front of them, wide violet eyes now matching the hair and looking at them with a stunned surprise coupled by rising hope.

Accompanied by a dreamlike feeling that *we just* did *this a few minutes ago*, Victoria said, "Ingram?"

"Y... yes?" the vision before them said. She looked down at Victoria. "Wow, I never realized what it was like to be *tall*." Then she glanced shyly towards Urelle. "Um... Urelle...?"

Victoria did not know what to expect. Urelle was a fine and thoughtful young woman, but this situation was not covered in any discussions she'd ever had.

"Ingram?" Urelle said, the word a soft, tentative question.

Their link strengthened, and for an instant, they saw the world through Ingram's eyes — and knew that no matter how high off the ground the eyes were, that it was still Ingram Camp-Bel who saw them, and surrounded each of them in his sight with a light of love and faith that could not be mistaken.

Urelle threw her arms around Ingram and hugged her tight. "I love your new look," she mumbled into the breastplate.

The four broke into peals of laughter that echoed across the broken landscape.

There was a sound of grinding stone. "How very *touching*," rumbled a voice from within the crater.

Victoria felt a stabbing pain in her chest as fear once more sent her pulse racing. *Too many surprises, too many battles, too much of everything.*

Massive blocks of stone shuddered and were cast aside, mere pebbles, as the figure of Ares, God of War, rose from the rubble.

Chapter 52
Raiagamor the Immortal

At last, I can let my rage free.

Raiagamor felt absolute *joy* at that thought — and, paradoxically, the joy let him hold onto his guise a few moments more. "You thought *that* was enough to stop me?" he asked, then spat blood. The four before him crouched into battle poses, but the pallor of Ingram the Spear, the shaking hands of the mage Urelle, the vibrating antennae-hair of the new Mother Quester, and the thin line of Victoria Vantage's mouth showed their fear and uncertainty — the exquisite taste of which *just* reached him from here, a hundred yards and more away.

"You thought *that* was sufficient?" he asked again, letting a bloody smile spread across his face. "Well, yes, it might have been... had I not been, as you say, a *false* Ares."

"What are you? Some other god? A demonlord?" Ingram's lips were pulled back from her teeth in hatred and fear.

"Such mundane guesses? Pah. And I hoped you might *entertain* me."

"For my part," Victoria said, and now he could scent her *pain*, and oh, my, how fine it would be to see her die before her friends, without another mark on her. "For my part, I would venture to say *Great Wolf*."

His own smile broadened. "Oh, bravo, old woman," he said. "As I said to Ares himself, the moment I slew him, you are — almost — right."

Holding precariously to sanity and control, he bowed with deep irony to the four Adventurers. "And I congratulate you, also, on forcing me to abandon imposture. It was my intent that, even to you, I would remain Ares, that no one in all Aegeia would have a chance to know who really had guided the fall of their 'eternal' Cycle."

He gestured to his near-naked form, the armor shattered to pieces that were scattered about and now within the fallen mountain. "But in truth, even Ares could not stand before you. Comfort yourselves in your last moments with that knowledge, that you could defeat a god!"

His eyes flamed green. "You demanded it, Spear of Athena — behold my true face!"

With a roar that made stone crumble from the edges of the crater, he let go his disguise.

***

Quester shrank back, a primal fear enveloping her and her friends as the thing before them... *changed*.

Black light burned around him as his form swelled from a mere seven to over nine feet tall, mighty chest broader than any human's, the golden fur on it a smooth expanse interrupted only by the forlorn stubs of the broken armor plate, massive arms coated with shaggy golden fur, arms ending in hands tipped with eight-inch diamond-glittering claws. His legs, too, bent and expanded, the springy limbs of a great cat tipped with crystal claws to rend the mightiest armor. His head distorted, stretched out in a muzzle, glowing eyes showing a blazing vertical slit of green fire within blue light, mouth now a cavernous maw filled with diamond blades. A tail with stiff yellow fur lashed behind him, and he laughed and spread his arms wide as the four Adventurers shrank back before his form and the menace he radiated.

"What in Athena's name *is* it?" Ingram breathed.

"I have no idea," Victoria said weakly, staring at the new monster with horror. "It looks... looks like some nightmare cross between a Great Wolf and some monstrous cat."

"What am I? Something *greater* than the Great Wolves," he said. "I am *Raiagamor the Immortal*, chosen child of the Queen of Wolves, Godslayer, Render of Souls."

Quester shuddered, a new and unwanted sensation. *A Queen of Wolves? I have never heard of such a thing, even the* Mothers *have never heard of it, save in the darkest and most ancient legends. And this Raiagamor's power is more than enough to justify his boasts.*

Raiagamor raised his immense arms, and the ground quaked beneath him. "Behold! The injuries you thought to have made are gone, as unreal as the form of Ares himself; you injured the *shape*, but the true power within was untouchable. And for you? I am your *death*, worthless Spear of Athena, feeble apprentice of the Wanderer, aged Adventurer of a bygone year, Mother of a doomed nest."

Quester set her new jaw and banished, as much as she could, her fear, and felt her friends doing the same. "Let us see how doomed we are, then."

Together, my friends. We can all see. We can all feel. We can all act — as one.

An instant of surprised understanding, as the three humnans finally understood what it meant to be Nestmates with a Mother.

The four sprinted forward, and Quester and Urelle sent a rampage of power ahead of them.

Magic and telekinetic power *vanished*, shredded by a contemptuous swat of one taloned hand, and the other came down, sent a blast of impact and hunger that swept the two aside.

But in the same instant, Victoria and Ingram slid *beneath* their flying comrades, slammed into Raiagamor with enough force to drive the creature back thirty feet, through boulders and rubble. Twin-Edged Fate cleaved its way deep into the monster's right shoulder, and the Spear of Athena drove her glittering silver namesake into Raiagamor's gut.

Raiagamor tore the axe from his shoulder and hurled it aside — taking Victoria with it. The spear... simply vanished.

Quester felt Ingram's shock even as the grinning monster caught up the God-Warrior and shook her.

"Conjured silver? Worthless even against my weaker brethren!" Raiagamor grinned edged death at them, the hideous smile widening at Victoria's stunned stare, seeing that the wound in his shoulder was already gone. "You thought the silver in your axe would hurt me? The sting of a bee, *less* than such a sting!" He hurled Ingram from him with such force that she flew in a flat trajectory and struck the cliff-face so hard that it left an outline of the God-Warrior in the stone.

But they had given Quester a chance to recover, and she hurled *boulders* at Raiagamor, one multi-ton projectile after another. *Perhaps he can consume my power directly, but he cannot change the laws of nature.*

He did not; instead, those terrible claws carved the boulders to pebbles with a speed and ferocity Quester had never imagined, and began to close on her, striding through the barrage like a man walking against a stiff breeze. "More! Come, o Mother of a freakish Nest, *more!* Show me your power!"

With an effort, Quester pulled up on both sides of Raiagamor and *slammed* a thousand tons of stone onto him from either side.

The monster burst from that granite prison as though it had been a bank of fog, talons glittering death as Raiagamor lunged for her.

But Ingram's golden boots took Raigamor in the head, the deadly claws inches short of Quester's face, and sent the monster tumbling.

Raiagamor rolled to his feet, but before he could charge, Urelle flew past, and a stream of silver coins flew from her back and through her hands, hands that glowed with a halo of electrical power, turning to a barrage of argent streaks, silver projectiles making the whipcrack sounds of the Camp-Bel coilguns as they slammed into the startled Raiagamor.

Did you see that, Quester? Victoria's thoughts were clear, though beneath was the sensation of an ominous ache in her chest.

With the question came understanding. *He* turned *to minimize that. He does not* like *silver, even if he claims it cannot kill him.*

Indeed, Raiagamor was now fully focused on Urelle, but she was floating, fading, moving from one point to another without always crossing the distance between, a flickering phantom whose reappearance was accompanied by a hail of silver death.

Yes! Ingram's mind-voice was tense but excited. *See, he's trying to cover that one side of his chest!*

Quester nodded, even as she and Ingram began to maneuver for the right angles. Victoria also nodded, and shifted her position — though she looked slower than usual. *Yes. See, the remnants of that armor plate. They remained with him even in this form. There was no* reason *for that — unless he was accustomed to keeping that* plate *always positioned over his heart. Urelle?*

I understand, Auntie!

"Then let's do this," Ingram said, her new contralto carrying the same clear conviction of the old tenor.

As Raiagamor made his own supernatural lunge, leaping the hundred yards separating him from Urelle, Quester leapt from one tumbled rock straight across, swiftsword and longmace taking the monster across the face. He stumbled and started to whirl, but Ingram slammed a fist into the golden-furred side. With that distraction, Raiagamor hesitated, and Quester bounded *back* from a second boulder, smashing Raiaga's head so hard it snapped all the way around. His attempt to slash Quester was blocked by a strike from Twin-Edged Fate, and then

Quester crossed his path *again*, longmace catching the back of the shaggy, fanged head.

Raiagamor gave an inarticulate snarl and splayed both legs out to brace himself, stretching his arms wide to catch two of his opponents at once —

And the stuttering snarl of the mystic silver coilgun ripped out again, stitching a line of holes entirely across Raiagamor's chest, halting at the small oval defined by the broken armor's anchors.

Raiagamor *screamed* — a bellow of pain and power that split the ears of everyone about, that might have been heard for literal miles — and staggered backwards.

Ingram caught his right arm.

Victoria caught his left.

Quester pulled the stone together around his feet.

And for one instant, Raiagamor was held still.

"Try a *thousand* bee-stings," Urelle said, and a hundred streaks of silver stabbed into the monster's chest.

Chapter 53
The Goddess of Wisdom

In that instant, Raiagamor cursed. *They have figured out my weakness!*

The curse was mainly for himself. When the *krellin* breastplate had been shattered by the incredible power of the Spear of Athena, it was no longer of any use; he should have overridden his habit of keeping it in any form. Raiagamor had no doubt that seeing the remnants of that plate — combined with his instinctive aversion to the pain, if not true injury, of silver — had given these King-damned Adventurers the clues they needed.

His chest was *afire* with the cold burn of silver, his heart writhing in agony.

But they lack one tiny element of the solution, he thought. *And have no weapon to deliver it.* Each bullet of silver through his heart *hurt*, indeed. But they didn't *stay* in the heart, and they were neither broad nor massive enough to finish the job. And that meant...

With a gutteral roar, he released a blast of godspower.

The four flew from him like shrapnel from the detonation of a bomb; Urelle's mystic shields shattered and she was sent careening over the stones, sliding up the hill and then back down. Victoria streaked straight into the side of the crater, striking with a bone-shattering *crack* and collapsing in front of the fallen ruin of the statue of Athena. Ingram moved in a split-second to help shield Quester, but the tide of deific force caught them both, plowed them into the stone not three yards from the great marble head of Ares' statue.

And then he unleashed his *Hunger*.

The four were not *quite* as close as would be ideal, but still they *sagged* towards the ground. Victoria's pain, already perfuming each breath Raiaga took, became richer and more intense, as he drained away the very life-force that fought against her body's weakness. The rich golden heaviness of godspower flowed into him, stripped bit by bit from the God-Warrior Ingram had become; the psionic powers of the Mother became a trickle of energy as refreshing as pure mountain streams;

and the infinite complexity of Urelle's magic also streamed into him, renewing his strength, ejecting the painful pellets of silver.

"Outplayed?" he said, an ironic smile directed at Ingram. "I think not, little God-Warrior. *Well*-played, I will grant. But even Athena knew nothing of what she faced. None of them did. And you, who have come closer than any to understanding? You will die, here, and *close* will mean nothing."

Despite his drain, despite the failure of their final gambit, the four were *still* trying to rise, to face him. Urelle was the first, swaying to her feet like a woman who had crossed a desert without water and, at the end of her strength, sees the salvation of an oasis still a mile distant. Ingram and Quester helped each other up, twin vines providing each other a momentary stability to rise before both would fall. Victoria had managed to roll to her hands and knees, but it was doubtful she could stand without help; under her dark skin her face was going gray.

But still she struggled, raising one hand, groping for anything to help, and her hand closed about the only thing nearby; a metal shaft.

Even to Raiagamor's inhuman perceptions, the world turned momentarily to pure gold, and the surge of godspower overwhelmed him, as though he had been drinking from a water-fountain and found it had suddenly become a firehose.

The mountain quaked anew and the golden light condensed about Victoria Vantage, coalesced into armor of gold, with a shield emblazoned with the the symbol of Aegeia and a great silver Spear, a spear twice her height and more, too heavy for a mere human to lift, a spear that had once been gripped in the hand of the Statue of Athena. A crested helm shimmered about her head, and her eyes flickered back and forth between blue and gray.

"No. No, no, no, *no, NO!*" he shrieked in fury at the reborn Athena. *If Athena is reborn, if the fools below are shown her, given her true words, the Cycle is repaired! All my work is for* nothing!

"Outplayed," Ingram said, the Spear of Athena staring with triumph at her namesake. "You matched yourself against the Goddess of Wisdom; how else could it have ended?"

Raiagamor snarled, but he grinned as well. "Ended? Oh, yes!" He gathered his Hunger once more. "I need merely slay *another* God — and give myself both triumph *and* power this day!" He let his smile widen, the crystal blades of teeth a threat and promise, and launched himself at Athena-Victoria, even as the incarnate goddess began to steady herself, repair the damage to her new mortal form.

"Now *that*," Ingram said, appearing between him and Victoria,

"-will *never*—" Quester contined, leaping to position next to her oldest friend,

"—*happen!*" Urelle, just behind them and between, blocking any path to the goddess, finished.

And a triple blast of power erupted towards him.

It was immense — more than he had *imagined* the three could project, drained as they were — and it was a *challenge*, for he had to consume godspower and psionic energies and what seemed the distilled *essence* of magic all at once, a surge that came near to touching the foundations of all reality.

But he *was* Raiagamor, ancient and powerful, and though the incredible blast slowed him, forced him to advance as through a fast-running stream, still he came on, seeing the God-Warrior and the once-Iriistiik's eyes widen, and he was *between* them, slapping out with both arms, sending the two flying, blood trailing their flight through the air. "So be it! The little girl dies first, and *then* the old woman!"

Urelle stepped back, horror writ across her face as he thundered towards her, and threw up one hand as though to stop him.

But in the moment, he would have reached her, the hand flipped around — and vanished.

Cold-silver agony *impaled* him, burning-frozen torment that spread, an icy conflagration, through Raiagamor. He looked down, seeing the mighty silver shaft of Athena's Spear projecting from precisely between the remnants of his armor.

He dragged his gaze up, his vision already beginning to darken, and understood. "She... swapped places..."

"... so you would run *yourself* onto my Spear, yes, with not a chance to dodge or parry." The voice was that of Victoria Vantage... yet it was not. It was stronger, younger, and filled with fury colder than the absolute-zero fire radiating outward from his heart — a heart almost entirely eradicated by the Spear that had penetrated him from front to back.

His fury and hatred were the only pieces of warmth left to them as sight narrowed to that hateful face, but strangely, his madness had departed. His mind was clearer than he could ever recall it, and that left him one final action to take.

"At the least, I deny you your brother," he breathed, and reached to consume the last of his tenant.

But Athena's godspower was *stronger* even than his Hunger, now, with silver through his body, and he *heard* her within him.

You will deny me nothing, least of all my favorite brother!

And the remnant of Ares vanished into the golden flames of Athena's soul.

Raiagamor felt his body toppling slowly backwards, to crash, unmoving, onto the crumbled stone of the Aegeian Path. As his consciousness faded, he sensed the Goddess of Wisdom standing over him... *no*. Not the Goddess. It was Victoria Vantage, still exhausted near to death, even with the power of Athena. Her lined, weathered face grim, she grasped the spear one more time, wrapping both hands around its huge shaft, and *twisted* it with the legendary Vantage strength as she shoved the spearpoint and shaft a full yard into the stone beneath, pinning Raiagamor to the ground like an insect.

The last thing he saw was the grim satisfaction in the old Adventurer's eyes.

Chapter 54
A Few Moments of Recovery

Victoria wanted to collapse to her knees, but the power within her would not permit it. *What? Can't an old woman rest, Athena?*

A smile came from within her, where she could see a tall woman, regal beyond imagination, with gold-touched tumbling curls that strongly recalled Berenike's to Victoria's mind. *Rest we both shall have, but it is not yet the time. Look to your friends first, and then my people — our people — must know what has passed here.* Victoria felt her head turn, both with and without her volition, and gazed out with more than mere human sight. *They have seen horrors and miracles and disasters this day; they must know that there is still hope.*

Victoria could not argue that — and she was grateful, at least, that she *could* argue with Athena if she chose. The Goddess of Wisdom had filled her, but had not *erased* her. Though she could already sense the truth of the Wanderer's words, months before, that this would change her beyond anything she had known.

And the *first* thing to do, was see to her friends.

Ingram and Quester lay where they had fallen after the double-backhand by Raiagamor had felled them. Bloody tracks were carved across both bodies, left by the bladed claws on the monster's huge hands.

Let me, Athena said. Victoria yielded full control of the body to the goddess, and now could see through her eyes.

There were night-black streaks across the bright-glowing souls of both the God-Warrior and the Iriistiik-turned-human Mother, cuts through not just their physical forms but their very essences, their *souls*, and Victoria felt her own nausea and anger echoing that of Athena as she gazed on the damage.

The souls themselves were *bleeding*, leaking their energy, their existence into the air and the black voids cutting across them. *By Myrionar, they're dying. Their souls are dying!*

They are, Athena agreed. *But — thank Father and the Highest — Raiagamor struck them merely to remove them as impediments. He did not direct his force to its fullest. There is enough remaining, and we learned, Cycles ago, the way of repairing this damage, at the side of Khoros himself.*

The Lady of Wisdom focused, and with her godspower drew out strands of Victoria's own soul, and some from Urelle as well, weaving those strands with infinite complexity and care into the godspower. From that mingling of mortal soul and godly energies, she generated blazing-gold threads and — as near as Victoria's mortal understanding could comprehend it — began, with inhuman speed and yet immortal care, to stitch the near-severed souls together.

By a clock's reckoning, it took a few scant minutes, with the auric godspower flaring about the three of them like a singing pyre; from Victoria's view within Athena — or the god's within her — it was hours of painstaking work, the darkness of the cuts seeking to strip away solidity even as they worked.

But finally, she rose, both Athena and Victoria shaky from the effort. *They will recover, though both must be cautious about the use of true power for many months indeed. Soul-wounds like this are the worst of all, and had we waited even hours, they would have been gone beyond even the gods' powers to retrieve.*

Ingram and Quester rose to their feet — unaware, Victoria thought, of the true nearness of their deaths — as she became aware of a hesitant movement near her, turned to see her niece.

"Auntie? " Urelle was staring up at her, wide-eyed.

A chuckle came from Ingram. Urelle snickered, and suddenly all four of them were laughing, laughing so loud the joyous sound echoed around the broken stone and curved crater walls, mocking the glaring, sightless remains of Raiagamor.

"Oh... oh, dear me, I think we all needed that," Victoria said finally; she also noted that she was obviously still human enough to need to breathe. "Yes, Urelle, Ingram, Quester, I am still myself. Athena is *with* me, but has not *replaced* me, as we were told."

Ingram looked sidewise at Urelle. "Are you going to change into something else, too? I mean, make it four out of four?"

"I don't *think* so," Urelle said after a moment. "Becoming the Wanderer's apprentice is the closest I'll come." She grinned at the others. "It *was* funny, though."

Quester nodded, her feathery hair-antennae bobbing. "It is indeed amusing. Three of the four of us, transformed in ways we really could never have expected, within minutes of each other." She raised a brow to Ingram. "Is this a permanent change for you?"

Ingram was studying her new body with amazement, now that the emergency had passed. "I... yes, I am pretty sure it is. I was a boy because they'd slapped a *whole* bunch of enchantments on me to make me one, and hide any *other* magic, so that no one would notice there was anything funny about me. I didn't so much get changed into a girl as I, well, *broke free* of my old body. Not that it doesn't feel... pretty strange," she said, with a visible touch of color on her olive-tinted cheeks, "but somehow it also feels *right*."

"Not surprising," Victoria said, feeling some of the words coming from Athena. "Your projection of Berenike was undoubtedly made so strong and convincing not just because of Berenike herself, but because a part of you could not be entirely fooled about its nature."

Ingram bit her lip. "I'm still not sure if I'm angry about this, happy, sad... it's really mixed up in there. The idea that something so *fundamental* to me was changed without my choice, without my even being able to make the choice, that... hurts. At the same time, I completely understand *why* it had to be that way. I'd have been killed years ago if anyone had suspected the truth."

"Victoria — or should I say Lady Athena?" Quester began.

"Oh, dear, Quester, let's keep *Lady Athena* for the formal occasions, or if you must address her directly rather than myself. She's there, listening, of course, but I am still very much myself."

"Hm. I believe this is, in fact, a question for Lady Athena. At the very end, I heard Raiagmor say he would deny you your brother. Yet Ares died *decades* ago, as I understand it."

Victoria let Athena answer; Quester was certainly correct as to who could answer this. "My brother was betrayed and murdered in his quarters decades ago, yes. But it turns out that our little monster had a particular appetite for pain and torment, so he stripped Ares of his power but kept just enough of his soul intact so that Ares could see what was happening and be powerless to stop it."

Urelle's brows came down. "That's *horrible*." After a moment, she went on, "Maybe he was inspired by the tales of Erherveria."

"Perhaps," Athena said, in that ringing voice that was just a bit stronger and younger than Victoria's had been in many years. "It does mimic much of Kerlamion's Curse in that sense. But I would incline far more to the suspicion that it is something the most powerful Great Wolves can do, and thus he was inspired by their King, or their Queen, who he claimed as his mother." She frowned, using Victoria's face, and shook her head. "That, in itself, is a valuable if frightening piece of information. Nowhere, not even in all my Cycles of memories, was there anything that truly pointed to the existence of a Queen of Wolves."

Victoria reclaimed her own face and voice. "Yes, and I suspect it was not meant to be known. He assumed there would be no witnesses to talk."

"Well, now what?" asked Urelle after a moment. "The bad guy's dead, the Xiilistiin are too, so... we're done, right? Adventure complete?"

The other three laughed. "Not quite so simple," Ingram said. "There's so much more to do, even if it hopefully doesn't involve fighting anything."

"Correct," said Victoria, looking down the mountain. The dust-fog from the collapse was still drifting down, obscuring parts of the city far below. "The people must be terrified, seeing the Path destroyed and hearing the strikes of the gods far above. Athena must let them know it is over, tell them the truth, and there is so much to do beyond that."

Quester waved her hands — first and second — around at the devastation surrounding them. "Rebuilding the Path?"

"Oh, that will have to be done," Athena agreed, "But until the people are reunited — until they know how close we came to falling, and how we were truly saved — I do not think their faith will support the rebuilding. They *needed* my aid, and were praying for it. But before the Aegeian Path can rise again, their trust in the gods must become as solid as the mountain they will see."

"Well then, I guess we'd better get to it," Ingram said, a sardonic smile crossing her face. "The Camp-Bels are going to need to adjust to their new Captain's face, too."

The four of them began to move towards the remaining landings and the city below, as Urelle laughed. "Yes, that'll be a surprise. I wonder... are there any problems with the Captain being a God-Warrior?"

Ingram bit her lip. "You know... I don't know. There's a possibility of conflict of responsibilities, even though both groups are theoretically ultimately loyal to Athena."

"Don't worry about it," Victoria said. "I am quite sure that we can find a way to adjust to it."

"And since you *are* Athena," Ingram said with a smile, "I guess you can say that and mean it."

They walked for a few moments in silence, before Quester spoke up. "What of the Seal? Has it been broken, now that the false Ares is done?"

Victoria looked within, found Athena there to help her look with the god-sight. "No," she said, hearing the surprise in her voice. "No, it is still up. Solidly so." She felt Athena gently nudging, let her take over. "And it shall remain so, until the damage has been healed enough for Aegeia to be itself again. This is the way the Seal has ever and ever worked, and even though it was invoked by dark beings indeed this time, still its basic nature remains unchanged."

"So, we are stuck here until then." Quester's words were more pensive than disappointed.

"Indeed, but there will be much to do here — some very much of the sort for Adventurers. The Swarm-Heart was destroyed, but there must remain *some* Xiilistiin hidden in this land — and such monsters must be eradicated. I have no doubt the false Ares had other vile allies hidden away; demons, at the least."

"At least," agreed Urelle, "and with everything that happened to the country, I'd bet that there's going to be factions out there that want to fight *everyone*, or who figure to prey upon the weak."

Ingram looked up — though not nearly so much as before her change — at Victoria. "Sounds like one of the duties of the Spear of Athena."

It was both Victoria *and* Athena who smiled fondly at the Camp-Bel. "One of them indeed. But for the next few days — and I suspect weeks — we will all have enough to do here."

They crossed the first landing, where the Camp-Bel bodies had already been removed, and came to its edge.

Below, *Rhyme and Reason* stretched across the Grand Plateia, hull bright and dark as the shadows of clouds passed across it. But what drew the eye was the crowd: before, behind, around the great ship were the masses of Aegis, from the oldest able to walk to the youngest, being carried by father or mother. To Victoria's newly-expanded senses, it was a tapestry of faces and fabric, every countenance clear and unique, every cloak or scarf or tunic bright and strong.

And every face was looking up, tense, filled with the fear that had been layered upon them, rumor by rumor, order by order, crime by crime, and the fear, sharper and more immediate, from the cataclysms that had just been shown them — a legend fighting the representatives of the gods, a battle on the mountain, and the mountain itself collapsing. It was the fear for your life, and the fear of the uncertainty of even what your life *meant*, when you had begun to question everything you knew, and could not be sure whether that was anything left to trust.

"It is over," she said, and the power of Athena sent her voice echoing across the entirety of the city.

"It is over."

Chapter 55
Salvaging Faith

Ingram, her own senses no less than those of the Goddess, saw a wave of relief pass across those assembled below... relief that faded almost as swiftly as it appeared. *Well... I guess we should expect that.*

Quester's mindvoice was grave. *Yes. This has not been one of your Cycles as told; it may have seemed that way at first, but Raiagamor and his servants bent it, twisted it to something darker, and took advantage of the position of Ares — one of those expected to direct the Cycle — to carry even the citizens who might ordinarily resist along with him.*

And by that, thought Urelle, with a sense of slow realization, *damaged their faith in the gods, especially with a false Athena to play an increasingly twisted part in his plans.*

"Who *are* you?" came a distant voice from below. The speaker was a woman, broad of build and perhaps fifteen or twenty years younger than Victoria; Ingram recognized her after an instant as Mother Ateos, one of the most respected members of the Symvouile, the council that advised the Kyverni. Ingram could also make out the Kyverni nearby; old Leonidas seemed content to let Mother talk.

"*I* am Victoria Vantage, an Adventurer who's had entirely too much adventure these last few months," she answered tartly. "But I happen to *also* be the current vessel of Athena."

A rumble of confusion and disbelief from below. "That's a lie! We know Athena is Artemisia Igemon!"

"You have been misled by a false Ares, who also gave you a false Athena, and other lies as well," Ingram said, feeling her own power giving her voice the same range and power as Victoria-Athena. *Though voice enhancement may be close to the limit of my powers right now, if my soul was as badly injured as Victoria told us.*

Those with better sight below were able to make out her unmistakable armor, and she immediately heard a whisper of "The Spear of Athena!".

That was a good opening. "Yes, I am the Spear of Athena, and what Victoria says is completely true. She *is* the Vessel of Athena."

Another great voice boomed out, but this one from the shining vessel lying in the plaza. "We do not see Ingram Camp-Bel among you," Reason said, and her voice was concerned. "Is our Captain dead?"

Ingram looked at the others and couldn't restrain a laugh. "*Rhyme and Reason*, I *am* Ingram Camp-Bel. As you could perhaps have guessed from the data you gave me."

A lighter laugh echoed from below. "As some of us suspected," Rhyme said, "but could not be certain until you confirmed it. Then to the people of Aegeia, we also confirm what is being said. General Aloysius, poor man, was not the vessel of Ares, but murdered and replaced by something that played Ares."

"And the gods did nothing? *Ares* did nothing against one using his name?" Mother Ateos' skepticism was echoed by the crowd.

In some ways, Ingram found this heartening. The people of Aegeia hadn't become broken or simply accepting of whatever they were told; they still had the spirit to question, to wonder, to *think*, and if Aegeia was to be reborn, that was *essential*.

In this particular case, though, it was going to be an obstacle. She looked to Victoria.

It was Athena who looked back, and sighed. "You know the way of the Cycles. The other gods cannot enter the stage unless and until the Great Play calls them; it is left to my brother and myself, and it is my brother who almost invariably begins the play." Her voice shifted to an anger that shook the ground. "And my brother was *murdered* before ever he reached the mortal world."

A whisper of shock and horror rippled through the crowd. "M... *murdered*?" repeated Leonidas, the word only caught through deific senses.

"Yes, murdered, in a manner more foul than any; his soul taken, his power carved away and used by his killer. The Ares you have seen all these years, since General Aloysius ascended, was a killer wearing the guise of his victim."

"And naturally," Ingram continued, "he had no intention of *allowing* Athena to appear. Raiagamor — for that was his true name — ruthlessly eliminated every possible threat to his power."

She tapped her chest. "I was targeted from the time I was a baby. Many of you remember the murders about fifteen years ago; he had a prophecy that warned of a particular child born at that time, and arranged for a killer to stalk our homes. He, and his forces, attacked and wiped out the Masters of Kyriarcnis — something even more of you will recall."

The four of them were now moving down the steps to the Grand Plateia — making it easier to speak, and also bringing themselves closer to the people, more visible, no longer distant and almost faceless figures.

"A stronger argument is more recent," Quester said, her voice also carrying far across the plaza. "Your guards, those who had of late become something more like your jailors; did not many of them die where they stood, but a short time ago?"

That brought a strong murmur from the crowd, and Mother Ateos nodded. "That they did. But that could be something dark from you, as much as we were resenting them then. Who are you, then?"

"It is wise to be suspicious," Quester said. "I am called Quester, and I, too, was a target of the false Ares, and a companion to Victoria and Ingram, as was young Urelle, here." She gestured to the small black-haired wizard. "But if you have those bodies examined, you will find they were not human, nor *Artan*, nor any ordinary species; they were *Xiilistiin*, parasites and shapechangers who prey upon others. They died when I destroyed their Swarm-Heart, defending these my friends from a fate far worse than simple death."

I thought we were expecting there to be some survivors, Ingram sent.

Most of those in the city were likely called to aid in my enslavement, Quester answered. *But those farther outside may well have had more immediate duties, and would have minimized their connection. It would have still been a shock, but not a lethal one.*

Ateos glanced about her, pointed to a gangly-looking girl wearing an eyepatch and carrying an assortment of bags about her. "Pempti, how long to find out if that's true? Does anyone know anything of these 'Xiilistiin'?"

"We do," Commander Eklisia said, her clear voice picked up and transmitted by *Rhyme and Reason*. "The Camp-Bels have fought them before in our history. If Xiilistiin were working in service to Ares, then a false Ares he would have to have been."

Pempti scratched her head. "If I've got permission to cut one of them open, I might be able to tell you if it's true or not in minutes, if we trust the Camp-Bels."

Mother Ateos exchanged some whispered words with the Kyverni and a few other members of the Symvouile, then nodded. "It is our opinion that if we cannot trust the Clan Camp-Bel, there are none we *can* trust in this."

"The Clan thanks you for your trust, Symvouile, Kyverni," said Eklisia, relief and gratitude clear in her voice. "Dykast Pemptikor, find an appropriate subject and we will assist in verifying — or disproving — the words of these four."

"Hold," Kyverni Leonidas said. "Eklisia, isn't it? Yes. Eklisia Camp-Bel, do you vouch for these?"

"Absolutely," she said, with an immediacy that warmed Ingram's heart. "These four traveled with us from Amoni Agapis all the way here, and aided us in awakening *Rhyme and Reason*."

"Hm. Then if we choose to believe you at all, I think we should believe you in this," the Kyverni said. "I cannot speak for all the people of Aegis — let alone the rest of Aegeia, with what has passed — but for my part..."

He stepped forward, ascending to meet them. Kyverni Leonidas was somewhat overweight, graying, and his body trembled some — possibly from all the shocks of the day — but he drove himself upward until he was only ten steps below them.

Then he knelt and bowed all the way to the stone before him, then rose and gave the two-gesture salute, arms crossed before him and then rotating so both were upright and parallel. "*Hail*, Athena! *Hail* to her Spear!"

Mother Ateos echoed the gesture and shout. Then the rest of the Symvouile took it up, and it spread, a fire ignited by a spark to bone-dry tinder, until the entirety of the Plateia shook, not to battle, but to the sound of thousands shouting in relief and joy the same great cry:

"Hail to Athena! Hail to her Spear! Hail to the Heroes!

"HAIL!"

Chapter 56

"You didn't seem as surprised as I'd have expected," Ingram said to Commander Eklisia.

"After you'd left — for victory or death — *Rhyme and Reason* released the data to the rest of us." Eklisia grinned, shaking her head. "It was... a bit much to take in, but it made sense of everything, Captain."

"Are you all right with my still being Captain?" Ingram tried not to sound hesitant — *I'm a* God-Warrior, *by the Founder, not the failure of the Clan!* — but it was really hard to fight a lifetime of uncertainty.

"If you'll be having enough time to *be* the Captain," Eklisia said, "the Crew will be just fine with it, Captain. If you won't, it would be more practical to designate someone else to take your place."

"Before she went to rest, Victoria — speaking as herself *and* Athena — said I should focus on the Clan, so I guess that means yes, I'll have time, at least for now."

"Then welcome back, Captain!"

With that decision, Ingram seated herself in the Captain's chair; by some technological trickery, it fit her new size and shape just as well as it had earlier; maybe better, since as a boy she'd been *tiny. No wonder it was hard for people to take me seriously; I never really grasped* how *small I was.*

"Yes, welcome back," Koragio Theros said; the Security Chief was wearing a bemused expression.

"What is it, Chief?"

An explosive laugh with a tinge of embarrassment was the answer. "Well, just seems like I won't need to worry about my Captain's safety, when she can probably lift *Rhyme and Reason* over her head."

"There are still a lot of things that can kill me, Chief, especially if I'm off-guard." Ingram raised her eyebrow. "So I'll expect you to still keep an eye or two out."

"Count on it, Captain." He grinned, his figure a shade less tense than it had been. "Truth be told, it's *Quester*'s transformation that's harder to take in."

"For myself as well," Quester admitted. "I am at least as much human, now, as I am Iriistiik, and still more besides, as I am a Mother. How that works with a human Nest... I have yet to figure out."

Urelle was completing a cautious circuit of the command deck, eyes wide. "This is *all* technology? Not magical?"

Rhyme, who had been following her, nodded. "Aside from a very few modifications or additions the Wanderer did — which, as I understand it, were necessary because the requisite components simply could not be made here — there is nothing magical in *Rhyme and Reason*."

"Amazing. I couldn't duplicate a lot of this with magic, or if I could it would take *years*."

"This vessel, however, is the culmination of *centuries* of work — both originally, and after the crash," Reason pointed out gently. "One of the primary advantages of magic is that a single person can walk that path from its beginning to its highest pinnacle; technology is the work of uncounted numbers over many generations." She surveyed the deck with her own analytical smile. "But it *does* have its own advantages."

"Primarily the way it can be used by anyone," Quester said.

"True, but only if it's *working*," Ingram said. "Which brings me to my first question: how bad is the damage, and how long before *Rhyme and Reason* can fly again?"

"Officer-Technical Actina and I have examined all affected systems," Reason answered. "It is our opinion that it will be a minimum of two weeks, as many as three, before we can raise ship and remove *Rhyme and Reason* from the Grand Plateia. Complete repairs to reach full functionality, approximately six months; there are some damaged components for which we will have to manufacture replacements."

"How many of the Clan will you require for the work?"

She gazed into the distance, gray-green eyes staring into nothingness. Despite the pause, Ingram had the impression she could have answered instantly.

After a moment, Reason said, "Depending on the precise task, between five and ten of the Clan. Officer-Technical Actina will be one most in demand, although both Rhyme and I will be able to perform many of the same operations ourselves."

That's good. "All right. Security Chief, I want you to take a hundred of the Clan and put them at the Kyverni's disposal; with nearly all the original guardsmen dead, we need *some* kind of recognizable force helping to keep order."

"Agreed, Captain. What about the rules of the prior ruler? Curfews and such?"

"Up to the Kyverni, not us. He's been here, we haven't. My own impulse would be to cancel them, but there's a lot of people out there who aren't going to be sure about the change; if there could be a fake Ares and fake Athena, the replacements could be fake too, even with the Camp-Bel support. So we leave that choice to the Kyverni and the Symvoile."

Theros shrugged. "As you say, Captain. I think it's a good idea, whatever the details." His eyes narrowed. "However, I'll be needing Quester."

Quester raised a feathery eyebrow. "I would, of course, be willing to assist in any way I can. What do you need?"

"All the guards died when you sent the Xiilistiin to Hades," Theros said, "but that doesn't mean there aren't some that were cut off and playing a role they had to stick to, right here in the capital. I need you to do a check on the Kyverni and the Symvoile."

"Good thinking. You'll have to explain it to them, but I think they'll understand it's necessary."

She closed her eyes and leaned back, then blinked as she became aware someone was speaking. "Sorry, what?"

Rhyme smiled down at him, but there was a crease of worry between her brows. "Captain, I think you should go to your own bed now. You are exhausted."

"I guess we all are. Quester, can you do what Theros needs now, or do you need to rest first? We don't need you straining yourself."

"I am indeed tired, Ingram," Quester said, the buzzing undertone somewhat blurring the words in a way that emphasized the Iriistiik Mother's weariness, "but if they are to put themselves under these others' orders, they *must* know the others can be trusted. It is not as though there are hundreds to examine, as with the Camp-Bels. I will rest immediately that we are assured we are not harboring spies within your local ruling body."

Just don't push yourself too much.

A hint of cinnamon and firespice. *As long as you* and *Urelle get rest also.*

Deal.

"So where *do* I sleep?" Ingram asked, finding it surprisingly hard to stand.

"The Captain's Quarters, of course," Rhyme said. "I will guide you and Urelle there."

"Wait, is there —"

"There is a guest bed there. If you both insist on greater separation —"

Urelle laughed as she followed them into the little room called an "elevator". "We've slept closer than that many times in the field."

"Very well." Rhyme smiled again and activated the elevator, which moved only a short distance before stopping. It opened to a short corridor, which ended in a door that opened at Ingram's approach.

"By the *Founder*..."

The Captain's Quarters were larger than Ingram had expected, knowing the usual way military commands were arranged. "A sitting room, a kitchen?, a bedroom, spare bed, entertainment area I guess... washroom... this is much bigger than I had expected, with the limited reading on ships of the stars that I had found — some of that clearly fiction in the old archives."

"*Rhyme and Reason* was a long-range scout and exploration vessel, equipped — in this case — for what was a perilous, possibly very long-term expedition. The crew were expected to live in the vessel for a period of years, perhaps. It was therefore designed as much for comfort as for scientific or military applications. The Captain, especially, was given additional room for their use." Rhyme saluted them. "Now, I will leave you to your rest."

The door slid shut behind her, and for the first time that day, Ingram just let tension *run* out of her. "By the gods, it's actually *done*."

"The worst part, anyway," Urelle agreed.

There was a silence for a few moments as they took off all their equipment, laying it out in order near their beds. Abruptly, Ingram said, "So... you're *really* okay with my... change?"

For answer, Urelle stepped over and kissed her. "Yes." She smiled — now up, rather than down, into Ingram's eyes. "You know, I never really *thought* about it, but I found out that I liked girls as much as boys when we were visiting Holly and her friends."

"I remember thinking you looked about as overcome as I did when we got our goodbye hugs." Ingram grinned. "And I'm not different *inside*. Aside from all the God-Warrior stuff."

"I know." She squeezed Ingram's hands between her own. "Now let's get some real rest."

The fogginess was heavier than ever. "I'll take *that* suggestion."

She wasn't even sure she remembered her head touching the pillow.

Chapter 57
Healing a Country

Quester finished examining Victoria with senses vastly extended from a mere day or two before. "You had seemed quite ill at the end of the battle yesterday, but I find nothing at all wrong now. You seem to be in superlative shape, in fact."

"Credit to Athena," Victoria said, leaning back in her bed. "She's stuck with this old body as her incarnate form; I suppose we can accept a bit of improvement."

There was that nigh-subliminal shift of expression and carriage that signaled that it was now Athena speaking. "Lady Vantage had long-term damage that even the quick treatment by the Camp-Bels could only mitigate. In truth, she would likely have died on the Path shortly after the defeat of Raiagamor." Somehow, she gave the impression of gazing sternly *inside* herself. "Some of your adventures pitted you against monsters and even *places* that left lethal marks upon you, Victoria. Fortunately, the power of a newly-awakened god is sufficient to that need."

"So, she will live for some time now?"

Athena laughed. "I certainly hope so, as I have so much to do! With my aid, I believe Victoria will find she has many more healthy decades ahead of her." Now the voice and pose hinted at both being present. "So, Quester, what news, before we emerge to become the spectacle they will expect?"

"The worst — and best — news is that one of the Symvouile was a Xiilistiin."

Victoria was instantly upright. "And exactly *how* is this the *best* news?"

"Because when revealed, he reverted to his true form, and we now have visible proof of our story of infiltrating monsters."

"What of Raiagamor's corpse? That, too, would be strong evidence," said Athena.

"I believe it is best to have an expedition *not* including any of our party ascend to find it, witness how it lies impaled by the actual Spear of Athena, and how it is like no other creature known.

"Speaking of which," Quester went on, with a slight hesitation, "Do we know *what* Raiagamor was?"

"My brother," Athena answered, "says that even within the monster he mostly saw only what Raiagamor *wanted* him to see. His mother was this Queen of Wolves; his father was something *not* a Great Wolf, but exactly what is unclear. What little Ares could gather was that Raiagamor's father did not know exactly what the Queen was, and was if anything opposed to the Wolves; his seduction was a ploy on the Queen's part, and a grand experiment.

"She apparently saw something in this other being that might combine well with the Great Wolf. I *believe* he was humanoid, but obviously with some features that were likely cat-like. The golden fur is clearly a feature from his father, as is the tail, since Great Werewolves are uniformly dark-furred and have no tails. Other than that..." She shrugged. "Powerful and strong of will and soul. No lesser being could possibly have attracted her attention, let alone been worthy of such a perilous experiment."

"As long as there are no *more* like Raiagamor," Quester said. "There are not, correct?"

"No, on that Ares is quite certain. Raiagamor was unique, and with his failure here, likely never to be replicated." She finished rising from the bed. "But enough of what was. We have a lot of work to do, and I have rested enough."

"What will become of Ares?"

"I am healing my brother within my own soul for now; once we can be sure that his temples will be filled again, I believe he can return. That, of course, means healing the damage Raiagamor has done."

"Yes. I hope I have not overstepped my boundaries, but I advised the Kyverni to send messages to the other cities immediately, summarizing the events."

Athena looked on her with approval. "Not at all; that was well-thought. The responses alone will tell us much of what work we must do."

"I suspect," Quester said, "that there will be quite a lot."

***

"What do you mean, we do *nothing*?" The Kyverni stared in disbelief at Athena. Most of the others in the impromptu audience hall, created by Athena's power from one of the damaged buildings, stared, silently echoing the Kyverni's reaction.

I cannot blame them, Victoria thought. *But you are, unfortunately, right.*

Aloud, Athena said, "Nothing *overt*, Kyverni. Yes, you and I — all of us here — know that the defiance by Talaria's current Kyverni is due to her being a Xiilistiin survivor — one who evidently has several others with her, perhaps enough to begin a new Swarm.

"But the doubts she plays on are very real, and as no one in Talaria was here to see what passed, nor to witness the other evidence we have, going in with banners flying could simply reinforce their suspicions."

Athena frowned. "The same is true of Demati, and if we are rumored to be forcibly conquering *any* of them, the other cities may easily be turned against us."

"And negotiating with the others is no easier," Ingram said; besides the Kyverni and members of the Symvouil, the three other members of their party and several of the Camp-Bel officers made up their current council. "I just returned from Lyra; they won't even *discuss* the situation without the return of their Great Library — which they define a lot more broadly than would have been true before the wars."

"But we cannot sit by and do nothing, Lady Athena," Kyverni Leonidas said. "I cannot argue that you are wrong — if we were to try to force our directives, we would prove them right to doubt us. But by the same token, we cannot idly accept this. If we do nothing, we look weak, afraid, or both."

Athena looked to Ingram. "Your position as Captain of the Clan Camp-Bel gave you no leverage, in addition to that of being my Spear?"

"Oh, *some* people were impressed," Ingram said, "but they weren't taking the Camp-Bel word as sacred truth, either."

"Not sure what the answer is," Security Chief Theros said. "Raiaga wanted to ruin things, he seems to have done a Founder-damned good job of it."

"I have an idea," Athena said, and Victoria found herself raising a figurative eyebrow, since even *she* couldn't see what the goddess meant. "But there are some details I need to work out. Until that time..." She let Victoria take back over.

"Until that time, I want us to maintain contact with the other cities. Assure them of our goodwill and give them assistance as we can to recover from the war. Talk with Lyra, see if we can negotiate on the size of the Great Library. If they aren't being run by Xiilistiin as well, they should be open to at least *some* kind of bargaining."

She glanced to Commander Eklisia. "Your transmission stations; is it possible to use them for communications with the cities, and others?"

"*Possible*, yes, especially if we build a few more, but they are limited to those who have receivers. We don't have that many of those available. But if you wish, Lady Athena, we will make a receiver available to the leaders of each of the other cities."

"Wait!" Urelle snapped. "All of them? Even Talaria? We can't hand your technology to the Xiilistiin!"

Officer-Technical Meresti shook his head. "That is the least of our concerns. Technology of that level is far beyond that known here, and would take decades for the Xiilistiin to understand, even with our assistance. Without it, they are magical talking boxes that don't even use magic." A thin-lipped smile. "*That* is also one of the advantages of technology. A wizard such as yourself might unravel even great works of other wizards within a year or three; but one untutored in the sciences and engineering needed will never understand a D-Comm transmitter; they will not even know where to begin."

"Then we will proceed with that. The first requirement to unifying Aegeia is communication. Only with communication have we a chance to reach understanding." Victoria saw Ingram trying to catch her eye. "Yes, Ingram?"

"I think we should also send out a call to the other cities for volunteers to repopulate Amoni Agapis," she said. "The worshippers of Hephaestus and Aphrodite are missing their main temple now; it needs to be reawakened and services begun. It's also a task I think all of them, except probably Talaria, will agree needs to be done."

"Well thought, indeed," Athena said. "It is an ideal way to get us working together despite differences; whatever we may think of each other, all of us should be able to agree that one of the great cities must not be left empty and forgotten. Propose this to the other cities at the same time we distribute the Camp-Bel communications devices."

The others agreed. Victoria looked inwardly to her newest companion. *And what exactly is this 'idea' that you have?*

One that may tip the balance in our favor — but I admit only if and when Talaria is dealt with. Honestly suspicious leaders, I can easily deal with; monsters who wish to expand and destroy us while wearing the faces of my people, not so easily.

And how to deal with Talaria, then?

An interior smile. *That, too, I have an idea for. But it should be discussed privately... with Quester and Urelle.*

***

"It is gratifying to have captured one the prior Swarm could not," the Kyverni of Talaria said; his smile was, as with some of the other Xiilistiin they had known, somehow both less and more than human. "And under your own will, as well!"

Quester spat, seeing a trace of her own blood in what came out, nearly as red as that of a human, and twisted in her bonds, but it was useless; if any knew how to restrain Iriistiik, it was the Xiilistiin, and they had stripped her of all her equipment, leaving only the few decorative gems set into her remaining carapace. "I suspected you were of the enemy, but what else could I do? If I resisted your people, fought them, I would have merely reinforced the suspicions of Aegis planning a coup. If I fled, the same, and made to look a coward as well. Besides," she glanced with trepidation at the crystal-and-web structures in the corners of the cell, structures also engraved with runes and complex symbols "I had assumed escape would be simpler."

"Of course you would. And had there not been several of the greater of the Swarm here, surviving, you would have been correct. But one of us was, as human, both a rune-master and a student of mind-power. The combination, you will admit, is extremely effective."

Quester could not argue; her mental powers, great as they were, could barely sense the presence of her enemy at a distance of five paces. "Killing me will not solve your problem. Aegis will send others, and eventually they *will* find a way to show your true face to the city."

"Given time? I believe you are correct. But there is a far better choice." The Kyverni's form shifted, expanded, became a Xiilistiin larger even than the one who had presided over Quester's awakening. Belying the 'father' appellation, a long, sting-like ovipositor extended below the abdomen. "While you managed to reject the invitation to become the first true Mother of the Xiilistiin, we now have a *second* chance to recruit you; you will become a grand Swarmfather indeed, and we can send you back to your friends with a new goal."

Quester struggled anew, horror on her humanoid face, but the bonds refused to give. "And Talaria?"

"Talaria will be an excellent place to establish a new, perhaps stronger, Swarm-Heart, one from which we can recruit the strongest while letting the weaker and stupider humans continue to shield us."

"Exactly as we expected," Quester said, letting her smile come through.

Halfway to Quester's abdomen, the stinger halted. "What...?"

Quester *vanished*, and through Urelle's eyes she now saw the Xiilistiin recoiling in shock. "How...?"

The young mage flickered with an aura of mystic energy. "One of Quester's gems was an enchanted channel. I used it to spy on you — and project the entire thing in the air above the town square. More than half the citizens heard it all." She grinned and brought up her hands, sparking with electrical death. "You're *done*."

Quester rose and strode towards the palace, where the rest of the little Swarm was just realizing its time was over...

***

"We have come as you requested," said the Kyverni of Lyra. "With the testimony of Talaria, and your other negotiations, you have gained enough trust to warrant that."

"But," Athena said with a wry smile, "not enough to call me by my name, Ilios?"

The man bowed his head fractionally, red braids nodding momentarily across his face. "I have heard you called 'Victoria Vantage'. I will call you by that name, Lady Vantage, but I — and my three fellow Kyverni — are reluctant to call you by a name we already know was held by an impostor."

Well, that's the name I would rather call you, Auntie, Urelle thought.

Hush, her aunt thought back, not without fondness. *I'd rather that name as well, but this is most certainly Athena's time.*

I'm ready.

"You have seen the body of the thing that masqueraded as Ares —" began Leonidas.

"-and monstrous it is," Agroti of Demati said, her face's tension making the scar on her face become white, standing out across one cheek. "But even if we grant you that it was the false Ares, it does not follow that you are the true Athena.

"Many pardons," she said, bowing to the others, "but with what has happened to Aegeia, can you fault us for caution? For, perhaps, even fear? Kyverni was in the hands of monsters. It appears you freed it — and well done — but the false Ares, also, performed many deeds that seemed wise and good."

Athena nodded. "Is there, then, any way you can think of that we *could* convince you?"

"For myself," said Toxoti of Velos, "I incline to believe that you are who you claim. Yet there remains *doubt*, Lady... Lady Athena, and without *certainty*, how can we return to urge our people to trust and believe in you?"

Athena rose from her seat. "Follow me, then."

The Kyverni — and Athena's advisors — followed her, as the tall woman with her ebony hair strode swiftly across the Grand Plateia — now no longer blocked by the immensity of *Rhyme and Reason* — towards the single set of stairs that were nearly all that remained of the Aegeian Path.

Ebony hair? Urelle blinked and looked again. There *were* still strands of silver, but far fewer, and as her aunt turned her head for a moment, Urelle realized that Victoria's face, too, was less lined.

I suppose this is not a surprise, Quester thought to her. *The goddess intends to be around for a long time.*

Well... yes, of course. But it's going to be strange to see Aunt Vicky young.

No stranger than it will be for me, I assure you, came Aunt Vicky's thoughtvoice. *I earned my white hairs and my lines, and now they're being erased!*

Athena's voice — in the telepathic link, more distinctly different, a young alto compared to Victoria's older contralto — responded, *Not erased, merely put into abeyance. You will earn them back, and more besides, I suspect.*

At last they reached the base of the Path, the broken statues still marking its end. "You all know what the Path represented," Athena said. "It led towards the sky, a symbol of our ascent towards the realm of the gods. Now it is broken, and the Path ends above."

She gestured upward. "Yet it still rises in our hearts — even in the hearts of those who wonder if the Aegi truly watch or care. This is the pathway of hope. And I believe, if we are strong and true, we can *open* that pathway — and receive proof of our hopes."

Ilios narrowed his eyes. "You believe we can open the pathway to the gods themselves?"

"I do. And I am certain, now, that it is the only way for us to resolve these conflicts in reasonable time."

"Perhaps you are right," Agroti said, "yet oft-times it is only time that will heal wounds of trust. What urgency is there, that you cannot take that time?"

"Because what happened to Aegeia is *not* an isolated incident," Ingram said. "The Sauran King was assassinated on his very throne." She continued, ignoring the gasps of disbelief. "The Suntree was felled, and the *Artan* driven from their homes. Urelle and Victoria's home country had the servants of *its* gods corrupted, as happened here. Artania was placed under siege, and for a year or more, the Black City itself was *here*, on our world.

"The Black City may be gone, for now, but that does not mean the rest is all made well; we are in the midst of a Chaoswar, and we *cannot* ignore it, nor wait in disunity and confusion as other powers rise to destroy Zarathan. It is during the Chaoswars that the strength of Aegeia is most needed; will you let us be weakened at the very time we must stand?"

Urelle watched their faces and saw their reactions: first the disbelief, then the worry, then the realization as they understood that dark, oppressive feeling that had engulfed the world for many months, and why it had lifted, the slow acceptance of the threat, and finally the stinging of their pride in the position that Aegeia had always held in the worst days of the world.

It was Daphni, the new Kyverni of Talaria, who spoke first. "No. I will not let us be weakened. If you believe this can be done... your Quester and this young lady, Urelle, risked themselves to unmask the monsters in my city. I can do no less for you."

Ilios bit his lip, then nodded. "I, as well."

"And I," Agroti said.

Toxoti of Velos sighed, and saluted the rest. "How can I turn aside from the path my fellow Kyverni show me? I am with you." His gaze shifted between Victoria-Athena and the other three of their party. "What would you have of us?"

"Your aid in *finding* the gods," Urelle said. "All you have to do — each of you — is focus on your own patron, the god who leads *your* city. We don't ask you to believe that *this* is Athena. Only that you believe, that you let yourself believe, that the gods themselves have not forgotten, and that *your* god waits above, waits for your call in this moment."

"That I can do," Ilios said, a smile warming his face. "I have no problem calling upon Apollo."

"Nor I on Demeter," Agroti said, "and I know the faith of Toxoti for Artemis, and trust that the newest of us has her faith in Hermes as yet untouched." Her own smile stretched her scarred cheek. "And all of us will remember Amoni Agapis, and believe in the Anvil and the Rose."

Daphni's mouth opened, then closed. She looked around at the others.

"What is it, Daphni of Talaria?" Athena asked in the voice that both was, and was not, Aunt Vicky's. This time it was gentle, inviting one who hesitated to speak their mind.

"Perhaps I misunderstand, or perhaps things are different now," Daphni said after a moment, looking apologetically at the others. "But it is my understanding that the Gods of Aegeia rarely, if ever, manifest... well, as *themselves* alone. They must be incarnate in a mortal body."

"You are correct," Athena said. "And if we are successful and we open the way, then those of the Aegi who choose to join us will find such mortals as suit their natures — as I did with Victoria Vantage."

There was a subtle shift of expression, and Urelle knew even before she spoke that this time it was her aunt. "It wasn't as though you had many *choices* at the time, Athena."

Another flicker of a different person's smile. "True, but you were not there entirely by chance. You may not have been of Aegeia, but I do not think you find me... in conflict with your essence."

Victoria ceded the point with a laugh. "No. And to finish answering your question, Daphni, I can *see* Athena, and what she knows, and the gods seek synergy. A pure compatibility that will not harm the chosen mortal, but make him or her *more* of who they already were."

"So while it might be a *shock*," Urelle clarified, "we don't think it will *harm* any of the people chosen."

The Kyverni exchanged glances. Finally, Ilios spoke. "That is indeed the way, and often the dream, of the Aegeia we have almost lost. It was my dream, when I was young. Perhaps... perhaps there are those for whom it still is."

Agroti nodded. "And so what else can we do, but give the dream a chance?"

"Then believe now," Athena said, and her voice shook the air. "Gaze upon the Aegeian Path, and *believe*."

The four Kyverni and Athena gazed upward, and through Quester, Urelle felt the *impact* of their faith. Athena the strongest, for she *knew* who she was, *knew* the Aegi watched from above. But the others' faith, too, was strong, and Quester *caught* it, caught the thoughts projected up and out, and funneled them to Urelle.

Urelle reached out with her own will, through her magic touched the great Circle she had made on the first landing, the only landing remaining, and into that Circle she sent the genuine belief, the faith, the *call* from the worshippers of the Aegi, and with it all her power as a mage, finding the resonance between faith and god, between belief and truth, between the world *here* and the world *there*.

In her travels through the fabric of the multiverse she had seen a thousand shifts of reality, half a hundred universes, each with its own unique essence, and had even watched as a Fae lord opened the Way between one world and another within his own reality, and with that ineffable and irreplaceable knowledge, she reached out to find the single and singular place that would *answer* these calls, the world within the world that was the seat and power of the Aegi themselves.

And into that circle, too, poured the power of a God-Warrior, Ingram Camp-Bel, the Spear of Athena, with her absolute, rock-solid faith in the goddess next to him, the wizard that she had come to love, and the Iriistik-become-human, and Ingram's power shimmered gold and silver atop the mount, rimming the marble with precious metal made light.

Without warning, a column of blue-white fire exploded into the sky, piercing the sky above with a shockwave that cut a perfect circle ten miles wide from the clouds. For long seconds the sapphire-silver flame raged, and then it struck *down* with a force that shook the entirety of Aegis, from the harbor to the Camp-Bel compound. A ring of pure starfire exploded from the mount, going both past and through the remnants of the Path and flying outward to the limits of sight and beyond.

For an instant, all was silent, those who had called standing stiff and uncertain at the base of the stairs, the city stunned, holding its breath at what this might mean. For long minutes they waited, and Urelle became aware that even the birds remained silent; there was not a movement, not even of air. The only motion visible anywhere, at the very edge of vision, was the eternal repeated surge and retreat of the sea on the shore.

Suddenly Ilios cried out and went to his knees as a dazzling burst of red-gold light enveloped him. Energy played about his form, and he rose, a strange double-vision surrounding him. There was, just visible, the original form of Ilios, the Kyverni of Lyra, squat and powerful, dark of skin, with his many red braids brushing his shoulders. But surrounding him was another figure, an immensely tall man with his gold-touched brown hair flowing in curling waves over bronzed shoulders, a pure white chiton emblazoned with the red and gold of the sunburst.

"*Apollo*," whispered Ingram, her own awe evident.

Apollo rose, and in the eyes of Ilios could be seen awe and revelation; in the eyes of the other, joy and anticipation. Apollo looked up. "They come. They have found themselves, and they come!"

And then a tall figure appeared at the edge of the landing. Another joined it, walking down, and another, and another, all of them limned with sparkling auras of power that smote the senses like a blow and a caress at once.

First came a woman, darker than Apollo, her hair even tighter of curl and wilder in aspect, her brown eyes sharp and dangerous, with a bow and spear slung over her shoulder; within that seeming was a hint of another, a woman whipcord-thin, with the aspect of a hunter.

Behind her came others, the raiment of a god each over a hint of mortality — a motherly woman with green and brown as her colors and a maiden of flowers and joy at her side, and on her other side a man of black flowing hair and stern demeanor that could not quite be maintained when the maiden smiled upon him; next, a slender young man dancing with almost irrepressible energy next to an older man of heroic build, his dark skin contrasting with blue-green hair that flowed about him like waves. Behind them, a man even more massively muscled than the others, limping slightly at the side of a woman whose beauty dazzled at a hundred yards.

Each of them walked with and about and within their own mortal forms — some expected, others not. Urelle saw that Aphrodite's mortal form was a very dark, curvaceous and short girl barely older than Urelle herself, with a spectacular head of wiry black hair, while Hermes' mortal form was *also* a woman, though one whose energy and figure seemed very much in tune with the energetic messenger of the gods.

And at last, a tall woman, straight-backed but seeming as old as Victoria, wearing a veil... and next to her, leaning on the woman for support, a whipcord-slender man with a narrow, mobile face, brown hair, and the symbol of the torch and sword across his tunic. Unlike the others, neither of them showed a hint of another presence within.

Athena started up the stairs, eyes wide. *"Mother... ? Brother!"*

The others parted, making a pathway for the last two; Apollo joined the line next to Artemis. Athena-Victoria slowed, her uncertainty clear as the figure that could be no one other than Hera, the Queen of the Aegi, descended in silence.

By the Founder, *I don't believe it,* Ingram thought, incredulity in every nuance of his thought. *Lady Hera was said to have gone into utter seclusion when Zeus vanished. She isn't even prayed to any more, to respect her wishes; if you refer to her at all, she's* "the One Who Remains".

Hera stopped a scant three yards from Athena and surveyed her, then gazed out at the city; still leaning on her for support, Ares did the same. Finally, her veiled regard returned to Athena.

"Daughter."

"Yes, Mother?"

"Show me the one who dared call the gods to the mortal world." Hera's voice was not angry; it was curious, though it was also iron. This was not a request. It was a Royal Command.

"That," replied Victoria, "would be my niece, Urelle Vantage."

The veil turned to Urelle, and she could *feel* the weight of the gaze of those hidden eyes. "You, child? *You* were the one who forged that circle and opened the way to the realm of the gods?"

"Not alone, Your Majesty," Urelle answered. "Without the faith of the Kyverni, the power of Athena, the psionic strength of —"

"Indeed, child, no great work is done *entirely* alone," Hera interrupted her. "Yet 'twas *your* will, was it not, that directed the power that sundered the barrier 'twixt this world and ours? That designed the Circle of Summoning, that sought to call the gods themselves to answer?"

"Yes, Your Majesty." Urelle saw the tension in all the others — even the other gods — at those words, and felt a leaden ball of fear forming in her gut. *Oh, by the Balance, I did, I summoned the gods!*

It was my *idea originally*, Quester thought. The Iriistiik stepped up next to her, as did Ingram.

Hera released her hold on her son, and Ares stepped back; Victoria caught his arm, helped steady him. Hera's boots rapped loudly as she stepped with measured, precise strides to Urelle, and looked down, ignoring the two flanking her. For a long moment, the Queen of the Aegi simply stood there, gazing at Urelle, and Urelle felt her heart beating faster with every passing second as the silence grew heavier and more fearful.

Then Hera's dark-skinned hand reached out and rested gently on Urelle's hair. "No hubris, after all. A child so earnest and filled with faith in the world, despite all she had seen, that she thought that if the gods were needed, then the only sensible thing to do was *call* them." Her head turned towards Quester. "And not alone in that, I see."

"We all agreed on this," Ingram said. "And like she said, it wouldn't have worked if the Kyverni hadn't accepted it."

A hint of a smile was visible through the veil. "No, it would not. Nor would it have worked had the Aegi not agreed with your need. Even I, in my isolation, felt my people's frustration and anger, as the Cycle trembled on the edge of dissolution and we, the Aegi, were unable to do a thing to save it.

"It was well thought of, Adventurers, and well-done." Hera's hand ruffled Urelle's dark hair, then lifted. "Come, my son. It is as we hoped."

"*Mother*, I *told* you! How could you doubt, after they saved me from that," Ares shuddered and went pale, then forced himself to go on, "that *abomination*?"

"I could doubt because I must. But let it be forgotten; all is well, all is well, and all shall be well."

Ares freed his arm from Victoria-Athena's grasp, then gestured. "Well, go on, go on, Sister, and Lady Victoria, I want you all together!"

With a smile on her face that was clearly Athena's — the fondness of an older sister; Urelle remembered the same smile on Kyri's face when they were younger— Victoria-Athena moved to join the other three of her little family.

Then Ares went to his knees and bowed all the way until his face touched the ground. "Sister Athena, Lady Victoria Vantage, Urelle Vantage, Ingram Camp-Bel, and Quester: I, Ares, thank you, thank you from the uttermost depths of my soul for rescuing, not merely my poor self, but the country we all love and protect, and the Cycle itself, from a monster beyond any of our imaginings." He rose to his knees and gave the crossed-arm to upright arm salute.

"Oh, get up, Brother," Athena said, helping him to stand. "By our missing *Father*, you're barely *able* to do this manifestation! Mother, you should have —"

"Be sensible, Athena. Has *anyone* ever been able to stop Ares from his theatrics, especially when it meant anything to him? He would have sulked in his rooms for *days*." Another subtle smile. "And he speaks truly. That is why we have answered your call... for we owe you more than even gods can easily repay."

"Excellent," came another voice, deep and resonant, echoing across the Grand Plateia. "For I may have need of your assistance."

Urelle had stiffened and then whirled at that voice, because she *remembered* it.

It was the same towering figure — seven feet in height, wearing a strange five-sided hat that shaded his face, an elaborate staff gripped in one hand. At the sight of that figure, to Urelle's surprise and consternation, the Aegi stepped backward, murmuring amongst themselves. Then Hera moved to confront him.

"Spirit-Mage," she said, "What do you seek here, Khoros?"

"I am merely carrying out a little errand for a... friend. Someone I owe a great deal to. It does not — directly — concern you or the Aegi, however. At the moment."

He turned to Urelle and her friends. "I see all has ended well enough. Aegeia will have her chance to recover, I think. The Wanderer and I congratulate you."

"Thank you," Ingram said. "Did you come all this way through the Seal to say that?"

"Oh, no, that was merely my own expression of appreciation for your hard and dangerous work, and for the prices you have paid. Adventuring, even if successful, changes one." The shadowed mouth grinned, and the tilt of the head showed he was looking at Ingram and Quester. "Some more than others."

"Did you *know* this - all of this - was going to happen?"

"*Know*? I *knew* relatively little of this particular problem, in truth. I could see, when I saw your souls, certain interesting indications, but how those would play out..." The mage shrugged. "Had I known and told you, would you have changed your course? Of course not."

He waved a hand, dismissing the issue. "But this is not what I have come for. I came for this."

He produced two elaborately and delicately painted envelopes, embossed with a crest of a tall tower surrounded by seven smaller ones. *Is that the symbol of... what was it... Skysand, that was it.* "For each of you," Khoros said, and handed one to Victoria and one to Urelle.

Urelle broke the seal and pulled out a beautifully engraved card with but a few lines written on it in golden ink:

Kyri Victoria Vantage and Tobimar Silverun

Request that you honor their wedding with your presence.

To be held in the Temple of Terian in the City of Skysand

At noon on the Anniversary of the Arrival.

Underneath the engraving was Kyri's looping, open writing:

None of the others reached you, Urelle

— hope Khoros can get this to you!

"Oh, by the *Balance*," she breathed. "Auntie, Kyri's getting *married!*"

Epilogue
A Queen's Loss

"What is it, my love?" she asked. "You call me from my court so suddenly. How fare you, after your terrible defeat?"

The King's smile was broad and glittering. "Oh, my dear, you know as well as I that such a defeat is worth many victories. I savor that novelty. But even more, I find that my return to Zaralandar was much to my advantage. The Great Seal was, indeed, broken, and few on this world would be ready or able to take advantage of it."

The surge of magic that even now must be reaching the other world would be incalculably immense. The King, she knew, intended to *consume* that power, as much as He could. "Then I am pleased for you, love."

"But I did not call you to speak of my own affairs. I am afraid I bear sad news. Your experiment has failed."

She froze. It was all she could do to keep her expression unchanged, and she suspected that great Virigar was not fooled in the least. "You mean poor Raiaga's plan has been upset?"

"Alas, completely so. As I warned him, heroes tend to find a way. My sources say the defeat was most... comprehensive. Athena was a better player of the game, in the end."

"But he has not called me. Surely he would..." She saw the King's smile widen and trailed off.

"He did not survive the failure, I regret to say. Oh, not *my* doing, though it was a possibility. They say his corpse is pinned to the remains of the Path by Athena's Spear. Adventurers are rather thorough in these instances, you see."

His smile dimmed and took on an edge of... not *threat*, exactly, but peril, certainly. "You understand, of course, that I would very much prefer you perform no more such... experiments."

She bowed her head. "As you wish, Majesty."

"Ha! It is good you understand when I speak from the Throne, as it were. Well, love, I have other work to do. Farewell!"

As swiftly as that, the image above her dresser winked out.

My Raiagamor is dead.

She was astounded — and not a little frightened — at how that knowledge *stung*, how she felt an ache that had no physical source. She had seen countless of her children fall, in battle, through treachery, or, sometimes, through their foolishness and arrogance, executed by their dread Father, the King of Wolves.

Never had any of those deaths wounded her. A momentary pang, a regret at the loss, but even those slain by her Lord and Father mattered little compared to His presence and regard. She found herself wandering, out of her most private rooms, wandering and wondering. The others had touched her barely at all, but Raiagamor...

"But he was *mine*," she finally murmured aloud, the words echoing about her apartments.

"Pardon, Majesty?"

She refocused her attention to the here-and-now. *Here*, she was the kind and just Queen Fenira of Shiramir, the Never-Wed, who had met her true love when he had saved her and the kingdom from the Lady of Shadow. He had entered the Fortress of the Beguiler, resisted whatever offers, threats, violence, or seductions the Lady could muster, and returned with the Elemental Source that was the heart of Shiramir's existence... and with Princess Fenira herself, who the Lady had taken to give her access to the Source.

It was no wonder that, passing through such trials, the two had become close. But the hero had been pledged to another, and could not stay, despite her pleading. Thus, Princess Fenira had sworn to wed no other, and had kept to that vow ever since.

Fenira shook her head. "My apologies. Please, convey my regrets to the Court, but I feel... unwell today."

Her servant bowed, but said nothing, bowing to the golden-haired woman who, many said, was more beautiful now than she had been years before, and then passing out from the Queen's apartments to the Throneroom.

Fortunately, those words, even if heard and remembered, could be innocently spoken. Part of Fenira's legend was that she would occasionally be seized by the memory of her loss, and need to retire from view for a while. This was convenient, as the Queen who went by the name of Fenira was also known here as the Lady of Shadow.

Once within her private chambers, a gesture and flicker of power transferred her to the suite of the Lady — as dark and ominous as Queen Fenira's were bright and sweet. She gave vent to a snarl, and as she left her quarters, her servants and aides gave back, ashen before her terrible countenance.

He was mine. The words were the essence of the truth. She had *chosen* to have Raiagamor, she had selected his father and groomed him, for he was unique on all the Earth and one connected to the very spirit of the world. It seemed to her that having a true child of such a being would make something new, something *powerful* in a way that even her own father and master would not have expected.

And he *had* been, his weakness to the terrible bright silver reduced to a single stroke, and his strength against the Hunger vastly greater than those many, many times his elder. He had been gifted with immense strength of body and spirit, a wide-ranging intelligence, and focus with courage.

However, he had also possessed the nigh-uncontrollable rage that had been inherited from his father's people, the rage that had, in the end, led to their extinction. The King had seen immediately that this was the potentially lethal flaw in Raiagamor's design, and suggested that she dispose of him. Now, of course, He knew He had been right.

With a startling twinge of difficulty, she banished any sense of resentment towards the King. He ruled as He had always ruled, since the Beginning, and it was not the place of any to judge Him.

Too, she would not permit herself to focus her anger on the Adventurers. They had done what Heroes do, and that was well and good; she had made great use of heroes over the years. That was one thing that kept her King amused.

No, the one to blame, the one who had *truly* murdered her only true son was no mortal; it was the one who had out-played Raiagamor in his own game and brought him not merely to defeat but to utter ruin.

It was *Athena* who was to blame, and now, at last, she allowed herself to give vent to a roar that echoed about the Hall of Shadow, changing to her true form; not even the bravest of the Court were foolish enough to remain, and within moments the Hall was empty and silent except for the sounds coming from the

Queen of Wolves, sometimes called the Lady of Shadow. She did not mourn, she did not cry. She was beyond such things, no matter the peculiar ache within.

But she *did* feel anger, and so very much did she desire to return the anger and pain ten thousandfold upon the source.

Athena.

Well, then, if Athena had deprived her of something so valued as her only true child, it would be only fair to take from her something as valuable.

But not now! Not now. No, they must think their victory complete, their recovery total. That meant delaying her revenge, but it was necessary for the full effect; a loss meant more when it was most unexpected.

Besides, there was a Chaoswar underway, perhaps the *last* Chaoswar, worldwide unrest that might last a thousand years or more. She smiled, and even her *son* might have cowered away at that abhorrent expression. Oh, yes. Aegeia would fall exactly as her son has intended. It would become exactly *what* he had intended.

She would just need a little time.

FIN.

Acknowledgements

No book is written without support from others. These are a few of the people who need the acknowledgement most!

First, and always, to my wife and partner Kathleen, without whom I'd never have the time to write these books… and in this particular case would definitely never have written the story in the first place.

Second, to my Beta-Readers, whose comments have always helped keep my books at their top form.

Third, to Vikki, my editor, who provides the extra critical eye needed to find the stuff I'm going to miss.

And a special acknowledgement to Ari Marmell, creator of Mick Oberon. Mick Oberon appears courtesy of Ari (who vetted his dialogue for me), and if you like the (non-canon) glimpse of Mick's world you get here, go out and buy the first Mick Oberon novel, Hot Lead, Cold Iron.

HISTRIA BOOKS

Other fine books available
from Histria SciFi & Fantasy:

For these and many other great books
visit
HistriaBooks.com

www.ingramcontent.com/pod-product-compliance
Lightning Source LLC
LaVergne TN
LVHW032047070526
838201LV00084B/4727